WANTED

WANTED

ALL THAT GLITTERS
BOOK 1

SHALAENA MEDFORD

Printed in the United States of America

Title Font: 403 Tarow Flare

Header Font: Ayres

Body Font: Palatino Linotype

First Edition: June 2022

Second Edition: March 2024

eBook ISBN: 978-1-970291-00-1

Wide Paperback ISBN: 978-1-970291-03-2

KDP Exclusive Paperback ISBN: 979-8-878366-54-0

Content Warning

Piracy
Alcohol Consumption
Graphic Violence
Death
Threats of Sexual Assault
Discussions of Rape
Mental Illness
Discussions of Slavery
Discussions of Child Labor

Table of Contents

Content Warning v
Maps viii
Pronunciation Guide xv
One 1
Two 11
Three 20
Four 29
Five 42
Six 54
Seven 62
Eight 73
Nine 83
Ten 97
Eleven 105
Twelve 115
Thirteen 128
Fourteen 135
Fifteen 141
Sixteen 146
Seventeen 154
Eighteen 169
Nineteen 178
Twenty 184

Twenty-One.. 189

Twenty-Two 196

Twenty-Three.. 207

Twenty-Four.. 224

Twenty-Five 233

Twenty-Six... 238

Twenty-Seven... 248

Twenty-Eight.. 258

Twenty-Nine 268

Thirty 275

Thirty-One... 284

Thirty-Two 292

Thirty-Three.. 300

Thirty-Four.. 308

Thirty-Five... 318

Thirty-Six.. 324

Thirty-Seven.. 337

Thirty-Eight... 353

Thirty-Nine 368

Forty 380

Acknowledgements 399

About the Author 400

Great Ocean
Armalinia
Jashedar

Andalise
Pishing
Kerriwen
Great
Ocean
Aibhànocht

Andalise
Anarchaia
Lund
Tarn
Garda

Screaming Cliffs
Blind Woods
Talegrove
Tamminpring
Shorton
Jashedar
Winterlands
Shoalpek

Kerriwen
Quodinlau Territory
Kal-Bar Territory
Pitique Territory

Pronunciation Guide

Aibànocht	EYE-van-AWkh-t
Aibhridh ain Thuirin	EYE-vrEE ahn hyOO-rihn
Anarchaia	An-ark-ay-EE-ah
Andalise	an-dahl-eEE-ss
Armalinia	arm-ah-lEE-nEE-ah
Darian	dAr-EE-an
Dashaelan	dash-AY-lan
Ebrinar	ebb-rih-n-Ar
Jashedar	jAA-sheh-dAr
Jiridamudor	jih-rih-dah-moo-dOHr
Kal-Bar	call-bar
Kerriwen	kAIr-ih-wehn
Kiikribandarija	kEE-k-rih-bahn-dAH-rIH-jah
kijæm	kih-jAm
Pishing	pihsh-EEng
Pitique	pEE-tEE-k-wah
Quodinlau	kwOH-dihn-lAA-oo
Shoalpek	shOH-l-pehk
Shorton	shOHr-ton
Stanjarbonima	stahn-jAHr-bOH-nih-mAH
Talegrove	tAl-grOHv
Tamminpring	tAm-mihn-prEEng
Tsingsei	sing-sAY

All that is gold does not glitter,
Not all those who wander are lost...

~J.R.R. Tolkien

One

S HE HAD ALWAYS LED AN ACOUSTIC LIFE — NOT THE LOUD AND musical kind, but rather the dull and somewhat muted sort, lacking electricity or thrill. The kind of life in which parties are thrown but smiles and laughter are stifled behind gloved hands holding lace fans; each button was done, each layer of her many skirts remained in place and her corset pulled tight enough to suffocate thoughts of freedom from the mind. Even as breathless as she was, Tsingsei Gould dreamed of a life free from such restrictions.

"You're seventeen," her mother chastised one afternoon as she led her into a beauty parlor. "You should be budding into a beautiful flower! Everything you eat should be settling on your hips!" She turned to the woman standing at a glass countertop pushing the rounded number keys on a bulky metal cash register. "Tell her I'm right!"

"I'm sorry, ma'am, but you'll have to wait your turn." The lady returned to the customer she'd been helping.

Mrs. Gould glared at the cashier, as though her blue eyes could slap her across the distance. She patted her neatly piled chestnut-colored hair, as though re-gathering her dignity. Tsingsei gave a triumphant sigh, though she hadn't won or lost the argument. It was satisfying to know that despite her mother's invitation, some people in this city had the audacity to not get involved in the affairs of a Gould.

Tsingsei sat on the nearest bench and turned herself sideways. She leaned back as far as she could, as though the angle might grant some minor reprieve from her torturous, tightlaced corset. She hated the new trend and wanted to burn her corsets in protest. Her mother would have lost her mind over the indecency—not that anyone would know if she'd worn a corset or not. Such was the unutilized perk of being a tall, narrow girl in possession of zero curves and a perfect posture forced upon her from the moment she could sit up on her own. She often thought it cruel to have been born that way into a world which found beauty in an hourglass figure. Unfortunately for her mother, Tsingsei rather liked her shape.

No doubt Mrs. Gould had hoped she would inherit the large breasts and perfect hourglass waist from her—perhaps she would have even settled for more feminine facial features. Instead, Tsingsei had gotten her ears, her small delicate hands, and her mouth's natural proclivity to settle into a frown if she stopped paying attention to her expression for even a second. Tsingsei always thought that if she were to cut off all her hair, she could almost double as her father. Which was, of course, unacceptable, and another cause for her mother to scoff her name as a hint to stop pointing out just how little femininity Tsingsei possessed.

"Tsingsei, what are you doing?" her mother gasped.

She didn't respond.

"Tsingsei, you sit up this instant or..." She thought for a worthy punishment, but Tsingsei interrupted her.

"Or what? You'll cinch this contraption even tighter and let me suffocate to death?"

Mrs. Gould sat beside her daughter so she couldn't lean back any farther, then scooted closer to push her upright. Tsingsei straightened to face forward on the bench.

"I don't know what I'm going to do with you," her mother griped. "How am I supposed to find a man who would want such a skinny, unladylike brat for a wife?"

Ever since she was little, her mother had used some variation of that complaint, accompanied by her exasperated tone to make Tsingsei stop acting out. It had lost its efficacy over time, and now it simply annoyed her.

She sighed and stared at the ceiling. "Easy. Don't."

Tsingsei had never admitted to anyone—though to be fair, she'd never had anyone to admit to—that she had never wanted a husband. All her life her mother, father—when he even bothered to make an appearance—and any house staff or partygoer who engaged Tsingsei in conversation had always found a way to squeeze in something about men.

"Men love a nice skinny waist!"

"Oh, the boys will be lining up to dance with you!"

"Once you've filled out, we'll have to fight the suitors off. Won't that be delightful?"

And on it went. Day after day, every chance anyone got, for all seventeen years and five months of Tsingsei's life. Boys, men, suitors, courting, wooing, marriage, and husband. But she wanted none of it. She never had, and she dared say that she never, ever would. And she never wanted to be told she was wrong for it.

But if Mrs. Gould ever found out, she might whisk her away to one of the strange people, who were both respected and feared, to have them 'fix' her. Because that's what her mother thought of things that didn't fit perfectly into her ideal world, where she was right and everyone else was wrong. It doesn't fit and so it must be fixed.

Tsingsei didn't want that. She didn't want a Touched to speak *kijæm* over her, calling on powers that even the ones holding it did not understand—for no one understood *kijæm*. They only knew that one day it did not exist, then three hundred years ago the skies darkened to a bloody hue and orange streaks clawed fissures across the heavens. The night sky became visible within these streaks, though it was the bright of day. As quickly as it had begun, it ended; the fissures closed, and the skies returned to their cheery blues. Over time, people who'd been ordinary one moment could call upon a strange new power in the next. Tsingsei didn't think even they had the power to make her be the way her mother wanted, but she did not wish to find out.

"Tsingsei Gould?" A woman with a plain dress and extravagant makeup called Tsingsei into the back room.

This was the part Tsingsei hated most—the poking and prodding, the powders and pastes, the combing and curling, the plucking and pulling. All in the name of being beautiful for one short evening out with her father—if that even happened.

Elroy Gould was a busy man with a penchant for standing up his own daughter. She did not get involved in her father's political business, but she knew he was both respected and feared among the masses. As a senator, he'd earned himself the nickname 'Pirates' Bane Gould'. All it took was his word, and a pirate would hang for their crimes—often without trial. Once he set his sights on a name with some notoriety, it was the beginning of their end. His actions over the years had made the East District the least friendly place for a pirate than any other in the entire world. In fact, Garda saw so few pirates, Tsingsei wondered if they avoided it, or disguised themselves.

Senator Gould's reputation and accomplishments were a point of pride for the family, and it had earned him some authority in other districts and even other countries. Everyone knew who Elroy Gould was—not that nobody knew who the most affluent family in the country was to begin with. And now, thanks to the gossip rags, everyone knew who his young daughter and beautiful wife were, as well as what they were doing and where they were going the moment they stepped foot outside the Gould Estate.

Tsingsei's mother seemed to think her husband's reputation gave her permission to shriek at anyone who dared get in her way. Everything had to be Annie Gould's way or no way at all. Which is why Tsingsei was being tortured for an hour, just in case her father kept his promise this time and spent the evening out with her.

When the women finished making Tsingsei over, she stumbled out to wait as her mother paid the receptionist. She caught sight of herself in the mirror and made a rude face at the pretty girl staring back. The powder on her tan skin was too pale for her, but the women always used it, anyway. She often wondered how her cousins in the country fared. Even the blonde ones had that darker tone one might occasionally see in the farthest north of Andalise, but never in Garda at the southern tip of the East District—except for Elroy and Tsingsei Gould.

Once outside the parlor, her mother sighed. "You look so beautiful. If only your father could see you."

"Father can't make it," Tsingsei guessed in a bitter tone.

"I received this telegram just after they called you back." She held up a folded paper, and Tsingsei glared at it.

"Then why did you let me endure all that knowing full well it was for naught?" she demanded.

"Because you look so lovely!" Mrs. Gould took Tsingsei by the chin, turning her head this way and that to observe the handiwork of the ladies.

Tsingsei sighed and stared at the cobblestones as they walked. Her mother hooked a finger and tugged her chin upward—a curt reminder to keep her head high lest others think her subordinate. But Tsingsei didn't care what anyone else thought. She'd been stood up by her father—again.

"So we're going home, then?" she asked, eager to get behind closed doors where she might loosen the ties of her corset to a fit she was more used to, or wash all the colors from her face.

"Your father asked me to take you to pick out a doll."

"Not only is he canceling our dinner, he's canceling his apology for canceling?" Tsingsei stopped in her tracks, appalled. It wasn't that she liked the dolls—on the contrary, she was sick of them. But when her father would bring the dolls to her room, it was almost the only father-daughter time they ever shared, if for only a few minutes while he reminded her that he is an important man with things to do and he can't pause everything just to spend time with her.

"He sent this note for you, already signed. All you've got to do is fill in the price."

"Then I'll get the most expensive one." Tsingsei snatched the note from her mother's fingers and smashed it in her fist.

"A lady does not publicly display her displeasure, Tsingsei," Mrs. Gould chided.

"I am not a lady. I am a daughter being ignored by her father."

Mrs. Gould's lips tightened as she stepped close to Tsingsei, her face close enough for her daughter to hear as she hissed, "You *are* a young lady and you *will* act like one."

Tsingsei set her jaw and straightened. "Then let's go get this damned doll and be done with our business in the city."

Her mother's eyes flashed a warning to mind her language before Mrs. Gould turned and stomped toward the nearest antiques dealer. Tsingsei followed, her mood thoroughly soured. She stopped outside to eye a doll in the window holding a sign that read:

Anything from Armalinia was bound to be expensive.

"'Scuse me, miss." A teen boy stepped around the corner, his eyes scanning the area in a paranoid fashion. "Could you spare a quoine or two?"

"Why would I do such a thing?" Tsingsei sneered at his filthy clothes.

"You see, miss, I'm tryin' to get somewhere on this here map." He flashed a folded paper at her. "This here marks the spot of the legendary Lost Treasure of Balamora. I only need a little more quoine to have enough food for my trip. Just one quoine'll do me."

Tsingsei turned away, unable to look into his sad green eyes. "I haven't any quoine, and if I had, I wouldn't give it to you."

She spun on her heel, stuck her nose in the air, and stomped into the shop. Inside, a thick, musky incense hung in the air. Much of the merchandise in the store was of Armalinian make—luxurious decoration and the finest silks. Armalinia was a desert country world-renown for intricate jewelry made from brightsteel—a white metal that shimmered in even the dullest light. Tsingsei took her time browsing the shelves of knickknacks and hooks with silk scarves, hangers with dresses and row after row of new and used books of every thickness. She wasn't allowed to even try on the dresses, let alone buy one. No one ever wore the clothing in public, and she half wondered if anyone even bought any to wear in private.

"Can I help you?" a woman with brown skin and black hair asked. She had a welcoming smile, and blue robes with a long, thick, purple scarf which wrapped around her waist and over a shoulder.

"I'm looking for the most expensive doll you've got," Tsingsei said. "Perhaps that one in the window there?"

"Oh, that one is very pretty, but it is not the highest priced." She held up her finger for Tsingsei to wait and disappeared through a doorway draped with streaming satin ribbons and glass beads. She returned a moment later, holding a small wooden crate. "Come."

Tsingsei followed the woman to the counter, where she pried open the lid to reveal a doll with blonde hair. The porcelain face was not made up with bold colors, as most were, just pale with soft pink lips. Over the eyes was an intricate metal mask like those worn to masquerades; the white dress with golden embroidery matched.

"The mask is pure gold, and her necklace is real pearls. Her dress is silk. She's the only one of her kind." The woman explained with excitement. It was clear she was desperate to make the sale, but Tsingsei had been sold by the price.

She wrote the numbers on the note from her father, adding two hundred to the sum. "I would like that extra given to me, please."

The shopkeeper bowed, rang up the sale, then gave her a small pouch with the extra quoine tied within. Tsingsei stuffed the quoine into her bodice and accepted the sealed crate from the woman. Her mother—who had been perusing the various books for something worth a read—came forward to purchase a rather large volume with a title that Tsingsei associated with something taboo, which any respectable woman would never be caught reading. Mrs. Gould paid with her own quoine and accepted the shopkeeper's offer to wrap the book in brown paper and twine. Every woman needed her guilty pleasure, Tsingsei supposed, whether it was reading naughty books in private or skimming from daddy's accounts.

When Tsingsei exited the store, the boy was still standing there, worrying his fingers across the face of the supposed map. He gave her a wry smile.

"Oh, come on, love, I know you got a bit to spare for old Altain."

"I have nothing and you will get nothing," she insisted.

He stood close and spoke low, so only she could hear. "What about that bit o' quoine you stuffed into your frock, there, miss?" His smell was something from a nightmare Tsingsei had never wanted to have.

"That is no one's business but my own," she growled. "Now be off before I call the authorities for harassment, you smelly little street rat!"

"If you ever change your mind, miss, I'll be right down here waitin' for you!" Altain winked and then slunk off into a narrow alley alongside the shop.

"What sort of riff-raff are you associating yourself with, Tsingsei?" Mrs. Gould demanded.

"Nothing worse than usual," she scoffed, eyeing her mother's new book.

"I imagine you meant that as a jest." Her mother's face soured as she pulled the novel closer to her bosom.

"I'm sure I did."

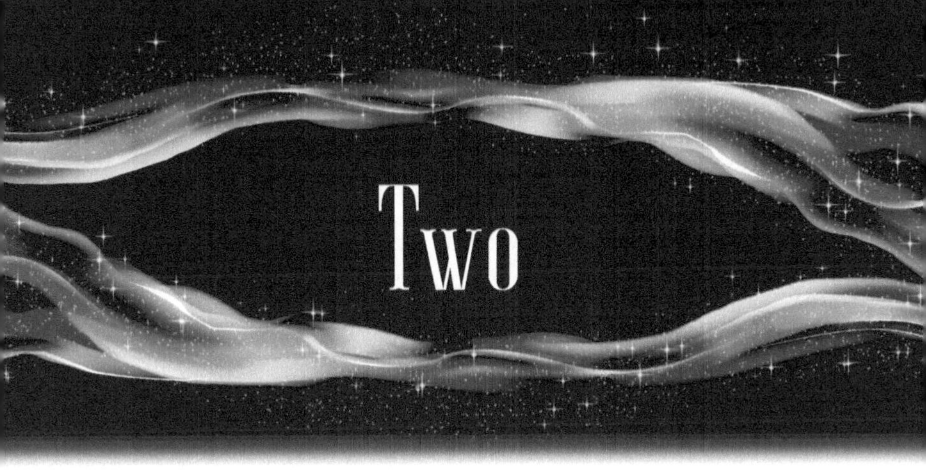

Two

TSINGSEI SET THE CRATE WITH THE NEW DOLL ON THE MAKEUP table in her grand bedroom and rang for her handmaid. Johanna was the one person Tsingsei found she could rely on without question. They'd hired Johanna as her second nanny when Tsingsei was four. Her job was to keep Tsingsei busy and out of trouble—tend to her studies, piano, and other arts. She had since taken on much more responsibility than a nanny typically would. Years ago, Tsingsei suspected she was kind because they paid her to be. Now she knew that Johanna's affections were genuine, and she was Tsingsei's only friend.

"You rang, Tsingsei?"

"I would like some assistance loosening the lacing of my corset, please."

"But the day is still young!" Johanna said.

"As am I, and I would like to breathe long enough to see tomorrow." Tsingsei turned around and gripped one of her bedposts. "Please. No one will see me being unfashionable inside my own home—no one who matters, at least."

"I know the tightlacing can be uncomfortable, but it serves its purpose." Johanna, at Mrs. Gould's request, was always trying to keep Tsingsei up to date with the latest ladies' fashions—sometimes even ahead, so that when she went out, she would be the talk of the town. It was always a matter of who was looking and what the presses would say.

The latest of these fashions was a particular type of torture called tightlacing. The idea was to give the wearer a narrow waist while pushing up their bosom. Unfortunately for Tsingsei, she had none to push up, and cinching in far enough to give her the illusion of hips made it difficult to breathe.

Tsingsei grunted as Johanna yanked at the tight cords on the back of the corset—just enough to give her a little more air, but not enough to free her fully. "If the purpose is to keep young women from being functioning people, it succeeds."

Johanna scoffed a laugh. "Beauty is pain, Tsingsei." She spied the crate on the vanity and scowled. "He canceled on you again?"

"I'd have been genuinely surprised if he hadn't," she said. "This time he didn't even bother to buy the doll himself, just sent a note with a blank amount."

"I hope you spent a fortune," she muttered, then caught herself. "I'm sorry miss, I just—"

"Newly imported from Armalinia, hadn't even made it to the display." Tsingsei lifted the lid to show off the doll. "The mask is pure gold, silk dress, real pearls and the finest porcelain."

Johanna whistled. "Must have cost enough to feed a large family for a month."

"Two large families, I'd wager." Tsingsei gave a wry smile.

She joined in the devious smile. "You have a good eye for rare items at…*reasonable* prices."

"I like to think so." She lifted the doll from the crate, pulling away stray pieces of packing hay with careful fingers. "Now for the real challenge… Where to put her."

They scanned the room. The armoire and dresser both had their tops covered with porcelain dolls standing upright on supports. Her floor to ceiling bookshelf that stretched over a meter across didn't have a single opening. They'd also filled the shelves lining the upper half of all four walls with dolls. As Tsingsei looked over the hundreds of porcelain faces, she felt an emptiness in the pit of her stomach.

"A girl your age should never have this many dolls in exchange for time." Johanna set a hand on Tsingsei's shoulder to comfort her.

She forced the knot from her throat—she'd promised years ago to never cry over her father's absence again. "I rather like them," she lied, her voice cracking just enough to betray her.

"Here." Johanna opened her hand to receive the new doll. She moved to the nightstand, where the oldest doll of her collection sat against her leather-bound journals.

"No!" Tsingsei shouted, gasping like she'd been splashed with cold water. She corrected her frantic posture to that of a lady unbothered. "Not Pim."

"I wouldn't dream of moving Pim. I was giving her a new friend." She set the two dolls together in the nightstand's cubby, then stood back to admire her work. "She doesn't look so lonely anymore."

Tsingsei stared at her oldest doll—a tattered second-hand thing her father had bought from a girl on the street. She'd been four at the time, and the doll had already been named.

But Tsingsei had loved her like she was new. It was the first time he'd bought her a doll when he'd been late home from the office. Now she wondered if her adoration of Pim had encouraged his replacing of time together with dolls.

"Thank you, Johanna. I don't know what I would do without you." Tsingsei wrapped her arms around Johanna and the quoine in her bodice clanked, shifting with the added room from loosening the corset. She fished it from her dress and retrieved one bronze-colored piece from the pouch, plopping it into her handmaid's palm. "You know nothing of this quoine."

She closed her fist around the piece and widened her eyes. "What quoine?"

"I'm getting to be a bad influence on you," Tsingsei said.

Johanna smiled and pocketed it. "It's time for your piano lesson."

"Pianos are so depressing," she said with a sigh. "You just sit there and press the keys. There is no fun in it. Now, if I could learn the violin—"

"Your mother would be hysterical if you even suggested such a thing!" She steered Tsingsei by her shoulders to the music room.

"So let her be hysterical!" Tsingsei wriggled free from Johanna's grip and lifted the violin from its stand. She set it under her chin and dragged the bow across the strings, creating an ear-piercing whine.

"Oh, what a foul noise!" Johanna tried to grab the violin from Tsingsei, who danced away and continued to drag the bow back and forth across the screaming instrument.

"See how easy it is to move and have fun with a violin? I would love to dance to my own music." She spun away from the woman again and lost her footing. She stumbled forward and rammed her toe hard into the foot of the grand piano. *"Damn it!"*

"Watch your language! If your mother were to hear—"

"Sorry." She massaged her foot through her boot, preparing to send Johanna away to fetch a button hook to check that nothing had broken.

"And that is why ladies do not frolic while playing the violin."

Tsingsei closed her eyes and set her jaw. "I'm not a lady."

"Your mother wishes you to be one, and so you must. Now, it is time for the piano."

With a grumble, Tsingsei allowed the woman to guide her to the piano bench. She then played through her day's piano lesson without enthusiasm. She'd been playing the instrument for as long as she could remember, starting with tiny pianos no taller than her knees now. Her mother had claimed on more than one occasion that her daughter could rival the best concert pianist in the country—but of course, that would never be put to the test. Tsingsei was above all that, and should never be caught lowering herself to the level of a musician.

If she'd been a boy, the world would have expected great things from her. She'd be watched to see if she became a senator like her father and her grandfather, or an explorer and cartographer like her great-great-grandfather. But as a woman, she was expected to marry a man who would do those great things, and all she had to do was look pretty on his arm.

She finished her lesson and set her hands in her lap, one over the other. She stared expectantly at Johanna. The woman smiled and nodded her approval.

The final lesson of Tsingsei's days was reading poetry for no reason other than to read it. Sometimes she and Johanna would discuss it, but most of the time, it seemed to be nothing more than a performance to while away the time. She didn't hate it as much as other lessons—she'd outright rebelled as a child when they'd tried to start her learning one of the other languages of the world—but she could have been doing so much more with her day, if only she was allowed to. She wasn't sure what she could do, but being given permission to come up with something else would have made a lovely start.

Mrs. Gould shuffled into the room partway through the poetry reading in such an excited state that Tsingsei thought she might swoon. She almost hoped she did, because at least it would be something different. They waited patiently for her to catch her breath, and of course she regained her composure—Annie Gould would drop dead before she would ever allow herself to faint.

"The Midsummer Ball," she said.

"What of it?" Tsingsei asked.

"They've asked your father to host it this year."

"Well, bravo for him," Tsingsei said, her tone heavy with indifference.

"You can attend this year. You're old enough now." Her mother's expression was one of pleading.

Mrs. Gould had always taken her daughter to formal balls where she was allowed, and Tsingsei had always scampered off to avoid dancing with boys. The Midsummer Ball, however, was the most prestigious event in the country, and no one under seventeen was allowed to go. It was an audacious affair where aristocrats wore their most expensive clothes and jewels, and more often than not, many marriage proposals would result from that night. Tsingsei liked the showing off part, but the idea of a betrothal made her queasy.

"I'm afraid I will be otherwise engaged that evening." Tsingsei lifted her book of poems to cover her face, as though it would force her mother to leave the room.

"You don't know what day it is," her mother growled.

"It's the Midsummer Ball. It's at the middle point of the summer, I assume."

"You're going."

"I can't."

"Why?" Mrs. Gould's eyes flashed a warning.

"I don't believe I will be feeling well enough to attend. Do give everyone my best."

"You are going and that is final," her mother snapped.

Tsingsei closed her book, the pages setting together as quiet as a whisper, and sat straight, adopting a dignified expression. "A lady does not publicly display her displeasure, Mrs. Gould," she said in her best imitation of her mother's voice.

With that, Mrs. Gould stepped forward and struck Tsingsei's cheek with the back of her hand. Tsingsei's head jerked to the side. She clutched her cheek and shot to her feet, letting the book drop to the floor with a thump. She shoved past her mother and all but ran to her bedroom, holding back all her emotions behind a fragile dam, lest the maids in the hall see her cry. Once inside, she locked the door and threw herself onto her bed, shoving her face into one of the many silk-covered down pillows. Tsingsei cried until she ran out of tears. Afterward, she lay in the fading light of the eastern sunset as it splashed pinks and purples across her room, painting the pale faces of every doll in its path a strange hue, which made them appear to be blushing, or bruised—or both.

She crossed the room to her armoire and from the bottom pulled out her little leather purse to sift through the quoine she'd acquired here and there by writing notes from her father for a little extra. There wasn't much—maybe a few hundred or a thousand. She assured herself she'd count it next time she pulled it out to stare at the glittering quoine— but it was a promise she made every time, only to break. One day she would count it, and maybe then she could figure out what she could do with it. Maybe she could buy herself a new horse, or her own personal carriage. Perhaps a fun holiday somewhere without her parents—whether they knew she was taking it or not.

She hadn't given much thought to what she would do with what she'd been skimming from her father's accounts. Tsingsei had only been trying to teach him some kind of lesson—though she was sure he had enough quoine to not even notice she'd taken anything. She tucked her purse into its hiding place and crawled into bed, pulling the covers up to her chin. She lay there for several minutes, staring up at the ceiling as the world darkened.

Daddy never notices the dwindling quoine… I wonder what else he wouldn't realize was gone? Would larger sums alarm him? If his collection of wanted posters for all the pirates he'd caught disappeared, would it catch his attention?

Would he even notice if his own daughter went missing?

Three

THE DAYS LEADING UP TO THE MIDSUMMER BALL PASSED, FOR the most part, uneventfully. As some sadistic form of entertainment for herself, Tsingsei spent some of that time being intentionally difficult. When her mother had apologized for slapping her, she'd also given Tsingsei permission to have any dress she wanted tailor-made for the occasion. She chose to have her newest doll's dress replicated. It wasn't that she loved the dress, or found it to be the most beautiful thing in the world. No, she chose it because making a full sized gown meant the exact details would never look the same. She refused it several times, claiming the cut or the embroidery was wrong; that the fabric was itchy, or it was the wrong shade of white. She didn't much care if it was correct or not. The only thing that mattered was aggravating her mother into flustered breathlessness as another week of preparations was wasted.

By the time Tsingsei had accepted the dress's completion, her mother's nerves had reached their end. Annie Gould was a woman who liked everything to go like clockwork, and for preparations to finish well in advance to account for any sudden problems, so she had time to fix them. And so, Tsingsei quite intentionally didn't accept the dress's completion until the day before the big event. The tailors didn't seem pleased with the whole debacle, but she decided it was worth it just to see the look on her mother's face each time. Besides, they were getting paid well for their time, and should have been thankful.

The day of the ball, everyone was bustling about, too busy to pay attention to Tsingsei, who sauntered the halls in silence, watching the activity. She'd donned one of her garden dresses—a plain blue thing with the skirt hem at her ankles so it didn't drag in the dirt—and mud boots with low heels. Even her mother was too preoccupied to notice she hadn't put on a corset under her dress.

Anytime she heard her name, she'd disappear into one of the many nooks and crannies through the house. She'd memorized them all. The cupboard under the stairs to the second floor. The linen closet down the hall from the ballroom. Even the ones she wasn't supposed to know about—seamless hideaways throughout the house where no one would even know a door to a hole in the wall existed.

Tsingsei exited one such alcove and quietly stole a tart from the kitchen. She hid in the garden to eat it in secret.

A bird left its nest perched high in a tree on the edge of the garden. Tsingsei ascended with care, one branch at a time. This was the purpose of leaving off her corset and wearing those specific boots—both made climbing trees much easier. She'd always been a climber. She had always loved being up in a tree, or walking along the roof of the mansion. There was something thrilling about being so high above the world. By the time she reached the top of the tree, flakes of bark clung to the front of her dress. She peeked over the rim of the nest. Inside were three baby birds, chirping for their mother's return and the meal she would provide. Johanna had always told her to leave baby birds alone, and so she moved away.

Tsingsei worked her way to a branch opposite the bird's nest that hung over the wall of their property. She pulled herself up to sit, and held fast to watch as the world bustled about. The Gould Estate was located at the top of a steady slope, which gave her the perfect vantage to look out over the rooftops and regular people going about their day.

The city seemed enveloped in a cloud, though the sun shone on the Gould estate. Puffs of steam spewed into the air as a whistle blew low and long, announcing the departure of a train. Horse hooves clacked against the cobblestone as wagon wheels thundered along behind them. A few steam cars bumped and clattered, honking at the pedestrians slowing them down.

Steam cars were a new invention, and one that many were not fond of. Her father had not invested in a steam car, even though Tsingsei did find them interesting. Many of the other wealthy families had, though. But he didn't see them as something which would propel the country into the future. On the contrary, he'd already decided they were a failed experiment.

"Death cars!" he'd said, waving a newspaper over the breakfast table. "That's what they are, death cars. They travel too fast and are unstable. Time-bombs, the lot of them."

"I would think them to be safer than a zeppelin," Mrs. Gould had said.

"Skyships are piloted by professionals and don't explode,

unless the zeppelin is exposed to flame. They are perfectly safe, Annie. These *death-traps* are driven by idiots who can barely control their horses."

Annie Gould had giggled into her fingertips and finished her meal in silence. Tsingsei, however, had hung on every one of her father's words. It wasn't often he had breakfast with the family, and so this time she was giddy with hidden delight. That had been five months ago, and he hadn't made it to breakfast since. Each day seemed to keep him away longer and longer until eventually, she thought, he would never return at all. Even with such a party being thrown, he was off at his office and would only return once the festivities had begun.

"What're you doin' up in that tree, love?"

Tsingsei jolted and gripped the branch tighter to keep from falling. Peering over the edge of the brick wall surrounding the garden, she spotted the boy from weeks ago who'd begged for her quoine—though, it took her a second to remember him. His short black hair stood straight on end from the filth of it, and nameless substances smudged his face. His clothes were too big and too small all at the same time. His pants were pulled tight with a belt, yet had short legs that ended too high over his ankles. He had on a baggy blouse and a jacket with long arms he'd shoved up to his elbows and buttons which strained to stay clasped over his wide torso.

"What are you doing at my home? How did you find me?" she demanded.

"Find you? Your home? Miss, I'm on the street and you're in a tree. I weren't searchin' for you. I was just happenin' by because I heard there was festivities in the works, here."

Altain put his hands in his pockets and scrutinized her. "Are you sayin' you're a Gould?"

"How do you know?" Tsingsei snapped.

"Oh, love, everyone knows about the Goulds. Even us street rats. You're, uh…the girl."

"Tsingsei," she growled, her brow lowering into a glare.

"Yeah, that's the one." He chuckled and squinted up at her. "So, miss, how about that quoine? Can I have one now? Not like you'll be missin' just one."

Tsingsei sneered down at him. "Why don't you get yourself a bath and an acceptable change of clothes, then you may have a quoine."

"But I need a quoine for a bath. Clothes'll be more!"

"Then I suppose you'll have to live without my quoines."

"It's a shame, really." Altain shook his head.

"What is?"

"That somethin' so lovely could be so cruel."

She was about to shout another snide comment back at him when Johanna came to the base of the tree, waving her down with such urgency that Tsingsei feared she may fall over.

"Your mother is on her way outside. If she sees you up there, it'll be the end of us both! Who are you talking to?"

"A street rat." She sneered at Altain, who bowed as though she'd introduced him as a lord. "I was just telling him to get himself a proper wash and clothes."

"Well, there is your act of charity for the day, Miss Gould. Now get down from there and go inside. It's time to get ready for the ball."

She climbed down the tree and sprinted to the mansion.

Johanna met Tsingsei in her room in time to cinch her corset and help her into her new dress; it had turned out identical to the doll's. But Tsingsei's hair was not blonde, nor her skin pale ivory. Her hair was a rich brown, so dark it was nearly black. She thought the only extraordinary part of her was her eyes, which were a piercing royal blue.

"Aren't you a sight," Johanna said after the beautician had finished with Tsingsei's hair and makeup.

"The good kind or the bad kind?" Tsingsei gave a cheeky smile and blinked her eyes against the dryness of the powder that had wafted beneath her lids.

"The perfect kind. The boys'll be waiting in line to dance with you."

"They can wait all night," Tsingsei snapped, setting her perfume down a little harder than she'd intended. "I mean…I am still young, Johanna. There is no rush for me to find a suitor."

"Well, you have five," her mother said, bustling into the room.

Tsingsei gaped at her. "Excuse me?"

"You will dance with all of them and choose one before the night is over."

"This is because of the dress, isn't it?"

"This is because you are almost eighteen and it is high time you marry. We should've started searching for new suitors after the Bartons changed their minds."

She vaguely recognized that name, but was in no mood to try remembering. "I don't want suitors! I don't want to marry!"

"And I don't want to hear it. You will dance with any man who asks, and that's final."

She squared her jaw at her mother, already scheming ways to get out of the requirement. Her mother stared at her with the same determined expression. Tsingsei stood as her mother left the room. She stared at herself in the full-length mirror on the inside door of her armoire.

We'll see who gets the last laugh.

Tsingsei strode from the room to stand beside her mother at the base of the grand staircase, welcoming guests after Leonard—or was it Laurence? Leeroy? She could never remember—announced them and they'd descended. She could tell by the way a few men gave her extra attention that these were some of the suitors her mother had spoken of— the oldest of which must have been in his thirties. Tsingsei avoided looking at them, adopting a disinterested expression as she'd turn her gaze anywhere but on them. The blatant snub caused at least two to scoff and stride away, angry. Her mother, of course, hissed a small noise to try getting her daughter in line, but being in public, she couldn't chastise her properly, and so Tsingsei continued the vexing behavior.

Some girls close to her age arrived. She was eager to speak with them, but had to stay put until her mother excused her. It was a lonely life being Tsingsei Gould; maybe just for one night she could have some friends her age. Even if none of them ever spoke to her again, at least she could pretend for a little while.

By the time Mrs. Gould relieved Tsingsei from welcoming duties, couples were already spinning around the dance floor. Guests were lining up along the walls where the tables with fancy foods had been arranged. Tsingsei glanced at the offerings. Oysters, snails, caviar—the usual sort of foods for these types of functions. She found the tarts and picked one up. It hadn't reached her mouth quite yet when someone pressed close to hiss in her ear.

"You put that back right now," her mother ordered. "You are not here to eat, you're here to dance."

"I would think I can do both."

"You don't want the suitors seeing you stuffing your face. It's unattractive."

She squinted at her mother. "You're afraid the men will know that I consume food?"

"Tsingsei—" She jolted in shock as her daughter shoved the entire tart into her mouth.

Her mother glared at her as she finished chewing, swallowed, then delivered a sweet smile.

"I'm not interested in men who are afraid of women with appetites," she said. "Now to wait and see how many I scared off."

She spotted a familiar figure descending the staircase over her mother's shoulder.

"Tsingsei—"

"Oh, look, Daddy arrived earlier than expected." She strode past her mother to welcome her father home. After that, she escaped, having successfully attached her parents together so her mother couldn't continue to hiss at her about how to behave in a manner pleasing to men.

She hadn't escaped for long before one of the suitors stopped her to ask for a dance. He couldn't have been older than twenty-five, which wasn't a terrible gap between them, but didn't add any favor from her. As far as men went he was…all right. Quite a bit too masculine for her tastes. She almost turned him down, until she caught sight of her mother's pursed lips.

As they danced, he dominated the conversation. He seemed perfectly thrilled to speak about his inherited wealth and small mansion, so she let him yammer on uninterrupted.

"Tell me about yourself," he finally said.

She released a dramatic sigh. "Oh, there's not much to say. My parents are trying to marry me off to a wealthy man who will be understanding of my lack of dowry."

"Lack of dowry?"

"Oh, yes. We've had a run of bad luck, but don't tell anyone. We had to cut costs where possible, and my dowry was the first thing to go. But you don't care about that, right? You're already wealthy enough for the both of us." She gave him a charming smile.

"That's quite…unfortunate to hear."

When the song ended, he bowed and left without so much as a glance behind. Tsingsei met her mother's gaze across the distance and she shrugged one shoulder, a smirk working its way across her lips.

Four

THREE GIRLS STOOD CLOSE TOGETHER AT THE CORNER OF A table, sneaking sips of champagne. Tsingsei straightened her white silk gloves and made sure her dress was smooth down the front. She smiled and approached, her nerves tangling together as butterflies formed in her belly. She kept her shoulders squared with a confidence she didn't feel.

"Hello, ladies," she said. "Tsingsei Gould. Welcome to my home."

The girl on the left had bright blonde hair and a dress such a dark blue that it shone like the night sky. Her blue eyes scanned the length of Tsingsei, as though finding things to judge. "I'm Isabelle," she said with an air of indifference.

"Kindra." The girl on the right had hair a rich golden color, and her dress was a soft pink. She barely glanced at Tsingsei before returning her sights to something in the distance.

"It's lovely to meet you, Miss Gould. I'm Marion Dermott." The last girl had dark hair and eyes, with medium brown skin. She reminded Tsingsei of the woman in the antique shop—she'd put money on Marion being at least half Armalinian. Her orange gown had a glittering sheer overlay that twinkled when she moved.

Tsingsei spent much of the night speaking with the girls—mostly Marion, who seemed to actually make an effort. Kindra remained mostly distracted, and Isabelle seemed determined to display the very opposite of interest or intrigue in relation to the event and Tsingsei. Many suitors asked to dance with them, and the ladies would either graciously turn them down, or take one turn around the dance floor. A young man approached and spoke nothings so sweet that Kindra was lost to his spell. After he'd whisked her to the dance floor, Tsingsei turned to the other two and made a face.

"I can't believe she fell for that."

Marion cringed. "I was about to."

Isabelle laughed. "Glad you didn't?"

Marion gulped down the last of a glass of champagne, keeping her gaze on the young man as he spun Kindra around the room, saying something meant only for her ears. "Probably not."

The three girls laughed and exited through the open double doors, where the guests had spilled out onto the patio.

"Come, let me show you the gardens." Tsingsei led the way to a serene patch, which shielded them from the party by a row of shrubs.

They dropped to the soft grass, giddy from the champagne. Dusk had given way into night, and now the three sat under a canopy of stars. Crickets provided their own music over the faint orchestra from the distant party. It was a perfect, warm summer night, and Tsingsei wished she could be enjoying it alone, without some silly ball or irritating suitors.

"Let's play a game," Isabelle said.

"What sort of game?" Marion asked.

She took a swig from a bottle of champagne she'd managed to sneak out in her skirt. "Truth or dare."

"How do you play that?" Tsingsei asked, accepting the bottle as it passed to her. Before this night, she'd only had a few stolen sips once or twice a few years ago. She'd had so much already that her words slurred the slightest bit, and she felt a bit wobbly, even sitting down.

"You will choose to either answer a question truthfully, or fulfill whatever task we dare you to complete."

"And if I don't?"

They stared at each other, trying to come up with something. Tsingsei had no idea what sort of punishments were appropriate for the game. She'd never played anything like it.

Marion held up the champagne. "You will have to drink the contents of this bottle…without stopping for breath."

The other two grimaced at the idea of such a stomachache.

"Who would like to go first?" Isabelle asked.

"It was your idea!" Marion squealed.

"We'll go alphabetically, starting with me." She closed her eyes and took a deep breath. "I choose truth."

"Have you ever been in love?"

Tsingsei snorted a laugh into the mouth of the bottle. Being in love at their age was a preposterous idea.

"Yes. I'm in love with someone I shouldn't be," she blurted, then smiled as though it was a relief to get it out in the open.

Tsingsei choked on the champagne in her mouth, pursing her lips to keep from spitting it back into the bottle. Perhaps Isabelle was a preposterous girl, or perhaps it was Tsingsei who wasn't as emotionally open as the other two—not that she'd ever had anyone who she could have tried with.

"Who?" Marion asked.

"An orphan. He lives in the shelter and works at the factory. He has to walk by my house every day and I live for the times he passes."

"Have you…talked to him? Or are you just in love with his face?" Tsingsei asked.

Isabelle gave her an impertinent look. "Of course I've talked to him."

"Is that the absolute truth?" Marion asked before Tsingsei could ask further.

"Yes."

"Will you swear on the champagne bottle?" Tsingsei giggled, holding it out.

Isabelle smiled, as though ready to forgive the previous question. She set her palm across the label and held up her other hand. "I solemnly swear, on the honor of myself and this bottle of pinched spirits, that I am telling the truth."

The three of them broke down into hysterical giggles.

Marion was the first to regain her composure. "I suppose it's my turn."

"Pick your poison!" Tsingsei said, taking a swig of champagne and passing it to Isabelle.

"I'll choose…dare."

Isabelle tilted her head back, draining the last of the champagne from the bottle. She stuck out her lower lip and gave the empty bottle a look of betrayal. "I dare you to go steal more champagne."

"Easy," Marion said. She stood, dusting off her backside and straightening her skirt. "Back in a mo'!" With a smile, she assumed the poised nature of the lady she was and returned to the folds of the party.

Isabelle turned her secretive smile on Tsingsei. "What will you choose when she returns?"

Tsingsei thought, trying to keep her mind on the task at hand rather than how pretty Isabelle was in her midnight dress. She did not want to choose to tell the truth and risk exposing the secret she held closest to her heart. If they dared her something as simple as a booze run, it wouldn't be any sort of problem.

She returned Isabelle's smile. "I choose dare."

Mischief painted the other girl's lips into a jester's grin. "When Marion returns, I dare you to kiss the most attractive person at this party...on the lips."

"When Marion returns," Tsingsei echoed.

Her head, light as a feather and full of cotton, chose to ignore this caveat. It also forgot proper public etiquette on how to lie without saying a word. For instance, Tsingsei thought she was sitting next to the most attractive guest, but she knew it was unacceptable for her to think such a thing about a lady and not one of the men. But her intoxicated mind did not care as it leaned her body forward and pressed her lips to Isabelle's.

Isabelle pulled away in an instant and Tsingsei teetered forward before correcting herself. The look in Isabelle's eyes told Tsingsei just how wrong she was to have been more attracted to Isabelle than to one of the young men within the ballroom.

"Why..."

"You're the only one here worth looking at," Tsingsei's mouth admitted before she could think of anything more clever.

"That's...that's..." Isabelle stood and brushed at the skirt of her dress. "Someone has to tell your mother, Tsingsei. That is not right. I can't believe..." With that Isabelle stomped off toward the mothers gossiping on the porch outside the ballroom.

Tsingsei stood and ran after Isabelle. "Please, wait. I didn't mean—"

"You're crooked and you must be set right," Isabelle said.

"Why am I crooked?" she asked.

"Have you ever wished to kiss a boy?"

Tsingsei shook her head.

"Only girls?"

She didn't reply.

"You're crooked... Backward!"

"Says who?" she demanded, knowing full well the answer was 'everyone'.

Isabelle stopped to think. "My parents. They say your kind are a twisted perversion."

"And what is your opinion?" Tsingsei asked as she started to cry.

Isabelle did not respond.

"If you say a word, I will tell everyone about your orphan boy." She fought to stop the tears, but they would not stop.

She thought for a moment before a slap stung across Tsingsei's face. Isabelle spun to continue toward the women.

Tsingsei didn't wait for the news to be shared. She ran through the gardens, taking paths which hid her from the patio, around the side of the house, and used the service entrance to avoid any partygoers.

"Oy, love!" a boy called from the step as she swept past him.

She didn't stop as she ran to her room. When she spun to slam her door, he slipped in at the last possible second and she locked him inside before she'd even registered him being there.

"Who are you?" Tsingsei asked.

"I look pretty good all washed up, don't I, love?" Altain tugged on the collar of his new shirt and shuffled his feet. He'd combed his hair back, and his trousers were a perfect fit—he even had shoes on. "You been cryin'?"

"My life is *ruined*," she sobbed, not to confide in him, but he was the first unfortunate person to ask what was wrong. But since she didn't know him, she bit back every detail she wanted to spill out to Johanna.

"Well, you could always start a new life. I did, and look where that got me!" He held his arms out as though his new second-hand clothes were something to be proud of.

"Where did you get those clothes?"

"Your lady gave me some of her quoine to wash up."

Tsingsei laughed through her tears at the irony.

"What's so funny?" Altain demanded.

"I probably gave Johanna that quoine!" As though the reminder compelled her to look, she sank to the floor in front of her armoire and fished into the bottom for her savings. The pouch was heavy in her hands.

He whistled as he eyed it. "With that kind of quoine, I figure you'd be able to start yourself a nice life, although it'd be much humbler than this palace you've got."

Tsingsei wiped her eyes as an idea struck her. "It could help pay for another life like this," she said.

Her mind worked quickly to think everything through. She couldn't stay in Garda if her secret had been told. Her parents would spare no expense to cover up the scandal, appoint her a suitor, and marry her off before the truth could catch up. She couldn't—wouldn't—marry some man. However, if she weren't in Garda anymore, perhaps it wouldn't be such big news. If *the* Tsingsei Gould were to be kidnapped by a suitor or some other man from the party, then her going missing was sure to cause more uproar than her taste in women and distinct lack of taste in men.

She couldn't ask this boy to kidnap her outright, though. Only an idiot would agree to be the villain in her disappearance. Her father would seek the highest punishment if they were caught, and it would be granted.

But perhaps she could trick Altain into it.

"Do you still have that map?"

Altain paused. "Why?"

She smiled, hoping it hid her devious plan. "I will give you every last quoine in here if you will take me with you to find the Lost Treasure of Balamora."

Everyone knew the legend of Balamora. A tragic tale of an inventor who took his riches and sailed off to the east and was never seen again. Several ships had been rumored to have gone after him and met a grizzly fate in the Great Ocean. With nothing out there but sea monsters and bad weather, the sailors likely either starved or drowned. The legend had been adapted into children's tales since then, and had remained as such for at least a century—even she had grown up having it read to her as a bedtime story. No fools sailed in search of the treasure anymore, though many spoke of what they would do with the quoine if they found it.

Altain gave the purse a covetous stare. "I didn't…plan on taking a partner, but…" He grinned. "Why not? When do we leave?"

"Immediately."

Tsingsei smiled as she pulled herself from the floor, kicked off her shoes, and shoved her feet into her pair of gardening boots. For a brief moment she contemplated changing out of her dress, but decided it would take far too long to remove everything; not to mention she would have to strip in front of some boy she didn't even know and didn't trust as far as she could toss him. Tsingsei did, however, remove the crinoline underneath to deflate the skirt. She searched inside her armoire and grabbed her favorite all-weather coat; a long, tan thing with golden embroidery and a high collar with a deep hood. If nothing else, it would cover the white silk gown and hide most of her face from view.

Tsingsei stared at the large purse of quoine she'd saved for no reason. Altain looked expectantly at her.

"You get it once we're safe," she said, slinging it onto her shoulder and securing the strap across her chest.

He sucked on his teeth and eyed it again. "Fair enough."

The pair climbed from Tsingsei's bay window at her insistence. Thankfully, he didn't argue.

Altain hopped over the balcony and dropped the short distance to the ground, losing his footing just enough to send him to his rear. He stood and brushed at his backside as he stared up at her. "Just let go," he said as she clung to the railing. "I'll catch you."

"You're shorter than I am!" she hissed.

"What's height got to do with it? I'm stronger than I look. Just let go."

It wasn't far to fall, but she feared that if she so much as twisted an ankle, he would leave her behind. Tsingsei squeezed her eyes shut and held her breath as she let go and fell backward. Altain's arms wrapped around her, holding tight for a moment longer as she lost her footing.

"See? I told you, old Altain's got you."

She straightened and rolled her eyes. He winked at her, though he had a strange expression of wonder on his face. They proceeded toward a small side gate. She led the way, peering around for any who might catch them as they hid behind bushes and idle carriages in the long gravel driveway which wrapped around a massive fountain.

She'd thought about circling the estate to the gate used for business and services. However, there would be more bustling at that side of the mansion, with the caterers and whatnot. With everyone inside, though, and most of the carriage drivers clustered together near the stables as they waited, the front gate was easily the most neglected entrance to the estate.

Once on the other side of the gate, Tsingsei let out a relieved breath. She remained tense, though, as they were still close enough for someone to spot them and cart her back to the party.

"Relax, miss. We're golden."

But she couldn't relax until they were away from anyone who might recognize her. One moment of lowering her hood, and she'd be caught. Everyone in this city knew her face—at least, they knew the face she had when painted with makeups like that night. She wondered how much easier it would be to not be recognized without the white powder and the blush, and eye makeup that made her eyes look wider than they were. In hindsight, she would have washed her face and changed her dress. But she'd been in a hurry, and there was no going back to redo that moment.

Now that they were outside away from her home, she let him be her guide. Altain led Tsingsei through dark streets and abandoned alleys to the docks, where ships sat anchored in the harbor. Massive towers loomed over the area with wooden walkways connecting them. Coastal cities had their harbors set up this way to make room for both seafaring vessels and skyships of all sizes.

She wasn't an idiot, so she knew the boy wasn't part of some crew they would be joining. She prepared herself to be a stowaway, though the idea sent shocks of fear through her. In another bout of hindsight, she decided she would have sneaked to her parents' room and stolen clothes from her father to disguise herself as a boy. Maybe sailors would be kinder to a boy stowaway than they were sure to be to her. However, Altain began the climb up a tower's stairs. Tsingsei hesitated at the bottom.

"Not afraid of heights, are you?" he asked.

"Where are we going?" Tsingsei was not afraid of the height; she was afraid of what he might do once there. A fall from the catwalk would prove fatal for anyone, and he just might care more about her quoine than her life.

"I have a skyship waiting for us."

"Seriously?"

"Would I lie to you, love?"

She blinked at him. "Yes."

Altain licked his lips and chuckled. "Fair. But…do you care about a tiny white lie more than escaping from the best life anyone could ever ask for?"

She clenched her jaw and stared at his outstretched hand. After a moment to think, she took his hand. "Get me out of here."

The wind at the top of the tower ripped at her coat and skirt. It flung her into Altain, who wrapped his arm around her to keep her steady.

"Get your hands off me," she growled.

"Don't you trust me?"

"No."

"All right, but, I was just making sure you don't fall."

She jerked away from him, then stumbled as another large gust tore across them.

Altain grabbed her again. "Just shut up and let me help you."

"What's stopping you from throwing me over?"

"If I wanted to push you, would I really be holding on for dear life so you *don't* fall?"

Tsingsei clenched her jaw. "Fine. But I still don't trust you."

"I get the feeling you don't trust anyone."

"You're surprisingly astute for a street rat."

He paused to look over one of the crafts. "Careful, love, that sounded dangerously like a compliment."

He led her along the walkway, passing skyships of various types and sizes. She'd never been so close to a skyship before. They were beautiful and daunting. Many were seafaring vessels repurposed, with zeppelins tethered on by ropes and chains. Some were built for speed, others for cargo, and a few just for style. Other vessels built for the sky had a flat bottom, rather than a pointed keel, and crows' nests hanging from the bottom, rather than being up top.

Altain stopped in front of a small skyship with a tan canvas zeppelin and a shining varnish over the oak woodwork. It was one of the smallest tied to the docks, and must have been a repurposed sailer, judging by the telltale keel. She doubted his claims to the ship being there for him, but kept her mouth shut and played along.

He stooped to slide the small board walkway onto the edge of the ship's side. Altain took Tsingsei's hand and led her across. He returned to the dock, glancing around like a madman as he unwrapped the ropes from the dock cleats and tossed them over. After rushing aboard and pulling the walkway onto the deck, he used a pole to push them away from the dock, then ran to the wheel to unlock the propeller and steer them away from Garda. Tsingsei sat on a small stool beside a short table behind the helm and watched as the city grew smaller.

"Miss it yet?" Altain asked.

"Not even a little," Tsingsei replied, wondering if she ever would.

Five

TSINGSEI SPENT THE NIGHT IN A SMELLY HAMMOCK STRUNG up in the galley. It took her hours to fall asleep as thoughts and fears plagued her—along with a bit of motion sickness from the swaying. Somewhere in the dark recesses of her mind, she knew she was a passenger on a stolen sky-ship, no matter how much she tried to ignore that fact. She'd never stolen anything in her life—if anything she'd intentionally overpaid to get her father's attention. Now she was an accomplice to theft. If they were caught, could she claim ignorance and leave Altain out to fend for himself?

Yes, she decided, she could.

"Where is your crew?" Tsingsei asked the next day as Altain dropped onto the stairs beside her.

He bit into a crusty bread he'd found in the galley. "I dismissed them. I was gonna get me a new crew before taking off, but you were in such a hurry we didn't have time."

She nodded, positive he was lying, but uninterested in forcing the truth out of him just yet. She'd spent the morning nauseated, but negotiating with herself on what she could accept, as far as being his accomplice. One of the things she hoped to establish between them was a promise of honesty.

The dark circles around his eyes told her to wait before bringing up such a serious subject.

Desperate for his own turn in a hammock, Altain gave her a quick lesson in flying. He explained the altimeter which gauged the distance the craft was above the ground, and the horizon gauges, which measured the tilt of the craft both forward and backward and side to side.

He instructed her to stay at a southwestern heading and make sure the horizon lines didn't move. Should the craft tilt to either side, it would put strain on the rigging. If the bow dipped, it would send them toward the ocean; if it rose they'd get lost in the stars. Neither was too sure about that second event's consequences, but flying into the stars seemed a good enough reason not to do it.

With a lazy salute, he disappeared into the captain's chambers to sleep. Tsingsei had bitten her tongue against admitting she was terrified of manning the helm. She'd wanted to come on this journey and so she had to do her part. Right now her part was helmswoman. Alone. The vessel and their lives gripped in the palms of her hands. She shook the thought off and stood resolute, keeping her sights on the horizon.

It was breathtaking, being up so high without a building in sight. The azure sky had bright white clouds dotted and smeared across it. The blue sky and ocean both stretched out around her as far as her eyes could see. They met somewhere in the distance and blurred together as a haze on the horizon. Tsingsei secured the wheel with the loop of a rope attached to the quarterdeck railing and walked to the side to peer down at the ocean. The calm water rippled and shimmered in the sunlight. Somewhere in the distance, a spout of water spurted into the air as a whale surfaced, before it dove back down, slapping the water with its fluke.

"I could get used to this," she said, leaning her elbows on the railing.

Tsingsei breathed in the salty air and tasted her freedom. It was magnificent. She felt as though a hunger that had been gnawing at her stomach for years had finally been satiated. With no one to scoff at her attire or demand she wear specific items, she undressed and removed her corset, then slipped her gown back on, doing her best to tie the back without her handmaid. She did a terrible job, but in the end decided it didn't matter, because who would even see it? Though, missing Johanna and the convenience of having her around was the first pang of regret which slapped her across the face.

The hours alone at the helm passed slowly as Tsingsei grew quite bored rather fast. She entertained herself by singing songs. When she grew bored of singing, she started telling a story about an adventurer who became world renown and so widely adored no one could tell her what to do. That's what Tsingsei wanted—somewhere out here in the open air. To find an adventure and make a name for herself that wasn't Gould. To be respected. Maybe even something of a hero in children's stories.

When Altain woke, the eastern sunset was painting the sky with its rosy pastels. He stumbled from the captain's cabin and walked to the edge of the deck to relieve himself over the side.

"Must you do that there?" Tsingsei demanded.

"Where else am I supposed to do it?"

A light blush crept into her cheeks. "I've been using a bucket."

Altain whistled low. "I bet you're missing that fine porcelain you're used to. And I bet you had to dump it yourself and everything."

She glared at him. "I'm sorry you find my comfortable life so offensive."

"Your life was more than comfortable, love."

"Would you stop calling me love!"

"Doll? Darling? Miss? Oh, how about 'your highness'?" Altain bowed low before taking the wheel and pushing Tsingsei with his shoulder.

"You're the most unbearable thing in the morning, you know that?"

"At least mine is only in the morning, your highness." He rubbed his eyes in a futile attempt to wipe the last of sleep away.

"Stop calling me that. I have a name, you know."

"Yeah, I know."

"So use it!"

Altain thought for a moment. "No, I don't think I will."

"Why?" she demanded.

"Because your name is ridiculous."

Tsingsei gaped at him.

"Your name is noise. That's what it is. It's like your parents thought you'd have a beautiful voice and so you'd *sing* things rather than *say* them. It's complete rubbish."

"There is nothing wrong with my name," Tsingsei snapped.

"There is everything wrong with your name. You've got a rubbish name."

"I was named after my great-great-grandmother!"

"Well, your great-great-grandmother had a rubbish name!"

She folded her arms and glared at him. "And what would *you* call me that's so much better?"

Altain sucked on his teeth as he thought. "Song."

"Now that's a rubbish name."

"Well, it was either that or Freedom, but I thought I'd stick with the noise theme your parents had going." Altain smirked at his own cleverness.

"You're naming me after the Song of Freedom?" She didn't know what to think about his choice.

"Well, yeah. You're free from everything now, including your under-things." He nodded at the little bundle on the deck. "Song just rolls off the tongue, too."

"Song Gould?" She made a face.

"No. You're not a Gould anymore, not out here and not with me. You're just Song now."

She played with the new name, letting it grow on her. "What about you? Should I give you a new name as well?"

Altain's brow furrowed. "Why? There's nothing wrong with my name!" He winked at her, then checked the compass, righting their course a small fraction.

"Do you even know where we're going?" Tsingsei tried to take the map out of his back pocket.

If she could just get it open and see that it was blank, perhaps she could admit to him she'd known all along, and they could start on that honesty she'd wanted that morning. He was on a wild goose chase for a fake treasure from a children's story, but Tsingsei had already found it in her freedom. But what would he do if she told him he was her kidnapper and nothing more? Would he take her home? Abandon her? Throw her overboard? She swallowed all her admissions as he caught her hand and took the paper back.

"Of course I know where we're going." He tapped her head with the folded paper, then slipped it back into his pocket.

She stared at him a moment longer, willing the words to come out. Instead, she shuffled away to watch the sunset and think.

Tsingsei stood beside the propeller for hours, watching the moon's reflection ripple across the ocean below. She ran a hand over a plank of railing. It was darker than the rest and rough to the touch, as though it hadn't yet been varnished to match. It was an unfinished bit surrounded by polished perfection. That was her. That was life in the city as a young girl with a secret.

The crooked daughter of the famous Goulds.

But no longer. Out in the air over the ocean, she was someone else. Someone who didn't have to follow rules or decorum. She was free. Her heart filled with an excitement she'd never thought possible. She wanted to scream her joy out to the sky. To make sure the sea birds resting on the bow railing knew how excited she was. Instead, she sang.

> *"Oh, there's a place on the horizon,*
> *A land that we'll call our own.*
> *You'll find me there where the sun rises.*
> *You'll find me there, in my new home."*

Altain wrapped a rope around the wheel and stood beside Tsingsei. He stared out at the sea and took a deep breath.

"Chain my hands and bind my body,
Shackle me to the ground.
Tie my flesh, but know my spirit
Will never be held down."

His voice was crisp and high, like a flute. A perfect contrast to Tsingsei's gentle alto—a voice her mother had deemed too low for a girl. Together they sang the final verse. She picked up the more difficult harmony the men had always sung, but it was within her range so she had joined in secret.

"Sew our lips and steal our voices,
You can rip away my tongue.
Try your best. You'll never silence
Our song of freedom."

After a long silence between them, Altain said, "I never got why something called 'The Song of Freedom' was so… depressing."

"It's sung by the slaves in Pishing," Tsingsei said.

"I never understood what it meant. Until…five years ago? Around my tenth birthday, think." He picked at the railing. "It was cold that winter, and I hadn't eaten much but stale bread from the garbage in days. I went into the factory where my brothers work, hoping to get a job. Just so I could buy myself a coat and a hot meal. There were boys as young as five and old granddads working. One of the younger boys tripped and fell against a hot steam pipe. It burned the skin right off his ear. When he started to cry, they spanked him and told him to get back to work."

Tsingsei didn't know what to say to this, so she said nothing.

"I left there and never went back inside. But once when I was passing it, I heard some of the workers singing that." He squinted out at the water. "Why are people so cruel to others that they have to go and write songs like that?"

Tsingsei shrugged. After a long moment, she asked, "If you've got brothers working in a factory, then why were you living on the streets?"

Altain sighed and scrutinized her. With a deep breath, he put a smile on his face and spun around. "So, this is the Dauntless." He held his arms wide.

"Altain, why—"

"You already know the helm, propeller, main deck and zeppelin," he continued. "And the galley. Let me show you my cabin." He took her hand and led her down the stairs to a door below the quarterdeck.

It was a cozy room. There were windows along the far wall with a cabinet beneath them. A mahogany desk with a green top sat a short distance away with its chair facing the door—a perfect vantage so as to never be caught by surprise. A leather-bound book and an inkwell sat atop the desk. There was a cupboard to one side of the room with a large chest beneath it. A padded hammock hung from the ceiling with a soft blanket and a round pillow heaped within. It was then that Tsingsei realized how tired she'd grown.

"I need to sleep," she said with an air of apology.

"Take my hammock." Altain smiled and held it open for her.

Tsingsei lifted her skirt and eased into the swaying fabric. "Good night, Altain."

He winked and left the room, closing the door behind him.

Tsingsei pulled the blanket to her chin, wrapping it around her. Like the night before, it took a while to fall asleep as she swayed in the hammock, listening to the propeller beat the air outside the windows. Her sleep was restless, and she felt half awake the entire time, tossing and turning, though this hammock was much more comfortable than the one in the galley. Frightful dreams plagued her. Fears come to life in never seeing her parents or Johanna again. Perhaps something terrible happening to one of them, and she wouldn't know, because she was off in the sky with some street rat liar she didn't even know. A stinging homesickness pricked at her heart until she sat up, a feeling of guilt gnawing at her stomach.

I didn't even leave a note.

A waxing moon lit the night. Tsingsei found Altain sitting in a small gap in the railing, dangling his feet over the edge.

She stood over him and sighed. "I think I need to go back home."

Altain picked some dirt from under his fingernail and squinted out at the water sparkling in the moonlight. "No."

"I know we had a deal—the quoine is still yours. Just take me home."

He didn't reply.

"I said—"

"I heard what you said, love. And I said no."

"Why?" she demanded.

"When I was nine—"

"I don't want another damned story. I want to go home!"

Altain looked up at her through his eyelashes, his expression stoic. He turned his attention back to the water. "When I was nine, I woke in the middle of the night and heard my parents arguing."

Tsingsei sighed and sat beside him. He would tell his story whether she wanted to listen or not, so she might as well listen.

"See, I've got three older brothers and one older sister. But I've also got two younger sisters and two younger brothers. My mum was having another baby and dad was worried about how they'd afford feeding another mouth." He grew silent for a minute. "They decided they were going to send me to the factory with my father and brothers."

"That's not so bad," Tsingsei said. "At least you'd be with family."

"But my brothers had all gotten to learn things. They didn't get sent to the factory until they were fifteen. Before that, they learned letters and numbers in the same living room down the street. They got enough learning from Miss Blanch that it was fine. But me? I still had things I didn't know. I deserved my time as much as they did." He sighed. "It wasn't fair. So I left."

"You've been living on the streets since you were nine?" Tsingsei gasped.

Altain nodded. "It was easy at first. People like helping the young ones. The older I got, the less they helped. I realized that other boys on the streets were out for themselves and no one else. They'd no sooner help you than a rich girl would give you quoine just because you asked nicely." His gaze met hers and she looked away, a clenching much like shame wringing her heart. "I also tried to go home, Song. But when I got there…they'd forgotten me."

"They didn't recognize their own son?" Tsingsei asked.

"I didn't go in, just looked in the window. Everything was continuing on without me. They didn't care, Song. If I'd gone back within the next few days, then maybe they would have missed me. But once I realized they were better off, I stopped thinking about going back home and instead tried to make my own."

"Are you saying I'll be forgotten, too?"

Altain released an airy laugh. "No one could forget you. I'm saying that you need to remember why you left and think if it would be better for you to go back home or continue on."

Tsingsei set her cheek on the banister and stared out at the moon. "I left because someone had discovered my secret and she was going to tell my mother. If my mother had found out…she would have put me through every torture imaginable, trying to make everything correct according to her own views on the world."

"How do you know?"

She shrugged one shoulder. "I just do. Mother doesn't like messes. And my…persuasion…would be a big mess for my parents to clean up like it wasn't true."

He scrutinized the side of her face. "There's nothing about you I'd change, Song. You were raised as a snob, but under that, I think you've got a good heart."

"A snob?" she demanded.

"Rich? Spoiled?"

"Ignored by my parents and given dolls as recompense."

"I would never give you r-rec…that." He took her hand in his, but she dragged it back into her own lap.

She gave him a sad smile. "They bought me off with dolls, Altain. A porcelain face in exchange for time."

"I thought it was odd to have such a collection. Were they expensive?"

"Some were probably worth more than is in that pouch I gave you."

He whistled low. "Bring any with you?"

She narrowed her eyes. "You know I didn't."

"Was worth asking!" He shrugged. "Song, my point is, I was being sold, and you were being bought… Why would either of us want to go back to that?"

Tears stung her eyes. He was right. She'd known her whole life, but it had taken him saying it aloud for it to really hit her. Her chin quivered, and she tried to hide her crying. Altain brushed a tear from her cheek and sighed. He pulled her to him and let her cry on his shoulder. As much as she wanted to pull away and slap at his hands, she really needed that embrace right then. She could be stronger later.

"It's all right, love. I've got you."

Six

OVER THE NEXT WEEK, TSINGSEI WORKED TOGETHER WITH Altain to run the skyship. She still had no idea where they were heading, but she stayed the course all the same. She did at least gain her confidence and corner Altain about his lies.

"I just want us to be honest with each other," she said.

He wouldn't look her in the eyes, opting to fidget with a wheel spoke. "What makes you think I'm lying?"

"You lived on the street. This is obviously not your skyship."

"Yeah, well, we're already on it, aren't we? Too late to change your mind."

Tsingsei growled in frustration. "If we get caught, I will claim I knew nothing about it being stolen, and I'll tell the authorities you kidnapped me."

His eyes rounded as he settled a hurt expression on her. "But that's a lie!"

"They don't know that."

"You wouldn't."

"Give me a reason not to throw you under the carriage, then."

Altain groaned. "Fine, fine. I don't even know who it belongs to, all right? I didn't have a bloody plan. I saw quoine and just made it up as we went."

"And the map?"

"Well, it is a world map. But that's about it. Found it in the garbage and thought I could trick a few people."

She folded her arms. "Did it work?"

"No."

"You and me," she said, pointing between them, "we're partners in this, now. No lying to each other. Lie to anyone else, but never each other. All right?"

He sighed in resignation. "All right, Song…partner."

She made a face at him. "Quit looking so smug."

"Sorry. I just never thought the richest person in the world would ever call me anything but an annoying street rat. Yet here you are, dangerously close to calling me a friend."

Her nose wrinkled. "Let's stick to 'partner' and see what happens."

"I'll take it."

Outside of their new understanding, they fell into a sort of routine. They continued to take turns flying—she during the day and him at night. It was rather lonely that way, except for the times when both were awake to have a conversation. Altain tip-toed around her sometimes, like giving her temper wide berth. Other times he seemed to be intentionally jabbing every one of her buttons.

Not that she wasn't doing the same, of course. She was trying to get a measure of him. Trying to figure out what sort of person he was. Would he drop all blame onto her without a thought, like she would do to him? Or was he the sort to go quietly?

He was not the latter. In fact, often he didn't know when to shut up. He loved telling jokes and making her laugh, but hadn't quite learned which jokes were anything but amusing to her.

And so, they continued to prod at each other to find the other's boundaries. Altain's seemed quite a bit more resilient than her own, as he laughed most things off. Every off-color comment about her upbringing left her straight-backed and glaring with indignation as he giggled. The only question now was would either of them respect the other's boundary once they'd learned it? Or would they cross that line just to cause the other the most anger or hurt possible? Only time would tell.

TSINGSEI WOKE WITH A START. HER MIND SCRAMBLED TO REMEMBER what had torn her from sleep. She got her bearings and looked around the captain's cabin where she and Altain now took turns sleeping. It was far less lonely to stay in there than in the galley or cargo hold. Her mind zeroed in on the sound that had woken her. Outside, a woman was screaming so loud she must've been on deck. The voice didn't stop for a second—not even to take a breath.

She leapt from the hammock and rushed to the chamber door. After a pause in consideration, she ran to the desk to search through the drawers. She found a small, stout dagger with a rounded T-shaped handle. She gripped the weapon in her fist, the metal cool between her middle and ring fingers. In one movement she opened the door and sprung onto the deck.

Empty.

At the helm, Altain stood pale and frozen with fear, his knuckles had gone bone white from gripping the wheel.

"Do you hear that?" Tsingsei shouted over the din.

"Of course I bloody hear that!" His voice cracked, betraying his terror.

She swallowed hard, forcing her panicked heart down out of her throat. "Well, what is it?"

More screams sounded in the night, permeating the thick fog that had settled upon them like a woolen blanket. Some screams were higher like a child, some low as a grown man, others were sorrowful moans. Altain shrugged, not daring to speak, lest his voice betray him again. Tsingsei stepped across the deck, her stockinged feet soft on the hard wood. No matter how hard she squinted, she couldn't see anything past the thick fog.

"You're too near the ground," she called out.

"Nowhere near it."

She growled in exasperation and strode to Altain's side. Tsingsei checked the altimeter beside the compass on the helm. Sure enough, they were kilometers over any sort of ground. Her heart pressed into her throat once again and thundered so violently against her vocal cords that any sounds she might've tried making were impossible. To be so high and yet shrouded in such a thick fog seemed impossible. She'd certainly never heard of such a thing. Then there were the screams. How could any sound seem so close, and yet there was no possible way for it to be there?

Tsingsei scanned through the fog, searching for anything besides white clouds. Something, perhaps a shadow, caught her eye. "Over there! Portside." She ran to the main deck and leaned over the railing, straining to make out any shapes.

Altain adjusted course to bring the skyship closer. The wind picked up, buffeting their clothing and forcing the air back into their lungs. Tsingsei covered her mouth and nose with one hand as her throat fought against the wind. The screams intensified, assaulting their ears and making them ring. The fog broke, revealing a rock wall stretching in all directions as far as the eye could see. Tsingsei gasped and skittered backward. She fell to the deck.

Altain spun the wheel, turning the craft to avoid colliding with the cliff. The wind exploded against them as they flew past a long, deep cavern that frowned with sorrow in the stone. A low moan emanated from its mouth, shaking Tsingsei's bones and bringing her windpipe to a nauseating close. Altain pressed his shoulder to one ear and used his free hand to cover the other. A woman's scream pierced the air as they passed by a thin, shallow scar against the stony face.

"What the bloody hell is that all about, then?" Altain shouted when they'd flown far enough away to hear their own thoughts, and the fog had swallowed the cliff once more.

"How the bloody hell should I know?" Tsingsei snapped, picking herself up from the deck.

"There are maps in the cabin. Get them."

Tsingsei sheathed the little dagger and slipped it into her bodice, deciding it was a useful weapon for a lady. The maps sat upright in a bucket, rolled and bound with ribbons. She laid them all out flat on the desk and scanned each one before sliding it to the floor. When she found the one she sought, she rolled it up, grabbed the lantern and rushed back out to the helm. She unfurled it on the map table behind the helm.

"This has to be it," she said.

The map depicted Armalinia, a desert country whose populations centered around oases and along the banks of the huge river. The land was world renowned for exotic spices and fine fabrics. Tsingsei had always loved items made there, but knew little else of it. Not that no one had taught her, of course. She had just never bothered to pay attention to her world lessons. Thinking back on it, though, she wished she had.

Ocean surrounded three sides of Armalinia's triangular landmass, but to the south was a stretch of mountains separating it from Jashedar—a country culturally similar to their home country of Andalise. On the Jashedar side, the Impasse Mountains tapered into the Blind Woods, but on the Armalinian side, there was a hard line and swirling pen strokes.

"The Screaming Cliffs," Altain read aloud.

"You can read?" Tsingsei gaped.

He pursed his lips and shot her a bitter glare. Altain squinted from the wheel. "What's that small bit underneath say?"

"Skyships beware: the Screaming Cliffs are shrouded in perpetual fog."

"Would make a brilliant place to hide," Altain said.

"Do you think maybe, I mean, if the legend is real... Balamora? I know it says he sailed east, but it could be a lie."

He thought about it. "No. Do you really think anyone could live with that racket for long? It'd drive me mad. Besides, this would have been too obvious."

"Then where do you think it would be?"

"Far and away," he replied as though beginning a mystical tale. "Where the red sun looms over the mountains, and the sky calls your name." He winked at her.

She gave him a playful shove for repeating lines from the children's story. "A real answer!"

"All I know is we won't find it until we stop looking."

"That's preposterous."

"I didn't make the rules."

She shook her head and stared off into the fog. "Should we actually try to find it?"

"Where would we even look?"

"East." Tsingsei shrugged.

He thought about it as his thumbnail ran through a crack in a wheel handle. "We've only been out a couple weeks. Let's have a few more adventures before we take on that particular legend, yeah?"

She let out a long breath. "I want to be the one who finds it."

"Hmm?"

"I want the entire world to know my name, Altain. But not Tsingsei Gould. They already know that. I want the entire world to know the name Song." She smiled shyly as he smirked over his shoulder at her. "I'm going to find Balamora's treasure. We'll find it together."

Tsingsei blinked as she thought a faint glitter like pale blue stars had managed to shine bright enough to permeate the fog. It disappeared, though, and she figured maybe she was just tired and seeing things.

"I should get back to bed."

Altain bent to examine the map one last time and adjust their course, then rolled it up and set it in her arms. "Go back to sleep, Song—future co-discoverer of Balamora's treasure. I'll get us away from this awful noise."

She returned to the cabin and dropped the map onto the desk. It unfurled and threw itself from the surface to join its compatriots. She stared at the mess for a moment longer, then shrugged and decided it was a problem for tomorrow. Tsingsei fell into the hammock with such force she paused to make sure it wouldn't rip from the rafters and send her crashing to the floor. When the bolt in the ceiling didn't so much as quiver, she dragged the blanket over herself and closed her eyes.

Dreams of a red sun behind a haze of dark smoke over a mountain made her sleep fitful. In the morning, though, the images were gone—chased away by strange voices whispering one word in a chorus over and over. She snapped upright, trying to catch her breath as the word echoed in her mind.

Song.

ALTAIN SAID NOTHING AS TSINGSEI EMERGED FROM THE cabin. He set his wooden stein of cold tea in her hands and stumbled into the chamber, shutting the door behind him. He had brewed it strong and unsweetened; it was bitter in her mouth as she gulped down the half he hadn't finished. She grimaced at the sharing of his mug, but they were low on dishes and tea, so they had to make do with whatever was available and not waste supplies—at least, that's what Altain had said. She'd begun to trust him as their honesty pact proved to be taking hold. So she had to trust that he knew a thing or two about stretching one's meals.

Tsingsei stayed at the helm for hours, thinking over the treasure and the legend. To ease her boredom, she talked to the air as though it could help her sort everything out.

"What do you think the treasure is?" She shrugged. "I couldn't say. Is it some fancy invention? A chest of quoine? …Power?" She smiled. "Something like the Touched, maybe. But better. More powerful." Tsingsei laughed into the breeze. "Whatever it is, I'm going to find it and claim it. No matter what."

Song…

She jerked to look over her left shoulder for the whispers, but there was obviously nothing there. After a few minutes, she realized she'd accidentally set the course directly west. On that heading, they would end up out in the middle of the Great Ocean. Without supplies and with just the two of them, it could have been their deaths. She righted the course to head northward.

"I think I'm losing my bloody mind," she said. "Oh, what makes you say that?" Tsingsei shrugged. "I don't know. Maybe it's that I keep hearing words in the wind. Oh, and I'm having *conversations* with *myself.*" She slapped her hands over her face and shook her head. "I'm so bored."

She wrapped the rope over a handle to keep it steady on course as she wandered about the deck. Ropes ran from the railing along the wooden ship body up to the sides of the zeppelin. They weren't connected to the netting which embraced the zeppelin, keeping it in place. Tsingsei pulled at one and discovered flaps which would open wide at the tug of the rope. She deduced that it was to catch the wind and push the skyship along faster.

As she rounded the bow, Tsingsei's stomach growled. She rushed below deck after checking that the course was clear, and peered around the galley. Dirtied dishes from days before lay strewn about, leftover food—unfit for consumption—clinging to them. She sighed at the burlap sacks and crates, then returned to the helm. Altain wouldn't be too much longer, she assured herself.

But he was. High noon had come and gone, but still Altain slept. Tsingsei could take no more; her stomach ached as though a small animal had gotten inside and was clawing its way back out. She set the rope over a handle then let herself into the cabin, where the boy sighed his snores through his nose.

"Altain," she whispered. When he did not respond, she poked his shoulder. "Altain, wake up!" she said a bit louder. She took his shoulder in her hand and shook him. "Altain!"

He jumped awake, his eyes scanning the room before settling on her. "What's wrong?"

"I'm hungry." As though to emphasize her point, her stomach emitted a painful moan that grumbled through the room.

He stared at her, gauging the seriousness of her desperation. "So eat."

"There's nothing to eat."

"I was in the galley last night, there is plenty to eat. Go make yourself some porridge."

"How?"

His face remained impassive as he studied her. After a long moment, he blinked, his eyebrows knitted together in frustration. "You put water in it."

"Which one is the porridge?"

"You can't be serious," he scoffed, rolling over in the hammock to present his back to her.

Without warning, Tsingsei broke down into desperate sobs. Altain craned his neck around to cock an eyebrow at her. She covered her face and gasped into her palms, catching tears on her fingers.

"You are serious?" He turned over and sat up, keeping his attention on the blubbering mess she'd become.

Altain examined her, taking in every little thing she'd looked at in the mirror for days on end. The scrutiny made her think over it all and cry for her wretched state as well as her empty belly. Her hair had lost its luster and fallen flat long ago, all the curls gone and replaced with knots. There were remnants of paling paste and powder around the outer edges of her face. Grease from the propeller machinery had smeared across her arms and shoulders. Her dress was fraying at the embroidery. She'd long since left her coat sitting in the chair at the desk, not daring to let it get so dirty.

He stood and pulled her into his arms. Altain didn't shush her, like she expected. He stroked the grimy knot forming on the back of her head and let her drop as many tears as she had onto his shoulder.

"It's all right, love. I've got you," he cooed. When her sobs quieted, he looked into her eyes and smiled through his bitter lethargy. "Have you ever seen uncooked food before?"

She shook her head. "I woke in the mornings to a large meal prepared by the cooks. I never went into the kitchens."

"Not even once?"

"Well, a few times, I suppose. But I never looked at anything, just stole some treats."

"You can't steal from yourself."

She frowned, and her stomach growled, objecting to his attempt at humor. Altain sighed and took her by the hand, leading her to the galley. It took some searching before he found a small pot that was clean. He showed Tsingsei how to light a fire in the sandbox—a shallow, square wooden box filled with sand and coal for fire—boil the water, and measure the porridge. They added some dehydrated mushrooms and sweet-sour berries for flavor. Altain returned to the helm while Tsingsei stirred the mixture, waiting for it to thicken. When it was a consistency Tsingsei recognized, she smothered the fire with sand, grabbed two clean spoons, and carried the pan out by the wooden handle.

"Here." Altain pointed to the deck at his feet.

As she approached, he pulled up on the lever beside the helm to stop the propeller. They sat on opposite sides of the pan and ate from it in silence. When Altain finished, he dropped the spoon into the pot and lowered himself backward. Sea birds cried somewhere far below them; the wind brushed against groaning ropes which pulled at the wood and held fast to the zeppelin overhead. There was the sound of a spoon scraping against the metal pot as Tsingsei did her best to scoop out every last bite. When she finished, the spoon dropped into the pot with a jarring clang. She sighed in satisfaction and lay back to stare at the underside of the zeppelin and digest her meal.

"Good thing your parents were rich," Altain commented after a while.

"Why is that?"

"Because I imagine it'd cost a small fortune to feed you."

Tsingsei pushed herself up onto her elbows to look at him. He was lost in thought, staring at the propeller blades as the wind pulled at them, trying to urge them back into motion.

"What's that supposed to mean?" she asked.

"You wouldn't know it, looking at you. I mean, you look half starved… But you eat like a derby horse."

"My mother thought I didn't eat enough. She wanted me to have wide hips with a skinny waist."

He made a face at the zeppelin. "I don't think eating more does that."

Tsingsei shrugged. "Certainly doesn't work on me, that's for sure."

"Is that why ladies wear their corsets so tight?"

She shook her head and shrugged. "Maybe some of them. It can make the waist narrower and push up…other things."

"That's cruel. Did you wear it tight like that?"

"Yes."

"Why?"

"Because that's the fashion." She made a face at the word *fashion*. "And my mother demands I keep up with all the latest."

"But you've got nothing to squeeze in or push up!"

Tsingsei gasped. "How dare you speak of a lady's body! You shouldn't even be looking!"

Altain flushed. "I weren't meaning no offense. But I'm also not blind. You're a girl, of course I looked at you. Not that there's much to see."

"What's *that* supposed to mean?" Her eyes narrowed, daring him to respond.

He accepted the silent challenge without hesitation. "I could put your dress on and look in the mirror and see the same thing."

Tsingsei picked a berry husk from between her back teeth as she contemplated this. "Maybe so, but I wear it better."

"No arguments there."

She stared at their last pot and sighed. "So, what now?"

"What do you mean?"

"We're out of dishes."

He sat up and shrugged. "We'll have to wash them."

She stared at him, her brow furrowed as she tried to imagine what washing dishes entailed. For Tsingsei, it was a foreign concept. She assumed it was something similar to taking a bath, but for dishes. But how did they get themselves clean?

"We've only one barrel of water," she said.

"We won't use our drinking water."

"Then what?"

"Look around us, Song! We're over the ocean!" He stood and offered a hand to her, which she took. He pulled her up and spun her to his side, where he wrapped an arm around her waist.

She glared at the silly grin that spread across his lips. As she shoved his hand from her side, he released the propeller brake. Tsingsei leaned over the railing to push the blades back into their rhythm.

"Right, then. Here we go." He grabbed a lever within a vertical slit beside the altimeter and the forward and backward horizon gauge. "Hold on to something." Altain eased the lever down and the nose of the skyship dipped.

Tsingsei gripped the railing beside the helm, planting her feet as her stomach somersaulted over the rapid descent. She gasped as the water rushed up toward them. Altain's smirk betrayed his humorous disposition as he pushed the handle back to the middle mark and the skyship leveled out, not far over the ocean's surface. She breathed a sigh of relief and straightened.

"Was it really necessary to make such a steep descent?"

He stopped the propeller and slipped the rope over a wheel handle. "No. But the look on your face was priceless."

He leapt away from her swinging fist and onto the main deck. Along the bow of the ship were three barrels Tsingsei had all but ignored; he strode to them now and lifted the lids. They were empty. Beside them was a bucket on a rope, which Altain took to the railing and tossed over the side. Using the rope, he retrieved the bucket and returned to the barrels to dump the seawater inside.

"Feel free to jump in at any time, love." He gripped the edge of the bucket in one hand and pushed his other fist into his waist.

"Into the barrel?" Tsingsei gasped.

"No! I didn't— Why would— Come and help me!" He tossed the bucket with exasperated zeal.

When they'd filled all the barrels, they gathered the dirtied dishes from the galley and took them above deck. He talked her through the process of washing them, ignoring the expression of horror which crossed her face as she realized she would have to touch them with her hands.

Tsingsei did her best to keep the unsavory bits of dried and rotted food from touching any part of her, but soon realized the dishes were not washing properly. She sat in silence for a long time, mentally preparing herself for the new levels of peasantry she was about to submit herself to.

"They're not going to get clean if you just sit there thinkin' really hard about it," Altain said. He dropped his brush and rinsed a dozen items, then set them on a cloth to dry.

"I'm…getting there," Tsingsei whined.

"What's the most repulsive thing you've ever touched?" he asked with a laugh.

Tsingsei didn't have to think hard, but paused on the reply. She glanced over her shoulder at him as he stopped midway to the helm to hear her response. "You." She turned her attention back to the filthy bowl she'd pinched between her thumb and forefinger, clinging to the only clean spot around the rim with not much more than her fingernails. Even the backside had been dirtied from being stacked within another dish.

"Me?" he demanded. "How can you…?" He paused and glanced down at his clothes, which were blackening in his filth. "Point taken." He strode to crouch beside her and took the bowl. "Look at it this way: you can always wash your hands after."

"But…" She tried to form a valid argument in her head, but failed.

Altain pressed the bowl into her palm. Her mouth dropped open and a faint cry gagged from her throat. Minutes passed as she stared at the bits of food touching her once-manicured fingers. She felt as though he'd thrown her head-first into a lake of freezing water before she'd even been allowed to test it with a toe.

"I can't do this," she gasped.

"You'll relieve yourself in a bucket, grease up the gears, sleep in a smelly hammock…but you draw the line at *dishes?*"

She shook her head, trying to form a better argument. Instead all she could muster was a repeated, "I can't do this."

Altain growled. "You're not princess of Garda anymore. You took my hand and ran away from all that. If you want to go back to being the pretty centerpiece of your father's collection, then fine, we'll turn around and get you home. But if you want to stay out here and do something that actually matters for once in your pampered, dull little life…then get scrubbing."

Tsingsei ducked her head as the words stung tears from her eyes. She felt as though everything she'd ever thought or done or aspired to in Garda was worthless. She was worthless. What was a pile of dishes compared to the adventures they'd planned? What would she do in the face of pirates, highwaymen, or slimy merchants with no scruples? The world was not a clean place, and never had been. But Tsingsei had never lived in the world. A high wall and iron gates protected her from the general population. Servants made sure she never had to do anything unseemly. Closed carriages kept her separated from the riffraff on the city streets.

"I'm not a Gould princess," she said.

"Then who are you?"

"My name is Song, and I'm a treasure hunter." She squinted up at him as the sun fell below the line of the zeppelin, removing all shadows from the deck.

Altain smirked. "Does Song the Treasure Hunter do dishes, or does she cry and wish she were back home in her silk sheets?"

"Song doesn't have silk sheets. She has an itchy hammock and rotten food on her hands."

With that, she turned her attention back to the bowl and began scrubbing until every bit of gunk had come loose. Altain stayed at the helm for most of the afternoon, occasionally stepping down to wash an item or two. After a while, he knelt behind her and began to comb all the tangles from her hair. She wanted to swat him, but at the same time, she was glad for the help.

"Song?"

"What, Altain?" She rinsed her last dish and raised an eyebrow at him over her shoulder.

He smiled and ran a final smoothing palm over her rippling cascade of dark hair. "Tsingsei Gould's got nothing on you."

THE HOME SICKNESS HAD DIMINISHED TO NEARLY NOTHING as they traveled—the thought of an adventure and a legendary treasure saw to that. The more she learned to exist comfortably without her handmaid, the less she missed her. Altain did his best to encourage her, though sometimes it felt a bit snotty. He would congratulate her for doing a simple job she'd had trouble with before, like dumping her refuse bucket into the ocean. Every so often it felt condescending, though, and so she would find bratty ways to congratulate him for managing to not be annoying. He took it in stride, though.

By the time they docked in a city called Lund in Andalise, she had grown rather fond of Altain. She no longer shoved his hands away if he tried to comfort her. By all accounts, she realized he was her friend, and she'd thought of him as one for some time, but hadn't recognized it. She was nervous, though, since she'd never had a friend besides Johanna. And she told him as much as they wandered the streets looking for supply shops.

His smile rose on just one side. "Are you really sure you can be friends with a street rat?"

"You're not a street rat, are you? You're an adventurer."

He nodded. "Aye. Same as you."

"Same as me."

"Well, I've been thinking of you as a friend for a while, now, too. So, I suppose we're friends."

"For better or worse."

"For better," Altain said at the exact same time she said, "For worse."

She'd given herself a good wash before dragging her coat back on to cover her dress and her face. They decided to rent inn rooms for the one night they planned to stay. In the morning, they would load up new supplies and continue to wander about until an adventure found them. They'd spoken of hiring a crew, but Tsingsei didn't want to hire any in Andalise who might recognize her and ruin the whole thing.

They ate a hot meal together in the tavern next door to the inn. Neither saying anything as they sat in a corner and hoped no one would bother them. Tsingsei took a hot bath that night, smiling and sighing at being able to submerge herself in warm water, rather than using a cold, wet cloth just to wash the most essential areas. She stayed in the tub until the water grew tepid, then climbed out to dress in her dirty clothes once more—though she had, at least, found a shop that sold pre-made knickers. She'd found a pair similar to her size, and forced herself to admit they were good enough.

She lay in the lumpy, scratchy bed and stared at the ceiling. Tsingsei tried for hours to drown out the noises coming from other rooms, and on the street. The sound of horses pulling carts along the cobblestone was foreign to her after such a long time being lulled to sleep by the gentle swinging of her hammock and the breeze pulling against the various parts of the skyship. Every footstep woke her. It was nothing like being on the Dauntless. Now everything she'd been accustomed to about the city drove her to the brink of madness. The smells, the sounds, the people—she wanted all of it to go away.

In the morning, she found Altain looking bright and rested, but felt as though she'd only dozed for a few minutes. They ate another hot meal before leaving to get supplies.

"Song," Altain hissed. "Put your hood up."

"Why?"

He yanked her hood over her head and pointed at a poster on an announcement board. There was a drawing of her with the word *MISSING* over it. To be honest, though, one would have to use their imagination to see a resemblance between her and the Tsingsei Gould named on the poster. Written along the bottom was *50,000 REWARD*.

She scoffed. "That hardly looks anything like me."

"I almost want to turn you in for that quoine," Altain said with a nervous chuckle. When he noticed her expression he said, "I'd rescue you right after, of course. We've got a treasure to find, after all."

But Altain and his jokes weren't what had her chest tight with apprehension. Tsingsei wrung her hands as she scanned the immediate area for anyone who might be looking in her direction and may recognize her.

Altain took her shoulders in his hands. "Go back to the Dauntless, Song. I'll get our supplies and be back before you miss me."

"Take your time," she said, trying to sound brave, though her voice betrayed her uncertainty. "I would never miss you." But she would, and she wished he would skip the supplies and return to the Dauntless with her—but they needed the food.

As she turned to leave, Altain took her hand and pulled her to him, then pressed his lips on hers. She was about to shove him when her eyes shifted to follow his gaze. A man in a green coat was watching them. His scrutinizing stare lingered a moment longer before he turned and sauntered away. Altain released Tsingsei, and she glared at him.

"Sorry, it was all I had," he said.

"Don't ever do that again."

"Not even to save you from being recognized?"

She thought about it. "Not even then."

Tsingsei left for the ship, leaving that embarrassment behind. Once aboard, she readied for departure, huffing around and throwing things with a little more anger than necessary.

"I should have slapped him," she said. "Never mind that I could have been recognized! I should have slapped him hard enough to leave a mark. Oh, I should still slap him."

"Slap who?" Altain asked as he carried a crate of supplies onto the deck.

Tsingsei waited until he'd set the crate down, then strode over and slapped him across the cheek as hard as she could. "Don't *ever* kiss me again, Altain."

"It wasn't that bad, was it?"

Tsingsei didn't respond as she pulled the walkway onto the ship and pushed against the dock with the pole. Altain took his place at the helm and guided them away from the harbor. They flew in a strange silence for an hour before he looped the rope around a wheel handle and sat next to her at the side of the ship, where she watched the ocean churn under her dangling feet.

"So, love, are we going to get this sorted or sail in silence from now on?"

"Don't kiss me. Ever."

"We've established that. Why not, though?" He turned his attention behind them, as he waited for an answer.

She took a deep breath, steeling herself to admit her dark secret. "Because…because I—"

Altain tapped Tsingsei's arm urgently. "Do you see that?" he asked, pointing toward a large object in the sky behind them, shrouded by a wall of clouds.

"What is it?"

Altain stayed silent, his eyes narrowed and searching. She leaned forward to look past his head. There were only a few things which could be in the sky behind them—another skyship or possibly a hot-air balloon. As the object broke the cloud wall, she was sure it was a skyship.

"Are they following us or is it a coincidence?"

"We need to outrun them," Altain insisted.

Tsingsei glanced around him. "Do you think it's…?"

"The owner?" He shrugged. "Better to not find out."

"Agreed. Let's lose them."

"And fast."

She nodded once and stood, gathering her skirt to run better. He shouted orders as they scurried across the deck, trying to make up for the fact that The Dauntless was meant to be piloted by a crew of no less than five. Altain disappeared below deck. Tsingsei ran to the bow, pulling on the ropes to open the first set of flaps along the sides. Midway down the ship, one of the larger flaps jammed and refused to open for her weak yanking.

"Altain!"

The skyship began turning and would soon be facing the ship they were trying to evade. Altain gripped the rope above her fists and pulled. It didn't budge.

"On the count of three!" he shouted. "One—"

"Two-three!"

They jerked hard, and the sail swung open to catch the breeze. Tsingsei sprinted back to the helm. Taking the rope from the grip and tossing it aside, she spun the wheel to steer them back east toward the sunset and catch whatever wind would oblige. The horizon gauge tilted, the tips of the double-ended needle drifting into the orange warning zone.

"You're insane!" Altain shouted, gripping the railing as the ship tilted and a box slid across the deck.

"You said we had to escape!" She kept steady on the wheel until a breeze caught the sails and the vessel lurched forward.

"Not fast enough!" Altain shouted as he sprinted below.

Tsingsei looked over her shoulder to confirm that the other skyship was still gaining on them. They'd done everything they could aside from ditching the heavier objects or cutting the entire vessel loose from the zeppelin—which even she knew was not an idea one should ever attempt.

A harpoon sprang from the other ship. It flew between the propeller fins and embedded itself into the deck beside Tsingsei. She pulled the knife from her bodice and began cutting at the rope. No sooner had she finished when another came careering through the air to catch in the boards just behind her. She spun on her knees and cut that one as well.

"Surrender the Dauntless and you shall live!" The shout came from the other skyship.

"We surrender nothing!" Tsingsei shouted, then cut the last bit of rope away from the harpoon tip. Two more harpoons shot into the deck around her. She stood, but could not move. "Altain!" She yanked at her skirt, which had been skewered into the planks. "Altain, help!"

More harpoons and four-pronged hooks shot onto the deck and wrapped around the railings. The other craft forced the Dauntless to turn as it sidled into the space beside it. Men swung across on ropes hanging from the zeppelin of their skyship.

"Find the rest of the crew!" A man shouted as he jumped down from a plank, which someone had set in place across the railings so he could walk from one vessel to the other. He was a handsome man with a five-o'clock shadow and tired eyes. His clothing was clean and expensive, down to the golden accents on his green coat. He spotted Tsingsei and smiled. "Ah, *Captain*, I'm afraid I must relieve you of your command." He gripped her skirt and yanked hard, tearing it free from the harpoon tip.

"I do protest!"

"How thrilling that must be for you." He wrapped his arm around her waist and carried her to the center of the deck.

"Sir, you board this vessel as a hostile party and I must ask that you explain yourself."

"I do not explain my actions to thieves," he scoffed.

"I am no thief." Tsingsei straightened to glare at him.

Another man came from below, gripping a squirming Altain by the collar.

"Let go of me!" Altain demanded.

"Captain Darian, I found this one below throwing things out of the portholes." He shoved Altain into Tsingsei.

"I called for you," she growled at him. "I was stuck."

"I'm sorry. I didn't hear you, love." Altain cast her an apologetic gaze.

"Where is the rest of your crew?" Captain Darian cocked an eyebrow.

She glared at him. "It's only us."

"Really?" He was unsuccessful at hiding his astonishment.

"Actually, the rest of me crew is invisible," Altain said. "Whenever we get into trouble, they disappear. They could be anywhere now, about to waylay the lot of you."

"Only two children are on board this ship, please don't assume otherwise." Darian sneered. "Tie them up and put the boy in the cage."

"What about her?" A man in a dirty white sailor's shirt set his hand on Tsingsei's shoulder.

"Take her to my cabin. I'd like her…company."

"No!" Altain shouted, fighting against the men trying to transport him below deck.

Tsingsei pushed away from the man holding her. She shoved the heel of her boot into his groin. He threw her across the deck. Her heels caught, and she tumbled. Tsingsei fell forward, unable to catch herself as she hit her temple against the railing with a *crack*. She collapsed, lying prone on the deck. The shouting men grew muffled. She couldn't have moved if she even wanted to. She couldn't blink, couldn't make a noise.

After minutes that felt like hours, her eyes slid closed, then opened again. She pushed up from the deck and the men fell silent. They stopped in their tracks to stare as she shakily got to her feet. Everything spun at sickening speeds as fog crept in from the corners of her eyes to blur her vision. The others' voices came distorted like echoes in a canyon. Altain's smaller figure struggled to break free as he shouted.

"*Em pleh-h,*" Tsingsei sputtered. Her eyes roamed, fixing on nothing and seeing blindness. "*Em pleh-h.*"

"Come to my voice, love." Altain leaned against the arms of the man gripping him. His hands stretched outward, but could not cover the distance between them.

"Why is she talking like that?" One man asked, drawing a sign over his torso to ward off evil.

"She seems to have had the sense knocked out of her," another replied.

"Well, catch her before she regains her composure," Darian commanded.

"*On!*" She threw her hands outward, and the men stopped. "*Em vais.*"

The two zeppelins collided overhead, though the breeze blew from behind. Tsingsei teetered toward the edge, catching herself on the railing. Another bump caused the Dauntless to tilt just enough to dump Tsingsei over the side.

"No!" Altain shouted.

Her scream clawed at the air. Sunset stained the sky a bitter red as the sun made its final farewell below the horizon. As Tsingsei fell from the skyship, the air spun around her. Whispers filled her ears and comfort filled her heart. Her rate of descent slowed, and she splashed into the water unharmed.

She couldn't be sure that what she was seeing was real or not. The water above her began roiling as though the air itself was boring a hole in the sea's surface. The whirlpool opened to encompass Tsingsei, cradling her in a spherical pocket of air. Water dripped from her wet dress, returning to the surrounding sea.

The undulating cocoon made of swirling mist and glittering blue lights moved through the ocean as though in constant motion to keep the waters at bay. It raced just under the surface, carrying with it the precious cargo. Tsingsei couldn't question these events. She drifted in and out of a fitful sleep in which she dreamed of the red sun and the whispers of *Song*.

Then, when the world had darkened, and the stars twinkled in the night sky, she was set down upon a beach of soft sand with a pillow made of seaweed. The bubble dissipated, leaving no evidence it had ever existed. Tsingsei fell into a dream of a cave with a strange structure like a huge four-pronged claw. A skeleton lay exposed on the other side of the room, and instead of being frightened, she felt like she'd finally gone home.

Song.

TSINGSEI WOKE IN AN UNCOMFORTABLE BED, COVERED BY scratchy blankets. The sun shone onto the worn wooden floor through a window made with warped glass. The sounds of domesticated animals—the low moan of a cow, the clucking of chickens, and the braying of an ass—filled the air, all but drowning out the chirping birds.

A girl in her mid teens entered with a tray on one arm and a large wooden pitcher in the other. She placed them on the dresser and arranged them like making a beautiful presentation.

"Who are you?" Tsingsei asked.

A butter knife clattered to the floor from her hand. She turned around with an embarrassed smile as a small blush crept into her cheeks. She retrieved the knife and wiped it on her apron.

"I'm Amelia." She fidgeted with the knife. "I brought you breakfast…in case you woke. And, well…you woke!" Amelia giggled nervously. "Who are you?"

"I'm…" She thought about giving her real name. But out in the world, with a large reward on her safe return to Garda, it was best to be the other girl that Altain had created. "I'm Song. Where am I?"

"On my family's farm, just outside of Lund. Where are you from? Can't be Lund."

"Why can't it be Lund?"

"Because three days ago you washed up on the beach." Amelia fluffed the pillows behind Tsingsei, urging her to sit upright. "Nobody from Lund washes up on the beach still breathing."

"Why not?"

Amelia set the tray on Tsingsei's lap. There was a thick porridge and a hunk of rye bread beside a small pat of butter on a tiny plate. Water in a wooden stein completed the dreadful meal.

"Debt collectors don't forgive forever." Amelia shrugged like it was an everyday occurrence. "Where are you from?"

"Garda," Tsingsei choked through the thick, sticky porridge.

Amelia's eyes widened. "I knew you had to be someone from one of those big cities with their grand parties and elegant gowns. Your dress is lovely."

It was then that Tsingsei realized she was naked beneath the itchy blanket. Her coat lay stretched across the foot of the bed. Someone had draped her dress over the back of a splintering chair. The skirt had been torn, and the fabric was dirty.

"Tell you what, if you can find me some new clothes, it's yours."

"Oh, no, I cou—"

"I insist. I don't even want it anymore." Tsingsei smiled and Amelia relaxed.

"Any of my dresses would be too short for you." She tapped her bottom lip in thought. "My brother's clothes are about your size!"

Tsingsei thought about it. In a boy's clothes, she might be able to pass as one. If she cut her hair, it would be several times easier. But Tsingsei didn't want to cut off her hair. She liked the length of it and all she could do to style it. Besides, if she then wanted to be a lady again, she would need to have the long locks again. However, if she kept her hair tucked in and her hood up, perhaps no one would be the wiser.

"I think they'll do just fine," she said.

Amelia hurried from the room and returned a few moments later with a pair of brown leather trousers and a long-sleeved tan blouse slung over one arm.

"I washed your underthings. I hope you don't mind. I didn't want to ruin your dress, though," Amelia said.

Tsingsei shook her head. "Oh, no, that's fine. Thank you."

"Would you like a bath after you eat?"

She ran her fingers through her greasy hair, which smelled like seaweed. "If it's no trouble?"

"None at all!" With that, Amelia disappeared from the room.

Tsingsei scraped the butter across the bread—it wasn't nearly enough, compared to what she was used to for her toasted bread back home. She had always liked a good layer of butter and sometimes she would add sugar over the top. Her other favorite way to have it was if the bread were hot and the butter melted into it and made the top half the littlest bit soggy while the underside remained crisp.

The bathtub was a round, metal thing in a room off to the side. Amelia apologized repeatedly for how long it took to heat water one pail at a time. By the time Tsingsei climbed in, the water was tepid at best. She scrubbed herself quickly, and washed her hair twice, then climbed out shivering. Never in her life had she taken a bath so cold. It was almost as bad as jumping into the lake at the country house during the summer.

She dried off and pulled on the clothes waiting for her on a stool. The trousers were a size too large, with a high waist with a row of buttons to fasten them closed. The ankles were tight in order to be tucked into boots. She opened the door, fidgeting with the waist.

"I'll get you a belt," Amelia said, and scampered into another room.

Tsingsei shoved the ends of the shirt into the trousers, then secured the belt once the girl returned with it. They walked together back to the room she'd been occupying. She pulled her coat on over the whole ensemble to look in the mirror and see how right her theory was. The collar of the coat covered her chin or lips if she dipped her head, and once the hood was raised, it sent her eyes into shadows. She could pull the edge of the hood down farther to cover her eyes, but it would limit her view to just meters in front of her on the floor. As she suspected, though, she could easily be mistaken for her father.

She dropped the hood back and knelt to force her foot into her boot. She caught sight of the tear in the skirt of her dress. It seemed an unfair thing that she should repay this girl's kindness with a tattered rag. She fingered the frayed edges, trying to think of a solution. Words formed in her mind. She didn't know what they were, but she understood somehow that they would accomplish what she wanted. After a moment testing the sounds, she glanced at Amelia, who watched her with a furrowed brow.

"*Sehrd sith skif*," she whispered.

Blue lights twinkled into existence from around Tsingsei. They converged on the gown, and settled on the frayed edges of the tear. It shone like a bright blue flame, blurred by a sort of misty quality. The torn edges lined up and stitched together, as though the threads had never been broken.

It didn't stop there, though. The blue mist crawled up the dress a little at a time and mended every frayed or damaged thread as it passed. Soon the dress was like new, a shining white and golden wonder. The mist dissipated like fog in the morning light as the blue sparkles faded out. The two girls gasped in shared astonishment. A grin of excited triumph spread across Tsingsei's lips.

"What in the world…?" Amelia cast her rounded eyes to her. "You're a Touched?"

Tsingsei didn't know what to say. It was new to her, and she didn't understand how or why it had happened. She shook her head, her mouth dropping open and closing again like a fish out of water.

"What's wrong?"

"I'm not Touched."

"But you—"

"I know." She shook her head. "I wasn't Touched three days ago, Amelia. Believe me."

"I believe you."

She nodded absently. "Good…because I almost don't."

"Try to do something else!"

"I'm fairly certain *kijæm* isn't supposed to be used for party tricks…"

"Says who?"

Tsingsei shrugged. "I don't know. I don't know the first thing about any of it."

"Well, if it is forbidden…I don't see anyone here who'll rat you out. Do you?"

"All right. Something small…"

Amelia dropped a handkerchief to the floor. "Pick this up."

Tsingsei furrowed her brow to think, and a phrase took shape in her mind. *"Ficherkdnæh-h ehth pu kip."*

The mist slithered into existence and wrapped around the cloth. It lifted it into the air to hover in front of Amelia. The girl blinked in confusion, then held out her hand. The mist lowered the handkerchief into her palm, then faded out of sight once more.

They stared at each other for a long time in a state of shock.

"Did you tell it to put it in my hand?" Amelia asked.

"No, I just said pick it up."

"How marvelous."

Tsingsei grinned and stared at her hands, as though her new power was written across her palms—even though it didn't seem to come from her, but from around her. Her gaze settled on the dress again. "Now you have a beautiful dress to wear to all the parties."

"I don't go to parties," Amelia admitted with a sigh. She ran her fingers along the delicate embroidery.

"Perhaps now you might find an excuse to?"

"Girls of my station don't attend parties, Song."

"Oh. Sorry. I didn't know that." Tsingsei fidgeted with the ends of her hair hanging off her shoulders. "Do you… know how to braid hair? I've never done it myself."

She grinned and urged Tsingsei to remove her coat and sit on the edge of the bed. She handed her a hand mirror to hold over her head. Amelia sat behind her and separated her hair on her scalp over her forehead into clumps. Tsingsei watched Amelia's fingers in the mirror as the latter talked her through how to braid her own hair. When she finished, she opened a jar of bandoline and smoothed the gummy stuff across Tsingsei's hair to tame the flyaways and keep the braid in place.

"I made it myself," Amelia said.

"Really? I never knew you could make it at home. We always just sent someone to buy more."

"I can give you a jar, if you like. It probably doesn't smell nice like you're used to, but it gets the job done."

She smiled and tried not to nod and disrupt the girl's work. "I'd like that. Thank you."

Tsingsei stared at the girl in the hand mirror, thinking how strange it was for her to be so kind to a complete stranger. She wondered if that was a common thing, or if maybe Amelia was just a kind person by nature. She would've liked to get to know her better, but the events of three days ago swelled to the forefront of her mind. Altain had been kidnapped for three days. She didn't doubt that he would have returned to rescue her, and so determination solidified in her mind that she should do the same for him.

Amelia finished and rinsed her hands in water from the pitcher as she poured it into the basin. Tsingsei studied her, trying to figure out if her attraction to the other girl was an actual attraction, or just a draw to her kindness. After Amelia finished, she accepted the hand mirror from Tsingsei, and stared at the gown on the chair.

"Is it silly that I want to try it on?" Amelia asked.

"Why would that be silly?"

She hesitated. "Because I'm dirty, and it's tailored to you."

Tsingsei stood beside her. "Yes, but who is here to see it?"

Amelia gave her a crooked smile.

"Put it on, then. Let's see you in it."

She blushed and shuffled to it. "Turn around."

Tsingsei did as she was told and waited, listening to the shuffling of fabrics. From the corner of her eye, she caught the girl's reflection in the mirror. She stared just long enough to catch the delicate curves of her hourglass figure. Muscles strained in her back and thighs, her biceps bulging a little as she bent her arm. Tsingsei averted her gaze, half captivated and half jealous of the body of this farm girl. Sure, she liked her own shape, but she didn't have muscles like that. Tsingsei was skinny and twiggy, and felt that she'd still yet to grow out of her childhood body. It was just more proof that Tsingsei was built for parties and pampering, while this girl was built for manual labor.

"How did you get me here?" she asked.

Amelia released a soft laugh. "I was collecting seaweed in a barrow—"

"A whole barrow?"

"We pickle it for the winter months. But I found you on the beach, stuck you into my barrow, and hauled you home. Why?"

"You did all that yourself?"

Tsingsei glanced over and spotted a blush in Amelia's cheeks.

"I did," Amelia said.

"You're quite strong."

"I'm really not. But thank you."

Tsingsei laughed. "But you are. You lifted me up? I can't even lift me up."

Amelia giggled as more fabric shuffled. "You weigh less than some calves I've had to carry."

"Oh, thank goodness, I weigh less than a *cow*."

The two laughed. Tsingsei turned as Amelia yanked the gown up to her chest and paused. There was a significant gap, which the cloth at the back could not cover, no matter how tight the ties were pulled. She tried to pull them before asking Amelia's permission, but the girl didn't object.

"You could fill it with another fabric," Tsingsei said.

"Or wear a nice coat over it."

"That could work." Amelia turned around once the dress was tied. "How do I look?"

Tsingsei stared at her from head to toe. Amelia was too short for the length of the gown, and so it dragged on the floor. The embroidery had been tailored to compliment a much less curvy body, and so now it looked a bit strange. But overall, the girl looked beautiful. When Tsingsei said nothing for a minute, Amelia frowned.

"Put a pauper in a pretty dress and she's just a pauper in a pretty dress," Amelia intoned.

As though woken from a daydream, Tsingsei shook her head. She turned around to grab the wash cloth and dip it in the basin of water, then walked over to stand almost toe-to-toe with her. She set her hand on Amelia's cheek to steady her face as she wiped away the bits of dirt the girl had acquired that morning. Before she knew it, she was a whisper away from the other girl, studying her features. Her gaze caught on Amelia's brown eyes, and she realized the girl was holding her breath.

"Why aren't you breathing?"

Amelia shook her head. "I thought…" She released a weak laugh.

"Thought what?"

"That…that you were going to kiss me."

"Do you want me to kiss you?"

Amelia blinked. "I…I've never kissed a girl. Have you?"

"Once." She swiped a bit of dirt from the side of Amelia's nose.

"Do you want to kiss me?"

Tsingsei stared over her soft pink weather worn lips. "And if I said yes? Would you let me?"

"You still haven't told me how I look."

"I think you look beautiful. And it's a shame you don't go to parties, because every head would turn to loo—"

Amelia's lips pressed to hers in a firm kiss. After a second, though, she lurched back, eyes wide. "I'm sorry."

"Why?"

"Well, you were talking, and I kissed you without asking."

Tsingsei chuckled. "I already told you I wanted to kiss you. Silly girl." She studied her bashful state. "Do you regret it?"

"No."

"Did you hate it?"

"Also no."

"That's a relief. The last girl I kissed slapped me and then threatened me."

"What if instead I just kiss you again?"

Tsingsei blinked down at her and smiled. "I think I'd like for you to do that."

This time they met in the middle. Their lips settled together in tentative pecks. Tsingsei wasn't sure how to kiss someone, but this seemed to be working, and was rather nice. She wrapped her arm around Amelia, setting her palm against the small of her back to push the other closer into her. Tsingsei's mind ran so fast she struggled to catch a single thought. One appeared over and over in the chaos, though, and that was that this was but a moment in which this young woman had been intoxicated by the compliments, and Tsingsei was dressed as a boy, and so she'd gotten caught up and confused. She would likely regret it later, but on the off chance she didn't, Tsingsei continue to kiss her.

"Amelia!" a woman called from another room.

The spell broke, the kiss ended, and both girls stood in a strange silence. Tsingsei stepped away from the girl, terrified to be caught by the person she'd had no idea was home. She'd been so enthralled by this girl's kindness, that she hadn't questioned the emptiness of the farmhouse.

"Amelia, where are you?"

"I'm in here, Sarah." She opened the door. "Our guest has woken."

A woman entered the room, scanning Amelia in her expensive dress and Tsingsei in boy's clothes.

"What are you wearing that fancy dress for?" Sarah tugged on the sleeve, adjusting it on Amelia's shoulder.

"I wanted to see how it fit," she said.

"I have a dangerous journey to make," Tsingsei explained. "It would be foolish for me to make it in such a dress. Amelia was kind enough to offer these, and as thanks, I gave her my gown."

"What sort of lady are you, that you would give away an expensive item to a pauper in exchange for tatty boy's clothing?"

To Tsingsei, it sounded like a challenge, but she couldn't be sure.

"The sort who is far from home and has no need of such a garment."

A man entered through the front door, dirty and sweaty. A bucket of water sloshed in his left hand and a dead chicken dangled in the other. He set both items on the table and lowered himself into a chair, which creaked in protest. The man was wide with thick muscles and a beard. He seemed to be lost in thought as his eyes remained fixed on the bucket he'd just brought in.

"Dear," Sarah caught his attention. "Our guest is awake."

"Oh, is she now? Good, good." After a brief examination of his fingernails, he squinted up at Tsingsei. "Good heavens."

"I gave her Caleb's old clothes," Amelia explained before he could ask. "Someone ought to use them."

He nodded, but it was clear his mind was elsewhere. "I'm Josiah," he said after a long silence. He stood to take Tsingsei's hand. "Amelia is my daughter, and Sarah is my wife."

"I'm Song." She gave a small curtsy.

"So, how does a young thing such as yourself come to be washed up on the shore?" He gestured at another chair and Tsingsei took the cue to sit.

"I was on a skyship. We were waylaid by pirates and I fell overboard. I'm afraid they still have my companion. Amelia says that I have been here for three days, and well, I really must go find him. There is no telling what Captain Darian has done with him."

"If the rumors are true about Captain Darian," Sarah said, "then your friend has either turned pirate or he's already been killed."

Tsingsei's insides chilled and her breath caught in her throat. Surely Altain would not have been murdered without so much as a thought. He was only a boy! "Regardless, I have to try," she assured, her voice sounding bolder than she felt.

"Your friend is lucky to have you." Amelia smiled.

"I suppose I should do the same for any friend. In any case, I must go. I've already lost too much time."

"I insist you stay. Just for the night, to finish recuperating," Josiah said.

Amelia perked up at the idea. "Yes, Song, please stay just a little longer. The road to Lund is long on foot, and you need to rest."

Tsingsei smiled back at her. "I suppose one night couldn't hurt."

That night, Tsingsei shared stories with the Sterlings of her month's escapades as they ate fresh, hot bread with a thin, almost flavorless chicken, seaweed, and barley soup. Amelia hung on every word, thrilled at the very idea of being on such an adventure. It was there that Tsingsei wondered if maybe she could convince this girl to go with her. Sure, they'd only just met, but she needed all the friends she could get. The world was a cruel place, but perhaps it didn't need to be.

Ten

THOUGHTS OF ALTAIN BEING LOST FOREVER PLAGUED Tsingsei's mind as she tossed in Caleb Sterling's uncomfortable bed. She hadn't realized just how much she'd valued him as a friend until they'd been separated. And what was worse is that it was all her fault. He wouldn't have been out in the world, wouldn't have stolen a pirate's skyship, if she hadn't convinced him to. Now everything was gone—her friend, her quoine, and her grand treasure hunting adventure. She had nothing left.

It would be so easy to return home, then. To run to a police station and surrender herself. She could send her father after Darian to get Altain back. But then she realized they would never let her go again. They would watch her like a hawk and make sure she stayed put. Her parents would lock her back in that gilded cage and she'd never get to go on another adventure.

No, going home was not an option. She had to stay the course and reunite with Altain some other way. Perhaps she could sneak onto the crew of another pirate ship and convince that crew to find her friend. Again, the thought emerged of chopping off her long, beautiful hair and disguising herself as a boy. She shoved it from her mind immediately. She loved her hair, and would have to make sure to always tuck it in and keep her hood up.

The door to the room creaked open and Amelia slipped in. She closed the door behind her and padded over the floorboards. She leaned over the side of the bed.

"Are you sleeping?" she whispered.

"No," Tsingsei admitted. "I'm worried."

"About your friend?" Amelia hugged herself, rubbing her hands over the sleeves of her nightdress. "Oh, blimey, it's cold!"

"Unseasonably so," she agreed.

"Probably just a draft from the sea. It'll pass."

Tsingsei lifted the blanket, signaling for Amelia to climb under. The girl slid onto the bed, shivering and trying not to put her freezing extremities against Tsingsei. But Tsingsei wrapped her arms around the other and rubbed a palm against Amelia's frigid arm.

"I'm afraid that my friend will have died when there was something I could've done to save him," she said.

"You really care about him."

"He's my friend. If I didn't care, then what kind of person would that make me? He helped me escape from the dreadful life I was living back in Garda."

"Was it a terrible life?" Amelia asked.

"Yes. I couldn't stand the expectations and the falseness of it all. Never allowed to laugh openly or share my own opinions, just agree with everyone else. I had to be pretty and perfect." Tsingsei stared up at the ceiling.

"Do you miss your family at all?" Amelia asked.

"I miss my handmaid. She's not really family, though she felt like it. I miss my mother, I suppose. Though I never felt like she really cared about what I thought. Isn't that what mothers are supposed to do? Listen to their daughters and love them?"

She nodded. "Mine did."

"Where is your mother?" Tsingsei asked.

Amelia was quiet for a moment. "She died when I was six. Our father was so sad that the farm started to fall apart. Sarah came to help us. It took her three years to convince Daddy to marry her." Amelia giggled. "What about your father?"

She paused, trying to think how to explain her father without giving away who she was based on what he did. "He's always been too busy with work for anything, even me. He's…a great man, but I wish he had also tried to be a great father."

"That's his loss."

They lay in the still of the night, listening to the chirruping crickets. She thought back on earlier that day, her eyes catching on Amelia's lips in the moonlight.

"Did you enjoy the kiss?"

Amelia averted her gaze. "I…think so. I'm not the most practiced in kissing, but it was nice."

"I'm not the most practiced either. In fact, you're the third person I've ever kissed—and both of those were horrible."

"You said you'd kissed a girl before…"

Tsingsei nodded. "Yes. I've…never wanted to kiss a boy."

She stared at her, an eyebrow raised. "Not once?"

"Not once."

"It's nice, though."

Tsingsei chuckled. "I'd still rather not." She paused, a thought playing through her mind while her tongue wrapped itself in the uncertainty of how to phrase it. "Amelia?"

"Yes?"

"May I kiss you again?"

Amelia stayed quiet.

"It's fine to say no."

"It's just so very confusing," Amelia said.

"Can I ask you something personal?"

"Sure."

"Do you like boys?"

She chewed on her bottom lip as she thought. "I do."

"Did you kiss me because you saw me as a boy?" Tsingsei asked.

"I...I don't know. That's why I'm so confused. Perhaps if we had more time together..."

A stupid thought entered her mind, and she blurted it before she could rethink it. "Come with me."

"What?"

"Come with me to find my friend. We were going to be adventurers and find Balamora's treasure."

Amalia giggled. "That's a children's story."

"I know. But it didn't used to be. All legends are based on some truth. I don't know what truth could be at the root of that tale, but wouldn't it be the most thrilling adventure? Whether you discovered something or not, it would be worth the journey." She grinned. "So, what do you say? Would you like to join me?"

She stayed quiet as she thought. "I...would like to..."

"But..."

"My father needs me here on the farm. I can't leave him."

Tsingsei stayed quiet for a minute, doing her best to hide her dejection. "I understand."

"Maybe one day you could come back and ask me again."

"Would the answer change?"

Amelia shrugged. "I don't know."

"Stay here. Stay with your father and step mother. Maybe marry a boy one day." Her nose wrinkled. "Have babies."

She giggled. "I don't know. Maybe."

"Well it sounds dreadful. I hope you love it." She laughed.

"And I hope you love your adventure."

She smiled and rested her head on the pillow. Even though she would never see Amelia again, her existence was encouraging to Tsingsei. If other girls were like her, then maybe she could find one who did want to follow her into untold adventures to the ends of the world. But that could wait. It would have to wait. First, she had to rescue Altain from Captain Darian's clutches—which might have been an adventure of its own.

TSINGSEI WOKE ALONE IN THE MORNING. THE SUN SHONE IN through the window, right onto her face. She dressed and entered the common area, discovering Amelia and Sarah cooking a morning meal of porridge, eggs, and buttered bread. Amelia smiled as she set a place for Tsingsei beside her own.

"You're up early," Tsingsei said.

Sarah laughed. "That's life on a farm."

"I churned this butter myself." Amelia set the butter dish beside Tsingsei's plate.

Tsingsei smiled as she bit into the bread, approving of the sweet flavor that swirled around her palate in creamy perfection. She ate as fast as she could swallow—ignoring the nagging voice of her mother in her head trying to force her to slow down and chew like she had a secret. She wanted to head out as soon as possible for the long walk to Lund. A few hours of daylight had already been wasted by her sleeping in.

Josiah said a warmer goodbye than the weary hello he'd managed the day before. He walked out the back door to start his day. The women cleaned the table and washed the dishes, then set about collecting things from around the house. Tsingsei stayed put as they urged her to wait instead of heading out immediately.

They stacked a change of boy's clothes, a spare set of underpants and socks, and some food—two apples, an end of a bread loaf, and a canteen of water. As though Amelia had just remembered, she rushed into the other room to grab the jar of bandoline for Tsingsei. They shoved all this into a battered satchel.

"Please," Tsingsei protested, "I don't need any of this—"

"We found you on the beach with no supplies of any kind and no quoine." She shoved the pack into Tsingsei's arms. It was clear there would be no negotiations on the matter. After a moment, Sarah hurried into another room, returning with a revolver in a holster.

"Oh, no, please. I—"

Sarah shushed her with a finger. "Josiah and I spoke about your predicament. If you're going after Darian, you'll need it."

"C.S." Tsingsei read the pale gold initials stamped into the butt of the mother-of-pearl grip.

"My stepson. Caleb Sterling." Sarah said.

"Oh, no, I can't take a boy's gun—"

"He died last winter. Consumption," Amelia said.

"I couldn't possibly—"

"Honor his memory and take it," she insisted, shoving the revolver back into the holster. "It's the only thing of value he ever had and it meant all the world to him." Amelia helped secure the belt around Tsingsei's waist and secured the thigh strap in place.

"I don't know what to say."

"Thank you is a good start," Sarah said with a laugh.

"Thank you."

Tsingsei lifted the satchel and settled the strap onto her shoulder and across her body. She was both restless to get going, and also sad to be leaving. At the door, she curtsied to Sarah, then froze as the woman enveloped her in a kind hug.

"Take care of yourself, dear," Sarah said.

"Thank you for your hospitality."

Amelia walked with her outside into the mid-morning sun. Tsingsei stared at her. She tried to memorize the beautiful girl's face. How her dirty blonde hair shone in the sun's light. The way her cheeks spread with pink embarrassment above her shy smile. She especially tried to remember the feeling of the kisses they'd shared, how Amelia hadn't pulled away or been disgusted.

"Perhaps chance will send me this way again," Tsingsei whispered.

"I hope it does," Amelia replied.

As Tsingsei turned away to take the first steps of her long journey, she released a long sigh. If this girl might have a mind for a woman's embrace over a man's, then perhaps there were others. She'd always thought herself to be so alone in the world, but Amelia made her realize she wasn't. Maybe for every outraged Isabelle, there was an Amelia, eager to let another woman kiss her. She just had to find them—after she'd rescued Altain.

Tsingsei smiled and quickened her step toward her next adventure.

Eleven

TSINGSEI DUCKED HER HEAD AS SHE WALKED THROUGH THE streets of Lund, keeping her hood up, hair tucked in, and her face down. She had no idea where to start. At the harbor, she pushed into one of the taverns, deciding if nothing else she could ask around about Darian. At most, she could think longer on her idea to join a crew to go after him. The problem would be negotiating her way onto one. She didn't know how to do much of anything, save for the way she and Altain had made things up and figured it out as they went.

She stared at the patrons scattered throughout the room—dirty men fresh into port who valued a hot meal and an ale over a bath. The stench was nigh unbearable, but she remained. She parted her lips to breathe through her mouth. Tsingsei found an empty table in a corner where she could watch for one she might be bold enough to approach.

"What'll ya have, love?" a barmaid asked, looking frazzled but smiling anyway.

Tsingsei noticed right away that she didn't pronounce the h on have. She hesitated in her reply, fearing that speaking would get her discovered. Her mother's voice popped into her head saying, *Speak higher, Tsingsei, lest someone think you're a boy!* She'd practiced for weeks until speaking at a higher, more ladylike tone had become second nature to her.

Tsingsei cleared the feminine pitch from her throat and replied, "I'm fine, thank you."

"Oh, you're just a boy, are ya?"

She avoided giving a triumphant smile. "Please leave me be, miss."

The barmaid scanned the tavern with a critical eye, then sat on the bench. "You lookin' to be a cabin boy, are ya?"

Tsingsei didn't reply.

"Word is Captain Krell over there is lookin' to add to his crew."

She pointed across the room at a man with hair like fire and eyes like ice. His coat and hat were black as coal, which made his skin appear pale as snow. The man was a range of extremes, each part at odds with the other. Tsingsei had never seen hair like his before. She almost wanted to touch it, to see if it was real—she couldn't fathom the existence of red hair, even while it stared her in the face. She barely acknowledged the blond man beside him, who was, for lack of a better word, uninteresting. The rings across the captain's fingers glittered in the candlelight as he lifted his stein to drain it.

The barmaid stood to retrieve his mug and returned it with a new foamy cap. She set a small glass of some amber liquid in front of Tsingsei.

"What's this for?" Tsingsei asked.

"Liquid courage." She winked. "Good luck, lad."

Tsingsei sniffed the contents of the glass; it smelled vile, but she took a swallow, anyway. It burned going down and warmed her stomach. She already wanted to vomit it up, but forced herself to keep her composure. She swallowed the bit of acid creeping into the back of her mouth. Whatever the woman had given her, it wasn't a drink she wanted to encounter again. As the blond man left the captain alone, Tsingsei stood and strode to Captain Krell's table before she lost her nerve.

Up close and personal, he was frightening and alluring all at once. His eyes bored into the soul. His face was handsome, though years on a ship had left their marks like crows had clawed lines into the skin beside his eyes. His forehead held the story of thousands of furrows. Captain Krell had probably been beautiful in his youth. Now he was weatherbeaten, though he couldn't have been any more than forty-five.

He looked up at Tsingsei as she stood before him, doing her best not to turn around and retreat to the corner. A flicker of a thought flitted through his eyes and then was gone, like a flash of lightning in the winter sky. He motioned at the bench across from himself and she sat.

"What's your name?" he asked, his tongue curled around his r's as though trapping them from escape.

"Caleb Song," she answered, having been prepared with the answer, since the initials were stamped into the revolver base. Surely Amelia wouldn't mind. "I go by Song."

"Captain Dashaelan Krell, but everyone calls me Dash. I assume you're speaking with me because my reputation precedes me?"

"I've no idea who you are, only that your crew is short and you need men."

"I need *men*," he emphasized.

"Well, I am worth three, at least," she insisted as he snorted in amusement. "Myself and one other crewed and flew the Dauntless for a month before she was seized and my companion captured."

His eyebrows rose in interest. "That was you?"

"Aye."

"Then why don't you go get the Dauntless back?"

"Oh, I intend to."

"And you want to use my crew and my skyship to do it," he guessed.

Tsingsei nodded, remaining silent while he contemplated the idea of not only allowing some child on his ship but also allowing said adolescent to make use of his crew in the apprehension of a vessel they'd already lost once before. It was a fool's errand, and he had every right to tell her no, but she hoped he wouldn't.

"I can make it worth your while," she said when she grew impatient for his decision.

"How is that?"

She didn't want to reveal the possibly nonexistent treasure she and Altain had sought for themselves, but knew it was the best way to gain this pirate's assistance. "My companion owns a map with the location of the Lost Treasure of Balamora."

"There are at least one-hundred fake maps which all claim the same thing."

"Those maps weren't drawn by Benson Gould."

His eyebrows rose with interest. "Benson Gould drew a map?"

"He did." It wasn't exactly a lie, as Benson Gould, the famous cartographer and explorer had drawn many maps—

in fact the Gould maps were the most widely used around the world—but to her knowledge he had never drawn a secret one.

He made a sound of thought and took a long drink from his stein, his eyes never straying from her. "Tempting, but that is just a legend. Why would I take a thieving brat on my ship for a manhunt and children's story?"

Tsingsei sighed but resisted showing how dejected she felt. He was right. Even she questioned the treasure's existence and wasn't sure it was an adventure worth risking.

An idea hit her. She'd been using *kijæm*—which she hadn't possessed before she'd fallen from the Dauntless. But it was there now. Why shouldn't she use it to suit her needs? Why couldn't she use it as a bargaining chip? A Touched could be an asset to any vessel.

She took the candle from the center of the table, placed it in front of her and snuffed out the flame. She set her hands on either side of the candlestick and stared at the wick, concentrating on what she wanted. As before, the words popped into her head as though she'd known them all along.

"*L'dnæk sith tyl.*"

The wick slowly lit to orange, and a flame flickered to life from it. Tsingsei watched through the flame as the man's face turned from annoyed disinterest to veiled astonishment. He licked his forefinger and thumb and suffocated the flame between them.

"Do it again," he said.

Tsingsei repeated the words. The wick relit and the veil on his astonishment lifted just a little.

"You've got yourself a deal!" he said, reaching across the table to clap a hand on Tsingsei's shoulder. His elbow bumped the candle, tipping it on its side and spilling wax onto the abandoned cloth napkin someone had left draped over the side of an emptied plate. Flames crept onto the cloth.

"*Shiugnit-skei*," Tsingsei hissed. The flame disappeared in a white and blue swirl as her *kijæm* extinguished it, before the mist dissipated as though it had never been there. She righted the candlestick and set it back in the center of the table. "When do we leave?"

"A little eager, aren't you?"

"My companion and I have been separated for four days. I cannot leave him in the hands of Captain Darian any longer than I already have."

The man's eyebrows rose high over his eyes. "Darian? Oh, your friend is probably already dead."

"I have to try," she insisted.

He sighed in resignation. "Well then, eh… Song, was it? I'll let you aboard and attempt in the rescue of your friend for three-quarters of the hypothetical booty."

"Dash, you must be joking. My man has the map. We rescue him or there is no treasure. You may have ten percent."

"Half."

"One quarter."

"Half."

"One third." She held up her hand, stopping his next offer. "My friend gets one third, as it is his map. I get one third as it is I who is enlisting you in this venture. And you get one third for your assistance or I move along to the next captain interested in making a deal for a share in the haul of a lifetime and the fame which comes with it."

Dashaelan chewed on the inside of his cheek, his eyes narrow and calculating. She knew he was studying her, trying to gauge if she really would take her offer elsewhere. She had already fooled him into thinking she was a boy; perhaps he would accept this offer so that she wouldn't be caught in her bluff. She doubted if she could negotiate and convince another captain, but she would have to if he sent her on her way.

"All right, one third," he surrendered. "We leave at dawn. Be on the Stars' Bounty, or be left behind with your damned suicide mission."

"I'll be there."

Tsingsei left the tavern and made her way toward the docks. The sun had set, throwing the city into an unsettling darkness. Ships lined the harbor as far as the eye could see. Above the docks were two towers connected by a long wooden walkway, much like Garda, though with less space. The skyships were arranged close enough together that if a hearty wind were to pick up, the zeppelins would bump against one another; far enough that no serious damage or injury would come of it.

She climbed into a clunky lift, immediately wishing she'd taken the stairs. The man at the control pulled the rusted gate closed, its sea salt bitten hinges screaming all the way. Every few seconds, the lift would jump and clang. For a moment, it stopped moving altogether before the hiss of steam came from below and it continued on its rickety journey. At the top, Tsingsei stepped free as though the cage would fall at any moment.

"I'm looking for the Stars' Bounty," she said.

"That one's five down on your left. Can't miss her, she's got a gold zeppelin." He closed the gate, then paused. "The lift will run for one more hour, and then you'll have to use the stairs."

Tsingsei nodded in understanding, but she had no intention of going back down or ever climbing onto another lift. The wind pulled against her coat, threatening to blow her from the high walkway. The ropes creaked as the massive skyships strained to escape. Her heels clacked along the planks, interrupting the otherwise silent darkness pressing in upon her.

She found the Stars' Bounty where the old man had said. The long, narrow zeppelin glittered as even the smallest bit of light caught the golden paint. The bow of the ship displayed a massive North Star—four large points in a t formation, and four shorter like an x—where sea vessels might have their maidens and serpents. Aside from the silver of the star and the gold of the zeppelin, the ship was rather dull in color, the body of it varnished over the natural fallow wood. It was larger than the Dauntless, built for cargo and plunder rather than speed. Her helm sat upon the raised quarterdeck, like the Dauntless, and the captain's cabin was housed below that. At the center of the deck was a thick mainmast, which ended at the zeppelin—the two secured together with a cat's cradle of ropes looped over hooks and nailed into the wood.

Tsingsei backed up to get a running leap at the side of the ship. She caught the side, but her strength gave way and she dangled from the balusters, her feet kicking in panic. The friction of her slipping grip burned her palms and the wind bit her face.

"*Lahf em tel t'nod,*" she whispered. A swirling cyclone of illuminated misty fog dotted with little blue specks of light wrapped around her legs. "*Puh em pleh-h.*"

Her muscles screamed as she pulled herself up. The lights concentrated at the soles of her shoes, propelling her upward. Tsingsei swung her leg over the railing and rolled onto the deck as quietly as possible. She stared up at the bottom of the zeppelin as she caught her breath—it was painted black with silver dots for stars. A snort at the helm caught her attention. There was a man sitting on a chair, his feet propped in the spokes of the wheel and his chin resting on his chest. Whoever he was, he was sleeping on the job.

Tsingsei made her way down the stairs. They took her to the connected kitchen and dining area, which housed a single long table with benches on either side. On the other side of the dining area through a doorway was the crew's quarters, where at least two more men lay in swaying hammocks—she couldn't tell whether they were awake or asleep. Turning her back on them, she found another staircase leading deeper into the ship's darkness. The third deck down was the cannon room with a cell like a prison on the far end. She found a secluded store room on the final deck. The ceiling was low, and the room was filled with barrels, crates, and sacks which contained anything and everything she could imagine a pirate ship would need.

She arranged a few soft sacks on a platform of barrels beneath a porthole and retrieved an apple from the pack

Sarah had given to her. It was sandy and bitter, nearing the end of its life. But it was food and so she ate it as she thought about the farm where that beautiful pauper lived.

She didn't know how long it would take her to find Altain, but perhaps after she found him she could return to figure out how Amelia was faring. Then again, it could take years. In that time Amelia could forget her. She could get married and have children. She could have a good life by then. And Tsingsei showing up out of the blue one day would just interrupt that. No. She had to let Amelia go.

She also needed to let Tsingsei go. Out in the world she had a bounty unlike any other—a bounty of her safe return. Thinking on it, she didn't much feel like Tsingsei anymore. She'd been on an adventure, and was starting a new one. Song was the adventurer.

My name is Song, and I'm an adventurer.

She played with the thought over and over. Let it settle in her mind. As she drifted to sleep that night, she let the thought solidify in her mind.

I'm not Tsingsei anymore. I'm Song. I feel more like Song, anyway.

Her eyes closed and that strange whisper in her mind floated into existence.

Song.

S HE WOKE TO THE SOUND OF BOOTS CLUNKING AGAINST WOODEN planks over her head. For a minute, she forgot where she was. She stared out through the porthole at the mid-morning sun and the ocean as far as the eyes could see. After she got her bearings, she paused to remind herself who she was and why she belonged there. She was Song, an adventurer, a treasure hunter…and now a pirate. The irony of being a pirate, given who her father was, was not lost on her. She had to wonder how he would react if he found out.

Better he doesn't.

Song tucked her hair back into her collar and lifted her hood before opening the door and ascending the steps on the balls of her feet to avoid making a racket. There were a few men in the hammocks of the quarters, some asleep and others looking at magazines. She ignored them and took the rest of the steps two at a time to get on deck.

"What the—" A man with a bald head and a bushy beard stopped what he was doing to gape at her. "Cap'n, we got a stowaway!"

Before Song could react, someone grabbed her from behind, pulling her arms back to leave her torso exposed. She kicked her heels at him, fighting to free herself. The man carted her up the steps to the helm, where Captain Dashaelan stood.

"Ah, my new cabin boy. I thought you'd changed your mind."

"I didn't want to be left behind," she replied.

"So you slept on board, did you?" He tugged her hood down and pulled her braid from her collar. "That's quite the mass of hair you have there—what was it…Caleb?" He pulled her hair hard enough to encourage a feminine scream from Song. "Take her to my cabin."

The man carried her as she kicked at him. Once inside the captain's room, he set her in a chair at an aged, wooden table, and shoved on her shoulders as though he could make her stick to it. Dashaelan followed soon after and dismissed the other. He said nothing for a long while as he busied himself at a liquor cabinet. He set a rocks glass with two fingers of red wine in front of Song, then took his own glass and stood to stare out the bay windows, his back to her.

"Tsingsei Gould," he said.

Song's heart skipped a beat, and she stopped breathing before forcing herself to regain her calm. "What about her?"

"There's a handsome reward for the return of Elroy Gould's daughter."

"She must be something special."

"Why yes, I believe you are," he replied, turning to study her. "You think you had me fooled into thinking you were a boy? In that fancy coat and those heels?"

Song didn't reply.

"I half recognized you last night after you mentioned the mapmaker—"

"Cartographer and explorer," she said with pride.

He responded with a dismissive grunt. "You put the name in my head, either way. It wasn't until this morning that I remembered seeing a poster for the girl gone missing from Garda. Have to squint to see the resemblance, but it's there."

"So you intend to turn me in for my father's quoine? What's stopping me from burning your ship out of the sky right now?" She set her jaw and glared at the wine.

Dashaelan swirled the whiskey in his glass and thought about this. He sighed. "I don't believe I know anything about a plan to return the daughter of such a wretched man to him. If she ran away, it was probably for the better."

"So you'll let me stay?"

"Oh, don't be so assumptive, dear girl. You see, I cannot be caught harboring such a fugitive unless they prove to me that they are worth their salt." Dashaelan sat in the chair across from her, his eyes stern.

"I've already proven what I can do," she objected.

"And then you threatened to blow up my ship. What I want to know is what can you do that will encourage me to keep you on? Every man on this ship has to pull his own weight—every pound of flesh is justified. So, what can you do?"

Song thought hard and came up with nothing. She shrugged and stared down at the glass.

"So *kijæm* is the only thing special about you?" Dashaelan drained his glass and sighed. "We'll be dropping you at the next port, then." He twisted in his chair to stand.

Song slapped her hands over the glass in his fist. "No!"

He stared at her in annoyance. "No?"

"You can't leave me. We had a deal! I know how to fly a ship!"

"But can you fight?"

She said nothing as Dashaelan stood and refilled his glass.

"I'm the best swordsman in the northern skies. I'll teach you to fight. If you're not good enough, then I'll be leaving you wherever we make berth."

"When do we start?"

He smiled at the over-eager young thing. "Welcome aboard, Miss Gould—"

"Song," she corrected. "My name is Song."

He paused, before nodding. "Welcome aboard, Song." He clicked his glass against the one in front of her and waited. She took the hint and lifted the glass. "To fortune."

"To pirates." She smiled.

He waved his hand in front of her as he swallowed the contents of his glass. "Don't be using that word, lass. We here on the Stars' Bounty are privateers." He winked.

"Privateers?" she repeated, her words barbed with disbelief.

He smirked as mischief sparkled in one eye. "As far as anyone off this ship is concerned, we're privateers, lass. Don't be calling yourself 'pirate' to anyone unless you fancy a thief's necklace for yourself."

"What…in the world does that even mean?"

"Gallows, Song."

"To privateers," she corrected. She raised her glass and swallowed a hefty gulp of her wine. It tasted like rancid pickles and ammonia. The flavor shocked her palate into coughing the liquid back into the glass.

"Kennington Private: thirteen-o-two," Dashaelan said. "Terrible year. Awful wine."

"Then why did you give it to me?" She gagged.

"Honestly? I didn't think you'd actually drink it."

Song gave him a dirty look.

He laughed. "Come." He stood and motioned for her to follow.

"Where?"

"You asked when we would start…we start now." He led her out to the deck and drew his sword.

"I have no sword."

"Gents, the lass needs a sword!" Dashaelan shouted.

The men roared and shouted and cheered. Two disappeared below deck, then returned a minute later with a chest, which Dashaelan kicked open to reveal swords of every length and width imaginable. She tried a cutlass, but the blade was too bulky for her to wield in any sort of comfort. She unsheathed a rapier, but it was longer than her arm and so she bungled the motion, catching the tip on the leather. It clattered to the deck, and she kicked it away in embarrassment. Nothing in the chest was the right size or length.

"Cap'n," the blond man from the night before shouted, revealing the likelihood of him having more toes than teeth. "What about them new ones?"

Dashaelan deflated. "But those are *mine*."

"What good is a sword if you leave it on a shelf its whole life?" Another with eyes and hair as black as night surrounding his pale face asked. He took a long gulp from a steaming mug, and eyed her with his tired gaze. His accent made her curious, as he spoke with heavy r's but a wide mouth—she'd never heard anything like it.

Dashaelan hesitated before nodding. The blond scurried into the captain's room, returning with a wooden display that cradled three swords of identical make, but varying sizes. Song took the one in the middle. It was not too long, nor too short. The wooden scabbard was stained a creamy tan; flakes of mother-of-pearl were set into the wood and outlined with gold. The opening was fashioned as a dragon's head swallowing the sword; its eyes were red and yellow rojed gemstones clutched by metal fittings.

"I couldn't possibly—" Song began.

"I've got two more," Dashaelan said as though convincing himself. "If you break that one, I'll have you walking the plank and let Davy Jones decide what to do with you."

"I've already been in Davy Jones's Locker," Song said and unsheathed the sword. The blade had a slight curve to it, one side razor sharp and the back wide like a wedge. "He sent me back."

Dashaelan smiled and held his sword out in front of him. "Ready?"

"Well, I—" Song held the blade over her head to stop Dashaelan's sword from coming down on top of her. "I wasn't ready!" she shouted.

"Lesson one: you will never be ready."

Song narrowed her eyes and dropped the scabbard to the deck, setting both of her hands on the handle of the sword. This time, she was prepared for the swing he took at her. After a few more hits, he scrutinized her.

"Sunshine, here." He pointed at the man with the dark eyes and black hair, bidding him to stand in his place. Once he was there, Dashaelan moved to Song, placing one hand at her waist and the other he wrapped around her sword hand. "Straighten…like this…no…like…would you stop squirming?"

"This is uncomfortable."

"I'm sorry, your highness, but this is how it's got to be. Now straighten up!" He pulled back on her shoulder and pushed the small of her back forward.

She fought the black-eyed man and the captain for hours until Dashaelan had had enough. Dashaelan took the sword from Song and inspected the blade—the steel shone as though still new. Satisfied, he sheathed it and set it back on the display.

"All right, you're safe from the plank…for now."

Sunshine clapped a hand on Song's shoulder. "You'll be one of us soon enough."

T HAT'S HOW IT WENT, DAY AFTER DAY, FOR WEEKS. S HE WOULD wake late in the morning and eat a meager breakfast. The men would train her on behaving like a boy—Toothy, the blond missing most of his teeth, went out of his way to make sure Song could belch with the best and give the rudest of insults with only a gesture—before Dashaelan would take her above deck to practice her swordplay. Every day he would threaten to send her over the railing for this or that, or to leave her stranded at the next port, but he never did.

In the solitude of the captain's cabin, she would practice her *kijæm*, perfecting the phrases and memorizing them. The words came to her faster, and she found that she began to think in both languages.

It was within the month when the men learned her rather unorthodox sense of attraction. She was trying to catch a few hours of rest in a high hammock when the hoots of the men had woken her. They were passing around their collection of women in immodest poses. The more they shared, the more naked the women became, until some images being passed around were downright lewd. Hairy—the man with a full beard but not a single hair on his head—was the first to realize Song was awake and peering at their pictures over the side of her hammock. He slapped the magazine over the bulge in his trousers—she was more offended by Hairy's groin than she was by the pictures.

"The least you could do," she slurred, "is pass a few magazines my way so I may share in your…enthusiasm."

"We ain't got no nudie men in these pages," one invisible said.

Song called those men invisibles because most of them blended into the woodwork and it was difficult to remember if she'd met one or if his resemblance to another was making her look the fool. In her mind, they were similar to her family's servants in that respect. So, she put little effort into remembering their names; they couldn't often stop to talk to her, anyway.

"Good, because I have no interest in men," Song replied.

The men hooted, and a magazine came sailing through the air toward her.

"Our lass is a lad!" shouted Hairy.

Song didn't open the magazine, nor did she correct Hairy. She was not a lad. She did not wish she were, except to make the act of relieving herself that much easier. Song liked being a young woman, and she loved the idea of being with other women. It had never even crossed her mind that maybe she should have been born a boy instead of a girl with a broken idea of who she should fancy.

The one thing her wry outburst had done was instill in the men that she would have nothing to do with them, as she was sure many had hoped would happen. They began treating her more like a boy, forgetting to censor their crude remarks about women. While it still offended Song, she said nothing. She would rather receive no special treatment than have the men walk on eggshells around her.

Captain Dashaelan was the only one who held his tongue and stayed respectful in the presence of Song. The more time she spent with him, the more she realized how similar they were. Dashaelan was a man of good character and strong morals, but something had turned him sour and so he'd become the most cunning pirate of the age—cunning enough to stay off her father's radar. He had a strict code of honor, which he followed to the letter. He took every opportunity to teach Song this code.

"Do not attack an unarmed man unless he still poses a threat."

"Never draw your sword on a woman or child unless they first have drawn a sword on you."

"Only a fool seeks revenge."

"A pirate can still be a gentleman."

He would say these to her at the most random times and out of context. But Song did her best to remember each one, because as Dashaelan said: "To live without a code is to sleep without rest."

THE FIRST TIME THE STARS' BOUNTY ENCOUNTERED ANOTHER vessel ripe for plunder, it caught Song unaware. First the whistle came—shrill and metallic, like a mechanical scream. All hands were on deck and armed. Every man was at his post; orders shouted and obeyed. The crew worked as a well-oiled machine, terrifying and awe-inspiring all at once.

"Song!" Dashaelan called to her from the helm. "Get you below deck and help with the cannons."

"But I can—"

"You can swim home or go to the cannons," he commanded.

In the ship's darkness, she stumbled and the lanky crew member named Thumbs caught her. Thumbs had rich, dark brown skin, with a mixture of tattoos and burn scars that marred his face. The largest tattoo was an animal skull of some sort in the middle of his forehead, it had spiraling horns that ended with sharp tips at his hairline. To look upon him was to know fear—until he tried to wield a sword. The reason everyone called him Thumbs was not only because his actual name was so long and difficult to pronounce that everyone would give up before they started, but because he was clumsy. There was no right reason Dashaelan kept him aboard, except that he was an excellent cook and always knew how to make a person laugh.

"Careful there, girly, or they be callin' you Thumbs next." His accent was strange, one Song had never heard. It was as though he couldn't say his 'th' and so substituted with either a t or a d, depending on the word. He took her hand and led her to the cannon at the end of one row.

"But then, what would they call you?"

"Hopefully not a cowardly dog, eh?"

Song's lips curved into a wry smile.

There were six cannons on either side of the ship, with two men to each cannon on one side, depending on where the enemy vessel was. So now, the other six sat empty in front of their closed trap doors.

Song's first ambush was rather uneventful for the cannoneers. They could hear the fighting above deck, but it wasn't very heated. The other vessel didn't even have its own cannons. So, Song and Thumbs passed the time telling riddles.

"What room has no doors and no windows?" Thumbs asked.

Song thought of every room she'd ever been in, but they all had at least a door. "I give up."

"A mush*room!*"

Song laughed. "All right, all right. Give me food and I will live. Give me water and I will die. What am I?"

Thumbs grinned. "A compost bin!"

"No, a fire," Song answered.

Thumbs thought for a moment. "All right, I have one for you. You use a knife to slice my head, then weep beside me when I am dead. What am I?"

"Umm—"

"An onion."

"Is everything all about food to you?" Song asked, exasperated.

"Maybe."

"All right then. What two things can you never have for breakfast?" Song challenged.

"Easy, lunch and dinner."

Later on deck, as they separated the looted quoine and a few items among the men, Song received her first wage.

"But I didn't do anything!" she protested.

"You followed orders," Dashaelan said. "Any man here'll tell you that following orders is key to not sending us all on a one-way trip to Davy Jones's Locker."

Sunshine held up a ladies' hairpin and cringed. "Well, ain't that just the most gods-awful thing you ever seen?"

It was a jewel-encrusted North Star with four long points and four short—a replica of the North Star carved into the front of their ship. It wasn't ugly in the slightest, but Sunshine acted like it had been fished from a cesspool. He leaned over and slipped the pin into Song's hair.

"Does it make me look pretty?" Song asked.

"If you mean does it make me look somewhere besides that dog's arse you call a face, then yes, I suppose it'll do." He gave her a wink.

Song smiled. She knew he was just a grumpy man reaching the end of his pirating years and finding reasons to hate it. With the new hairpin, she felt like she was not only part of the crew, but a part of the ship. It was her new home, and these ragged ruffians, her new family. Never mind that they still had no idea who she really was—and Dashaelan made sure it stayed that way.

Every time they treated her in this teasing manner, it made her compare how everyone previously had treated her. In Garda, no one dared talk to her without invitation. Her mother very rarely said a kind or encouraging word. Her father was distant, but would assure her he loved her—sometimes it felt like they were just words with no meaning behind them. Johanna would never have said a mean thing in her life. That woman didn't have a rude bone in her body, though she had some choice opinions about things, which she would mutter. But never about Song. She only ever had kind words and encouragement for her.

Sunshine's muttered insults were a sign that he even knew someone enough to say something. He didn't direct jabs at much of the crew, just her, Dashaelan, Toothy, and two invisibles she recognized as more than the woodwork, but still hadn't managed to pin down who they were. Dashaelan's show of caring was the lessening of the threats. Day by day he'd made fewer comments about throwing her overboard, and had switched to her having to scrub the latrine with a boar bristle toothbrush and her own spit. Toothy's was obvious in the way he made sure to share all the dirty words he knew and teach her how to be the rudest pirate aboard after him. The captain, however, was not as amused nor excited as Song.

That night, Dashaelan gave Song her own hammock in the weapons room, away from the others. He said it was because they could use an armory guard, but she knew that was as truthful as Sunshine's critique of the hairpin.

Thirteen

IT WAS OVER A MONTH LATER WHEN DASHAELAN GAVE SONG her first turn in the crow's nest. She'd never known there was one until then. He handed her a small pouch with a long strap. Inside the pack were a telescope, a sailor's whistle, a flask of water, a hunk of hard bread, and a small cloth pouch of dehydrated fruits.

"When you see another vessel, you blow once for all hands prepare to board, twice for pirate, and three times for foul weather. The fouler the weather, the longer you hold the third blow."

She nodded in understanding.

"Now, when your shift is over, I'll call you down like this." He covered the small hole at the front of his whistle and blew out a flat note; then, on the same wind, released so the whistle's sound shot up to an ear-piercing range. "Understand?"

Song hesitated. Dashaelan raised his eyebrows, urging her on.

"Why is there a crow's nest?"

He laughed. "I asked Captain Garmont the same thing."

"And?"

He took her to the center of the deck. "Spin around. Tell me what you see."

Song spun. "I see the ocean."

"And?"

"And what?"

"You see a mast, a bow, the quarterdeck. You see crewmen to distract you from lookout."

"Point taken." Song smiled, nervous, as she repeated the previous whistle instructions over and over in her head.

Toothy came into view, climbing down the cargo net that stretched up to the top of the zeppelin. The bags beneath his eyes were dark, and he seemed about to fall over from exhaustion.

"Careful up there, lass. Something in me bones says bad weather is a-comin'." He set his finger on the side of his nose and patted her head before making a determined line for a hammock in the quarters.

"Should I be worried?" she asked Dashaelan.

"He's never wrong."

Song nodded and swallowed hard against the dryness in her throat. She made her way up the cargo net. A round wooden tub sat atop the golden zeppelin. Up there, the sun had bleached the paint to a pale yellow and there were spots which had thinned from exposure. Dashaelan had said something about patching up at the next port, but it hadn't occurred to her this was what he meant.

The crow's nest was a virtual oubliette—once Song was there, she felt forgotten. The sun and the wind, the clouds and the occasional sea bird were all she had atop the zeppelin. She tried not to think about the pocket of potentially explosive gasses sitting beneath her, though it was unnerving.

The sun was warm and the crow's nest cozy. Song leaned back, draping her legs over one side and resting the back of her head against the other, making sure to keep her eyes on the horizon. It wasn't long before Song's leg jumped, waking her from the sleep she hadn't known was beginning.

She sat in the calm and let her mind wander. She did not notice she had fallen asleep again until an icy breeze slapped her face, waking her from a pleasant dream. Sitting upright, she stretched, stopping with her arms over her head as she saw what was on the horizon. Clouds, black with anger that released flashes of light to emphasize the danger held within them.

Song dumped the contents of her pouch at her knees and grabbed the whistle in her fist. She blew hard, but the sound was flat and muted. Removing her finger from over the hole, she tried again. This time, the shrill note screeched through the air.

One. Two. Three—

She held the third note as long as she could, then drew breath and blew again.

One. Two. Three—

The skyship was on a collision course with the head of the storm, both speeding toward each other with dangerous determination. Song waited and then blew again.

One. Two. Three—

The storm was nearly upon them when she heard the low and high whistle blow, sounding over and over in repeated urgency. Song scrambled to collect her things as the first drops of rain smacked her face like cold pebbles thrown by a scornful child. She began her descent down the side of the zeppelin, panic shaking her to the core. As she neared where the net widened, a gust of wind struck the skyship, knocking her over. She dangled from the net, her foot caught between the rope and the canvas. Dashaelan yelled orders at the men to secure this and tie down that and 'for gods-sake someone take a rope up the net and get Song untangled!'

Toothy grabbed a rope and set it in his mouth, where his last remaining teeth gripped it. He climbed the net from the inside; his ascent was slow as he gripped each rung securely in his fist. Once he reached Song, he stretched around to hand her the rope, which she wrapped around her wrist. He then began to work her foot free.

The release of Song's foot was sudden, and neither she nor Toothy could have reacted fast enough. One minute she was wiggling her foot this way and that to aid him in her rescue, and the next her boot decided it'd had enough and released her. She fell face-first toward a churning ocean hidden behind thick sheets of rain. She couldn't even scream as the heavy rainfall threatened to drown her in the air. The rope around her wrist caught, and the skyship pulled her along behind it.

"Da—" Song tried to shout but choked on the water. She took a deep breath and angled her face away from the oncoming storm. "Dash!" she shouted. "Dash!"

"Pull her up!" Dashaelan shouted.

Slow and steady, the rope made its journey to safety. But Song's arm had ripped from the socket and she could feel her grip failing. One quick slip and the rope burned into her palm and cut the top of her hand open. She screamed from the pain of it, but held fast. The distance between herself and the ship closed faster, as Dashaelan himself took hold of the rope and pulled. She reached out to him with her other hand, catching his fingertips as her right arm lost all strength. The rain had wet Dashaelan's fingers and her hand slipped from his grasp. She fell backward into the darkness.

Song did not scream as she fell. Instead, she summoned the strength and courage to demand saving. The words were choked from her twice as the rain filled her mouth every time it opened. She shielded her lips with her hand and said, "*Em t'keht-orp!*"

The first time the strange bubble had shielded Song, it had bored a hole in the sea. This time, it seemed to explode from around her as though her aura had detached itself and become a shield. The protective barrier undulated with a mysterious light that was in constant motion as it fought with the elements. The little dots of light in the glowing mist circled around her feet, pressing against the soles of her shoes to keep her suspended in the air. Song cradled her injured arm and breathed her panic out of her throat, calming herself.

"*Pish ehth oot em kait,*" she murmured.

Song didn't know if she was moving. She trusted her *kijæm* to do as she asked, grateful that at least that would always be predictable. The Stars' Bounty came into view as she sped toward the vessel as though nothing stood in opposition. The lights slowed and lifted Song over the railing, setting her on the deck. Before it could leave, Song made another request.

"Pish ehth t'keht-orp. M'rots sith oorth suh del."

The lights hesitated, blinking in randomized spurts, each dot flickering in and out of existence, as though processing this command. Then it spread outward to encompass the skyship. Dashaelan let go of the wheel as it lit with the blue light and it took control away from him. He stared down at Song.

"I thought we'd lost you to Davy Jones's Locker."

The laugh she gave him was humorless. "I told you, he doesn't want me."

Looking around the ship, Song realized that this was the first time any of the crew had seen her use *kijæm*. Dashaelan moved to her to inspect her arm. Toothy came next to crouch by her other side, setting the retrieved boot beside her.

He studied her, bitter apology knitting his brow together. "I shouldn't have let you fall."

Song remained quiet for a moment, shocked that his main concern, considering what he'd just seen, was her having fallen. "I should've gotten down faster. It's not your fault."

He wrapped his arm around her head and pulled it to his chest to hug her. "Next time, use your Gift before you go falling into the abyss."

"I'll have to remember that."

When Toothy let go of her, Sunshine reached forward to adjust the North Star pin in her hair. "Aren't you just a glittery ball of surprises?" He took a swig from his flask and disappeared below deck

Dashaelan wrapped his hands around Song's wrist and put his foot on her ribs, then yanked her arm outward. Her shoulder popped back into place and Song screamed, then fainted from the pain and the effort of the day.

Fourteen

Song felt the hands of time pulling at her, reminding her of the original plan to save Altain. As each day ended and another began, she started to lose hope of ever finding him.

"Dash, may I speak to you in private? Please."

"Hairy, take the helm!" Dashaelan shouted.

"I fear we have tarried too long in searching for my friend," she said once they were in the privacy of his quarters.

"How so?"

"It has been months since I first joined your crew and all we've done is train and pillage, train and pillage, every day."

"Sit." He pushed Song onto the chair at the table and poured her a glass of rum, something she'd found she could stomach well enough. "You're below deck when we seize the other vessels," he began, sitting across from her. "But we've been interrogating the crews for information on the whereabouts of Captain Darian and your precious Dauntless. Of course, hardly any of them know anything, or if they do, they're too scared to say anything."

Song rested her forehead on the tabletop. "I have failed him."

"Naw, he was probably run-through the day you took your little swim."

"That's ever so encouraging."

"Point is, you've done more than anyone else would do in your place. You stole a skyship from one of the most ruthless pirates in the world and evaded him for the better part of a month before he caught up with you. And even then you nearly got away! Two runnin' a ship made for five grown men. If I was Darian, I'da killed you both on the spot."

"But you're not Darian." Song smirked at him. "But maybe, just once, Darian was like you. Maybe he couldn't kill someone so young, like you can't."

"I could have ended you on the first day," Dashaelan said.

"Then why didn't you?" They sat in silence as Song sized him up. "You could have tossed me overboard and kept right on flying. You keep saying you will, over and over, but I don't think you could."

Dashaelan's lips hooked in a sideways smile. "And why is that?"

"Because you still have some scrap of decency."

"I have a code, girl."

"And to live without a code is to live without honor." Song tapped her glass against Dashaelan's and took a bitter sip. "I'd like to stay above deck for the next interception." She caught his gaze and held it.

He drained his glass and studied her. "Do you think you're ready for that?"

"I think I'll never be ready. But neither is any man until he actually does it."

"Except Thumbs." Dashaelan poured himself another finger of rum. "Bless that clumsy dog and his damned stew."

THEY MADE PORT THAT AFTERNOON TO RESUPPLY. SONG KEPT HER hood up and her head down with every intention of buying new, less conspicuous clothing.

As they'd docked, Sunshine had leaned close to whisper to her. "A block from the inn is a tailor. She don't ask questions. A pirate's quoine is as good as any, she says."

And so Song found herself entering a small building called 'Stitches'. A beautiful woman in a simple blue dress approached and began taking Song's measurements.

"Ello, love. You can call me Stitch. It's not my name, but I'm sure I won't be seeing you again, so what's it matter?" She spoke with a somewhat frantic tone, as though her mind was switching subjects in such rapid succession that she had to get them out before she lost them. Stitch dropped the h's on all the words that started with one and skipped over her t's, so they became more of a harsh pause or stutter.

"How do you know—"

"You come in here smelling like sea salt and sweaty men and you ask how I know what you do? Cheeky little thing." She lowered Song's hood and stopped, her brow furrowing before she re-assumed her hurried hush-hush manner. "And a girl! Well, darling, I can tell you now that a tan coat with such fine embroidery is not what I'll be doing for you. Though this style is rather becoming…" She wandered away in thought and began picking through her rolls of cloth.

"I was hoping for something less...fancy."

Stitch tapped her lips in thought. "Give me your coat."

"Excuse me?"

"I'll make you another, but I need to see how it's put together."

Song shifted in her discomfort. Stitch took Song's chin between her thumb and forefinger, lifting her face to get a good look at her. After a long moment, she sighed and pulled a long brown cloak from beneath her drawing table. Song removed her coat and handed it over. Stitch wrapped the cloak around Song's shoulders and secured it with a simple broach. She lifted the hood and smiled at their secret.

"Keep your hood up and your face low, child. There's a price on your head."

"How do—"

Stitch pressed her finger to Song's lips. "Shh! I don't know anything. Just a simple seamstress making new clothes for a customer."

"I'll be at the—"

"Tavern down the way. I know. Hurry off. I'll send for you when I'm ready."

When Song entered the tavern and took a seat beside Dashaelan, the others eyed her. She squirmed under their scrutiny but said nothing.

Thumbs spoke up. "Trying your hand at being a highwayman?"

"A highway-madam!" Toothy corrected just loud enough for their table to hear.

"Stitch get you all squared away?" Sunshine asked.

"She did, thank you."

"What *is* with the cloak, anyway?" he asked.

Song cleared her throat, but it was Dashaelan who replied. "A young lady in the streets without an escort is a tempting target for men without honor."

"But where is your coat?" Thumbs demanded, then intoned, "I loved that coat."

"She's making another for me," Song replied. "I left it with her so she could copy the design."

Thumbs smiled. "Good. I love that coat."

Three men approached their table. Dashaelan held his hand up as a warning for Song to keep her head down and her mouth shut. The rest of their crew at a nearby table sat at attention.

"Word is you're short on crew," the short, pretty one said. He had an accent like Amelia's, soft and yet betrayed their low status in society.

"Word is wrong," Dashaelan replied.

"We're three good men who know their way around a ship. We'll work hard and earn our keep."

Song choked on her ale. He was the prettiest man she'd ever seen, and the mere idea of one such as him knowing anything about crewing a pirate ship made her scoff into her palm.

"Pimples was talking of staying in Tarn," Toothy said.

Dashaelan swirled his mead as he thought. "Can you follow orders?"

"Aye," the blond man said.

"We leave in two days at dawn. Be on the Stars' Bounty or stay here in Tarn."

Song peeked out from under her hood to watch the men

leave. The pretty one was short compared to the others and dressed above his means; his vest alone would've fed him for a week, with its fine embroidery and elaborate cut. The second man was tall and slender, with a sword in a red leather sheath at his side. His clothing was modest and unimpressive; dark trousers, battered boots, and a linen shirt with a collar. His hair was long and rich auburn, pulled into a loose ponytail at the nape of his neck. Again, Song stared at the color—darker than Dashaelan's, but still red. The third man was a hulking figure with broad shoulders in dark clothing. Beneath his burnt-brown hair was coppery brown skin and mean black eyes, which he trained on Song for a moment longer before following the other two.

"That beast-man gives Song another look and I'll castrate him," Sunshine muttered into his mug.

"I do *not* like his crazy eyes," Toothy agreed.

Dashaelan nodded. "If he causes trouble, then all three will find themselves swimming home."

"Do you just idly threaten to throw everyone overboard?" Song asked. "Or have you actually done it before?"

His eyes bored into her. "Don't go trying to find out."

IT WAS LATE THE NEXT NIGHT AND SONG WAS THINKING OF retiring to her room when a young boy entered the tavern and ran straight to her.

"Miss Stitch sends for you," he said, his voice confident.

There wasn't an ounce of fear in the boy, and Song found that admirable. In the presence of pirates and highwaymen, he'd run in without flinching to deliver his mistress's message. Song finished the wine she'd treated herself with and stood to follow the boy. Dashaelan took her elbow.

"Keep your head low."

"Aye."

In the shop, the boy scampered through a door as Stitch came from the other side.

"Thomas." She stopped him.

"Yes'm?" He stood attentive.

"Get yourself a sweet from the counter. You may sit in the corner and eat it so the others don't get jealous." She smiled and patted him on the bottom as he ran back into the front room, retrieved his sweet from under the drawing table, then ran to sit on a stool at the back of the room. His eyes watched Song as he nibbled his treat, savoring every second he had it.

"You have many children?" Song asked as Stitch urged her behind a folding wooden room divider, which served as a dressing room.

"Orphans," Stitch replied.

Song stripped and began pulling on the clothes, starting with a sleeveless beige undershirt that was tight around her body, like a ribless corset. "Do they work here?"

The next shirt buttoned partway down the front, the collar accented with golden lace. Stitch stepped around to have a look, then urged Song to stand on a nearby stool. Thomas kept his eyes on Song, gears turning behind them.

"They live here," Stitch replied as she bent to check the hem on the pant legs.

"Live here?" Song tried not to squirm as Stitch shoved the fabric upward, crinkling it just below the knees.

"I give them a roof and three hot meals a day in exchange for labor. It's the only way I can guarantee such fast clothing to overnighters, such as yourself." She buttoned the cuffs on the sleeves of the shirt and tucked the tail into the top of the pants, sliding Song's own belt through the loops to secure them in place. "Rather narrow for being eighteen." Her eyes swooped over Song's figure.

"I'm seventeen," Song corrected.

"Dear, you haven't been seventeen for almost a week." Stitch winked and turned to her table to retrieve a vest of deep charcoal-colored fabric with golden swirls embroidered into it. The front reached just below her ribcage, the back rose a little higher. "Now, I said I wouldn't do anything fancy, but…" She swung the vest over Song's arms in one practiced movement. "Been dying to use this fabric for a while now, just never had the right customer." She fastened the clasps across the front and nodded in approval.

Stitch picked up a black replica of Song's tan coat. It was nothing fancy, just black leather with a soft cotton lining. "This will be more durable. I made this one myself, didn't trust any of my children with a new pattern like this." She backed away a step and admired her handiwork. "These coats will sell like hot porridge on a cold morning."

"I'd rather my coat remained unique." Song replied, reaching into her bag for the quoine to pay for the clothes.

"Oh, I'm sorry, of course… Perhaps you'd allow me to sell similar variations?" Her hopeful smile urged Song into agreement.

"As long as you make sure those orphans stay fed." She looked back at Thomas and couldn't help thinking of Altain alone on the streets. She set an extra quoine in Stitch's hand and leaned close to speak low. "Give him an extra sweet from me." She winked at the boy in the corner and took her leave.

"If you're ever in Tarn again—"

"I'll be sure to get some new clothes." Song pulled her hood over her head and stepped out into the night.

Her new coat was warm and comfortable; the hood was deep and cast much of her face in shadow. The trousers were a strange material Song had never encountered—they were tough like leather, but breathed like cotton. When she reached the tavern, much of the crew had gone. Sunshine and Thumbs still sat with their chins on their hands, looking like they'd run out of things to talk about, but neither wanted to retire for the night. When they caught sight of her, Thumbs smiled and Sunshine sniffed his indifference into his nose.

"I love that coat!" Thumbs said.

Song laughed. "So I've heard."

Thumbs reached out to touch the supple, black leather and whistled low. "I bet you lost a pretty quoine on that."

"Worth it," Sunshine snapped.

"I did not say it was not," Thumbs said.

"I didn't say you said it wasn't. I'm saying it was. Stitch's clothes are always worth it."

Dashaelan cleared his throat behind her and set a pair of tall black leather boots with low heels onto the table. Then he set a strange utility belt with two pouches and a gun holster clipped onto little brass rings next to the boots. "Happy birthday." He shoved them in front of Song and nodded at the other two. "Get some sleep Thumbs, Song. Dawn comes early."

"Thank you!" Song called after him as he left for the rooms above. He nodded and ascended the stairs.

"It is your birthday?" Thumbs asked.

"I didn't even know…supposedly it was days ago." Song removed her fancy boots and pulled on the new ones. They laced up the back and would need to be broken in to rid them of stiffness, but the fit was close to perfect around her feet. The belt matched—the initials C.S. had been pressed into each of the pouches and the holster. Dashaelan had taken the liberty of sneaking her revolver from her trunk and securing it within.

"What does the 'C' stand for, anyway?" Sunshine asked as she secured the belt beneath her coat.

"Captain," Thumbs said; Sunshine and Song both narrowed their eyes at him. "What? Captain Song has a nice ring to it!"

"I have no intentions of being a captain. It's Caleb."

"That's not your sidearm, is it?" Sunshine stated.

"It is now."

He nodded in agreement.

Sixteen

THE WORLD WAS STILL BLACK, THE HORIZON NOT EVEN HINTING at the sun's rising. Song hadn't slept for long when Dashaelan barged into her room and shook her awake. She stretched and rubbed her eyes, which were dry and rough as though filled with sand. It took her a moment to catch the urgency with which he was pulling her from the bed and shoving her boots onto her feet.

"What's—"

"You've been made!" he hissed.

"What do you mean?"

"Sunshine was in the tavern—"

"This late?" Song let Dashaelan pull her coat over her shoulders.

"He's used to it, stayed as lookout. You're not exactly a forgettable face, with so much quoine offered up as reward for your safe return."

"That poster doesn't even look like me."

"It looks enough like you that desperate fellows will see the similarities."

"Why don't you just turn me in?"

"I've grown rather fond of you," he said. He led Song out into the hallway, where she scurried on the balls of her feet to a door at the end. "Go in there. Hairy is waiting. I'll be to the Bounty shortly."

"But—"

Voices echoed near the staircase and footsteps started up.

"Go!" Dashaelan hissed.

Song spun into the room, closing the door with a gentle *click*. Without warning, a rope wrapped around her waist and Hairy scooped her into his arms.

"Hold tight," he whispered as he raced to the balcony. "To the rope!" he said when she gripped his shoulders. As Song grabbed the rope in her fists, Hairy lifted her over the railing. "Don't scream."

"Wh—"

Song gasped, her breath catching in her throat as he tossed her over the side. The rope caught, and she swung toward the building. Thinking fast, she turned to plant her feet against the stone wall. Hairy fed the rope outward as she rappelled down to the street below where Toothy caught her and Thumbs untied the rope. Once it was free from her, Hairy pulled it back up and waved them away.

"Tuck in your hair and put up your hood," Toothy hissed as he set her down and urged her to the opening of the alley.

One invisible stood at the end of the alley. As they approached, he waved them through. Constables stood guard at the front of the tavern, but they had turned their attention inside. As they walked away, the blond invisible fell into step on Song's heels, blocking the view of her from behind.

"Oy," he whispered. "What's so special about her?" His accent was eerily similar to Sunshine's, though she still had no idea where the latter was from.

Toothy shrugged. "Captain's orders. I didn't ask."

"Kill a man?" he continued, nudging her shoulder.

"Sneakin' off in the night to leave us behind, are you?" The three new crewmen stepped from the shadows. The blond stood to block their path as the other two hung back to assess the situation.

Thumbs looked over his shoulder to make sure they hadn't brought any unwanted attention to them. "We are not leaving no one behind as long as you keep your voice down and help us get our cabin boy to the ship."

The large man fixed his gaze on Song again, and her skin crawled. The short man noted his compatriot's attention to her.

"What?" he asked.

The big man glared sideways at the other and grunted.

"He dangerous?"

He scoffed through his nose.

The blond turned his attention to Song. "Bounty on your head, lad?"

"A large one," Toothy replied.

"Then we'd better get going."

The hulking man first turned his attention to the third companion, who seemed to think on the subject. When he nodded his approval, the men all circled her, the biggest straight behind. His every step clenched her heart further into her throat until she could hardly breathe through her fear. There was something about his wild eyes, which he kept fixed on her, that scared her in ways she could not explain. The short one stood to her left; she had at least a hand on him in height. The other on her right had a hand of height on her—she guessed him to be a hand shy of two meters.

When they reached the skyship, the short man turned to extend his hand to Song. "I'm William. Friends call me Bill."

She stared at the offering, but didn't shake it.

"Pretty Boy, got it," Toothy smiled at him.

William gave him a long look before deciding to ignore his comment. "This is Leslie." He jerked a thumb at the slender one, whose gaze swept over the docks as he kept watch and ignored the introductions. "And this is—"

"I'm Brute," the hulking man said. He never took his eyes from Song, who kept her gaze trained on the deck at her feet.

"You're going with Brute?" William asked.

Brute shrugged.

William took a moment to process before shaking it off. "I'm Toothy, this is Thumbs and—"

"Caleb," Thumbs blurted. "And these blokes are Pinch and Ponce."

The invisibles—one tall and muscular, with white-blond hair, the other Song's height with brown hair—gave small waves as they busied themselves readying the ship.

"Caleb, with me." Thumbs took her by the elbow and dragged her to the pantry.

"Why did you tell them my name is Caleb?"

"Best they know nothing until Dash says so," Thumbs replied. "Now, I want you to keep an eye out that porthole. If anyone official-looking comes poking by, hide yourself in here." He lifted a trapdoor hidden beneath sacks of potatoes; it led into a narrow crawlspace between the pantry and the weapons hold one level down. As he turned to leave,

Thumbs stopped and cast a curious eye on her. "Why is there a bounty on your head?"

"Would it change the way you think of me?"

Thumbs twisted his lips in thought. "I do not think so."

"Then I'd rather my secret remain mine."

He chuckled. "Not a good secret if the entire world knows it."

"I don't care about the world. I care about my friends."

"Good. Because we care about you, no matter your past."

Thumbs returned to the main deck, and Song turned her sights on the porthole. When someone came near, it was not the authorities, but rather the crew. Some time later, Sunshine came into view, looking irritated as ever—maybe even more so. With Sunshine being the last of the crew to board, the skyship left port. Moments later, he let himself into the galley. First, he leaned against the door and studied her, then he sighed.

"Was it Stitch?" Song asked.

"No. It was Thomas, her courier. She's sendin' him back to the orphanage in the mornin'. She sends her deepest apologies and her finest brooch." He held a small, gem-encrusted swirl out in his palm. It looked like a sparkling vortex.

"I paid for that little brat to have an extra treat!" Song growled. "That little scab!"

"The constables gave me a strange name when they came searchin'."

Song swallowed.

"I didn't recognize the first one, but the second… You'd have to live under a rock to not know who the Goulds are."

Song's heart beat in her ears.

"It's funny that they should go lookin' in a pirates' inn for someone bearin' such a famous name—a pirate hunter's name at that."

She took a deep breath. "What did you tell them?"

"I told them the truth." He pressed the brooch into her palm. "Ain't no Goulds here. Just a load of ruddy pirates." He kept her gaze for a moment longer before turning to open the door. "Captain wants to see you."

Song sank onto a sack of potatoes and let a rush of air pass through her lips. Her secret had reached a second crewmate. She wondered how long it would be until everyone on board knew. She picked herself up from the sack and pocketed the brooch before lifting her hood up and heading to the captain's cabin.

Dashaelan was pacing when she entered. He had a glass in one hand and a bottle of whiskey in the other, but he had yet to pour any as though he'd forgotten he held them. Song eased the items from his grasp and poured two fingers, which he finished in one swallow, then held out the glass for more.

"That was too close, Song."

"It was the boy," she said.

"It was too close."

She retrieved a glass for herself and poured three fingers in.

Dashaelan eyed her. "That's more than you usually take."

She tilted her head and swallowed the contents. "I don't usually get thrown from a window with constables at my tail, either." She sat down and set her face in her hands.

"We can handle the law."

"I'll remain on board when we dock in the future," she said.

Dashaelan stared at her.

"We're both thinking it."

He shrugged. "Fair enough. What's your opinion of those three?"

"What does my opinion matter?"

"Let's just say I respect it."

Song tested her words. "The small one, William, he seems the sort we can trust. Honorable. Though he seems a bit pretty to be crewing a skyship. The other one, Leslie…he's quiet, reserved. I don't know what to make of him."

"He's dangerous."

"How do you know?"

"It's always the quiet ones…" He paced a few more times. "What about the big one?"

"Brute." Song ignored the chill that ran down her spine. "He stares at me like he can see right through me. Something about him sets me on edge. I suppose it's a good quality for him to have for intimidation, but how am I supposed to crew with him if he uses it on me?"

Dashaelan nodded. "I'll have to ask him to keep his eyes on his feet, or lose them." He sighed and pulled his palms down his face. "I want you to sleep in my quarters tonight. I'll be locking the door from the other side."

"I didn't have to sleep in here with other new crewmen!" she objected.

"The others didn't have a behemoth staring you down, either. You're sleeping in here, Song. And that's final." Dashaelan didn't wait for her to object again. He stormed out of the cabin and locked the door.

Song sighed and removed all but her undershirt and trousers, then fell into his hammock. Whether by exhaustion or whiskey or some mixture thereof, she fell asleep almost instantly.

Seventeen

For the next few days, Song kept her hood up, never speaking in the presence of the new hands. Brute had taken to inspecting his fingernails while eyeing her in his peripherals. While it still made her uncomfortable, she learned to ignore it. William didn't have time to bother with Song, as the rest of the crew kept him busy. According to Toothy, there was nothing going on behind that pretty face of his. Leslie was still the wildcard. He kept to himself, doing as he was told without question. His eyes, an icy-blue similar to Dashaelan's, were always watching, always aware of his surroundings.

Dashaelan wanted to get a read on the three himself before making proper introductions. The wildcard was making it difficult. No matter how she begged to return to her sword lessons or be given something exciting to do, he would growl at her to keep her mouth shut and her head down. To keep out of the way, she set herself in the galley with Thumbs, much to his great pleasure.

"No one ever wants to learn to cook," he complained as they peeled potatoes. "All them up on deck just want booty and adventure. But you know what I say?"

"Everyone's got to eat," she replied. This was the fourth time in two days he'd said some variation of the complaint.

"Damn right everyone has got to eat. No one ever thinks of the cook until their belly is grumbling for a meal. Dash says swordplay is an art, well, so is food." He began slicing his potato into medium-sized squares.

"Thank you for teaching me," she said, holding back her chuckle.

Thumbs dropped the potatoes into the cauldron of water suspended over the sandbox. At its center were coals waiting to be kindled with a modest fire. He was not a fan of large open flames, not when a skyship could be so unpredictable. Right then, the pile of coals was waiting for Song to ignite it, rather than tinder. Every hot meal she'd helped him with, resulted in his vocal adulation of her for making his job that much easier.

"I think I will treat the boys to fresh mushrooms tonight. What do you say?"

Song smiled. Fresh mushrooms were a rare treat, which she looked forward to. "That would be delightful."

"I think I have got a sack in the hold. Mind grabbing them while I get this meat cut up?" He reached into a bucket of water where strips of meat had been soaking to restore some juices and wash away much of the salt used to preserve it.

"It would be my pleasure." She dumped her potato pieces into the water and wiped her hands on a cloth.

"And do not go sneaking any, either." He eyeballed her. "Do not think I do not know you help yourself to one every time you go into the hold!"

Song slipped him a sly smile and entered the hold. They'd obtained fresh mushrooms in Tarn, which she enjoyed much better than the dehydrated ones they usually kept on board. Her stomach fluttered at the prospect of fresh mushrooms in the night's stew. Grabbing the sack, she paused and twisted her mouth sideways in devious thought. She found a small mushroom and popped it into her mouth, chewing fast to get rid of the evidence as she tied the sack. Someone entered the room behind her and she spun around, ready to deny Thumbs's accusations of mushroom snatching. But it wasn't Thumbs, it was William. Quick as a snap, she yanked her hood over her head.

He tutted. "Ahh, too late. I've already seen your hair, girly."

Song said nothing.

"When Brute first suggested there was something the matter with you, I thought he meant you were dangerous. After all, there is a bounty on your head." He strode across the room and yanked her hood back. "Not a bounty…" The gears worked behind his eyes. "I've never had anything quite as expensive as you."

Song's eyes went wide as he pressed himself against her. "Thumbs!"

Cold steel set against her throat as William leaned in closer. "I'm afraid he's on deck with the captain."

She opened her mouth to shout again and felt the knife press deeper into her skin, stinging it open as a warm trickle made its way to her collar.

"I'd try to be quiet if I were you." His other hand found her gun, un-holstered it, and tossed it onto a far sack of grain.

"Don't touch me," Song growled.

"Or what?" he scoffed. His free hand began working to undo the utility belt at her waist.

"I will break your hands."

William leered and pressed the knife further into her neck. "One more word and I cut your throat."

"*Em pleh-h*," she whispered, flinching as the blade stung into her flesh.

She'd never felt so helpless, pinned against a crate and unable to speak. Her speed and *kijæm* had always been her strength, but without movement or words, she was nothing. Her eyes memorized his face as he fought against the belt holding her trousers up. He was determined and unapologetic; cold and dishonorable. He avoided her accusing gaze as though he knew deep down that he was making the biggest mistake of his life.

The door burst open behind William. Startled, he slid the knife along her skin, extending the line he'd already cut into her neck. A gasp hissed through her teeth at the sting of it.

Brute stood in the doorway, wild eyes taking in the scene. Song knew her chances were slim, but if she could at least get away from William, then she could use her *kijæm* to force Brute out of her way and escape. She shoved William away and threw herself sideways. As she turned, Brute wove his fingers together and swung his fists, making contact with the side of William's head. The small man's body rag-dolled against the wall before falling into a heap on the floor.

Brute turned his wild gaze on Song. After a long moment, he extended his hand, and she took it, allowing him to pull her to her feet.

"Song," she said as her mind went blank with her shock.

He nodded, acknowledging the offering of her true name. "Bruce."

He bent to grab William by his belt. As Brute dragged the other man through the door, Song let her shaking knees send her back to the floor. Thumbs appeared beside her and pressed a cloth to her neck.

"What happened?"

"Brute… William…"

Thumbs lifted her from the floor and led her on shaking knees to the main deck. Brute was ascending the top steps as they approached. Once on deck, he dropped William and nodded at Dashaelan.

"What's this?" he asked.

"He attacked Song," Thumbs shouted.

"What?"

A low whistle came from the bow of the ship where Leslie sat polishing his blade. "Funny thing about William, he never could resist a pretty girl…or an ugly one, for that matter. Even the occasional fair-skinned boy would catch his fancy." Leslie's voice was a strange duality of low and high as it passed through his nose and lips at the same time. It was melodious and frightening all at once. Quiet as his voice was, it carried across the deck and urged trust from those who listened. His accent was the purest Andalisian, the kind found in the upper class of Garda, like Song—but she would have remembered a man with hair like that, and so distrust wove through her gut.

"Why didn't you warn us?" Toothy demanded.

Leslie fixed his icy-blue eyes on Toothy, his demeanor calm. "I was told the cabin boy's name was Caleb. Had I known he was, in fact, a cabin *girl*…I would've thrown William from the ship before it left port."

"I thought him to be honorable," Song admitted. "He looked it, at least."

"Looks can be deceiving."

William groaned into the deck.

"You may want to tie him up." Leslie returned his attention to his sword, running his rag along the blade. It was a methodical action, as though some personal ritual inspired him to take such care in his weapon.

The blade itself was a strange one Song had never seen the likes of before. It was dark as onyx with a double edge, which gleamed silver in contrast. The hilt was wrapped in leather braids, red as blood to match the scabbard. They tied together at the pommel, where the short strands hung from the end. It seemed more for ceremony or formal occasions than for combat.

As Song watched them bind William's hands and feet, her courage returned. She approached Dashaelan, who lifted the cloth to see her wound. "What do you intend to do?" she asked.

"Toss him over," Dashaelan growled.

"What are you waiting for?"

"I want to see the look in his eyes as he falls into the ocean."

A steely calm settled over Song as ice pumped through her veins. "I'd like to speak with him before that."

He cocked an eyebrow at her. "What could you possibly have to say to him?"

"*Ng-edelb ehth pawts.*" She pulled the cloth away as a blue mist collected beside her neck, then turned to orange as it settled on her skin. The wound burned shut and the blood stopped flowing. She cringed at the pain as the bittersweet smell of burned flesh reached its rancid fingers into her nose. Never taking her eyes from his, she handed the cloth to him. "I can think of a few things."

She strode to where Brute sat beside Leslie, his eyes trained on her, though his face was angled down at the blade in Leslie's hands. She waited until he turned his head, giving her his undivided attention.

"You saved me."

Brute nodded.

"How did you know?"

"I knew." His voice was like a grunt.

"You knew I wasn't a boy?"

He nodded.

"How did you know to save me?"

He paused. "I...knew."

Leslie sighed. "What he's saying is that he was told, right?"

He nodded.

"By whom?" Song asked.

Brute shrugged and pointed at his head. "Help me."

"He heard you ask for help," Leslie translated. "In his mind?" He eyed Brute, who nodded. A flicker of realization lit his eyes as his eyebrows rose. "Well, there you have it."

Song turned her attention to Leslie. "How put-out would you be to lose your dear friend William?"

"Dead men pay no debts." When Song said nothing,

he elaborated. "William owes me. I'll be sad to lose the quoine promised."

Brute turned to the other. "Song." He pointed at her.

She smirked. "You've joined a pirate crew, mate. Cause no trouble and you'll be repaid tenfold."

He stood and sheathed his sword with a flourish. "I accept your terms and offer you my services."

Brute grunted in agreement.

"I'm not the captain, you can pledge yourselves to him."

"That's not how this works, dear girl. His debt is now yours. We will not pledge to the captain nor to you. But trust me when I say we will not let you out of our sights until we've been repaid."

She swallowed hard. "What if I refuse?"

"Darling, you're on a pirate ship. A cut of the booty is ours, anyway. Just think of us as hired muscle to help keep your virtue intact." He tapped her nose with his index finger. He froze, a strange expression crossed his features, before he straightened and held out his hand. "Do we have an accord?"

Song thought before nodding and shaking his hand. "I believe we do."

"You little harlot!" William called behind her.

"Excuse me. I've some business to attend to."

"We'll be watching."

Song approached William, calculating each step before she took it. His glare was dangerous, but his eyes betrayed a hint of fear. She crouched in front of him, looking into his cold eyes.

"I'm not afraid of you, little girl."

Song smiled as she took his thumb in her fingertips. "*Mu-th si'h kairb.*" The bone of his thumb gave an audible crack inside his flesh as it splintered, before his screams filled the air. She waited until his noise died down to desperate whines.

"He sounds like a little puppy!" Hairy laughed.

William's breath hissed through his teeth as he looked into Song's eyes. The fear was stronger now, stretching across the smooth green of his irises and reflecting at her in his dilated pupils.

"I should have locked the door behind—"

"*Rg-ngehf skehdni si'h kairb.*"

William's screams filled the air once more as the bone of his index finger shattered. One by one, Song broke each of his fingers, waiting for his screams to subside before moving on to the next one. She sat back on her heels. His nose ran, tears streamed from his eyes, sweat ran in little beads along his face, spittle dripped from the corner of his mouth.

Sunshine, eyes dark with disturbed sleep, tapped Song on the shoulder and gestured with his head for her to go with him. "Why are you doing this? This isn't you, Song."

"I promised to break his hands," she replied.

"Why?"

"He tried to force himself on me."

"But he didn't succeed."

"No. But he might've." She pulled her collar down to show the long slice across the side of her neck. "According to him," she made to motion at Leslie, but he and Brute had disappeared. "According to the new crewman, Leslie, I am but one of many."

Sunshine inspected the wound with his fingertips, his face growing sour. "Break his other hand." He caught her gaze with his own.

Song nodded and removed her coat as she returned to where William hunched, red-faced, his breath coming in ragged gasps from his pain. She tossed her coat to Toothy for safekeeping.

Turning her attention back to William, she crossed her arms and stroked her bottom lip in thought. "How many, William?"

He spat on the deck in reply.

Song knelt in front of him and took his unbroken right thumb in her fingertips. Her gaze caught his; there was nothing but fear left in his eyes.

"How many?"

He didn't respond.

"Mu-th si'h kairb."

His thumb cracked, and he shrieked.

"How many girls, William?"

"T-twenty," he sputtered.

She took his index finger. "How many boys?"

"Seven!" he shouted, panic forcing his voice to a higher octave.

"Twenty-seven. That's how many. *Rg-ngehf skehdni si'h kairb."* She waited for him to go quiet again before grabbing his middle finger. *"Sith kairb."*

He kicked at the deck, his voice shrieking through the air around her.

"How many fought back?" She shouted over his screaming. "All of them?"

He shook his head.

Song whispered, "How many did you kill?"

The fear in his eyes warped into a blind hatred as he sneered at her. "Three. And they deserved—ahh!"

Song whispered and his ring finger broke in her grasp, followed by his pinky. William spat on her cheek.

"As I should've done you! I should've slit your throat first and then taken all I wanted. Save your parents the trouble of paying out some ransom for their little harlot!" He pushed onto his elbows to better yell at her. "You will burn, little girl. If not for your own transgressions, then for your father's!"

"That's enough of that!" Dashaelan shouted. He picked William up by his collar and glared into his eyes.

"You've never thrown a man overboard, Krell. Everyone knows it's because you're soft. After all, you're harboring a G—"

William's accusations cut short as Dashaelan dumped him over the railing. The crew scrambled to watch him fall. The faintest twitch tugged the corner of Sunshine's lips upward and Thumbs cheered as the water turned white in a splash so far below they could not even hear it.

"His limbs were bound," Song said.

Dashaelan nodded. "Aye. His fingers were broken, too."

"Think he'll make it to shore?"

"If he's very, very lucky."

"But he isn't," Song said. In a whisper, she used her *kijæm* to make sure he never made it out of the ocean alive.

THAT NIGHT, SONG STARED UP AT THE CEILING OF THE WEAPONS hold, counting each time her hammock swung left or right. When she slept, it was troubled, and she woke covered in a thick sweat, her stomach roiling in disgust. She ran out on deck and leaned over the railing to heave into the ocean. When she'd finished, a hand settled on her back as though alerting her to the person's presence, and a flask entered her line of sight.

"Care for a rinse?"

"Thank you, Leslie."

He gave her a strange look. "And thank you for not calling me Whispers."

Song took a swig from the flask as she cocked an eyebrow at him. "This is water," she coughed, her palate shocked. "Why Whispers?"

"The men have given me the nickname Whispers. Apparently, my voice is too quiet for some of them." He lifted his flask and tipped his head to Sunshine, who stood at the wheel.

Sunshine did not make any gesture, just kept his scowl trained on Leslie.

"He doesn't like me."

"He doesn't like anyone." Song sat against the railing and folded her arms. "Why do you have water in your flask?"

"You never know when your throat will dry." He sipped at his water, then replaced the cap and pocketed the container. "I prefer to stay away from alcohol—it awakens demons better left in the dark."

"You have many demons?"

He smiled—it was clear his secret was his own. "Besides, it muddles the mind and slows the senses, leaving you vulnerable." He leaned on the railing beside Song. "Speaking of vulnerable, you really need to bolster your defenses."

"I have a gun," she replied.

"Where is it?"

Song flinched. "In my footlocker below deck. But I know how to use a sword."

"Is your sword also below deck?"

She poked the boards with the toe of her boot. "I don't exactly have one. I borrow one of Dash's to practice."

"So right now you are completely unarmed," he said.

She straightened. "I have my *kijæm*."

He breathed a laugh through his nose. "Where was that *kijæm* when William pressed that knife to your throat?"

"I can protect myself." Song pushed away from the railing.

Leslie followed her. "Then stop me from getting your hairpin."

"What?" Song spun around and threw her hands over her head, but she was too slow. "Give it back," she demanded.

He held the pin over his head. She wasn't too much shorter than him, but it was still out of her reach. After a moment, she stepped back.

"Take it from me." He held it out in his palm.

Song reached for the pin, but he took her wrist and spun her around, twisting her arm upward along her back. She grunted, and he spun her away from him. She leapt at him and, in an effortless movement, he slammed his palm into her belly, knocking her to the deck.

"Song?" Sunshine called from the helm.

"It's fine, Sunshine," Leslie said. "I'm teaching the lass to fight."

Song coughed, gripping an arm around her middle as she pushed to her knees. "You're bullying me," she growled.

"I'm watching you, Whispers," Sunshine said, then spat in a long arc over the side of the ship.

Leslie smiled at him. "Good, then you can tell Song what she's doing wrong."

"She's aiming for the pin when she should be aiming at you."

Leslie set his finger on the side of his nose and smiled at Song as she clambered to her feet. "Did you hear that? The shortest way to your goal is not this way." He made a line with his free hand, gesturing from Song to the pin on the other side of him. "The fastest way for you to get what you want is to go *through* your obstacles." He pressed his fingertips under her chin so he could catch her gaze. "Set your anger aside and focus on your goal. Now, take your hairpin from me."

Song mimicked the motion he'd used on her abdomen. He grunted but didn't move. She wrapped her other hand around her wrist and cursed.

"You cheated!"

Leslie smiled. "I didn't cheat. I anticipated your attack. You were too slow. Your form was poor, and you injured yourself."

"Fine, I don't know how to defend myself. I am nothing without my weapons or my *kijæm*. Is that what you wanted to hear?"

Leslie held the hairpin out in front of her. "Would you like to learn?"

Song tensed the muscles in her jaw as she studied his face. He gave no hint at retracting her pin and so she took it from his open palm. Leslie snapped his fingers closed around hers and she pulled against him. He bowed his head and set a delicate kiss on the top of her hand.

"Sleep now, and tomorrow, I will begin turning you into a weapon."

She pulled her hand from his grasp and chewed on the inside of her bottom lip as she thought. For all she knew, he could be just like William, but more reserved. He could be tricking her, gaining her trust just to hurt her later. His eyes were gentle, yet veiled what might have been darkness — perhaps it was the demons he spoke of.

But she couldn't afford to ignore the opportunity of learning to defend herself. Besides, after William, any man would be a fool to try hurting her. After giving him a curt nod, she turned, slipping her pin back into her hair. At the helm, Sunshine smirked at her. She scoffed and stomped back below deck.

Eighteen

Song's stomach churned through the morning with a bitter mixture of excitement and disgust. What had she done? She'd tortured a man and ensured his demise. *Isn't the world better for it?* she thought. Of course it was. But that didn't make her feel any better for having done it.

And where was Leslie? She'd woken earlier than usual and gone on deck, but he was not there. Nor was he in the hammocks where Sunshine had retired for the day.

It was near midday when Dashaelan blew his whistle and Leslie came slithering down the cargo net from the crow's nest. Song remembered her first—and last—time atop the golden zeppelin. She'd gotten tangled in the ropes and fallen from the sky; Leslie looked as though he was climbing the most stable of ladders, never faltering or missing a step. Toothy ascended as Leslie retrieved his sword from nearby the helm.

"Is that where you were supposed to be last night when you were bullying me?" Song asked, folding her arms as she stared at his back.

"I was simply enjoying the night. I volunteered this morning after Sunshine retired and Bells became too tired to keep watch."

She scowled. "Who is Bells?"

Leslie scrutinized her. "The… The chap with the bells on his boots. He's been part of the crew for two months. How do you not know this?"

"I don't have time to socialize, neither do many others," she explained. "Did you sleep at all last night?"

"Why are you so concerned with me when you don't even know half of the men on this ship? Do you even know how things work around here, or are you just along for the ride?" Leslie turned and made his way below deck.

"Where are you going?"

"The galley."

"Why?"

His laugh was without humor. "Thumbs'll have lunch ready now. And no, I wasn't up all night. I just function on less sleep than most." He jammed a finger into her sternum. "And everyone sleeps less than you."

"What is that supposed to mean?"

"Oh, princess—"

Song glared at him. "I'm not a princess."

"Then why do you sleep later than everyone else? You're not part of this crew, Song, you're a decoration."

A lump knotted in Song's throat. She spun away from him and stormed back above deck before the tears could spring from her eyes. On deck, she marched to where Dashaelan stood at the helm with his eyes closed and a lethargic smile on his face.

"What do you need, Song?"

"How did you know it was me?"

"You walk softer than most men aboard, but your heels click."

"You know everything, don't you?"

"Someone's got to." He winked at her. "What d'ya need?"

"A word in private, please."

Dashaelan nodded, then motioned with a tilt of his head for the man sitting behind him to take the helm. She didn't know this man, either. Guilt panged at her gut as she followed Dashaelan to the captain's chamber. Once the door was closed, she let everything out in the open.

"Do I sleep longer than everyone else?" she asked, but didn't pause for Dashaelan to answer. "Am I really given special treatment? Am I just a decoration rather than part of this crew—which I don't even know half the names of! I don't even know who Bells is! He has *bells* on his *boots*. How does anyone miss something like that? I didn't even see the truth about William until it was too late. Why are you keeping me on board? Am I some pretty little thing—a bauble for you to toss on your collection of treasures?"

He took a deep breath and set his hands on her shoulders, pressed her into a chair, and strode to the liquor cabinet. Dashaelan took his time getting drinks for both of them, a pensive twist to the corner of his mouth. After taking his seat across from her and sliding her glass across the table, he sighed.

"It is true that I allow you to sleep longer than the others."

"Why are you giving—"

"If you're going to interrupt me, then I'm not going to speak." He folded his arms over his chest and stared her down.

Song also sat back and pursed her lips.

"You're done then?"

She nodded.

"I've been letting you get more rest than the others because you train hard. Every day you're out there with me or Sunshine, and every day it gets harder for us old men to keep up. You help Thumbs in the galley, you practice *kijæm*, and you follow orders. As for the crew, sometimes I don't know who is who with names. They all change around. The ones who are worth remembering will be remembered, or stay aboard for good." He took a sip of whiskey and rolled it through his mouth as he thought. "There's a man wearing bells on his boots?"

"The men call him Bells. Apparently he's been on board for two months!"

Dashaelan's eyebrows rose. "I knew there was someone named Bells, but I never figured out why. The lad at the helm's been here for a month. I still don't know his name."

"He's been at your back the whole time," she gasped. "How do you talk to him?"

"I don't." He shrugged. "I just say 'You there!' and people respond."

Song snorted on a laugh. "And here I was thinking I was an awful pirate."

He eyed her. "Even Thumbs isn't an awful pirate. The awful ones go into taverns off the beaten sailor's path and brag of their conquests. A good one keeps his—or her—head low. You may not remember all the faces and all the names that go with them, but you'll make sure every man is fed and gets a fair share of the loot. Fates willing, you'll also get them all home safely."

She shook her head and sipped her rum. "I'll leave all of that to you and just focus on training."

"Speaking of which, Whispers spoke with me. He says he'll be training you to fight without a sword."

She nodded. "I don't always have my usual weapons at my disposal. I should learn to fight without one."

"Well then, you'll understand when I say you're not coming above deck for the next heist."

Her mouth dropped open. "That's not fair! You said—"

"I remember well what I said, girl. And I'm telling you now that you will stay below at the cannon with Thumbs."

"Why?" she snapped.

"For one, Whispers is right, you need more training. Two, and this one is very important, you're still being recognized. We need you to be forgotten, missy. Then you can join us above deck."

Song thought for a moment. "Let's say, hypothetically, the reward posters started...disappearing."

"Then hypothetically people might stop trying to find you."

She flicked her eyebrows in interest and finished her drink.

On deck, Song found Leslie sitting at the bow of the ship, polishing his blade. Before she could say a word, he lifted a bowl of mixed grains garnished with a nut paste and raisins. She didn't ask questions, just took the offering and sat beside him to eat. When she'd finished, she set the bowl beside her and leaned back to look up at the stars painted under the zeppelin.

"You have fifteen minutes to settle your stomach before we start," Leslie said.

When the fifteen minutes were up, he stood, sheathed his sword and removed it from his belt, setting it on the small stoop. Song followed suit, removing her utility belt and setting it beside his sword.

"Remove as many layers as you can," he said, tugging her coat sleeve. "You want to move freely." He eyed her vest while she shifted under the uncomfortable scrutiny. "That will have to do."

"Why am I learning to fight wearing less than I usually do?"

"I want you to learn the movement before encumbering yourself. Once you've built up some muscle, then we can add layers back onto you." He stepped back. "Are you ready?"

"Lesson one: I will never be ready."

His eyebrows rose. "Good, though you must always be on your guard." He lunged toward her, catching his arm across her chest and hooking one leg behind hers, sending her to the deck. "You never know when you'll have to defend yourself."

Song clenched her jaw as anger flared in her chest. There couldn't have been an actual point to him dropping her like that. And the crew on deck had been watching. Her pride and the back of her head had both taken a painful blow. She would train with him, if for no other reason than to pay him back for the embarrassment.

He then spent the next hour teaching her how to stand and shift her weight to provide a defensive advantage. He even taught her how to fall without hurting herself. Leslie wanted her to learn how to defend herself and reduce the chance of injury before moving onto offense. By the end of his lesson, much of the crew had gathered and stood back, watching.

After what must have been several grueling hours, Song fell to the deck and refused to stand back up. She stared at the constellation on the zeppelin, tracing the lines and trying to figure out how those stars could, in any way, be a large feline.

"We'll resume tomorrow," Leslie said as some form of dismissal.

"Uh-huh."

"Song," Dashaelan hollered from the helm. "Get yourself up here."

"Is that any way to request the presence of a lady?" she asked, a wry smile twisting at the corner of her lips.

He barked a laugh. "Get your scrawny hide up here before I toss you overboard."

She tilted her head to look at him, standing on the ceiling of an upside-down world, grinning at her like a proud father. At least, that's what she thought a proud father might look like. Her real father had never given her that smile as far as she could remember.

"But I'm so very tired," she whined.

He flinched as the tone in her voice grated on every one of his nerves. Even she couldn't stomach the whines of a spoiled brat—the girl she'd been before Altain had rescued her.

Dashaelan stomped to her side and wrapped a hand through her belt, lifting her from the deck. "Won't you be very tired after swimming home?" He carted her to the railing.

Her arms and legs shot to attention, her fingers dug into

his arms and a giggle forced its way up her throat. "Unhand me, you scoundrel!"

In one motion, he set her on her feet, spun her around, and shoved her toward the helm. She tripped up the steps, shooting a glare at the man behind the wheel, who was laughing at her expense. Dashaelan joined her at the helm.

"Lesson one about flying—"

"I know how to fly a ship," she interjected.

He raised one eyebrow and lowered the other in a warning. "You know how to fly a little puddle-jumper. If you haven't noticed, the Stars' Bounty is quite a bit larger than that tiny thing you flew before. I've seen the Dauntless. That ship is held together by ropes and prayers. Look at the Bounty, what do you see?"

"Ropes?" she said. "Prayers?"

"Ropes reinforced by braided metal. A mast that ties to the zeppelin, acting as an anchor to keep the blasted thing in place. Mistreat a skyship like this and you might come out of it with your life. One wrong move on a little thing held together by spit and sheer determination, and it could very well be the last thing you do."

"So if flying this one is easier, then why do I have to have a lesson?"

"I never said it was easier. The Stars' Bounty is less likely to fall from the sky during a storm. But she steers like a blind cow—wide turns and slow reactions. She takes patience to pilot correctly."

Song shot him a devilish grin. "You called your ship a cow."

He eyed her, trying to think of a smart retort. A small ringing caught their attention. They turned to discover the sound. A man with mousy brown hair and a shaggy beard emerged from below, a patch over one eye and two bells on each boot, attached to the laces and clinking together. Song and Dashaelan turned their gazes back to one another, their eyes meeting in a shared epiphany. Then they burst into uncontrollable laughter.

Nineteen

SONG WAS FAST ASLEEP WHEN THE QUIET FOOTSTEPS approached her hammock. They stopped beside her in the darkness. Dreams of adventure held her captive within her mind, and so she didn't see or feel as a man reached down, gripped the edge of her hammock, and jerked it upward. Song tumbled out with a scream, sprawling onto the floor in a tangle of hair and blanket and limbs.

"It's time to train," Leslie's soft voice said in the darkness. Before she could respond, he turned and strode from the room.

She dressed quickly, a silent fury building in her chest. She ran up the stairs toward the main deck.

"What the bloody hell was that about?" Song shouted as she stomped toward Leslie.

He sat, polishing his blade. The sun hadn't risen yet, though its light dimmed the stars and heralded its arrival.

"Time to train," he repeated.

"No. That's not good enough. Why couldn't you just gently shake me? I would've woken!"

"I suppose if the ship were ever to be boarded by a hostile party, they'd at least have the decency to shake you gently to wake you before raping and killing you."

Somehow, the gentleness of his tone set her on edge. Fear tingled its way up her spine and pulled tight along her scalp. "No, but—"

"No. No 'buts'. You ride with pirates, you take their risks. All is fair in love and war."

"This isn't war!"

"Well, it definitely isn't love," he said.

"I dunno," Sunshine said from the helm, "I sure do *love* me a nice pile o' loot." He winked at Song, then shot a glare at Leslie, who twisted one corner of his mouth into a smirk.

"Be that as it may, other pirates are not your friends. They do not care who you are or what you mean to this crew. They care what is between your legs and how it can best please them."

Song swallowed hard. "Is today's lesson that I am merely a whore in the eyes of men?"

"Today's lesson is: be ready to fight every hour of every day. Let your guard down and you could lose everything."

She reached behind her head, where her tangled hair hung loose around her shoulders; she pulled it into a messy braid and secured it. "I'm ready to fight."

Leslie smiled and slid his sword into the scabbard. Standing, he righted her positioning, then stood before her. They trained hard, Song fueled by tired anger, until the sun had cleared the horizon and threatened to blanket the land in a suffocating heat.

"Good," Leslie said. "You did very well today."

"Are you going to throw me out of bed tomorrow, too?"

He gave her a small smile, but said nothing as he retrieved his sword and disappeared below deck. A hand clapped on

Song's shoulder and she jumped, turning her head to see Dashaelan's grinning face.

"You learn quick."

Song groaned. "Do I have to work on swordplay now?"

"No. Get yourself some grub, then meet me at the helm."

She nodded and followed the smell of Thumbs's sweet-mash below deck. Song took her time eating as the hot food warmed her from the inside. Her eyelids were heavy, and she found herself experiencing what were best described as long blinks.

"Meal not exciting enough?" Thumbs asked with a laugh.

"It's wonderful," she smiled. "I like these berries."

"I like them too." He grinned and scooped himself a bowl of mash.

"Why do you wait to eat last?" Song asked.

He shrugged. "Someone has to. I figure if I serve everyone the same amount, then no one will get too much, and no one will get too little. Leave it to each person's judgment and you will always find that one man who takes more than is available and leaves another to starve."

"There is still some leftover," she said.

"Brute will come take that off my hands any minute."

Song swirled the contents in her dish, pushing a berry this way and that. "What do you make of him?" she asked.

"Brute?" He sucked a berry husk from between his teeth and furrowed his brow in thought. "I suppose he is a good man. Does not say much. Does not get in nobody's way… But there is something about him that can set a man off-kilter."

"It's the way he looks at you. Like he can see straight through you."

"Like he knows everything in only that glance."

"Tums."

The grunt came from behind Song, making her jump and nearly spill what was left in her bowl. She stared up at Brute. A shy smile was plastered across his lips as his eyes remained focused on the pot.

"It is all yours," Thumbs said.

Brute lifted the entire pot, took the spoon offered by Thumbs, and found himself a comfortable corner to sit in. Thumbs caught the look Song was giving him and chuckled.

"Since introducing myself, he has called me 'Tums'," he said, low enough for only her ears.

"Because that's how you say it," Song guessed.

"And I do not have the heart to ask Whispers to correct him."

Afterward, Song met Dashaelan at the helm. His mood seemed to have soured as he set her at the wheel, then stomped to his cabin.

"What's that about?" she asked the man behind her.

He sat on a low stool beside a table nearly as low, with a map spread open across the top. Small pins held each corner of the map in place.

"He tried to out-chart me while plotting a course to Talegrove." He gave a triumphant grin.

"Are you some sort of nautical savant?"

"They call me Maps," he said, holding out a hand for her to shake. His grip was firm and sure. "Navigating is my trade." Maps wore small round spectacles that curled behind his ears and left a glare over his green eyes.

"I'm—"

"Song. I know. The men talk about you all the time." His accent was a strange one somewhere between Andalisian and Dashaelan's.

She narrowed her eyes. "What do they say?"

"Just that you have exquisite taste in women and you're a wicked good Magic."

"Oh, so all good things."

"Pretty much." He shrugged. "Say, have you learned to do that far-seeing thing?"

"The what?"

"Well, rumor is, some Magics can see things in other rooms. On rare occasions I've heard tell of Magics seeing from one country to another!"

"How would I even begin to teach myself that?" Song asked herself aloud.

"Word is you have to picture a person you've met or a place you've been. Something you know. Then you just… I dunno, see it?" He shrugged for emphasis.

"Why do you call me a Magic?" She turned back to the helm, her mind turning the idea of far-seeing over and over.

"That's what you are, isn't it? At least that's what they're called in Jashedar."

"Is that where you're from?"

"Aye."

Maps chattered on behind her for the next hour about the wonders of Jashedar. The Blind Woods along the northern border, which had claimed more travelers than had been counted. Nestled in the darkest part of the high mountains on a sheer cliff was Talegrove, an uncharted pirate haven shrouded in fog and guarded from the sea by a forest of massive boulders.

He spoke of the man in charge of Talegrove, repeating stories he'd heard. The rumors made him out to be more god than man; his skills were the stuff of legends. According to what Maps said, the man was a better fighter than Leslie, a better swordsman than Dashaelan, and less forgiving than Captain Darian. Song didn't want to meet a man like that.

When Dashaelan emerged from his cabin, Song excused herself to practice her *kijæm*. She pulled closed the curtains over the bay windows, which opened to the propeller blades and a sudden drop into the ocean. Song sat on the cushion of the bench that stretched beneath the windows, legs crossed and eyes closed. She focused on her breathing and thought of her target: Amelia.

"Amelia *em osh*," she whispered.

The fatigue began in her fingers, numbing them and bringing sweat into her palms. An ache within her skull accompanied it, dull and throbbing, but manageable. She'd never had to put effort into using *kijæm* before. Every command was always obeyed without incident—carried out as though by another entity. But this was different. Tiring. An image unfurled within her mind of a muddy girl fighting a squealing pig. Then the image was gone.

Song's clothes were sticky with sweat. It trailed down from her forehead and stuck her hair to the nape of her neck. She opened her eyes to find she was not alone. Dashaelan had her by the shoulders and was shouting. But she heard nothing.

"I...saw..." she sputtered, before giving in to the darkness.

Twenty

LESLIE WAS SITTING ACROSS FROM HER AT DASHAELAN'S TABLE, polishing the blade of his sword, when she woke. She wanted to knock it from his hands and slap him across the face and scream that it was just a stupid sword and he didn't need to see his own reflection in the metal. Instead, she turned her back to him.

"How are you feeling?" he asked.

"Go away."

"No. I'm staying until you're up and about. Captain's orders."

She sat up on the bench, then stood. "See? Up and abou—oo…" She sat back down as her head spun and her vision spotted. When her senses calmed down, she glared through her eyelashes at him. "Go away."

"Why are you suddenly so hateful toward me?" he asked.

"You threw me out of my hammock. You bully me and you bruise me. And would you put that damned sword back in its sheath and let the bloody thing rest for a moment? Keep at it and there won't be any blade left!"

He smirked; a small scoff of a laugh exited his nose as he trained his eyes on his sword. "Do you know what metal this is?"

"Does it matter?"

"This is Pishing sorrowstone."

"I thought you said it was metal."

He smiled at her. "It is. Sorrowstone is a special metal. It's black," he ran his fingertip along the black center of the blade, "but with certain treatments, it turns silver. They call it sorrowstone because the substances they use to silver the blade cause severe burns to living things. The sorrowstone reacts as though it can feel what is being done to it."

"I ask again if it matters."

"Sorrowstone is temperamental. If it lies neglected for too long, then it becomes brittle and one sword stroke would shatter it. But if you oil the blade, it is stronger than any other material in the world. Long ago, some used blood to sate its thirst. And thus the rest of the world calls it sorrowstone for another reason." He sheathed his sword and wrapped his tin of congealed oil and cloth together, slipping them into a small pouch on the scabbard. "To own a sorrowstone blade is to take pride in your weapon. It will never fail you if you take care of it."

Song stared at her palms in her lap. "Sorry I snapped at you."

"Would you like to tell me why Dashaelan has me in here watching over you?"

"Maps told me about this thing Magics can do…"

"Magics?"

"That's what he calls us."

"Ah, he must be from Jashedar. My people call them Gifted. Andalise—"

"Calls them Touched."

A spark of a thought caught in his eye. "Andalisian? I should've known."

"Is that where you're from?"

He chuckled. "Far from it. In any case, that is irrelevant. *Kijæm* is an effortless thing. What were you doing?"

"It was only for a moment and—"

"You were in here for hours."

Song swallowed away the panic at losing so much time when it had felt like none at all. "Maps calls it far-seeing. I was trying to see…someone I met once."

"Where is this someone?" he asked.

"Near Lund."

Leslie shook his head and pinched the bridge of his nose between his thumb and forefinger. "I don't know much about *kijæm,* but I do know that is too far for your first time. Those who far-see start with merely closing their eyes and viewing something hidden within a nearby cupboard."

"I would like to try again," she said.

He strode to sit beside her, spinning her to face him on the bench. "If you pass out again, I'll tell Dash you never woke from the first time." He winked.

"I'll try not to let it get that far." She curled her legs beneath her and closed her eyes.

"If it gets too difficult, stop. Don't force it. Try finding Dash on deck."

She let her thoughts go blank, her body relaxing and falling into the rhythm of the propeller just outside. Then the world fell silent and her limbs numbed once more. She opened her eyes, and she stood in the galley watching Thumbs peel potatoes. She didn't want to find Thumbs. It was a silly thought—that Thumbs was not sufficient proof of her skill. But she had to see Dashaelan, to prove to herself that she could control the sight.

Song willed herself up the stairs to the deck, high above the other men, looking down at them from an unfamiliar angle. She moved straight to the helm, where Dashaelan argued with Maps over who was the better navigator. She watched for a minute before Dashaelan turned to look up, staring straight into her eyes.

Song gasped and broke from her meditative state so fast she shivered from the shock of it. He'd looked at her, but she hadn't been there. Leslie wrapped a blanket around her and forced her to look at him.

"What is it?"

"He looked right at me!"

His brow furrowed. "That's not how it works, Song. He must have just looked in that direction and it merely seemed like he saw you."

Song shook her head. "Maybe." But she knew in the pit of her stomach that he had looked right at her. Dashaelan had known she was there.

On deck that evening, as the sun made its way to the horizon, Dashaelan had Song going through the usual motions of swordplay. He was taking it easy on her, though, since her episode—she and Leslie had kept the second between the two of them. Frustrated with the passive way he wielded his blade, Song let her emotions get the better of her. With a few quick moves she'd learned from watching Leslie that morning, she disarmed and floored Dashaelan. The men watching grew quiet as the pair stared each other down.

"Stop treating me like I'm fragile!" Song shouted over him. "I'm not a lady. I'm one of your crew. Now treat me that way and let's get on with it!"

Dashaelan nodded, a thrilled smile spread across his lips as she helped him up and handed his sword back to him. They sparred, then. It was intense and Song could feel the electricity of it shock across her skin, infecting every pore and buzzing through her veins like a lightning strike. He'd taught her well, and she was proving it as he fought her like he'd fight another pirate.

For a split second, her mind grew bold and her limbs became overconfident. Dashaelan's blade nicked across the back of her hand, urging the sword from her grasp and a shocked gasp from her throat.

"Confidence will kill you, son," he said. After a pause, he caught his mistake. "Song."

Twenty-One

Song tumbled through the air. The world slowed until it all but stopped. All she could see was darkness. And then his face. Determined and unapologetic, lips pursed in concentration. Her mind clicked into gear and realization struck. She braced for the impact, but it didn't hurt any less. Scrambling across the floor, she gripped her boot and threw it with all of her tired strength at the back of Leslie's head. It fell short and to his left.

"It's time to train," he said, unfazed.

"I won't always miss!" she shouted, then threw herself to the floor in a frustrated and sore heap.

Every day began like this, and Song slept lighter at night, stirring at the slightest footstep above deck. By the time morning came, she was so weary that she stopped bothering to throw her boot; she never made impact with it, anyway. In an attempt to outsmart him one night, Song slept on the floor—it was a terrible mistake as every small motion of the ship rocked her this way and that. It was the worst motion sickness she'd ever experienced.

When Leslie came to wake her, he smiled at her green complexion and sleep deprived eyes. He crouched low and set a palm on her cheek. "It's time to train."

Song let go of all control, allowing herself to cry—ugly, desperate sobs. "Why are you doing this to me? Did I wrong you in another life?"

"I know it doesn't seem so, but I'm helping you. This is part of your training."

"And what is the lesson?" she growled.

"When you figure that out, I'll stop."

"You're a bully!"

"No, you just complain too much."

He left her with that. He didn't reprimand her for taking her time arriving on deck, just handed her a ginger root and gave her a few minutes to ease her tumultuous stomach. Her queasy frustration made her limbs sluggish and clumsy. Leslie gripped her wrists and spun her to the deck. The back of her head met the wood with a sickening crack, causing her ears to ring. Her tears returned against her will.

"Stop that!" Leslie hissed.

"I can't!"

He leaned in close so only she could hear his words, his breath tickling across her ear. "You are weak. You're going to die if you stay aboard this ship. Why don't you just go home?"

"No!"

"Why not?"

"I can't!"

"You have a lot of 'can't' in you. But I think you're using the wrong word. You won't. You won't fight me, you won't go home…you won't survive on this ship."

"Yes, I will!"

"Then prove it. Stop acting like a spoiled little princess. This isn't a palace, sweetheart, and we are not your servants," he hissed in her ear. When he lifted his head to look in her eyes, something was hiding just beyond the blue of his irises—a dare for her to retaliate.

"Get off me," Song demanded.

"Make me," Leslie said.

"I can't."

"You won't. Take all your anger and ball it in the pit of your stomach. Every emotion you have ever felt is a weapon. Use them."

Song did as he said, collecting her emotions into the pit of her stomach. Then she let it loose, forcing her arms free of his grip as she rolled away from him. She sent her fist into his abdomen. He grunted, and she hit him again, then used her free foot to kick him away from her.

But her rage took over. He'd called her weak; a decoration; a princess. She leapt at him, pinning him beneath her, and punched at him. With little effort, he shoved her off himself and snaked out his arm to slap her across the face.

"Don't let your anger rule you, Song. Use it, yes. But do not let it blind you."

That afternoon, she legitimately bested Dashaelan at swordplay. The crew grew quiet. Dashaelan smiled with pride and took her into his arms. She'd never been hugged like that before—like she mattered so much to someone.

She didn't want to cry again, not in front of anyone. So she waited, holding it in a knot at the base of her throat until she retreated to the weapons hold to wash the sweat from her body with the small barrel of water she had just for that purpose. She gripped the rag and let herself sink to her knees, smiling as the happiest tears ran to her chin.

As time wore on, she bested Dashaelan much faster. He was the greatest swordsman in the world, according to the stories—which he said were utter codswallop—and yet age had slowed him. Leslie, on the other hand, was still in his prime; his strength and agility had not begun to wane. He taught her to use what little weight she had to her advantage. Both bearing narrow builds, he was the ideal teacher, knowing just how to manipulate her movements to provide advantages. Every day she learned something new, and every day she acquired more bruises.

It was a perfect day. Leslie had woken Song in the usual way. She was getting used to it—though that didn't make it hurt any less. On this morning, she'd tried to be awake on time. He found her lying in her hammock, staring up at him.

"Good morning," she'd said.

"Morning." He'd then dumped her onto the floor, as usual. "Time to train."

They were in heated combat when the whistle blew; a single note ringing through the air. She caught Dashaelan in the commotion and begged to stay above deck. One stern look told her that wasn't happening and she slunk away below deck. Thumbs welcomed her excitedly, pointing out the cannon doors on the other vessel.

"We may see some action yet!"

But they didn't. The fighting above deck was loud and Thumbs began a commentary with a swabby named Ponce at the next cannon over on what might have been happening— it turned into tales so ludicrous Song tuned them out. The deck above grew quiet. None of them could see anything through their trapdoors.

"It is too quiet," Thumbs said.

"Let me look," Song whispered.

"Captain said—"

"I'm not going anywhere. Just trust me."

She closed her eyes and concentrated on the upper deck. Her vision rose from the barracks, up the stairs, and onto the deck. Shapes formed, coming into focus as men scattered loosely around the decks of the two skyships. All eyes stared at one spot on the enemy ship where Sunshine held one man at knifepoint; another had a revolver trained on Dashaelan's head.

"All I'm saying," Dashaelan said, "is that no one has to die today. I'll go in willingly, but only if you spare every member of my crew."

"Captain Krell in exchange for an entire ship of bloody pirates?" the man asked.

"And this bloke's life," Sunshine said.

"I suppose it is a fair trade. Your crew is useless to me, but *you* have a high value." He turned his attention to Sunshine. "Return to your ship and leave. If you follow us, we will blow your vessel out of the air."

As Sunshine swung across, Leslie approached where Song's consciousness looked on in horror. "Bruce wh—" His confusion transformed into revelation.

Song forced herself from the trance as Leslie rushed below deck. He intercepted her near the weapons hold door, wrapping his arms around hers to pin them at her sides. She fought against him.

"Let me go!" she screamed. "Dash!"

Leslie covered her mouth with his palm and held her closer. "He's protecting *you*," he hissed in her ear.

He didn't release her for a long time, even as she bit into his palm. Once free, she punched him in the jaw with the entire weight of her body and ran above deck. Shoving Maps out of the way, she grabbed the wheel, scanning the horizon for the other skyship. Sunshine took her by the shoulders of her coat and threw her down the stairs, converging on her to pin her down.

"I know you weren't plannin' on goin' after them," he said.

"We have to—"

"No! You be quiet." He slapped her lips like a child who'd used foul language. "You go chasin' after that ship and we're all dead men—includin' Dash."

"But he—"

Sunshine popped her mouth again. "I said shut up. I didn't say we're leavin' Dash to the hands of the law—which *will* see him hang—but we're not gonna go in half-cocked and get ourselves killed."

"Song." Maps had returned to the helm and trained his eyes on her. "That ship…she flew Jashedar colors."

"What of it?" She struggled under Sunshine's weight.

"They were law."

"And?"

"And when they catch criminals, or pirates, they always take them to Tamminpring. Sometimes they are then extradited to Andalise."

Sunshine let her up. "They have a process, you see. Lots of bureaucratic nonsense tied to Senator Gould."

Maps smiled. "We have about a week to spring him before he's moved or sees the noose."

"Better get crackin' on a plan," Sunshine said.

Twenty-Two

THE STARS' BOUNTY DOCKED IN TALEGROVE AROUND DAWN. Icy air bit into Song's cheeks as winter winds seeped through her clothing and settled in her bones. The pirate haven in the northernmost part of Jashedar's Blind Woods, where the trees clung in desperation to the steep mountainside that came to an abrupt stop at the first of many cliffs, was nothing like Song had anticipated. The perpetual fog that blanketed the city, casting it in an eerie gloom, was the only thing she'd expected—the Blind Woods were on the southern side of the Screaming Cliffs, which she'd encountered over a year before with Altain.

She'd imagined Talegrove as a city filled with filth and lawless barbarism. Instead, the streets were paved with cobblestones, men behaved themselves, and the establishments—even the obvious brothels—were well kempt.

"I don't understand," Song said to Sunshine as they made their way to a tavern across town, where they'd been told a shipkeep was having his morning eggs and rum.

Sunshine grimaced. "This is the only safe place for pirates. If you cause trouble, you can never come back. Keeps a lot of men in line when there is that much to lose. That and the man in charge. Showed up out of the blue and changed this whole place around, eight years ago, making it more respectable. At least for pirate standards."

"Maps told me he's the most skilled and ruthless man in the world."

Sunshine nodded in agreement. "That's what the stories say. He has a code—just one. Mind yourself or he'll kill you."

"That's quite the code. Though it's not really an actual code, so much as a threat."

"It's a promise, lad."

Song spun to look down at a man at the shorter end of whatever ugly stick he'd been beaten with. It wasn't so much that he was ugly, but his nose had been broken several times and scars streaked across the pocked skin of his face. He squinted up into her hood and smiled.

"Lass?"

She wanted to lower her head more, but the angle at which to keep him from looking at her would have been impossible.

"What business have you in Talegrove?"

"Who's asking?" Song demanded.

"They call me Shadow."

"Why?"

He lowered his brow, and an expression of sarcastic mischief crossed his face. "Because I am barely tall enough to cast my own, of course."

Song hissed a laugh through her teeth.

"I ask again what business you have in my city."

"Oh, so you're the man in charge, then?" she asked, tone barbed with disbelief.

Sunshine's eyebrows rose in mild amusement.

"Astounding, isn't it? Answer the question." His palm settled over the shining black handle of a revolver nearly the length of the thigh it was strapped to.

Song looked to Sunshine. He shook his head, assuring he'd have no part in it. This was her rescue plan, and she was in charge.

"I've come to requisition a skyship."

"For what purpose?"

"I believe that is my own business."

"Only if the ship you commission returns safely and does not bring trouble to Talegrove. So, I ask again, what sort of purpose?"

Song thought, testing her wording. "Retrieval of an item of great import." She wondered if a person could be called an item, and if Dashaelan would scold her for it.

Shadow gauged her, scrutinizing every aspect of her demeanor. After a moment, he smiled. "You are either a pretty boy or an ugly girl, child. I'll figure it out, eventually. But you seem an acceptable sort. You don't want to commission one of Keenan's ships; he's a drunkard and many of them are unreliable and have…reputations. Speak with Ambrose. He's a friend of mine. You'll find him on the lower docks." He motioned to the edge of the cliff which Talegrove was built on, where a single metal lift sat in wait for passengers.

Song held back a shudder. "Thank you, sir."

"Remember, child, whatever trouble you get into, do not bring it back to Talegrove." With that, he sidestepped around her and continued on his way.

When he was out of earshot, Song let out a breath. "An ugly girl or a pretty boy? Seriously?"

Sunshine avoided the subject as though he hadn't heard anything. "Lower docks, then?"

They set off, but Song wasn't finished being indignant. "I mean, really, is it so strange that a girl could be a pirate?"

"Actually, there's a few that crew a schooner called the Jolly Jane," Sunshine said. "Any woman who's a pirate travels with them."

"And what am I, then, if I do not travel with those women?" She stopped in her tracks and stared at him.

"An exception."

"Apologize!" A disturbance across the city center caught their attention. Shadow was shouting up at an inebriated man while a woman gripped her torn dress.

Sunshine tutted. "Now that's what not to do in Talegrove, go and try takin' a whore without payin'…"

Their voices lowered. Song couldn't hear what was being said on the other side of the fountain, which marked the middle of the area. In the blink of an eye, Shadow had the man on his knees and screaming in pain. An argument rumbled between them, distorted by the distance.

Song heard the boom of the shot before her mind registered the quick movement of Shadow's hand as he retrieved his sidearm and aimed between the man's eyes. It was too late to look away and she couldn't erase the image of the man's brains spraying out the backside of his head. Without missing a beat, Shadow searched the man's pockets and tossed the discovered quoine purse to the prostitute.

Song stood petrified, her fists balled at her sides. "He just…just like that…"

Across the distance, Shadow caught Song's eye. He nodded once as a warning to keep her in line.

"Yes," Sunshine said, "just like that. Let's go." He steered her by the shoulders to the lift, forcing Song's hesitant feet over the threshold. "You all right then?"

"Is there another way down?" she asked on a frightened whisper.

"I doubt it."

He closed the gate, and Song's heart clenched. She pressed herself into the corner as he pulled the lever for the lift to make its descent.

He eyed her. "What's got you so bothered?"

"I don't like this," she squeaked.

"You fell from the Bounty, and a little ride down a cliff has you lookin' like you saw a ghost?" He scoffed.

"It's not the height, it's the—" The lift lurched and bumped as the flow of steam adjusted itself. A small scream squeaked out of her mouth and she gripped the metal grating behind her. "I can't save us if it falls."

He leaned against the other side, folding his arms over his chest and studying her terrified state. "If this bloody thing falls, then you worry about you. I'm an old man and I know what happens to old men. Just promise me you won't stop for nothin' until you have Dash safely out of Tamminpring."

Song looked between her boots through the grating; no ground was yet in sight. "I'm sure we haven't far to go…"

"You just worry about you, Song."

She pursed her lips and gave him a curt nod. When the metal cage bumped to the ground and hissed to a complete stop, Song shoved her way past Sunshine to open the gate and leap out onto solid ground. She rubbed her sweaty palms against her thighs and gave him a weak smile.

"See? Nothing to worry about, right?"

He shook his head and strode after her.

They found Ambrose at the end of a dock, reclining in a wicker chair beside several fishing poles. Each pole had a bell attached at the tip and had been secured so their lines could sit in the water, waiting for a bite. Ambrose himself was unimpressive in a white linen shirt, thick brown trousers and vest and boots made with grey fur. A furry cloak rested on his shoulders. Smoke curled upward from beneath a wide-brimmed woven straw hat.

"You gonna stare all day? Or do you have some business with me?"

Song looked to Sunshine for support, but he used his shoulder to shove her forward. It was clear he was not helping her with any of her plan.

"I w-would like to req-requisition a skys-ship." She stuttered over the request, then pinched her eyes closed, flinching in humiliation.

He observed her. "No need to be nervous, boy." He stood and tested his lines. "Where will you be going?"

"What does it matter?"

"Well, the only skyship I've got available is a small cargo transport. However, I do have some sailers available that may suit your needs better."

"Tamminpring," Song said.

"Ah, land-bound. Skyship it is. That'll be five hundred quoine per day, plus a mortem deposit."

"A mortem deposit?"

He nodded. "Just in case you don't return. Come back and you'll get it back—so long as my ship is still intact. It's two thousand."

"I'll be returning it!"

"That's fine, but if you don't, I won't be left hanging. No mortem deposit, no ship." He folded his arms over his chest and set his jaw.

Song turned to Sunshine to consult in private. "Thirty-five hundred is steep," she whispered.

"I say it's a fair price, given our need for it."

"I brought two thousand," Song hissed.

Sunshine reached under his coat to untie his small purse from his belt. He opened it and counted out the missing sum and dropped them into Song's purse. She waited as Ambrose re-cast a line, then handed over the required quoine. He withdrew a pre-written contract from a leather satchel, filling in the pertinent information, and waited as Song signed it.

Ambrose read the signature. "Pleasure doing business with you, Captain Song."

"I'm not a captain."

"You are now."

Tamminpring was a large city, land-bound at the center of Jashedar. Maps accompanied Song as she walked through the streets wearing a black funeral dress, her face covered by a veil. It was common for women of Jashedar to hide behind such garments for months after the death of a loved one, which gave Song the perfect disguise, and no one would even question her. She'd taken a select handful of crew with her, all dressed in clean clothing, posing as traders.

They settled at an inn out of the way—something not too flashy, but not a hole-in-the-wall where a pirate would stay. Maps knew the place, and assured they were a business which could help them out, as they were no friends of the law. The crew gathered in Song's room that night to go over the minor details of getting Dashaelan out of prison without losing their own lives in the process. Sunshine sat in the corner reading the paper. It was his most predictable habit—to pick up a paper wherever they made berth, and read cover-to-cover about the goings-on in the world.

"What we need is a distraction," Toothy said.

"Could stage a robbery," Thumbs suggested.

"We're trying to get Dash out of jail, not add more of us to the cells," Leslie said. He was sitting in a chair, his blue eyes trained on the world outside as he kept watch.

"It has to be big," Song said. "Something that would draw the attention of all the guards."

"Something like a big ball raising quoine for orphaned children?" Sunshine asked from behind his paper.

"We don't have time to organize something like that," Maps said.

Sunshine scoffed. "We don't have to." He strode across the room and laid the paper out on the bed before Song.

"It'll already be heavily guarded," Song said. "But how could we get more to go there and leave the jail vulnerable?"

"You know what always draws attention?" Sunshine sat beside Song, keeping his gaze fixed on her own. "A Gould."

Song did her best to hide her own panic.

Thumbs tapped his lower lip in thought. "The benefit is in two days. It would take longer than that to send a message to Garda."

"That would go swimmingly," Bells said. "'Dear Elroy Gould, you don't know me, but I would like to extend an invitation to a benefit for orphans, which I'm sure you couldn't care less about. I myself am not invited but I need a distraction so I can jailbreak my dear captain who has been taken on charges of piracy.' He wouldn't be able to resist."

"Fools," Sunshine scoffed. "Elroy ain't the only Gould."

Song held her breath, willing Sunshine to stop talking. Since joining the crew, only two had learned her true identity. She wanted it to stay that way forever, but to think it would be was naïve, and she knew it.

"Are you suggesting we find his missing brat?" Thumbs asked.

"I can't," Song whispered, so only Sunshine could hear.

"That girl was right to get away from him, else she'd be just as corrupt," Toothy said.

"You can," Sunshine said as low as Song. "You just won't."

"Mark my words," Bells said, "that girl is nothing but trouble."

"Don't," Song hissed. "Don't make me."

"Why do you say that?" Thumbs asked Bells.

"Not even for Dash?" Sunshine whispered to her.

"Well, look at her father! What's his count for innocents hanged as pirates, now, eh?" Bells said. "Rotten, the lot of them. They look on commoners as disposable pests and refuse to help them out of the squalor *they* put them into. Won't do nothing for no one. Never have, never will."

Tears stung Song's eyes, but she refused to let them do more than that. "All right. Fine. For Dash."

Toothy nodded in agreement with Bells. "I'm not saying I hope she's dead, but the world could do with less of her kind."

Leslie's brow furrowed as he eyed her. "Quiet, all of you! Song, what's wrong?"

She realized the tears she'd denied release had broken free, anyway. "I suppose hearing these things bothered me more than I'd expected."

"You sympathizing with a Gould?" Thumbs asked.

"You idiots," Sunshine growled. "None of you ever questioned her so-called bounty?"

"No way a girl so untrained could have accrued a sum against her," Leslie said.

Song wiped away her tears. "It's not a bounty. It's a reward for my safe return to my father…Elroy Gould."

An awkward silence fell over the room. Bells stared at his feet. "Well, don't I feel a right git."

"So, you really are a princess," Leslie said.

"No—"

"May as well be," Sunshine said.

Song took a deep breath, determined to get the subject away from her. "So then, what's the plan? I can't go in alone. A lady never attends a function like this without an escort."

The men looked around at each other, acknowledging that each of them would be overly conspicuous at such an event.

"Send Whispers," Thumbs said.

"We need him at the jail," Song argued. "He's our best fighter."

"He's also the prettiest of us all," Sunshine said with a smirk.

Leslie said nothing for a long time. He gave Sunshine a look. "I'll go."

"What's the story, though?" Bells asked. "Who are you? How do you know Tsingsei Gould? And where has she been all this time?"

"I have a story," Leslie replied. "Just worry about getting Song into a lovely dress."

Twenty-Three

Song sat still and patient as the women surrounded her, making her up and twisting her hair into a popular fashion. Sunshine would arrive at any moment with her tailored gown, and then she would be off to play the role she'd abandoned long ago. A woman entered and scrutinized her face. She let out an exasperated sigh and glared at the women.

"She's supposed to look like a lady, not a whore. Scrub her face and do it again." Then she left.

They scrubbed her face until it stung, and then reapplied the pastes and powders. They finished with her hair, and let her look in the mirror. The way they'd put her hair up, she could take it down by removing a single long pin at the back. It was ideal for a quick disguise. She realized that her naturally golden skin was darker now—kissed by the sun, Johanna would have said. But the ladies had used powders to pale her face and neck, as was considered attractive in Andalise and Jashedar. She still hated the way she looked with the paler skin, but at least it made it harder to recognize her without it.

Sunshine entered and stopped to stare.

"How do I look?" she asked.

He regained his composure and gave an indifferent shrug. "Not ugly."

After ensuring she would be ready on time, he left once more, and the women helped her into the dress. It was bright blue with dark blue embroidery — a flowery pattern Song wasn't fond of. From the top of her bust to her neck and wrists, the fabric was a lacy sheer that made her skin itch. Someone threw a cloak over her shoulders to combat the chill in the air; she felt like a partially wrapped present in the shining blue material.

She met Leslie outside where a carriage, driven by Maps — wearing a fine cabbie uniform — sat waiting. Leslie had dressed in an expensive navy blue suit with a lighter blue shirt. His attire matched her dress rather well. Once the door closed on the rest of the world, Song leaned forward.

"So, what is the cover?" Her voice rose to the pitch she'd used for the benefit of her mother, as though the presence of the corset urged the lady-like tone into her.

"You ran away with me because you were afraid your parents would not approve of the match."

She wrinkled her nose. "Not likely."

He sighed. "Come up with something better and I will accommodate your story."

Her mind immediately blanked. "So, where have we been hiding this whole time?"

His brow furrowed as he studied her. "Are you falling ill?"

"No," she said. "I'm fine. Why?"

"Your voice is…different. Higher?"

She swallowed and stared at her hands. "I hardly think that is as pressing as our cover."

He sighed in exasperation and gave her this secret. "Pishing. I have an estate there. A large one."

"Do you?" Song asked, astounded.

"My cover does. We need to act as though we have been courting since you left. Comfortable around each other."

"I'll do my best." She braced herself for a different sort of contact between them than combat. "Why am I coming out of the dark now? And why here?"

"I'm showing you the world. We have a mutual soft spot for orphans and couldn't resist an opportunity to help."

"Did you plan all this out, or is it just coming off the top of your head?"

"Mostly off the top of my head." He smiled.

"You're an excellent liar."

"You have no idea."

The coach stopped and Thumbs jumped from the back to open the door, holding out a hand for Song to take.

"You clean up nicely," she whispered as she passed him.

"Not so bad yourself, m'lady." He bent at the waist and Song had to suppress an amused giggle. "M'lord." He bent again as Leslie exited and made a face at the honorific.

Inside, a doorman took Song's cloak. Leslie stared longer than was comfortable.

"You look beautiful," he said. The tone in his voice was one of astonishment, like he was seeing her as a woman, rather than a pirate boy, for the first time.

"Not so bad yourself," she said. "Stop making a scene and let's go."

They first had to walk up a tall set of stairs where they waited behind other guests who produced invitations for the man at the top of the descending stairs to announce their names.

Realization struck Song, and she hissed into Leslie's ear. "They have invitations."

"So they do," he replied.

"We d—" She stopped as it was their turn.

Leslie reached inside his jacket and produced a finely made invitation.

"Miss Tsingsei Gould of Andalise accompanied by Lord Roman Duchamp of Pishing," the man announced.

Song's stomach knotted around itself as every eye in the room turned to stare. As predicted, there was immediate movement of the officers in attendance. One made a swift exit. Song hoped he returned with backup. The more officers at the ball, the less there would be at the jail. Now she just needed to act natural. It was only a matter of time before she was apprehended and taken into protective custody—or at least before the officers attempted it. They descended the stairs as Song's entire body shook.

"Remain calm," Leslie whispered beside her.

"They're all staring."

"I don't blame them." He smirked as she shot him a look. "Ignore them."

When they reached the bottom of the stairs, ladies curtsied and men bent at the waist, as though the revelation of her existence was an honor bestowed upon them.

"Are they bowing at me or you?" she hissed.

"Possibly both. Just keep smiling."

He set his palm on the small of her back to steer her toward the dance floor. Once there, he took her waist, and she set her fingers in his palm. After they started dancing, everyone seemed to forget they were there and returned to their own business.

"You're an exceptional dancer," Song said after a while.

Leslie smiled. "I learned to dance before I learned to fight."

"And when did you learn to fight?"

"When I was very young."

Song grew silent as they spun around the room to the music. She caught the stares of others and she could ignore her most burning question no longer. "Who is Roman Duchamp? Is he real, or did you make him up?"

"Roman Duchamp is very real, and I suspect if he knew I was impersonating him, he might grow cross."

She gave him an impertinent glare. "Cross?"

He didn't reply.

"How do you know about him?"

"We were raised like brothers, though he never liked me."

"Tell me the whole story," Song demanded.

He chewed on the inside of his lip. "It's really not that grand of a story."

"Tell me, anyway."

Leslie let out a long, thoughtful breath, his eyes meeting hers as though hoping to stall. But she was having none of it as she pursed her lips and urged him on with raised eyebrows. With an exasperated sigh, he relented.

"All right, fine. But only because you look so divine tonight." He gave her a playful wink, and she snorted, falling out of her ladylike posture for a split second before straightening her back again.

"Continue," she urged, sobering into a dignified expression.

His lips twisted into a devilish smirk. "You look like the sky on a perfect summer—"

"With your story," she hissed, shooting a smile at a nearby couple spinning close enough to eavesdrop for a moment before their path carried them back out of earshot.

"Oh, that dreary thing?" He flinched as she stood on his foot. "Right. When I was little, I went to live with the Duchamps, a sort of playmate for their son, Roman. But he had a very crooked definition of 'play'."

"Did he hate you?"

"Oh," Leslie gave a short, bitter chuckle, "I don't think hate is even a strong enough word." His eyes swept the room, passing over the balconies. "Would you like something to drink?"

"Not particularly," Song grumbled.

He smiled, all handsome charm, and set his hand on the small of her back, guiding her to a table with small champagne coupes. Leslie lifted one and set it in her fingers. She sipped the bubbly liquid as he made conversation in a strange accent more similar to that of Dashaelan's, with his curling r's and heavy o's. He spoke with confidence, making sure every curious ear in the vicinity heard their cover story. Song smiled at appropriate times or hid her lips behind her fingertips to giggle. When he set his hand at her waist to pull her closer, she leaned into him and allowed the kiss on her forehead.

In all honesty, Song thought she should receive some sort of award for her impeccable performance. For just this one night, she allowed herself to be that glowing damsel her mother had been so desperate for her to be, hanging on a gentleman's arm and overflowing with such affluent grace that not a single soul went un-enthralled by her.

"Miss Gould," a man bent at the waist beside her.

"Or is it Lady Duchamp?" a woman nearby asked.

"Just Miss Gould," Song said.

The woman's eyebrow arched with interest. "How scandalous!" Her smile told Song just how delicious this sort of gossip would be.

Leslie cleared his throat. "Miss Gould is an *honorable* young woman."

"Mm, I'm sure." That devilish smile returned to the woman's bright red lips. Her brown eyes swept over Song.

The man cleared his throat. "I am Percival Kent of Schoalpek."

"Schoalpek?"

Leslie leaned closer to her ear. "The Winterlands."

She cocked an eyebrow at him.

"South."

Percival laughed. "Extremely south, indeed. Tamminpring is mild in comparison."

Song gaped. "You mean there are places with winters worse than this? And people live there? By choice?"

Leslie cleared his throat. "Mind your tone, Miss Gould."

Percival smiled. "It's quite all right, Lord Duchamp. It's a shock to anyone, I can imagine. I was wondering, Miss Gould, if you might join me for a dance?"

"Oh, I—"

"Of course she will." Leslie pushed her toward Percival.

"I couldn't possi—"

"Don't be silly! Enjoy yourself." Leslie gave her a wink.

"Cheeky bas—"

Percival took her hand and yanked her into his arms so fast it caught the breath in her lungs. They fell into step with the sweeping tune.

"You're a good dancer," Song said after an awkward amount of time.

But Percival wasn't looking at her. He was glancing toward the tables, where Leslie stood watching them with a devious smirk.

"Mister Kent?"

"Hmm? Oh. I'm sorry. My thoughts carried me away."

She let him stare a little longer. "What's got you so bothered, sir?"

Percival pursed his lips. "You seem like a wonderful young lady."

"Well, thank you—"

"That's not Lord Duchamp."

Song forced her smile to remain and her feet to continue dancing. "I beg your pardon?"

"That man is a Jinjur."

Song blinked, unsure what he meant. "I don't follow."

"A Jinjur will never be a royal of Pishing. And if by some unholy act, one is, and that man really is a Duchamp, then you're in even more danger."

"Whatever do you mean?"

"I don't know what would lead a lady such as yourself to run away with Lord Duchamp, but you should go back home."

"I think that is my own business, Mister Kent."

"You need to get away from him, Miss Gould," he insisted.

She pursed her lips. "Yes, you said that. You failed to explain why."

"Ask him what happened to Lady Duchamp."

Song leaned closer. "What happened to—"

"Tsingsei," Leslie stood beside them, "there are some prestigious individuals begging for a word with you."

"Of course."

"Miss Gould." Percival kissed the top of her hand and she curtsied. The man turned away and wove through the crowd.

"What did he want?" Leslie asked the moment he'd gone.

"He was warning me about Lord Duchamp. Told me to ask you what happened to Lady Duchamp."

Leslie cleared his throat as they neared the people gathered to speak with her. "That depends on which Lady Duchamp he is referring to."

"Oh! Miss Gould! Just look at you." An older woman bustled up to them and set her palms on Song's cheeks. "Are you eating enough, dear? Is this lord starving you?" She winked up at Leslie.

Song turned her grimace into a smile. "I eat well enough, thank you."

"Either way, you *must* try the hors d'oeuvres."

Song held a plate and answered every question asked of her while taking delicate nibbles of the food shoved onto the dish. Each item was just big enough to eat in one bite, but she kept her composure and remembered to chew like she had a secret, as her mother had always told her to. Her discomfort rose as the minutes passed and the questions continued. The food had only made her hungry in an unpleasant way and she was tired of the tittering ladies. She set her plate in the hands of a waiter and wrapped her arm through Leslie's, waiting until he finished speaking with another man. Leslie leaned closer to her to listen.

"Darling, could we have another dance?"

Leslie eyed her, a kind smile curving across his lips, while a spot of humor twinkled in his eyes. "Of course, *darling.*"

Once they'd returned to the dance floor, Song raised an eyebrow at him. "Using aristocrats to avoid finishing your story? How shameful of you."

His shoulder raised in a shrug of innocence. "Was worth a try. So, where was I?" He'd returned to using his usual accent, which was similar to Song's.

"You were taken in as a playmate for Roman," she reminded him.

He gave a bitter frown. "Right."

"And he hated you."

"Ah, yes. Well, when his father grew ill, Roman was all but signing the order for my immediate execution. Caius thwarted his attempt by granting me my freedom. And now here we are…poking the bear, as it were."

Song didn't realize she'd taken an involuntary step back and paused in the path of the other dancers. But she had, and she couldn't call up the command to make her feet move and her spurious smile return. Leslie's smile to the others came forced.

"Song."

"You…" It was all that came gasping from her lips.

He took her back in his arms, squeezing her fingers hard in his to pinch her back to the present. "Wake up, princess."

She blinked and let him lead her back into the steady waltz.

"Can't slip anything past you, can I?"

"You were…" she said.

"Say it, Song."

But she couldn't. Her lips refused to say that Leslie was once a Pishing slave. Song turned her gaze from his, a shudder of pity crawling into her heart. She knew, though, that pity was never something he would kindly accept. She didn't want him to see that in her eyes for even a second, and so began counting the officers lining up around the room and on the balcony, speaking with the hostess and clearing people away to reduce injury of innocent bystanders.

"Strange how quickly your opinion of someone can change once you've discovered their past."

"How do you mean?" She tried to maintain a casual tone.

"A moment ago you looked at me like the lord I'm pretending to be. Now you're afraid."

"What could I possibly be afraid of?" She forced a laugh.

"That I'll see the pity in your eyes." His lips twisted in a knowing smile as she glanced up at him. "There are things you learn to recognize when in the lowest station known to man, and pity is one of them."

"I'm sorry."

"Don't be." His eyes swept the room and Song realized they were alone on the dance floor. "Time's up." Leslie set his cheek against hers and whispered in her ear. "I hope there is still some damsel in distress left within you."

Song gave a shy smile as though he'd been whispering sweet nothings. When the police force rushed forward, they grabbed her and dragged her away from Leslie. She gasped, her heart clenched into her throat as genuine panic set in.

She'd thought she would have to put on another show—thought she would have to pretend that being torn from his side was the most terrifying prospect imaginable. But the anxiety came of its own accord. It tightened around her heart and made her breath come in quick gasps. Her hands stretched for him, stretched for the security of returning to the Stars' Bounty tucked away in Talegrove and the promise that she would not have to go home to Garda and expectations and suitors and marriage.

The surrounding voices blurred together. Officers told her it would be all right, and that she was safe now. A woman shouted her objections at such aggressive treatment of a lady. But when Leslie shook free of the guards and shouted a commanding "Stop!" everything froze. The room grew silent in anticipation. He strode to her and tore her away from the officers.

Song collapsed against him, tears trying so hard to spring from her eyes. After she lost the battle against them, she decided they would aid in the performance she knew she had to give. She wrapped her arms around him and clung to him for all she was worth. She turned her tears on the approaching lawmen.

"You can't take me back!" she shouted.

"Miss Gould you need to—"

"No!" She slapped away an outstretched hand.

"You're frightening her," Leslie insisted.

"You can't take me away from him!" she shouted, then for dramatic effect she added, "I love him!"

Maps came into view on the balcony, nodding that it was time to leave.

"We need an exit now," Leslie whispered in her ear before kissing her on the cheek.

"Miss Gould—"

"I can't…I can't…breathe." Song forced herself to hyperventilate, just until her vision spotted. "You can't… I won't…" She allowed her legs to buckle beneath her and went limp in Leslie's arms.

"She needs air," he said. He cradled her and shoved through the officers.

"You barbarians! Let her be!" It was the hostess of the party, a plump woman in the finest silks. "Come, dear, bring her here." She led Leslie to a room upstairs, away from the ballroom, where he set Song on a chaise.

"Stay as long as she needs."

"Thank you for your kindness." Leslie shook the woman's hand as she left. He closed the door on the gathering officers and locked it.

"You're frightening her?" Song demanded.

"It worked, didn't it?" He strode to the window to check that it was unlocked. "Nice waterworks, by the way. I nearly believed it." He pulled his suit jacket off and tossed it onto the chaise.

Song blushed. "I don't want to go back, and if they had taken me…"

He considered her from across the room, then delivered a gentle smile. "I wouldn't have let that happen." He paused in thought. "What about the other part?" he asked.

She raised an inquisitive eyebrow as she began working to remove the gown.

"The part where you announced to the world that you love me. Is that true?" Mischief twinkled in his eye.

She rolled her eyes. "Hardly. Oh! Blast it all!" The dress was not cooperating as it should have, as Song tugged it this way and that. "*Smes ehth pir.*"

The dress fell away from her in chunks as the seams holding it together split open in a flash of blue light. Beneath the gown, Song wore a black corset and trousers. She pulled the pin to let her hair down. Leslie opened the window and turned to stare at Song.

"Nice corset…"

She walked past him and to the window. "Nice cummerbund."

He stared down at his waist and ripped the garment from his middle, then freed his neck of the silver bowtie.

There was no security in sight, so Song ducked out and gripped the sill, shivering as the winter air bit into her bare shoulders. By some stroke of luck, there was a trellis just within leaping reach. To her dismay, the vines weaving through were some sort of brier.

"Blast," Leslie grunted above her as they made their way down. "Frostthorn. Only plant that grows in the cold of winter here. Bloody—ah!—painful."

"Keep your prickings to yourself or you're sure to get us discovered."

When they reached the bottom, Song's palms stung where the little thorns had coaxed small spots of blood from her skin. Leslie's palms were no better. She wiped her hands on her trousers and he on a handkerchief as they set off at a jog around the side of the mansion.

Thumbs leaned against the side of the coach, his top hat low over his eyes and a lit pipe smoking in his hands. When he spotted them, he spun around to assess the surroundings, then opened the door and waved them inside. With the world on the other side of the door, Song opened a box sitting on the bench beside her. With Leslie's help, she donned the funeral garb she'd worn to sneak into the city. Leslie pulled the ribbon from his hair and ran smoothing fingertips through the auburn cascade.

"That won't do much good," Song said.

"What?"

"Your hair is a notable color."

He narrowed his eyes. "Not all of us can be so plain as to be forgotten quickly."

"Forgotten quickly?" she demanded. "You call this forgotten quickly?"

"Fair enough." He observed her in a long silence, broken only by the horse's hooves and the wheels on the cobblestone street. "Song."

"Yes?"

"Please…don't tell anyone what I told you about myself."

She gauged him. "If you're such a good liar, then why not lie to me?"

He met her eyes through the black sheer. "Because you deserve better than that."

Her heart softened. She lifted the veil to hold his gaze. "My lips are sealed, Leslie. I promise."

When they arrived at the inn, they ducked inside and the hostess ushered them to a trapdoor beneath the bar. Song descended the ladder first, pulling the veil away from her face to see better in the darkness. There were cots in a row as the only furniture. A figure sat on one, leaning against the wall, another figure sat adjacent.

"Song?" Dashaelan's voice came through the darkness.

A lantern flame turned up to illuminate him sitting on the cot against the wall. She ran forward, throwing herself into his arms. He gripped her tight for a long time. When he let her go, Leslie had found himself a cot, and they'd been shut into the darkness. Sunshine, sitting across from Dashaelan, handed Song a bundle—her clothes. She found a dark corner and began removing the plain black dress, her progress made difficult by the injury to her hands from the frostthorn.

"I was starting to think I'd see the gallows," Dashaelan said. Song and Sunshine scoffed in unison.

"Thank you." He directed it to Sunshine.

"Don't thank me," Sunshine said. "Wasn't my idea. I mean, I wasn't gonna just leave you in there, but damned if I could come up with a plan as good as this one. Your thanks go to Song."

"I just had to be a Gould for a while." Song shrugged. "Don't ever let me do it again. That Tsingsei is just awful."

"I think we all prefer you this way," Dashaelan said as she sat beside him.

"As do I. What about you, Leslie?" she said to the figure lying in the shadows, staring at the floor above them. "Would you rather always be Lord Duchamp?"

Dashaelan eyed her, his expression distorted by the flickering, dim lamplight. But he said nothing.

"I would die a thousand deaths before I would choose to be Roman for any longer than I pretended to be." There was something dark in his tone, and it worried Song.

"You're troubled," she said.

"Nothing is without repercussions." He turned his head away from her.

Song stared at the others, who stared right back. She shook her head in confusion.

Twenty-Four

THE NIGHT WAS BITTER, HIDDEN AWAY IN THE DARK CELLAR. Song shivered alone in silence, her arms wrapped around herself as she lay fully clothed under two blankets. The wind howled against the inn above them. It froze the ground and sucked what little heat there was from the room. After staring at her quivering figure for a long time, Leslie stood and bundled his blankets. Before she could object, he spread them over her, then returned to his own cot to lean against the freezing wall and rub his hands together.

It wasn't long before Song sat up. Without a moment's hesitation, she wrapped the blankets around herself and crossed the room to sit beside him, covering them both with all four blankets. He wrapped an arm behind her shoulders to keep her away from the frigid wall and closer to his own body's heat. She nuzzled into him as her shivering subsided just enough so she could relax.

"Well, don't you just look nice and toasty," Dashaelan grumbled from across the room.

"Room for one more," Leslie said.

"I'm fine over here."

"Dash, I did not save your life just to watch you freeze

to death in this bloody hole. You don't have to cuddle me. Just come share our blankets," Song said.

He grunted and stared off toward the ladder.

"Dash," she warned, "don't make me throw you overboard."

His lips cracked into a smile, and he chuckled. "I'd like to see you try."

Song left him alone and concentrated on trying to keep warm. A short while later, he stood over her, his arms overflowing with pillows and blankets.

"Put these behind your backs or that wall will suck the heat right out of you."

He set a pillow behind Song's back and handed Leslie another. After a moment of thought, he spread his blankets over the others, then climbed onto the cot on the other side of Song. She leaned over to lend him some of her warmth, and he grumbled.

"You said I didn't have to cuddle with you."

Song laughed. "Quiet, old man. I'll shove off once you're not nearly frozen solid." She kept her promise. Once he'd warmed to a reasonable temperature, she let go and leaned away from him.

Song's eyes opened sometime late in the night as a board creaked. Sunshine leaned off the ladder to check on them. The other two were fast asleep. Dashaelan's arm was wrapped behind Song, hugging her close; Leslie leaned against her with an arm encircling her waist, head on her shoulder. She blinked at Sunshine. Neither said anything. He ascended the ladder, and she closed her eyes and fell back asleep.

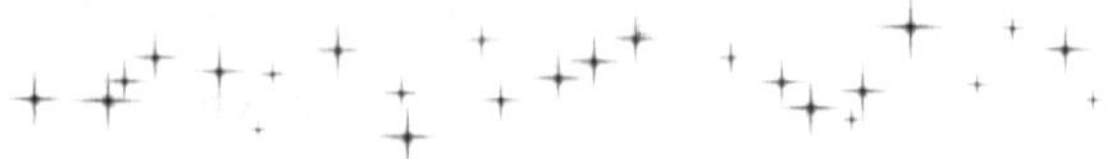

AN UNCOMFORTABLE QUIET HAD CAUGHT THE TAVERN IN ITS trembling fingers. Song sat at a table beside Leslie. She kept her hood low and her eyes on her food. The two had opted to eat their lunch in the warmth of the dining area; Dashaelan had taken his below as a precaution. They jumped and turned as the door opened, but it wasn't the law—Sunshine would have warned them. Their eyes met and as one they returned to their meals, determined to finish faster.

"Leslie?" The man who had entered stood over them. He was a short man with a crooked jaw and a sideways smile. He wore a brown flatcap and his mousy brown hair stuck out around his ears.

Leslie glanced up. "I'm sorry, you've got the wrong man."

"Right, so, you're just another soft-spoken Jinjur who looks exactly the same as the Leslie I knew."

"I'm not a Jinjur."

"Hair as red as that? You're a bloody Jinjur, mate." He sat across from them and stared at Leslie in excitement. "You haven't changed a bit!" He glanced at Song. "Who's this, then? New bird?"

"This is *Caleb*," Leslie said.

His eyebrows rose. "Oh, oh! I'm so sorry, lad. You have lovely hands. Assumed…"

Song replied with a rude gesture.

"What are you doing in Tamminpring, Ollie?"

"I run the show here, now. It hasn't been the same since we lost you," Ollie said in a hushed tone. "I understand why you had to leave…"

"Don't," he snapped.

"Right, of course. Either way. The gents all miss you. I mean, who wouldn't? You were the best!" He punched Leslie's shoulder.

He stared at his shoulder, then at Ollie. "You talk a lot more than I remember."

"Ten years," he barked. "I haven't seen you in ten years. Excuse me if I'm a bit excited."

"You lived in Jashedar?" Song asked.

Leslie growled out a breath. "Shorton. Are we done here?" He clenched his jaw at Ollie.

"Yes, you are," Sunshine said over them.

Leslie bolted out of his seat, but Song hesitated. Sunshine picked her up by the back of her coat and shoved her toward the back room.

"Right, I get it! I'm going! I'm going!"

Sunshine glared down at Ollie. "You ain't seen nothin' or no one."

"Just enjoying my stew," he replied, dragging Leslie's bowl to where he sat.

"Toothy," Sunshine motioned across the tavern for him to sit in Song's place.

He rushed to the back and followed Song down the ladder as the officers entered the tavern, shutting out the blowing snow behind them. Thumbs and the barmaid moved a large box over the trapdoor, then slipped back into the main room without making a sound. Song looked up at the floorboards, squinting to see through the narrow cracks between them. The officers stopped in the middle of the room.

"Ollie! Fancy meeting you here," one said.

"If meeting me is fancy, then you've got to get yourself a better social life."

"What's a guy like you doing in a place like this, anyway?"

"Talk to me like that and you'd better be buying me a drink."

"Answer the question," another voice said.

"It's cold out and I like the stew here. Is stew a crime?"

"That depends on how you answer the next question." Papers shuffled across a tabletop. "Have you seen any of these individuals?"

Ollie whistled low. "Lovely girl. Who is she?"

"Tsingsei Gould of Andalise. And this one is Roman Duchamp of Pishing. They attended the benefit together."

He coughed out a laugh. "This ain't Roman Duchamp."

Song had the urge to run up the ladder and throttle Ollie. Sunshine gripped her upper arm in warning.

"But he said—"

"What a man says and what a man is are two completely different things. And this man ain't no Duchamp. And good thing for that Gould girl."

"Not this again," one officer growled.

"Roman Duchamp is a monster," Ollie insisted.

"Rumors."

"Facts! Saw him with my own eyes, I did. And this terrible drawing is not Duchamp."

"What about this one?"

"Who's that one?"

"Dashaelan Krell, captain of the Stars' Bounty."

"What's he doing in Tamminpring?"

A long silence followed before the first officer spoke. "He escaped from jail the night of the benefit."

Ollie barked a laugh. "That must have been some benefit!"

"Just answer the question."

"I ain't never seen that man before."

"Ollie, if you're lying to us—"

"I know. I know. You'll shut me down and give me the thief's necklace."

"So, I ask again, have you seen any of these individuals?"

Song held her breath and waited. He must have been looking long and hard at the pictures. Every frightening possibility zipped through her mind and she readied herself for a fight, reaching for her revolver. Leslie set a hand on her shoulder and shook his head.

"Yeah," Ollie said. "I think I may have seen these two. Headed south out of town."

"And this one?"

"Never seen him. But I'd guess he'd head for the coast. Stars' Bounty is a skyship, right? If it were me, I'd get myself onto a sea-faring craft just to throw you coppers off the scent."

"As usual, Ollie, you've been the most unbearable help imaginable."

Boots scraped across the floor as they collected the papers.

"A pleasure," Ollie replied. "Don't freeze to death out there. Or do. Either way, don't come back."

The door opened to the icy wind, then shut on it once more. The four under the floor breathed a sigh of relief. Leslie waited just long enough for the officers to be out of earshot before climbing up the ladder and shoving his shoulder against the trapdoor. A scrape came from above and Thumbs opened the door to let them out. Song followed, a hand on her sidearm. Leslie lifted Ollie by the collar.

"You're a rat now, Ollie?"

"Oy, you got no right getting irate over what I do with my business. You left, remember?"

Leslie sent his fist into Ollie's jaw with enough force that the other lost his footing.

"Oh, brother, you have not lost your touch one bit."

"No. But I *am* losing my temper."

"You and I both know you never had one of those, except—"

Leslie smacked the back of Ollie's head. "What did I say?"

"Don't talk about it. Right. Whatever you say, brother." He gulped down Song's ale and slammed the stein on the table. "Could really use you, Leslie. Business is good, but not as good as when you were the main event."

"I have more important things to do."

Ollie observed Song with a critical eye, thoughts whirring through his eyes. He shrugged. "Suit yourself, mate. Good luck getting out of Tamminpring alive." He dropped some quoine on the table and sauntered to the entrance. "Lunch is on me…*fellas*." He winked at Song before disappearing into the whitened world outside.

Song thought about what he'd said. "He's right. The only way we're getting out of Tamminpring is in coffins."

"Aren't you just full of hope," Dashaelan muttered behind them.

"No, she's right," Leslie said. "That is brilliant, Song." He grabbed her into an excited squeeze of a hug before she shoved him away. "Sunshine, find us a cooper." With that, he descended back into the darkness below.

"You've all lost your minds," Toothy said, shoving a spoonful of stew into his mouth.

"Good stew?" Song asked.

Embarrassment spread across his face before he brushed it away. "Quite excellent."

She rolled her eyes and climbed down into the cellar. She sat beside Leslie and he reached across to wrap her in the blankets. Song knew she shouldn't ask, but the curiosity gnawed at her.

"What aren't you telling me?"

Leslie made it a point to ignore her, as though she'd said nothing at all. It wasn't until hours later, when the three huddled together in the darkness, that Leslie broke his silence.

"I don't want either of you to get the wrong ideas," he said.

"We all have pasts we'd rather not claim as our own," Dashaelan said.

"Tell me about Roman," Song urged. "What did he do?"

He remained silent for a long time as the wind howled its mournful cries outside, warning of another freezing night. Leslie reached out of the blankets to tap the tip of Song's nose. "It is a long and dreary story, best left for another day. Get some sleep."

"But—"

"Goodnight, Song. Captain."

Dashaelan grunted in reply, but Song deflated in curious irritation. She sat in the darkness for a long time after the other two had succumbed to sleep, their breathing deep and steady around her. Each had their heads resting against her shoulders and it comforted her, somehow, to be set between those two. When her eyes could stay open no longer, she let her curiosity go and joined them in sleep.

Twenty-Five

TWO DAYS LATER, A FIGURE IN A MOURNING GOWN ESCORTED two caskets to the skyship towers. Constables who'd been more than just kissed by the winter winds stopped them at the bottom.

"I'm sorry, miss, but we need to check inside."

"But…mother and father…" Song broke into fake sobs behind the veil. "I'm sorry, it was just so sudden."

"Officers, you may not want to open these," Maps replied from the back of the cart. He strode forward to pull Song into a comforting embrace. "Doctor said our parents died of the fever. That we were lucky not to catch it."

"Are you saying your parents had Forrest Blight?"

"That's the one," Maps replied.

"I miss them so much." Song faked a ragged breath, which sent saliva straight into her windpipe. Her throat tightened, and she fell into an uncontrollable coughing fit.

The officers stepped back several paces and paled.

"Get out of here. And burn those damned bodies!"

They allowed them to pass and load their cargo onto the waiting skyship.

"You can stop coughing now," Maps said as they left port.

Song tossed the veil over her head—her eyes were red and watering. She covered her mouth and forced her reply through the coughing. "I wasn't…faking."

"Are you all right?"

"Choked myself." She smiled, and her laugh came out as another cough.

A pounding came from the left coffin, followed by Dashaelan's muffled protests. Toothy worked to get the lids free of the coffins with a pry-bar. Dashaelan strode straight to the side of the ship, releasing a grateful sigh as he relieved himself. Leslie joined Song, sitting on a crate of supplies. He held out his flask of water and she snatched it up to wash away the urge to cough.

"So," he said, "am I your mother or your father?"

She delivered a devilish smile, then broke into laughter, which broke into another fit of coughing.

In Talegrove, the crew celebrated at an inn. The drinks came and were drained at an alarming rate. She'd already recounted her story of what had happened at the ball, leaving out the entire conversation with Percival Kent.

Ponce waved a hand at his cheek like an excitable lady. "Oh, my, my," he said in a falsetto tone, "that is quite the adventure Miss—*Oof!*"

Thumbs shoved his elbow into Ponce's ribs.

He gripped his side and abandoned his mocking of ladies. "Oh, right. Sorry."

"Her secret is all ours now. Keep it or I will cut out your tongue." Thumbs kept his face so straight that Song snorted a long laugh through her nose.

"I'd like to see that!"

"Well," Toothy said, slamming his wooden stein on the table with such force that ale splashed out, "while you were off having the time of your life, we had a right near bollocks at the jail."

"What happened?" Song leaned closer.

"Well, you went snoopin', right? Told us where he was with your…" He wiggled his fingers as though that explained her *kijæm* without words.

"Right, and?"

"Well, he wasn't!"

"Then they moved him! It's not my fault!" Song said.

Toothy laughed. "And then in come these coppers shoutin' about Miss Gould and apprehendin' her and I'm shoved in this broom closet, touchin' noses with Ponce—"

"Bloke tried to kiss me!" Ponce shouted with a laugh.

Toothy ground his elbow into Ponce's other side.

Ponce crossed his arms over his torso to hold the injuries. "You lot're cruel."

They fell silent to gape at him, then broke into raucous laughter. It wasn't long before the drunken singing started.

"That's enough of that," Dashaelan said.

He stood, but wobbled on intoxicated limbs. Song slipped under his arm as support and he let her steer him toward his room. He flopped onto the bed and leaned against the wall to stare at her. She pulled his boots from his feet, then propped them at the end of the bed. She could feel his eyes on her, but didn't say anything.

"I'm proud of you," he said.

"Thank you," she replied.

"I wonder if my son is someone I can be proud of," he mused.

Song stopped to stare at him. "You have a son?"

"I had a wife once, too."

"What happened to them?"

"Leonna died in childbirth. She was an amazing woman." His brow furrowed as his eyes fixed on a distant point. "I can't remember what she looked like."

"What about your son?"

Tears filled his eyes. "I was so young. So stupid. He was four years old and had to pay for his father's mistakes… I can't remember him, either."

"What did you do?"

"Oh, Song, it doesn't matter now, does it? Point is I was unfit, and he was taken from me. That's how this all happened." He waved his fingers at the room. "I couldn't carry on alone anymore. I did what you did…"

"Approached a dangerous man in a tavern and lied your way into his crew?" She gave him a cheeky smile.

"Made promises of usefulness to convince a man who didn't want anything to do with me to take me on board." He eyed her, and she stared at her feet. "I wanted to toss you out of that tavern," he admitted. "Your persistence bothered me."

"Do you wish you had?"

"Not even a little! Your persistence is an excellent quality and I'm alive now because of it. I'm not an educated man, Song, but I'm not stupid."

"I never said you were."

"I've spent three decades trying to be better than the man I was when I lost everything."

"Blimey…" Song sighed. "You're old."

He groaned. "And don't I feel it!"

"What was your son's name?" Song asked.

"Wesley." A smile spread across his face. His smile fell and was replaced by a frown of determination to not lose his composure. "I failed him. I should never have let him go."

Song sat on the bed beside him and wrapped him in a comforting hug.

"I didn't ask to be cuddled, Song."

"Shut up, old man."

Twenty-Six

Song left Dashaelan snoring in his room. She returned to the tavern below in time to see Leslie exit. She followed. Night had fallen and the street lanterns were lit. It was snowing big fluffy flakes like cotton balls—it groaned underfoot and stuck to her clothing.

"Why are you following me, Song?" Leslie asked on the other side of the city center.

"Why are you sneaking out of the inn when it's freezing out and you've a bed inside?"

"My business is my own."

"As is mine."

He turned to look at her. "Except this isn't your business. This is mine. Get out of it."

"No."

He pursed his lips to contain whatever comment was forming on his tongue and turned away. She fell back into step a distance from him; giving him space—but not enough to evade her. The cold crept through her coat and seeped into her bones.

Leslie stopped again. "Go back inside, Song. You'll freeze out here."

"At least I've got a coat," she said. "What are you planning on doing once the cold catches up with you?"

"Does it matter?"

"It matters if you don't come back."

He spun to look her in the eyes. "Who said I wasn't coming back?"

"I'm not stupid," she replied.

"What do you care if I return or not?"

She chose not to reply to that question. "The crew is in high spirits."

"Aye."

She approached him. "And you are not."

"What of it?"

The bite of whiskey hung in the air between them. "Instead, you're out here letting loose demons."

He sniffed, his nose red from drink rather than cold. "You're not my keeper, Song."

"No, but I am your friend, and—"

"*You?*" he hissed. "My friend? I keep many secrets, but none so big as yours, Miss Gould."

Her eyes darted through the night for any prying ears. "Leslie, please, could we—"

"Oh, no. No, we couldn't *please.*" The upper-class Andalisian accent was failing, giving way to curling r's and puckered o's, like the accent he'd used in Tamminpring. "You could have anything you wanted, and you chose this." He threw his arms out, motioning at the city.

"Leslie, stop it."

"Do you know how hard it was to fall into the shadows? To get Roman off my scent after Shorton? I thought I'd never stop—" He rubbed his hands over his face. "He's going to have all of Ebrinar after me."

"Leslie—"

"So what's a few demons matter, huh, *Miss Gould?*"

"Don't call me that."

"Why not? Do you prefer Tsingsei?"

"Leslie!"

"Yes, *Tsingsei?*"

Song readied a punch. She twisted at the waist as though she were about to leave, then turned back around. Her feet spun on the snow. Her momentum caught him off guard and her blow knocked him to the ground. He didn't bother getting up, just sat in the snow. Defeated.

"We're done," she snapped. "Since we're not friends, you and I are finished. No more training, and no more deals. Enjoy your demons."

Song didn't return to the tavern. She didn't look behind to see if Leslie was going to follow her—part of her hoped he did. But then he would see her tears. He would see that she was not angry, but that she was hurt because he would not open up to her about the things that really mattered. Once across the wide open area, she turned to see if he was still sitting in the snow, waiting for his death to catch him, but he was gone.

"Lover's quarrel?" The voice came from a dark corner and made Song tense. "Didn't mean to frighten you." Shadow stepped forward and studied her.

"That's why they call you Shadow."

"Did you really believe it was because of my height?"

"Not even for a minute."

"That was a fantastic punch…for a girl."

"Right." Her laugh was without humor. "I'm an ugly girl."

"All girls are ugly," he replied.

"Would you rather I was a pretty boy?"

His eyes scanned her from head-to-toe and back again. "I would." His smile was genuine. "What is a maiden such as yourself doing traveling with a load of men? Aren't you afraid of improprieties?"

"There would be more improprieties if I rode with women."

His smile warmed as they established a common ground. "Have you ever shot that?" He gestured at the gun strapped to her thigh.

She shifted, and it was enough to tell anyone the answer.

"Come with me…what was your name again?"

"Call me Song. Caleb Song if anyone asks."

He turned to eye her as he led her across Talegrove, his long furry cloak smoothing the snow in his wake. "You don't look like a Caleb." He stopped at the edge of the city, where it nestled against a cliff. There was a shooting range set up, where targets stood with their backs to the rock, arms wide as they welcomed oncoming gunfire. "But you do look like a Song." He held out his hand for her sidearm. She let him inspect it. "Good revolver. Cheap, but a suitable model, nonetheless. How much ammunition do you have?"

"Only what's in there. It was a gift."

He handed the gun back, then took her hand and wrapped her fingers around it in a proper fashion. "Your fingers are ice!" Shadow produced a pair of gloves and offered them to her.

"They won't fit."

"Please, I'm a small man and you have small hands. They'll fit."

To her astonishment, they did. As she worked with Shadow to get the best angle and find the most comfortable way to stand, she forgot she'd fought with Leslie; forgot the events in Tamminpring. She even forgot that it was snowing and her coat was not thick enough for such weather. She found that angling herself to shoot sideways was easiest. Shadow commented that her narrow build would be a difficult target that way.

She eyed him, and he lowered his brow in question. She shook off her curiosity for a moment before turning to face him. "I don't understand."

"What?"

"The stories people tell of you…"

"You don't believe a man of my stature could do such things?" He thought about this. "I'm not a patient man. I don't have the physical acuity to wield a sword or lay a man flat in a single punch." He smirked up at her. "What I do have is a gun and a temper shorter than I am."

"So you just…shot everyone, then?"

He laughed. "Hardly. I bested one drunken idiot in a bar fight. He did the rest."

Song set her revolver in her left hand to shoot at the target a few times while facing him. "How do you mean?"

"Insult leads to tall tales to rescue a wronged man's reputation. I don't have to be good at anything, really. The rest of the world just needs to believe that I am." He grew quiet and watched her practice for a few minutes. "Are you sure you've never shot a gun before?"

She smiled. "Quite sure."

"It agrees with you."

"I'm just a quick study."

"I don't think that's true."

She eyed him. "Why not?"

"How old are you?"

"Eighteen," she replied, before adding, "-ish."

"Running on pirate time can get confusing. A month-ish; a year-ish." He chuckled. "And in eighteen-ish years, you never learned how to be a lady." They shared a moment of silent understanding. "Get back to your inn before you catch your death." He set a pouch of bullets in her hands. She began to remove his gloves, but he stopped her. "Keep them."

"Oh, I can't—"

"The world is a cruel place for an unattended girl, and you have pretty hands."

"Thank you."

"And thank you for keeping your troubles with the law out of Talegrove." He turned from her and headed off another way into town. "Oh, and Song?"

"Yes?"

"Remember, the only thing more insulting than being beaten by someone like me is being beaten by a woman." He winked at her.

Song blinked, and just like that, he was gone. Another shadow under the buildings.

She held out the revolver and took another shot at the target. A rock tumbled nearby, the sound grew faint as it descended the cliff. She pulled back the hammer on her revolver. Another rock tumbled its way down the cliff. After a moment of hesitation, Song set the hammer back in place and holstered her sidearm, then tied the pouch of ammunition to her belt.

She made her way through the thick night, the swirling snow dancing before her. A figure became apparent, standing at the edge of the cliff. His arms spread wide and palms to the open air as one at a time he kicked stones over the side, then waited as they clattered downward.

"Leslie?"

He didn't move. His proximity to the edge sent her jaw into a tight clench.

"Leslie, what are y—"

"I wonder…how high it is."

"What?"

"This cliff." He toed another stone off the edge, then paused to listen. "I can't hear them hit the bottom."

"I don't understand."

"If I could just hear them hit the bottom…"

"Why does it matter how high up we are?"

"Did you know that there are equations for timing a fall?" He gave a small snort. "I could tell you, per pound, how long it will take me to hit the bottom…if I could just hear the bloody stones."

Song rushed for him. "Leslie, stop!"

He turned to cast a curious expression at her. She grabbed his shirt, spun him to the ground, and pressed him into the gathering snow.

"What the hell are you doing?" she shouted from atop him, her nose an inch from his.

"The stone isn't any better than the sticks," Leslie whispered.

"What are you on about?"

"In another life, I had everything. In another life, you had everything. Only one of us is here by choice."

Song growled. "I wasn't happy."

"I was."

"And calculating killing yourself with a long fall will make it suddenly better?"

"It isn't the fall that kills you. It's the landing." His eyes held tight on hers and there she saw them, the demons, twirling away in the sorrow he'd unearthed with drink. They danced in the street lamps and rolled from his eyes as tears.

"Stop it," she hissed. "If you want to fall, that's fine by me. But don't you go looking for a landing. I've enough *kijæm* to catch you and any other fool I call 'friend'. So just stop it."

He closed his eyes and took in a deep breath that lifted Song on his chest. "And what of Roman?"

"If he wants you, he can come get you himself. Until then, all of Ebrinar can try and try, but we'll keep fighting them all off. Right? You and me." She fished for her handkerchief in her pouch and dabbed at his tears. "Until then, no more whiskey. For you, anyway."

"That hardly seems fair."

"I'm not the one calculating speed of descent."

"Point taken."

Song stood and held out her hand to him. He took it and let her help him up. He gripped her hand a moment longer before pulling her into his embrace to hug her as tight as he could without breaking her. His fists wrapped behind her back and gripped her coat as though she was the only thing keeping him from falling into darkness.

The cold crept into her bones. With one word a red-orange sphere encircled them, the warmth of it dried them and melted the snow at their feet. Leslie stared in wonder, reaching out a hand to touch the cocoon. It rippled beneath his fingertips. He pushed his fingers through; the sphere spread around them, then closed back into place as he retracted his hand.

"It's freezing on the other side."

"It's snowing on the other side," she said, laughing at his amazement.

"How does it work?"

"I don't know. I just say things and they happen." She ran her fingers along the sphere, smiling as it rippled beneath her fingertips. It had a strange texture, something solid and yet pliable, constant, but temporary. "It feels like I'm making vague requests of a separate entity, and it guesses how to carry it out. The more I use it, though, the more we understand each other."

"So, this?" He motioned at the red sphere.

"I asked for warmth, but didn't specify beyond that word. I didn't know it would put us in a bubble, but it does the job I asked for."

The wind blew a furious gust, which attempted to knock away their protection. The snow fell harder around them.

"We should probably go back," Leslie said.

Song hesitated. "Are you sure you'll be all right?"

He shrugged. "I've never been all right."

"How do you do it?"

"I'm just very good at lying."

He extended his elbow to her, and she wrapped her hand around it, letting him escort her like a lady back to the inn. Their sphere of warmth stayed with them, dissipating of its own accord after they entered the tavern.

"Leslie," she stopped him as he entered his room. "If you ever need a friend…"

He regarded her in silence, then nodded. "Good night, Song."

"Good night."

Twenty-Seven

WHEN SONG WOKE IN THE MORNING, SNOW HAD BLOCKED the view from her window. In the tavern below, men were standing at the open door marveling at the white world beyond, where the snow had accumulated to waist-deep. Dashaelan sat in the corner, looking sour. She joined him.

"This is bad, Song."

"Don't want to be stuck here?"

"Besides that. The Bounty is not a winter-weather skyship. She needs more canvas on the zeppelin. That snow will keep coming and weigh her down until she cracks and falls into the ocean."

Song drained the mug of hot tea the barmaid set in front of her. It burned the flesh all the way down her throat and sat as molten slag in her stomach. "I suppose someone will just have to go clear her off and put a cover over the zeppelin." She stood and jogged back upstairs to knock on Leslie's door. He didn't respond.

She opened the door, careful to not make a sound as she peeked in to see if he was sleeping. Sweat trickled across his brow. It had soaked through his clothing and left the bedding damp. He shivered, though the room was comfortable enough. Without hesitation, she ran downstairs and grabbed Maps, dragging him back to the room.

"Is this that sickness?"

Maps checked Leslie. "No, thankfully. But it appears he was caught in foul weather."

"He was outside without proper attire last night. How do we fix it?"

"He needs more blankets."

Song rushed to the tavern and spoke with the innkeeper. He was large—fat off his own food and drink—but a good man. He instructed one of his maids to tend to the ill, getting him whatever he needed.

Once she'd handled Leslie, Song asked her crew for help with clearing the Stars' Bounty. Hairy rubbed his bald head and frowned. Thumbs volunteered, but Song saw a vision of him slipping in the snow and falling down into the fog to find the lower harbor. Bells stepped forward, wrapped in a borrowed fur coat. Song called upon the warm sphere from the night before; it melted the snow in the doorway and several feet ahead of them as they made their way to the Stars' Bounty, armed with two snow brooms.

"I suppose I didn't need this after all," Bells chuckled.

"I don't want to warm the zeppelin too fast," Song said. "You'll need that when we get there to knock the snow off."

Bells grumbled. "Bloody bad weather."

"Where are you from?" Song asked.

"Andalise."

"North or south?"

"About middle-ish. Bad winters. Worse than Garda, but better than this."

"Aye, Garda winters are much milder than this." They arrived at their skyship and Song sighed in preparation. "Are you ready for this?"

"No." He laughed.

"Me either." She braced herself and took in the warmth one last time. "*Thmrah-w ehth pawts.*"

The shield fell away and the suddenness with which the icy air hit Song's lungs choked her. It froze with such force that it burned. Bells lifted his hood and pulled a scarf over his nose, then set to work. She rushed inside first and fished an old shirt from her trunk, tearing it just so and tying it behind her head to cover her mouth and nose. It wasn't the ideal sort of scarf, but it was all she had.

They worked as fast as they could. First, they cleared the deck, then they climbed the netting to bat the snow from the zeppelin. Bells secured a rope around Song's waist and twisted it around his forearm. He planted himself in the crow's nest as she walked to each end of the long zeppelin to shove the snow. It created a chain reaction, pushing all the snow in an avalanche over the side and down into the consuming fog below. They brought large canvas pieces up from the cargo hold to wrap around the zeppelin and secure underneath with twine. Song used her *kijæm* to speed the process.

"It's not the prettiest fix," Bells said as they stood on the dock to catch their breath before returning to the tavern, "but it'll do."

"If Dash says it's not good enough, then he can come out here and do it himself." She laughed.

Bells nodded in agreement. "Let's get inside before we lose precious body parts."

"*Thmrah-w.*" The sphere of warmth surrounded them, and their muscles relaxed. "It's gotten higher," Song observed as they reached the main street. Their previous path had been filled-in a ways, and the walls on either side were higher, running abreast with Song's bust line.

When they entered the tavern, Song dove into the hot grain-and-game soup Dashaelan set in her hands. She finished three bowls before heading upstairs to see how Leslie was faring. His room was stifling hot with a roaring fire in the hearth and thick curtains over the window to catch any drafts. They had moved his bed beside the fireplace, where he lay covered in a stack of thick blankets and furs. Yet he still shivered underneath.

Maps had gone below and another man had taken his place. She recognized him from their crew, but had never had the chance to speak with him.

"How is he?" she asked.

"Ah, yes, Song." He stared up at her as though she had appeared out of thin air. "Sorry, off in my own world." His eyes were small, his hair losing its color and his skin was weatherbeaten. He noticed her scrutiny. "I'm not as old as I look. Dash just aged better than me."

"You're the doctor," she said.

"And Doctor is what they call me. You're very good at staying away from me. Partly because Dash just *has* to tend to you himself. You're like his little pet, aren't you?"

She folded her arms over her chest and clenched her jaw. "How is Leslie?"

"Sorry, didn't mean to offend. Whispers—Leslie—should be fine. He needs a day or two to sweat it out and then a few more to recover fully, but it's not going to kill him."

"I'm sure he'll be fine by the time we're able to leave port."

"How is it outside?"

She held her hand out against her sternum, palm parallel to the floor to indicate how high the accumulated snow was. "And still falling."

He shook his head and shivered despite the heat. Song let herself out, shutting the door to keep the heat in. A door at the end of the hall groaned, then rumbled as a pounding set upon it from the other side. She stepped with apprehension to it, then yanked it open. Standing atop the snow, looking winded and grumpy, was Shadow.

"Don't just stare! Although a short man stuck in a door is quite hilarious. I'd like to get *out* of the cold." He reached a hand up and she took it, planting her feet on the door frame to pull him up.

"Why is there a door up here that leads outside?" Song asked as she shut out the wind.

He looked from her to the door, then back. "You're really asking that question?"

She shrugged, embarrassed. "What are those?" She pointed at strange flat things secured to his boots.

"Snowshoes. They keep you from sinking in and getting lost until spring."

"Why did you come to this door?"

"How many questions can you possibly ask?" he grouched, then sighed. "I overestimated the height of the snow. I thought it would at least be high enough for me to reach the knob."

She pursed her lips, preparing to say something she knew would put him out. "Last I saw, the front door was clear enough to enter."

The look of desperate frustration that spread across his face made Song bite back a laugh at his expense. "Of course it is." He tossed his snowshoes at the wall and strode to the stairs. "I'm here for men. I hope you and your lover will volunteer."

"I'm sure you know he's not my lover, and he is actually very ill."

"No matter. Come."

She followed him to the tavern below, where he stood on a table and shouted for attention.

"The snow is getting deeper by the hour." His voice boomed through the room, demanding a respect one of his stature would not command in normal circumstances. "If we do not do something, the roofs could collapse and everyone will die." He let that sink in before continuing. "I need men to go out with me to knock the snow from the rooftops and clear it away from windows and doors."

Song waited to see who volunteered. A few men raised their hands. Bells shrugged his shoulders up to his ears and turned back to the fire, where he was keeping warm. Of the thirty-odd men in the tavern, only five volunteered. It was not a pleasing number, and Song could see the frustration pawing at Shadow.

"You don't need any men," a voice rasped from the stairs. Leslie leaned against the wall wrapped in a fur, looking spent but determined to get where he was going. His lips were pale and cracked, his skin was white as snow, and his hair stuck to his face, though he was no longer sweating.

"You should be in bed," Song chastised. She hated that for a moment she sounded like her mother. "Where is Doctor?"

He smirked. "Couldn't take the heat, I suppose."

Song helped him to a chair.

"Before you kill yourself with overexertion, tell me, friend, what could I possibly need more than men?"

Leslie motioned at her. "Song." The barmaid gave him a bowl of broth and some hot tea and that was the end of anything he would say.

"Is the man delirious?" Shadow asked. "Or is there more than meets the eye with you?"

"No," Dashaelan barked his objection. "I won't have it."

"I've never done anything…quite like this," she admitted.

"Song can't do it," Dashaelan growled.

Thumbs rubbed his lower lip with the side of his thumb. "I think Song can, Dash."

"You're not doing this. That's an order."

She turned to face Dashaelan, stubbornness setting her lips in a hard line. "You heard what he said. The snow's got to be cleared. I can do this."

"If you disobey this order—"

"You'll throw me overboard. I know." She looked up to where Shadow waited for them to finish. "I'll do it. Stay inside. Stay warm."

"Here," the barmaid rushed up to shove something in Song's hands. "A bloke left them ages ago. That cold'll freeze your eyes in their sockets."

What she'd given her was a pair of strange goggles with gear work on the sides. A small knob on one gear turned all the rest and moved secondary lenses within. She assumed they worked like a telescope. She pulled them over her eyes and adjusted them so she could see.

"Nice look," Thumbs said, but she caught the hint of a laugh in his tone.

Ignoring him, she pulled the scrap of shirt back over her mouth and nose, then opened the front door of the tavern. The snow had risen, and she had to lift her knees high to step over what had filled in their path from earlier that day. She found a suitable spot where she could see every building within the city center. Turning her eyes to the roof of the tavern, she concentrated.

"Faw on-s ehth olb."

She waited nervously as nothing seemed to happen. Then the wind over the tavern picked up, swirling in a spiral made visible by the snow blowing within it and the streaking lines of white and blue light. It rose like a tornado until the roof shingles became visible, then it hovered in wait.

"Nehsho ehth oot."

The column turned at its middle and angled toward the cliff overlooking the ocean. Like a snake, it slithered away before plunging headlong over the side. Song stood in astonishment. She'd done it. She'd cleared the roof. But her exhilaration was short-lived as she counted the number of roofs in Talegrove.

"Ti vu law, on-s ehth relk."

It started as a low breeze on her hood. As the snow lifted around her, it intensified. It was beautiful. She was at the center of an illuminated, living snow globe. For a moment, she forgot where she was as she watched the snow spin around. The cobblestones became visible, and she laughed. She'd done this. She had cleared the snow away, and it was now swirling around her in gale-force winds like a blizzard at the mercy of her every whim. It should have blown her away, she knew, but it didn't. She remained with her feet planted on the ground.

Or did she? Curiosity took her over, and she lifted one leg. Then the other. She jumped just a little. Then she spun around for momentum and jumped higher. Her feet always found their way back to the street below. She lifted the goggles, resting them atop her head to see the glory of her accomplishment unhindered. She threw her arms wide and spun in quick circles. The snow shifted and spun opposite. She threw both arms left; the snow swirled together in a funnel and passed so close in front of her, she could touch it. She pointed her arms straight right, and the serpentine snows changed direction to follow where she indicated.

Laughter filled the air as the winds took her own and blew it around, echoing it from the buildings and the street. Her voice should have been lost, she knew, but it was amplified and sent back to her. Song began to dance. She danced alone, but the snow danced with her. It spun around her in excited circles, lifting her into the air and twirling her like a music box ballerina. It turned her this way and that as she moved in cadence with a tune only she and the *kijæm* understood. Then it set her down on the cobblestones. She slipped on a patch of ice; the snow column spun behind and pushed her back upright before she fell. She was breathless and tired as she pulled her mask down around her neck so it could see her smile.

"*Oowe k'naith.*" She curtsied, and the snows gathered into a thick column which bent as though bowing. "*Nehsho ehth oot.*" She pulled the goggles back over her eyes and adjusted them so she could better see the spectacular plummet of an entire village-worth of snow over the side of the cliff. The winds stopped, and the snow returned to falling in the lazy way it had been before.

It was then that she noticed her audience, which had gathered in the doorways and windows of the various buildings across Talegrove. She set her mask over her mouth once more, this time to hide her slightly embarrassed face. Song picked her way back to the tavern, avoiding ice patches left behind. She entered the doorway, keeping her head low.

"I've seen a lot of things in my years," Shadow said, a bright smile across his face, "but I have never seen a Magic dance with their *kijæm.*"

"Happy to oblige," she said.

A few steps into the tavern, she began to feel strange. Her skull seemed to vibrate as pain radiated within it. She fell to her knees and held her head in her hands. It burned behind her eyes and blinded her. It forced a scream from her throat before she fell to the floor, unconscious.

Twenty-Eight

SONG WOKE TO A POUNDING IN HER HEAD. HER VISION WAS foggy, and she felt as though her entire body was weighed down. As far as she could tell, she was alone. She wished she wasn't. She wanted a glass of water for her cotton-dry mouth and she wanted someone to explain to her what had happened.

"Hello?" she called, but her voice sounded far away and muffled.

Determination took hold, and she began rocking side-to-side until she was able to roll over using the momentum. One arm flopped over the side of the bed to dangle above the floor, while the other became trapped beneath her. Tearless little sobs of frustration humphed through her nose. Slow footsteps approached her. She tried to look up but only caught sight of a boot dragging its sole across the floor. Hands set upon her and rolled her onto her back.

"You should be in bed," she said to Leslie.

He sat beside her, tired from the small adventure, though he looked much healthier. "You called for help and now you're chastising me? I can roll you back over."

She let out a defeated sigh. "Thank you."

"Where were you trying to go?"

"I want a drink of water."

He patted his pockets and furrowed his brow. He held up one finger for her to wait, then left the room. A short while later, a barmaid swept into the room with a pitcher of water; a chunk of clean, white snow melting in the center. She moved a small table to the side of the bed and set the pitcher and a glass on top. Once the barmaid had gone, Song set about drinking three full glasses of the water; the cold soothed the burning in her skull and cooled down to her stomach. It was a bit longer before Leslie crept back into her room. He backed in, checking behind him as he closed the door.

"Doctor has her making sure I stay in bed," he explained as he sat beside her once more. "She's so busy making sure the men coming in from outside get something hot to drink that she hardly has any time to throw me back into bed."

"Have you been wandering about?"

"Mostly just in and out to check on you."

"How long was I out?"

"Overnight and the better part of a day." He took in her nervous expression. "I'm sure you just overexerted yourself with that…quite extraordinary display of power yesterday. Did you tell it to do all that?"

"No, I only lifted the snow. The rest just…happened." She smiled at the memory. "It was absolutely amazing."

"It was quite spectacular to watch." He motioned beside her. "Mind if I…?"

She scooted sideways. "By all means."

Leslie lay beside her and stared up at the ceiling. "Song?"

"Hmm?"

"You were right."

"I'm always right. Except when I'm wrong."

A chuckle hissed through his teeth. "Well, this time you were very right. I should've gotten a coat."

"Gloating just doesn't feel right in your current condition."

They stayed in a comfortable silence for a minute, both staring at the ceiling as footfalls moved across it.

"So, tell me about Tsingsei Gould. What sort of woman is she?" he said.

"Why? Do you fancy her?"

"I am merely curious."

"She was born in Garda to Elroy and Annie—"

"No, not like that. I don't want what the history books will say when we're all gone. I want to know about *you*. How does the girl who has everything end up pirating her way across the globe, terrified of returning to her comfortable life?" Leslie's eyes searched hers, and she felt he may find the answers without her having to say them.

"It's no secret among the men that I fancy ladies. But in Garda, admitting such a thing means the end of your social standing. It would mean shame on my mother and father—shame neither of them would abide. A girl I'd only just met discovered how I felt. I was terrified of my secret coming to light. So I ran."

"A simple secret is not a reason to run from all of that. Your parents have the means to cover up the scandal." He shivered and pulled some of her blanket over to share.

"My father, if he had the time to pay attention, would have hired someone to cover it up. My mother would've tried to fix me."

"I don't think that's something you can fix."

"I didn't want to find out." She stared at the ceiling for a long moment in silence. "I never felt right in that life. All the expectations and the formalness of it. 'Keep your chin up, Tsingsei.' 'Don't climb the trees, Tsingsei.' 'Ladies do not play the violin.' 'Ladies do not dance like that.' Mother even had me practicing speaking higher."

"What's wrong with your voice?"

"'It's too low for a lady.'" She balled a fist in anger.

His eyebrows rose and Song assumed he'd made the connection to how she'd spoken in Tamminpring.

"She fed me as much dessert as she could, hoping I would fatten up and fit into that perfect little mold all the ladies are formed in. And always, *always* having to stay up to date with fashions, and the tightlacing…it made me hate corsets."

"A woman should never be judged by her figure," he agreed. "There is nothing wrong with you, Song. The way Andalisian aristocrats wear corsets now is unnatural, anyway. Dangerously tight. You know, they don't even wear them in Aibhànocht, Armalinia, or Kerriwen? Then again, the latter are both desert countries and it's much too hot for…" He grew silent and observed her. "What did I say?"

Song blinked tears back into her eyes. "Just nice to hear someone say it, I suppose."

He wrapped his arm behind her head and gave her shoulders a comforting squeeze. "You are who you are. No one should say you're wrong for it."

She let him comfort her for a moment before shoving him. "Don't get all sappy on me now."

He chuckled and removed his arm from behind her. "Right, sorry. Forgot you abhor men."

"I do not," she growled.

"When they touch you."

She punched his shoulder. "That's not how it works."

"Then how does it work?" he asked.

She glared at him.

"I'm serious! I haven't really met anyone like you before… that I know of. Well, none that would answer questions."

"I don't find men attractive, is all." She shrugged. Her eyelids were growing heavy, but she fought against them.

"What about a very pretty man?"

"Are you asking for yourself?"

He scoffed. "I'm not pretty."

Oh, but he was, Song thought. Perhaps not as pretty as William had been, but she could see how other women might fawn over him. She snorted on a laugh, then turned to hide her amusement in his shoulder.

"What?"

"Give me a moment."

"Are you saying I am pretty?" he demanded.

She laughed harder and shook her head. "No, not nearly pretty enough." She took a few controlling breaths. "Besides, I'm quite sure I could never be attracted to any sort of man, pretty or not."

They lay in silence for a minute before Leslie took a contemplative breath. "What about a handsome woman?"

Song didn't try to stifle her laughter this time as she shoved against him. He joined in her humor, smiling as he batted her hands away. Song stopped, realizing the exertion was too much for her.

"I'm just going to rest my eyes for a moment," she said, closing her eyes as she rolled onto her back.

"Song?"

"Hmm?" She didn't open her eyes.

"I'm sorry…about last night. I don't know why I—"

"Shh."

"I just want you to know—"

"Resting now. Shut up."

"I'll keep watch," he said.

But her lips refused to make another sound.

Song woke some hours later, the world outside still grey and boots scraping along the roof above her. She turned over and stopped short to avoid colliding with Leslie's back. She realized right off that he was sleeping and decided not to wake him. As she thought of a way to exit the bed without jostling the man, she stared at the back of his head. His hair, usually tied low over his neck, was loose and falling to the side to reveal something hidden behind. She lifted her hand to push his auburn hair to the side. She bit into her cheek to control the gasp that tried to explode from her.

At the center of Leslie's neck was a mark. It stood out as a scar but had been tattooed over in black. She knew she shouldn't touch it, but she did anyway. She traced her fingertip along the outer line of the circle, which encompassed a strange symbol like a bird. Leslie's hand shot to hers, gripping it so tight her fingers ached against each other. Neither moved as Song bit back the pain in her hand.

She swallowed and choked out the only thing that came to mind. "I'm sorry."

He didn't say anything, just released her hand and sat up to rub his palms along his face, keeping his back to her.

"What is it?"

He looked over his shoulder, an eyebrow raised at her curiosity. "What does it look like?"

"A tattoo…and a scar."

"Well, that's what it is." He stood and strode to the door.

"What's it for?"

He took the doorknob in his hand and stopped, staring down at it as though the metal held his answers. "It's how they tell who you belong to." His eyes met hers.

She did her best to hide her shock. "Will we be resuming training anytime soon?"

He smiled. "I thought you were done with that?"

Song swallowed her pride. "There is still much I don't know."

"True." He thought about it. "We'll resume once we're back on the Bounty."

"Brilliant!"

He cocked an eyebrow and opened the door. "Good morning, Song."

"Good morning, Leslie."

Song was enjoying a hot breakfast down in the tavern, though it was past noon. Shadow hopped onto the bench beside her. She acknowledged him, but continued to shovel food into her mouth. He asked for a warm cider, then smirked at Song.

"That's quite a lot of food for such a small girl," he said so only she could hear, humor pinching his words.

She swallowed what was in her mouth. "I've been asleep for a day."

"Even so."

They sat in silence for a long time after he received his cider. He sipped it, pinching his lips against the heat of it.

"How goes the snow-clearing?"

"Nearly done, since the storm let up."

"Need me to—"

"Don't even think about it. Dashaelan would skin me alive. He's quite fond of you."

"And I of him."

Shadow turned to face her. "Your crew speaks highly of you."

She scoffed. "Flattery, I'm sure."

He leaned closer to whisper at her shoulder. "And is a fifty-thousand quoine sum on your apprehension also flattery?"

Shock rippled through her. Song didn't reply as she picked at her eggs, glad he could not see the roundness of her eyes for her raised hood.

"Few can change the entire nature of themselves to be completely unrecognizable from who they once were. I applaud you."

"Who said I changed my nature?" she replied, thinking back on their conversation days before.

"Habits, I suppose, would be the proper word. Patrician to pirate."

"You know everything, don't you?"

"I make it my business to know everything."

"Then you know of Captain Darian."

Shadow scrutinized the side of her hood. "What interest have you in such a man?"

"He tried to kill me once."

"He's not known to have ever failed at killing."

"I was knocked overboard. My *kijæm* saved me."

Shadow smiled. "I'd like to see the look on his face to discover his failure at killing a mere girl."

Song returned his smile. "He took my companion, a young boy. Fifteen at the time."

"When was this?"

"About a year ago, give or take."

"He's docked here in that time. What would this boy have looked like?"

She opened her mouth to answer, then stopped. She'd never memorized Altain's face, and it had been so long. "Time seems to have worn my memory to almost nothing."

"Think on it. Even the smallest details could help."

"Green eyes. Dark hair."

"Name?"

"Altain."

"Altain, what?"

She pursed her embarrassment between her lips. "I don't know. He never told me. He's the one who took me out into the world for an adventure."

"On a stolen skyship. Did you know it was stolen?"

She laughed. "I'm not an idiot."

"Well, I'll keep my eyes open for a green-eyed boy named Altain. If I see him, should I deliver a message?"

"Only that Song is looking for him." She rolled a piece of egg around her plate. "Everyone else says he's probably already dead."

"Maybe." Shadow tipped back his mug to finish the contents.

"I can't accept 'maybe'. It's torture, living like this. In my mind, Altain is both alive and dead. He's in a state of suspension until I know for sure."

"And what's the harm in searching for the answer?"

"Is there harm?"

"None at all." He spun around and hopped from the bench, dropping a quoine by his mug. "Good day, Song."

"Good day, Shadow."

Twenty-Nine

AFTER A WEEK STRANDED IN TALEGROVE, THE CREW PACKED up and made a swift escape for warmer climes. Leslie had recovered; the zeppelin remained intact; and Dashaelan wasn't stuck in a perpetual sour mood because of the snowfall.

A week out in the open air later, Song woke to the sound of Leslie's boots on the stairs. She'd learned to recognize the way he balanced on the balls of his feet, the heels barely tapping at the wood underfoot. Regular footsteps, like the slow stomping of Sunshine or the light and springy steps of Bells, didn't wake her. Only those soft ones, which could be mistaken for any old noise a skyship might make. She gritted her teeth in annoyance. Their vacation was over. They were no longer friends, having civilized conversations, and attending grand parties. She should have expected it when he said they'd resume training, but somehow her mind had left this part out.

This morning, she decided she would not allow him to throw her from the hammock. Silent as a breath of wind, she hopped from her hammock onto the balls of her feet, crossed the room, and hid behind a cannon. He came in and glanced at the hammock, realizing right off that it was empty. He scanned the room. Once he was turned away from her, Song leapt at him, landing across his back with her arms around his neck, trying to drag him to the floor. He gripped her wrists and lurched forward, throwing her over his shoulder and onto her back.

Song didn't wait for him to make the next move. She threw her leg up to kick him away, and rolled onto her feet to run at him. She jumped to kick him in the chest, but he caught her ankle and threw her back to the floor. A growl rumbled through her chest as he dragged her. Rogue splinters pushed their way through her undergarments into her shoulder blades and right buttock. After wriggling free, she rolled backward onto her feet.

They fought, jabbing at each other with fists and flattened palms. Song landed a well-timed kick to his stomach, knocking him to the floor. Without a second thought, she clambered to straddle him and pinned him down. One hand wove through his hair as the other searched in the darkness for some sort of weapon—she only found a fuse wrench. Their eyes locked as their breathing broke the silence in the hold. His skin shivered under the cold steel of the two sharp prongs pressed to his throat.

"Time to train?" she asked.

Leslie smiled, set his hands around her waist, and lifted her off him. After pushing to his feet, he extended a hand to help her up. "Good morning, Song." He released her hand and left the hold.

"That's it?" she called after him as he began up the stairs.

He smirked over at her but didn't stop.

"That's all you wanted?" She threw the fuse wrench to the floor in frustration. "Wait! Are we going to train?" She pulled one of her oversized shirts over her head, shoved on her boots, and stomped out on deck.

Leslie sat, polishing his sword.

"Explain yourself."

He cocked an eyebrow at her. "I think you're the one that needs to explain their attire." He stared at her bare knees.

She shifted uncomfortably. "I got splinters."

"Where?" he asked.

She pursed her lips and looked away from him.

He raised his eyebrows in understanding. "Would you like me to—"

"No."

"But I'm trained in—"

"No!" She spun to stomp away.

"Song." He trotted after her, taking her by the elbow. "They can get infected, you need to—"

"Bugger off!"

Sunshine snorted from the helm. An entertained gleam sparked in his eye as he caught her gaze. "As much as I hate to agree with Whispers, he's right."

"See?" Leslie said. "Now, please let me help—"

"I will not be stared at like one of those paper prostitutes!"

"Ugliest prostitute I ever seen," Sunshine said.

"You," she turned and pointed a threatening finger at him, "button it, old man!"

Dashaelan exited his cabin, looking disturbed and rumpled. His gaze swept over Song and his brow furrowed. "What the bloody hell is going on out here?"

"Song's got splinters," Sunshine announced, as though it was the juiciest gossip he'd ever heard.

"Where?"

She said nothing, but Leslie's expression gave it away.

Dashaelan's eyebrows raised in embarrassment. "Do you need help?"

Song pinched her lips together as her eyes flashed a warning. She balled her fists and held them up in frustration before stomping below deck.

"They could get infected, you know!" Dashaelan shouted after her.

Song knelt before a lantern, her shirt raised and her underpants lowered beneath the injured buttock to assess the damage. Boots scraped in the doorway. Leslie stood just inside, holding a steaming bucket of water. She dropped her shirt, ignoring the uncomfortable position of her underpants just long enough so she could tell him to leave. But he didn't.

He strode to her, set the bucket down and wrung out a clean cloth that had been soaking within. The water smelled sweet, like honey. Without a word, he wrapped his arm through hers, gripped her bicep, and jerked her to him. She didn't have time to be indignant over the rough treatment as he lifted her long shirt and set the hot cloth on her buttock. She gasped at the heat and tried to pull away, but he held her tight. Then he released her arm and forced her hand to hold the cloth in place.

"How dare you!" she said.

He didn't reply as he swished another clean cloth through the bucket.

"How dare you treat a lady so obscenely!"

His eyes caught hers as he took the other towel flat in his palm. "Where else?"

She pursed her lips, refusing to answer.

He began pulling her shirt up, and she gripped the bottom. "My shoulders!"

He shoved her forward. She supported her weight with her free hand and gritted her teeth in embarrassment. Leslie lifted her shirts high enough to discover the splinters while keeping the front low to prevent any indecent exposure. The hot cloth spread along her shoulder blades before he sat back on his heels, turning to look away from her.

"I don't see any ladies on this ship," he said.

She huffed at him.

He smirked, glancing over to meet her glare. "She got left behind in Jashedar."

"You still shouldn't be looking at me."

"Did I actually *look* at you, though?" he asked. "Pride is fine, as long as you don't go killing yourself over it."

"I wasn't killing myself."

"Stronger men have died to less."

She let out a breath of frustration. "Thank you."

"You're welcome. That will help clean the area, but it won't remove the splinters. You can either let one of us—"

"One of who?" she demanded.

"Dash and I have some medical training, but your best choice is Doctor."

"My best choice is myself," she said.

"Song, you need to trust me. All of us. We're not out to make some lewd display of you. You're our crew mate. Some of the men call you lad."

Song chewed on the inside of her lower lip. "I'm still getting used to such indecency." She whispered to her *kijæm,* and the swirling mist and blue lights converged on her injuries. Her flesh stung as the splinters pushed out from within her skin. She winced as it continued to sting.

"All set?"

She cringed. "Didn't feel any better coming back out."

He pulled the cloth from her shoulder blades, hunching over her to assess the damage. "This floor has been neglected. I'll tell Dash to get a swabby down to smooth it."

"Thank you." She sat up as he pulled her shirt down. Song held her palm to his chest. "I think I can check this one on my own, thank you."

"I honestly wasn't even going to offer."

"So," she began, brushing leftover splinters away from her skin, "you learned all this in Pishing?" She pulled her underpants up and stood to dress.

"Yes, I used to visit an orphanage and my—... Someone I knew was training to be a nurse under Madam Pim."

Song stopped to stare at him. He stopped and stared right back. Neither said anything for a long while. Leslie swallowed.

Song took a small breath. "Pim?"

Leslie breathed out, as though relieved. "Yes. She was a great woman."

"But her name was actually Pim?"

He chuckled. "Not everyone hides behind an alias, Song." He studied her carefully. "What's wrong with Pim?"

"Nothing," she said. "It's just not a name one typically hears."

"Have you heard it?"

"I have."

"Where?"

Embarrassment settled on her cheeks as she busied herself with her coat. No way was she going to tell Leslie of her collection and her first and favorite doll, not when he was finally treating her like a woman rather than some brat who didn't belong on a pirate skyship.

"Are you hungry?" she asked as she strode past him. "I'm famished."

"I could really use a bite, yes." He stood and busied himself with the bucket.

Neither made eye contact as they made their way to the galley, as though secrets could be read in their eyes.

Thirty

Pirates. That's what was on the horizon. It was a small ship. Song half hoped it was the Dauntless. Though being honest, she had no idea what she would do once she found Altain. She didn't want to leave her new family or her new life. But there was also the possibility at the back of her mind that maybe Altain really hadn't survived the first day.

She grumbled and made her way across the deck to descend, knowing Dashaelan would tell her to get on the cannons. Leslie hooked an arm around her waist and carted her away like a child, then deposited her behind the mast.

"You stay here. Use the mast as cover."

"But—"

"That's an order," Dashaelan said behind her. They exchanged smiles as he handed over the flatblade she used for practice. "Whispers."

"Captain?"

"Anything happens to her—"

"I won't let it."

Dashaelan sized him up, then gave a curt nod before striding away to bellow orders to his men.

Song clasped her belt once she'd secured the scabbard. "Did you—?"

Leslie tapped her nose and smiled. "You've earned it. Just don't go proving me wrong. It took a lot of convincing to get you up here."

"I won't let you down," she promised.

"Good, I'm counting on you to have my back." He flicked her hood over her head and turned to scan the horizon.

"Go, I've got your back."

"Song," he set a hand on her shoulder, "I trust you. Trust yourself."

She smiled as he ran to the railing and gripped a rope to swing over. Everything moved like a symphony. They shot the harpoons to catch the other vessel and pull it closer, and helped secure it with grappling hooks. She'd seen that method when Darian had apprehended the Dauntless. The men swung over and the fighting began in a clash of glinting swords and ferocious shouts.

There wasn't much Song could do from her position, so she lowered her goggles and extended the view to see the action better. Toothy, at the bow of the enemy vessel, had a man pressed against the railing. Another man emerged from below deck and approached from behind. Song unholstered her sidearm, aimed, and squeezed the trigger the way Shadow had taught her. Her mouth twisted down at the corners in horror as her bullet entered the man's forehead and exploded out the back.

Toothy glanced behind himself, then at Song, his mouth agape. "What the bl—" he mouthed before the man against the rail interrupted him with a punch.

"Careful not to hit our own, Song!" Dashaelan shouted.

"Aye, captain!" she growled back, trying to keep her voice as boyish as possible.

The other crew realized their main competition was Leslie. Soon they surrounded him, and Song couldn't get a clean shot. Dashaelan had told her to stay put, but she'd also been told to watch Leslie's back. She unsheathed her sword and raced to the edge of the ship before Dashaelan could stop her or she changed her mind. She launched herself over the side into the open air between the vessels.

"*Saw'rkuh em er'æk,*" she whispered. Her *kijæm* swirled beneath her, propelling her over the distance and setting her on the deck.

"Song!" Dashaelan barked.

She ignored him and began fighting her way to Leslie.

"I told you—"

"To watch *your* back!" She brought her sword up to block the man aiming for Leslie.

Leslie held up his own sword over her shoulder to stop another aimed at her. "Watch your own back!"

"How about we watch each other's?" she said.

They spun to stand back to back. The men came at her, swords slashing. She spent more time parrying and blocking their blades than fighting. The muscles in her arm grew tired and sore from the impacts, which vibrated through her bones.

"Would you like to end this fight already?" Leslie asked.

"What?"

"*Kijæm.*"

"I thought you'd never ask." She called up the words to knock the men away.

An enemy pirate ran across the ship and tackled Song. Her sword skittered across the deck, out of reach. She kicked him away and rolled to find a weapon. A stray dagger lay abandoned, so she took it in her hand. When the man came at her again, she kicked him in the chest and slashed at his throat. His trachea split open, and he fell to his knees. Song took him by the hair, but faltered and released him. He fell to the deck, gagging on his blood.

Song's frown returned as she stared on in horror. "Why isn't he dead?" she said. "I slit his throat! Why isn't he—" She had to fight back the vomit creeping up her own throat as he continued to gag at her feet. "I'm sorry."

Leslie pushed her away and knelt. "I'm so sorry," he said to the man, then slit his throat in one swift movement. Then he stood, casting a stern gaze on her. "We'll practice that later."

Dashaelan swung across as they worked to bind the enemies. He took Song by the back of the coat and shoved her to the helm, where he pointed a finger in her face. "You were told to stay at the mast."

"I was—"

"Don't! Don't you make excuses, Song. You disobeyed an order and you could've gotten killed, or compromised your crew."

"But I didn't!"

He hit the flat of his palm on the back of her head. "Just because it didn't happen this time, doesn't mean it never will."

Song studied him, their jaws squared at each other. "You're just mad because I scared you."

"No—"

"You don't want anything to happen to me."

"That's not what I—"

"You love me!" She threw her arms over his shoulders. "Admit it, old man, or I'm not letting go."

"All right, all right! I love you, Song."

She released him.

He hit his open palm to the back of her head again. "Don't do it again."

"No promises. Hey, can I help with the interrogations?"

"Killing two men isn't satisfying enough for you?"

She gave a coy shrug and followed him down to the main deck.

The others had tied up the enemy crew, who were now kneeling on the deck. At the bow, someone had deposited the dead. She studied the faces of the defeated men as Dashaelan asked them questions. The rest of her crew looted the sky-ship's cargo. As Dashaelan had said, the men insisted upon knowing nothing of Captain Darian's whereabouts. Song scoffed and kicked her heel into the planks. But something caught her attention, the way one of the crew fidgeted. It was a fashion similar to the way Pinch would squirm when playing cards and he had a good hand.

Her gun was out as she crouched in front of the man, pressing the barrel into the soft flesh under his jaw. "What do you know?"

"Nothin'!"

"Song?" Dashaelan growled from the end of the line.

"He's a liar," she insisted.

"I don't know nothin'!"

"You're lying!"

"Song, would you—"

"I ain't lyin'!"

"Song!"

"Stop—" she hit the butt of her revolver against the side of his head, "—lying!"

"I ain't—"

"Song!" Dashaelan's hand wrapped around hers as she raised it to hit the man again. He ripped the gun from her grasp.

"*Gehl si'h kairb!*" Blue-lit mist erupted from her, converging on the other man's shin.

The crunch of his breaking bone set everyone else in stunned silence, but him into painful screaming.

"Stop lying to me! You know where Darian is?"

"All right!" the man beside him shouted. "I know something!"

"What?"

"He's got the Dauntless docked up. Been flying another skyship."

"Which one?" She pressed her palm against the break in his leg.

"I don't know."

"Why?"

"He's evading you lot! And no wonder!"

Song growled. "What about a boy? Is there a boy on his crew?"

"I don't know his crew. I only know rumors."

She pointed a finger between his eyes. "Next time, speak up when you're asked a question."

He leered and spat at her feet.

She stood and ripped her gun from Dashaelan's hand. "I wasn't going to shoot him. I'm not an idiot."

"After earlier, I couldn't be too sure."

She pursed her lips at him, and he chuckled. "At least I got an answer."

"And how true of an answer do you think it is?" Dashaelan asked. His stern gaze bored into her, and she pursed her lips.

"Why would he lie?"

"So you'd stop."

"Who are you, boy?" a man on his knees asked.

"Song," she replied. "Caleb Song."

"Watch your back, Song."

She smiled. "Is that a threat?"

"You go searching for Darian... When you find him, you'll be sorry you did."

"No. He'll be sorry he ever crossed me." She turned her back to him and walked with Dashaelan to the edge of the ship.

"I never had the stomach for torture," Dashaelan said.

"Because you have honor."

"And you don't?"

She watched the men load their haul into the cargo net to be swung back over to the Stars' Bounty. "I'm sure if I had more patience, I might have honor. But until I find Darian, I'll use whatever means necessary to find my friend."

"How well did you know this boy you seek?"

She thought over her answer. "I only knew him a month. We swore to be partners and to stick together no matter what. He's the only friend I've got."

He chuckled. "You've got me."

"And you see what I did for you. All right, he was the first friend I ever had."

"You're loyal to a fault, Song."

Footsteps pounded on the deck behind them. Toothy shouted from the bow. The man who'd answered her questions shoved Dashaelan sideways and tackled Song from behind. They tumbled over the railing.

"*Em chæk!*" The bright mist swarmed around her and turned her upright.

The man clung to her coat to keep from falling to the mountains below. As he tugged on her coat, she wrapped her fingers around his fists and pried at them, but he was determined to hold on. He pulled himself up high enough to punch her jaw. She reciprocated, landing her own blow directly on his nose. They exchanged more hits as he clung to her. He'd slip down, then work his way up her torso.

She unholstered her gun and set it under his jaw. "You should've stayed kneeling."

The top of his head exploded as the boom of her revolver shattered the air. Blood splashed across her face. He tumbled through the air. His corpse found the edge of one of the crevasse lips, then slid sideways to be swallowed by the black scar on the mountainside. Once back on deck, she kept her revolver gripped in her palm and glared at the others.

"Anyone else want to have a go at me?"

"Song!" Dashaelan strode to her. With the flick of his wrist, he pulled her hood back over her head.

"The infamous Krell traveling with a woman?" a man scoffed.

Song strode forward and pressed her gun to his forehead. "My name is *Caleb* Song. Do you understand me?"

His breath came hard as he contemplated this. "Yes, *sir*."

"Good. May you have a long and boring life spreading the word that Caleb Song is looking for Captain Darian. And I *will* find him. When I do—" she shoved her toe into the other man's broken leg, "—he'll wish I went this easy on him." She spun to find Dashaelan eyeing her. "Captain."

"Song."

She strode to the edge of the ship and let her *kijæm* carry her across. As calm as she could, she walked below deck. Once out of sight, she rushed to the galley and grabbed a bucket to vomit into. When she finished, she found a rag to wash her face. It was getting easier, that much she could admit. Her stomach settled much faster than it had after she'd tortured and killed William. But was that a good thing? Or was she slowly losing herself to cruelty? She could feel Brute behind her and turned to smile up at him.

"Careful," he said.

"What?"

"They don't like it."

"Who?"

"The glitters." He took the rag from her and rubbed at a spot in her hairline, then down across her cheek and on her ear.

"I don't understand."

He smiled and gave his grunting laugh. "You will."

Thirty-One

IT WAS LATE IN THE EVENING. LANTERNS ILLUMINATED THE deck of the Stars' Bounty—their yellow glow cast the crew in strange, misshapen shadows. Leslie took Song by the elbow and they walked to the bow side of the mast, where they could be alone.

"Now, before you mutilate any more men—" he stooped and pulled a narrow double-edged dagger from his boot, "the easiest way to get the angle you want is to be behind your target. Do you trust me?"

"Of course I trust you."

He grabbed her wrist and spun her around, pinning her back to his chest. His arm slid beneath hers and wrapped over her shoulder so his palm could press against the back of her neck. He reached his right arm across her body and set the blade to her neck. A chill ran through her as she remembered all too well the last time a man had set a knife to her throat.

"Let me go." She couldn't hide the urgency in her whisper.

He released her. "I'm sorry."

"It's not your fault." Her fingertips found the scar on her neck.

Leslie lowered her collar to look at it. "This will never happen again, Song."

She shook off the dark memories and smiled. "I know. I have an excellent teacher."

"You're not talking about me, are you?" Dashaelan said behind her.

"You, too."

"Well, then, let me teach you something else." He grabbed the dagger from Leslie and pinned him against the mast with his forearm. Dashaelan set the dagger to Leslie's throat, just behind the bend of his jaw. He stared Leslie down for a minute before turning to make sure Song was paying attention—it was the first time she'd noticed they were near the same height. "If you're going to get a man from the front, make sure he's pinned. Start at one side—" he traced the tip of the dagger across Leslie's throat and to the other side, "—and go all the way around. Ear to ear." He released Leslie and turned the handle of the dagger to him; the latter accepted the offering. "They'll bleed out faster that way."

"We can practice tomorrow, if you've a mind for it," Leslie said.

"Yes, please."

"Goodnight, Song." He bent at the waist. "Captain."

When Leslie was below deck and out of earshot, Song laughed and turned her smile on Dashaelan. "You scoundrel!"

"What did I do?"

"You didn't want to show me how to slit a throat! You wanted to threaten Leslie!"

"Why would I do such a thing?" He turned for his cabin.

Song followed. "Because you're jealous?"

He scoffed. "Codswallop."

She thought about it. "Agreed." She made herself comfortable in a chair at the table to wait as he poured her a drink. "I don't know why you did it, but I know it wasn't to teach me."

A sheepish expression crossed his face. "Had to remind him who's in charge, is all."

Song gaped at him, then laughed. "He knows who's in charge!"

"Yeah, and now he's been reminded!"

"Leslie isn't the sort that needs reminding. He knows his place."

Dashaelan let the whiskey rest in his mouth before swallowing to answer. "What exactly does that mean?"

Song ran her fingertip along the rim of her glass. "Just trust me, Dash. He's no threat to your position as captain."

"That's not what I'm worried about. My crew is loyal to me. But men with his skill are a great asset, or a great danger."

"He's an asset." Song crossed her ankles on the tabletop.

"As long as he doesn't go getting ideas."

"What sort of ideas? Like taking on a military envoy or sacking a sailer?" She laughed. "Oh! We should sack a sailer!"

Dashaelan coughed into his glass. "Skyships do not sack sailers."

"Why not?"

"Because the logistics of it are a nightmare."

"Unless someone were to jump onto the sailer and incapacitate it so the skyship could hover overhead."

He furrowed his brow. "How did you get to think in such ways?"

She shrugged. "I suppose I'm just ambitious."

"You'll make an extraordinary pirate one day. Terrifying, even."

"I'm not a pirate now?"

"You're not terrifying now."

"So we can sack one?"

A laugh barked from his lips. "Not on your life, Song."

"But—"

"Find a man foolish enough to go onto a ship alone to incapacitate it and maybe, just maybe, we'll see about taking one."

"Does it *have* to be a man?"

"Song, you're not—"

"I'm sacking a sailer."

"Song," he warned.

"Dashaelan." She mimicked his tone.

He pointed a finger at her, then withdrew it to think.

"I'm doing it, Dash. You can't stop me."

He pursed his lips. "Get yourself to bed, Song."

"Goodnight, Captain," she singsonged.

"Goodnight, Song."

THE DAY CAME WHEN SONG DISCOVERED DASHAELAN'S GREATEST obsession. She entered his cabin unannounced and uninvited to find him and Sunshine sitting side-by-side at the table. Books, papers, and maps covered every inch of the surface. When they saw her, they began scooping up the items as though she'd caught them in some licentious secret. Before they could clear all of it away, she snatched up a paper and scanned the contents.

"Who is D.C.B.?"

"Don't worry about it," Dashaelan said, holding out his hand for it.

Song narrowed her eyes and kept the paper clutched in her fingers. "Who said I was worried?"

"Forget about it."

"You and I both know I won't do that."

Sunshine sat back and crossed his arms over his chest. "We've been poring over this rubbish for years, Dash. A new set of eyes couldn't hurt."

Dashaelan spread the items back across the table and motioned for Song to take a seat. She sifted through the pile, scanning the pages and assessing the maps.

"Duke Carey Barton," he said.

"*Barton?*" she asked. "As in the Bartons from Anarchaia?"

His brow furrowed. "You know them?"

She swallowed and forced a single shouldered shrug. "Just in passing, it's nothing too terribly interesting nor helpful to your cause."

Her mind drifted to her connection with the name. Somewhere in Andalise was a man she was supposed to have been married to right now, but it had been called off. She almost wondered if this man was her almost-husband, or if there was a brother. She hadn't bothered to pay attention at the time, and given the chance to go back in time and do it again, she probably still wouldn't.

"Proceed," she said.

Dashaelan cocked an eyebrow at her, but seemed to let it go. "Every year he makes a trip around the world in his unsackable skyship, giving audience to the most important people in the world so they may look upon the largest rojed known to man."

Song's eyes snapped wide. "The Jewel of Castildi!"

"Aye."

Years ago, her parents had allowed the duke into their home so they could view the red and yellow gemstone. They hadn't allowed Song to see it, but they'd said it was beautiful—and authentic, according to her parents' jeweler. In all the years in his possession, no one had ever stolen the Jewel. The few raids on his skyship had been disastrous failures.

"We've been collecting this information on him for years," Sunshine said, "and in all this, we still don't have any way onto that bloke's skyship. It's a damned fortress crewed by the finest officers."

"What about his home?" she asked.

"Even more difficult. From what I could gather, it's a fortress of a mansion in the middle of Anarchaia."

"That's the largest city in the South District of Andalise. It would be incredibly hard to get into, if not impossible."

She flipped through a journal belonging to some other man she'd never heard of as the two detailed a few of their ideas on how to take his ship. The feet of the chair clacked against the floor as she stopped tilting backward and sat upright, an idea forming in her mind. She turned the book and set it in front of them. Dashaelan cleared his throat. On one side was a rather detailed drawing of a nude woman;

across from it was Barton's greatest weakness revealed—women. Dashaelan tried to close the book.

"I didn't draw—"

Song stuck her index finger on the page to keep the book open. "I'm not interested in the drawing. Dash, this is your in!"

He read the other page and scowled. "What are you on about?"

"It's her," Sunshine said.

"Who? Her?" Dashaelan motioned at the nude drawing.

"No." Song laughed. "Me. I'm your in."

He pursed his lips. "And how would you propose we go about that? Use you as bait?"

She shrugged. "Doesn't matter what you call it. I already know how to be a damsel. All I'd need is to be in distress."

"What sort of distress?" Sunshine asked.

Song's eyebrow rose high over the other as she stared them both down. "Are you serious?" She laughed. "Please. Gents, I know you're at least a little more imaginative than you're being now."

"I won't allow it," Dashaelan growled. "Not even as pretend."

"You would pass up the Jewel of Castildi to preserve the mere notion of my virtue?"

"I will not allow the honor of a lady to come into question!"

"Dash, you're being an idiot," she said. "Who cares what anyone thinks of me, a nameless woman who will disappear from all memory the moment word spreads that Captain Krell is the first man in history to steal the Jewel of Castildi? No one will care if there was a woman involved, let alone if she was chaste or spoiled. It only needs to look like I'm in danger. You and I both know if anything were to get out of hand, the crew would have my back."

"Whispers would lay waste to every man in sight if anything happened to you," Sunshine said.

She gave him a strange look. "Only because Dash keeps threatening him."

Sunshine shrugged in reply.

Dashaelan sighed. "We'll talk more on this later, then. Flesh out a plan and make sure we can pull this off without a hitch. No lives lost, and no chastity compromised."

Song snorted and drank the whiskey in his glass. "What makes you think it hasn't already been?"

He barked a laugh. "Because of a man previously known as William."

"And if it were a woman?"

Sunshine snorted. "Please, you blush at the mere thought."

She laughed with them as they returned their attention to the maps and documents, studying them as they thought of the perfect plan.

Thirty-Two

THE HEIST WAS GOING FROM BAD TO WORSE, AND FAST. THE merchant vessel they'd intercepted was larger than the Stars' Bounty, with a crew at least twice their size. Several of Song's crew mates had sustained injuries. Cuts zig-zagged over Toothy's arms. Sunshine had a small nick on the back of his hand. Leslie had a deep gash in his shoulder.

After forming a swift plan, Song pulled her goggles over her eyes and took her sword in hand. She stepped with borrowed confidence from behind the mainmast to the center of the deck. She planted her feet and whispered to her *kijæm* so her voice would carry.

"I am going to say this only once." Her voice echoed across to the other craft and caught the attention of the fighting men. "Lay down your weapons and surrender your ship and all its cargo to us…or all of you will be swimming home."

Most of the other crew laughed, a few dropped their weapons on deck.

"We surrender nothing to pirates!" one shouted.

"Not true, I surrendered." One man with his hands in the air kicked his sword away as an example.

But Song had the answer she was looking for. *"Drobr'vo oork ehth kawn."*

A wave of spiraling bright mist and blue light blasted forward from all around her. Leslie and Sunshine each grabbed a man who'd surrendered and dragged them down to the deck; others followed suit. The wave hit the rest of the crew and knocked them up into the air to tumble end over end as it pushed them from the deck of their skyship and dropped them into a free-fall over the other side. Her *kijæm* spared those who'd surrendered, but had remained standing. They threw themselves to their knees, relieved to still be on deck.

Song smiled at Dashaelan. "Your turn."

He strode to her, lips pursed and fingers grasping for words. "I'm not saying you didn't do good," he said, "but we're not over the ocean."

"I…gave them a choice…?"

"Yes… There is that." He strode to the edge of the ship and swung across with one of the waiting ropes.

Just then, a deep boom shattered the air. It knocked Song from her feet as something impacted the side of the Stars' Bounty.

"Cannons!" Dashaelan shouted. A group rushed to get below the other deck, but Song was quicker.

"*Ryf-kæb.*"

Another boom sounded, but it didn't hit the Bounty. Shouting came from below deck. She rushed to assess the damage. The blast had taken a chunk out of the weapons hold, blown her trunk open, left a cannon dolly damaged, and reduced crates of various contents to shreds of sticks and metal. The cannoneers from that side of the ship collected themselves in a daze.

"Help!" the shout came again. It was Thumbs, hidden somewhere beneath the rubble.

"I'm here," she said. Splinters shot themselves into her palms as she grabbed the broken planks, scrambling to find Thumbs. A piece of wood had buried itself in his thigh. "Right, uh."

"Get Doctor."

"Yes, that. I'll do that." She ran to the cargo hold where the doctor usually stayed during skirmishes. "Thumbs," she shouted, "he's got a stick in his leg."

All calm, Doctor set down his book and grabbed his medical bag. "I suppose we'd better fix that." He smiled and patted her shoulder as he passed. "He's still at the cannon?"

Song nodded, taken speechless by his placidity.

She helped with the collection of cargo from the other vessel—a trade ship that hadn't yet reached its destination and so was filled to bursting with goods. They took only the most expensive items. The injured gathered in the weapons hold, where Doctor stitched their wounds. As the cargo hold neared full, Song carried a sack of fine silk dresses into the weapons hold. She stopped to stare at the bandaged men. Leslie and Thumbs leaned against the wall, their wounds covered, yet blood still soaked through the white dressings. She sat beside Thumbs and blinked as the two finished their conversation in a language she'd never heard before.

"Hello, Song." Thumbs wrapped an arm over her shoulders to pull her into a sideways hug.

"What in the world were you saying?"

They exchanged a look.

"Nothing important," he said.

"Thumbs was just explaining things to me," Leslie said.

Song shot Leslie a bitter look. "In another language?"

Thumbs laughed. "Kerri is easier on the tongue than Common."

They exchanged a joke in Kerri, and Song rolled her eyes. Leslie spoke the language as though it was native to him. Those around them paid no mind, as though used to the Kerri discussions between the two.

"You're still bleeding," she said after a few minutes.

"Do that thing," Thumbs said. He pulled his bandage down to show her the wound—it was rough and angry, trying to break open against the stitches.

"What thing?" she asked, holding back the urge to gag.

"The *kijæm* thing like you did to your neck. Please."

She whispered the words and a flurry of blue light converged on Thumbs's wound, then pulsed to orange. He gripped her shoulder and squeezed until it stung tears from her eyes. His breath hissed through his teeth and he grunted, knocking the back of his bald head against the wood behind him. The mist finished its task and dispersed.

Thumbs released her shoulder and patted it. "Sorry."

"Hurts worse than you expected?"

"A little, yes."

She directed her attention to Leslie. "Would you like—"

"Don't even think about it."

"I'm just trying to help."

"No."

She left to finish helping with whatever needed doing above deck. They were pushing off from the other vessel when Brute found her.

"Hello." His greeting was gentle, but his eyes were dark with worry.

"Hello, Brute."

"Help Leslie."

She squinted up at him. "Is he still bleeding?"

Brute nodded. "He's scared."

"Of?"

"Fire."

She realized why he'd refused her aid. Of course, he'd be wary of any sort of flesh-burning heat. "We're all afraid of something, Brute."

He laughed. "I didn't tell."

"I have no idea what you're talking about." She winked at him.

He followed her below deck, where she found Leslie glaring at Doctor; stubbornness had set his jaw square beneath his angry face. The bandage on his arm was filled and his blood now seeped down his bicep. Doctor strode to Song, a bitter smile stretching his lips thin.

"And how are you—"

"How is Leslie?"

"Defiant."

"His temperament?"

"Slightly drugged, though he fought it."

"And his wound?"

"Deep."

She scoffed. "I'm fine, thank you. Are the other men all right to leave?"

He shrugged. "Yes, they're all fine."

"Return to your posts," Song shouted.

Ponce and Pinch stopped securing the rough patch-job of planks over the hole and stared at her.

"Will it hold?" she asked.

"Should," Pinch said.

"Right. Leave. Come check it later. I need this room."

The crew filed out, Brute lending aid to Thumbs, who promised fresh stew for the night. When everyone was gone, she stood over Leslie. He stared up at her.

"I'll be out of your hair in a moment," he said. "I just need to…" He pushed against the floor.

"You're staying right there." She knelt over him, straddling his legs and sitting to pin him. "Do you trust me?"

"Song, don't."

"I trust *you*. Do you trust me?"

"Get off me."

She wrapped one hand under his jaw and squeezed until he looked into her eyes. "Pride is fine, so long as you don't go killing yourself over it."

"This isn't pride."

"Fear, then."

He pursed his lips. "Song—"

"I won't tell a soul. Just let me help you."

He glared at her and reached out to grab a stick from the rubble, which he wrapped in spare gauze and stuck between his teeth. With a curt nod, he signaled that he was ready.

"Smerks si'h snehl'ys."

Blue mist hovered around Leslie's throat and mouth, ready to quiet any noise he made.

"Dnoo'w si'h zy'ertawk."

Blue-lit mist slithered to his injury as she untied the bandage, letting it drop to the floor so she could press his shoulders down. He gripped her arms, pulling her closer on one side and pushing her away on the other. His wound was deep, and she thought maybe his fear was amplifying the pain. He bit into the wood and let loose a silent scream. Once finished, she released his voice and pulled him in a comforting hug.

"How old were you?" Her hand found the brand on his neck.

He didn't stop her from running her fingertips along the outer circle. "I'm not sure," he said. "Five, maybe six."

She growled in her throat and stood, leaning him backward against the wall. "Your country is full of barbarians."

"Not my country anymore."

"What do you call home, then?" She stooped to collect her belongings, which had been strewn about from the cannon blast.

"I had a flat in Tarn," he said. "But now? This is home."

"A bloody pirate ship?" She laughed.

He chuckled. "Not just a bloody pirate ship." His eyes fluttered. As he drifted closer to losing consciousness, his usual accent failed, like it had in Talegrove. "Something about *this* one. It's home. It's family."

She chewed on the inside of her cheek. "You might be delirious…but you're not wrong. I think it's Dash."

"It's not Dash," he murmured. "It's you."

"What do you mean?"

But he was too far gone to get any more answers from. With Brute's help, they moved Leslie into his hammock. She followed the smell of the stew Thumbs had promised into the galley. Song sat at the table with the injured men, making eye contact with each and acknowledging the truth in what Leslie had said. This was home. These were her brothers. She smiled and dug into her bowl of stew. The others returned her smile as they tucked in. No words needed to be said, not when they had the best stew of any ship, and each other. They were family.

Thirty-Three

 ONG MANNED THE HELM MORE OFTEN. SHE LOVED THE FEELING of being in control of the ship. Deciding where they would go—or at least having the illusion of deciding. Much of the time the captain chose, and she just steered them there. Of all the duties she'd participated in around the ship, this was easily one of her favorites. She closed her eyes and let the wind wash over her face as she breathed in the crisp morning air.

"Song?" Dashaelan shouted from the doorway of his cabin.

"Aye, Captain?"

"Happy birthday!"

"It's your birthday?" Toothy asked behind her. He and Maps hunched over the map of the world pinned to the table.

She shrugged. "I wouldn't even know what day of the week it is."

"How old are you, then?" Maps asked.

"Nineteen."

Their silence bothered her. She turned to eye them.

"I thought you were older," Toothy said.

"Older?"

"Just a couple of years."

She scoffed. "And how old are you?"

He opened his mouth to answer, then stopped. He counted on his fingers, but blinked as his expression remained confused. Toothy stood and scanned the deck below them. "Oy!" he shouted toward the bow. "Oy, Ponce!"

"What?" Ponce, the brunet swabby, shouted back.

"How old am I?"

Ponce stared at him for a long time, then lifted one hand to count. He paused the same way Toothy had and stared back at them. "I dunno! Twenty-five-ish?"

"Are you sure?"

"No." Ponce returned to scrubbing the deck.

Toothy shrugged. "We'll call it twenty-five."

Dashaelan emerged from his cabin some time later and took over the helm. "What say we celebrate your birthday properly?"

"You never celebrate the others'."

"Then we'll all have a birthday."

Sunshine ascended the stairs, rubbing a fist into his tired eyes. He dropped onto the stool Toothy had vacated and swallowed several gulps of tea from a mug.

"Sunshine, Dash is trying to show me favoritism," Song whined.

He scoffed. "Trying? He already does."

"I just want to give her a proper birthday celebration."

Sunshine leaned over the map on the table. After a moment of scrutiny, he stuck a pin in the western edge of Pishing. "There's an inn here. Don't ask no questions—"

"No!" Song and Dashaelan barked in unison.

Sunshine blinked at them. "I have to ask…"

"It's a rotten country, and I'd rather not pay any sort of visit," Dashaelan said.

"I know your reasons, Dash. But Song?"

She shrugged. "Yeah, what he said." To explain why she preferred they didn't go to Pishing was to betray Leslie's secret—which wasn't hers to tell.

"Liar." He pulled the pin from the map and stuck it into the land mass below Pishing. "Haven't got any problems with the savanna in Kerriwen, do you?"

"That'll do," Dashaelan said. He pointed. "You—"

"Maps," Song hissed under her breath.

"Maps, get us there." He gave Song a wry smile and let her take the helm. With a nod to each, he returned to his cabin.

Some hours later, without a word, Leslie lifted the pin from the map and moved it to a new location within Kerriwen. He patted Maps on the shoulder as the latter set to work adjusting their course. Leslie gave Song a small smile, and disappeared below deck.

They continued flying toward a huge conic mountain, which Maps told her was an extinct volcano on the edge of the country. They'd passed over it months before, she remembered. It was the mountain with the huge crags which had swallowed the man after he'd tried to drag her over the side of the ship to her death.

"Song!" Thumbs called.

She rushed below, leaving the wheel to Maps, to see what was so urgent. Thumbs gave her a bright smile and held out a pale blue silk bundle.

"What's this?"

"A gift. I found it in the cargo."

She unfurled the cloth to discover it was a dress. "It's beautiful!"

He smiled at her admiration. "I was not sure you would like a dress."

"I love dresses without the Armalinian corsets," she said. "There's just no place for wearing one aboard a pirate ship."

"Wear it now! For your birthday."

She smiled, and he grinned at the excitement glittering in her eyes. Song disappeared down the stairs to the weapons hold, where she stripped all but her knickers and pulled the article over her head. The dress was a style she'd never seen before. A panel of cloth covered her front, and it had a high collar that tied behind her neck, though it left her upper back bare. *Downright immodest*, her mother would have said. Song bit her lower lip to reign in the excitement that fluttered through her belly—an excitement caused by the mere notion that her mother wasn't there to stop her from wearing it. She replaced her boots and belt under the skirt—without the pouches but with her sidearm strapped around her thigh—then returned to Thumbs.

"It is Kerriwen fashion," he said. "It suits you beautifully. Brings out those beautiful blue *tirikurusan* gems you have for eyes."

Song blushed at the compliment as Thumbs unbraided her hair so it hung loose in waves around her face.

He whistled. "Most beautiful star on the Bounty."

She scoffed. "Now you're just flattering me!"

"A compliment is not the same as flattery." He winked at

her. "Get yourself back to the helm before the power goes to Maps's head."

She laughed, curtsied, and hurried up the steps to return to the wheel.

"I like it. Suits you," Maps said behind her.

Hours later, the plucking of strings caught Song's attention. She gave the helm over to Maps and strode to discover the sound. On the bottom step of the starboard side staircase sat Sunshine, tuning a weather-beaten violin. She smiled and sat beside him to admire the beautiful instrument in his grasp.

"I didn't know you played."

"Usually everyone's asleep. Figure I'll play in Kerriwen."

"Will you play now?"

He cocked an eyebrow at her.

"Please." She delivered a charming smile.

"One song."

"Of course!" She nodded.

When he'd tuned the violin to his liking, he set it to his chin and pulled the bow across the strings. It was a quick tune, like a jig, but not quite as fast, though not slow enough for the sort of dance she was used to. Song stood, overcome by the beauty, and spun around the deck in a dance somewhere between a ballroom dance and a jig she'd once learned. It differed from a waltz and required more fancy footwork than she'd been willing to learn, but some of it had stayed in her memory.

The bright notes urged crewmen from below deck. They stood at the bow and around the railing to watch Song and enjoy the tune. A recorder's sweet, high notes rang across the deck in a beautiful accompaniment with the violin. Leslie winked at her as his deft fingers picked out the tune by covering the little holes in his hand-carved instrument. Much like Sunshine, he'd never even pulled out the instrument during the days when other crewmen sometimes would.

An arm interrupted her astonishment as it wrapped around her waist. She spun in a quick circle as Dashaelan took her into his arms to dance. He was far from graceful, but the smile he gave her as they spun around the deck made her forget there was ever such a thing as formal dancing. They stepped on each other's toes and tripped on their heels, but that didn't matter as he twirled her so fast her skirt fanned out around her ankles like a bell-flower.

Thumbs and Leslie were wrong. Song wasn't the heart of the Stars' Bounty—not in her mind, anyway. Dashaelan was. He was the sun in her sky every day, when the days were too long to bear. He'd been there at her side every time she'd needed him. And he always knew the right things to say. If this was what having a loving, attentive father was like, then Song wanted more of it. She wanted every day to be music, dancing, happiness, and Dashaelan. The rest of the crew, her brothers in arms, were the sweet-cream topping on an already perfect dessert.

She never wanted the song to end. She wanted to spin forever like a little girl pretending to be a ballerina. She wanted to share Dashaelan's laughter over their poor footwork until the sun set in the east—even then she never wanted to stop. Damn the rewards and the bounties. Damn the pillage and the plunder and the treasures. She was home. And this moment was perfect in every way.

But like all songs, this one had to end. After Dashaelan straightened from bowing and kissing the top of her hand, she threw her arms over his shoulders and hugged him long and tight.

"Thank you."

He returned her embrace with a chuckle. "Of course, my dear. Of course."

As they crossed the border of Kerriwen, Dashaelan took the helm. He steered the skyship over the savanna, its tall grass swaying in the winds. Animals set off at a run, spooked by the low-flying craft. Song had never seen such creatures outside of a book. Their brown coats gave way at their rumps to tan and black stripes; they had cloven hooves and tall, spiraling horns. Another pack had white and black fur, with manes that stood on end like the bristles of a brush. There were even more, varying in pattern, color, and horn type, but they wove so fast between each other that Song's eyes crossed and they blurred into one mass of colors and dust.

Dashaelan eased the propeller to a stop before reversing it to slow the ship and let it coast above the savannah until it had slowed enough to send men over the sides with ropes to secure it to sturdy trees. The men pulled a long ramp from the side of the ship at the bit of railing which lifted up out of the deck to create an opening, and tilted it down to the ground. Wheels at the bottom of the ramp kept it from breaking or falling away, should a gust of wind jostle the craft. They'd never used this ramp before, and Dashaelan informed her it was for situations like this, in which there was no dock for them to anchor to. Sunshine emerged from below holding a large crate of spirits. He shoved the clanking crate into Ponce's hands and sent him away with a wave of his hand.

Thumbs appeared at Song's elbow. "Would you like a hand down?"

"I'm sure I can manage."

"Please?" He smiled at her and she knew it was more favor to him than anything.

"Only because you asked nicely."

She set her fingertips in his palm and let him lead her down the ramp.

Dashaelan laughed from the top. "You're trusting Thumbs to keep you steady?"

"No, sir. She is keeping me steady!" He turned his head far enough to smile up at Dashaelan and managed to lose his footing.

Song squealed as they fell over the side. The two landed in a heap with Leslie and Toothy beneath.

"*Y'banzi!*" Thumbs shouted with a smile. He sat up and clapped a hand on Leslie's shoulder.

"*Y'ditta.*" Leslie stood to help Thumbs up before dusting himself off.

Toothy stooped and picked Song up by her armpits and set her on her feet. "Ha! Caught you this time. A little warning wouldn't hurt, though."

She smiled and straightened her skirt. "If I ever go tumbling over the side of anything again, you'll be the first to know."

Thirty-Four

IT WAS LATE IN THE EVENING. THE CREW HAD BEEN DRINKING and laughing for hours. Music played on and off, courtesy of Sunshine, Leslie, and Pinch—who played a concertina. Toothy would join on a battered guitar for short songs, but he wasn't as skilled with his instrument as the others.

"At least I know how to tune it!" he shouted as a few men teased him.

"Well then, you're halfway there!" Ponce laughed from beside Pinch.

Toothy set the instrument aside and pulled Song up from the ground to spin her in a lively jig. When the song ended, Song laughed and dropped to the ground beside Leslie.

"Is there anything you can't do?" she asked with a laugh. Since meeting him, it seemed he knew everything there was to know and had done everything there was to do.

He directed his sad smile to the ground. "I can't fly."

Brute chuckled from the other side of him.

"But you do on the Bounty," she said.

His lips curled into a small smile. "I can't sing."

"Rubbish," she scoffed.

"I really can't."

"Oh, codswallop."

"What?" Dashaelan asked as he lowered to the ground beside her.

"Leslie here says he can't sing."

He stared at him. "That's one of the easiest things *to* do, and you can't?"

Leslie shrugged. "I was just never any good, so I thought I'd leave the singing to others."

"Hence your recorder," Song guessed.

He smirked and tapped the tip of her nose.

"Play us something to sing to, then!" Toothy shouted, having been eavesdropping on their conversation.

Leslie thought, then set the recorder to his lips and began the first bittersweet notes of a soothing song, which seemed to begin with a gentle hello and made Song smile.

Dashaelan smiled, too. As the tune circled to start again, he sang.

"Deep in the Winterlands where the cold wind blows,
I met a bonnie lass that I yearned to know.
She said 'Come take my hand, I'll show
*   you such wond'rous things.*
I'll take you to a land where the mountain sings.'"

His voice was rough and weatherbeaten, but sure and steady. It was low, like sorrow, and deep, like heartache. Song found that listening to him brought tears to her eyes, but not because of the song.

"Lost in the desert skies, met a maiden fair.
She had bright, sloe-black eyes and long, ebon hair.

She said 'Come follow me. I will take your pain.
We'll lay beside the sea and will never hurt again.'"

Dashaelan allowed Leslie a small verse before continuing to the end of the song.

"Now I'm at journey's end, where I longed to be.
I cross the river bend and a plain girl, I see.
She says, 'Come kiss me dear, rest your weary head.'
My heart was always here in my own warm bed."

The music ended like a soft goodbye in the warm night. The fire crackled as applause in the following silence. Each of the men observed the other or stared off, lost in thought.

"I don't have a plain girl," Pinch said. "I've got a lovely woman with angel's curls in her hair and a wicked smile." He chuckled, thinking about his maiden of sinful beauty.

"Whores don't count," Toothy said.

Pinch shot him a look. "You'd know, she's your sister!"

"Why you smarmy—" Toothy leapt at him and the two wrestled in the dirt.

Song laughed.

Sunshine cast his dark eyes on her. "What about you, Song? Have you got a plain girl waiting back home?"

She smiled. "Not back home, no. But I fancied one once."

"Why sigh after a plain girl?" Bells asked. "Why not find a beautiful maiden to go home to?"

"Because I am a plain girl and it is best I stick to my own kind," Song said.

Dashaelan barked a laugh and clapped her shoulder. "If you find yourself a beautiful woman who will remain loyal to you when you've gone for so long, then wife her. Never so rare is a flower who lets but one man pluck her."

"I never thought you could make flora sound so perverse," Sunshine said.

Dashaelan turned his light chuckles on Leslie. "What about you, Whispers? A man like you must have a lady watching the skies for your return?"

Leslie kept his eyes on the ground between his feet and shook his head.

"Oh," Toothy wailed, straightening his shirt after the scuffle—beside him, Ponce reached up to pluck a weed from Pinch's white-blond hair. "If Whispers ain't got no bird, then there's no hope for any of us!"

As intended, Leslie's lips curved into a half smile. "I'm just making sure you boys get first pick before I swoop in to take the best of them."

"Song is not going anywhere with you," Thumbs said, "no matter how much swooping you do." He winked over at Song and her cheeks warmed.

Leslie chuckled.

The silence that followed was strange as the men continued in their thoughts, some eyeing her in the light of the fire. Maybe contemplating what Thumbs had said. But she was not the best of all women. She was the worst of them. *It's a good thing I fancy women, because no man would ever want me.* The thought burned through her, angering something in her heart. Even though she'd never wanted it, she was furious that she couldn't have it. Not in a sincere manner, at least.

She gazed around the fire at the men. They were not all ugly for men, but they weren't the most attractive of the gender—save Leslie and perhaps Dashaelan, if he shaved that bird's nest of a beard. That's where she belonged, away from romance and silly notions of a woman—or man—awaiting her return. She was happiest never sitting still, always flying somewhere or nowhere, always on the move. Such a life made even the idea of a family impossible. A small smile tugged at the corner of her lips as she realized her being the worst of all women was not a bad thing. It was perfect. She'd been born to the wrong parents in the wrong walk of life. Everything about her fit into this wonderful nomadic existence.

Song blinked out of her musings to see Dashaelan standing over her, a hand extended in invitation. Pinch had started another song on his concertina—this one had a waltzing rhythm. She smiled and took Dashaelan's hand. As bad as he'd been at the other dance from earlier that day, he was worse at waltzing. She bit her lips together to keep her laughter at bay.

"What?" he demanded.

"You're not supposed to watch your feet."

"If I don't watch them, I'll step on your toes."

"You are, anyway!"

With a scoff, Sunshine strode over to them. "Let me show you how a gentleman dances with a lady."

"Ha!" Dashaelan moved aside to let him cut in.

"Oh, a real live gentleman?" Song teased.

Sunshine was a better dancer than Dashaelan by leaps.

His movements were sure, but clunky and unpracticed. He only stood on her foot once.

"So how is it?" Dashaelan asked.

"Much better."

"Best you've ever had?" Ponce gave a wicked wink.

"Not nearly."

Sunshine feigned insult. "Who could possibly have danced better than me?"

"Leslie."

"How much better?"

"He makes you look like Thumbs."

Thumbs smiled beside the fire. "You mean devilishly handsome?"

"She means clumsy!" an invisible laughed, smacking the side of Thumbs's bald head.

Thumbs laughed and reached out to hit the other in the chest—the blow knocked the invisible to the ground.

"Well, if he's so grand, then why doesn't he dance with you?" Sunshine said.

All eyes turned to Leslie, who was staring into the fire, lost in thought.

"How about it, Whispers?" Dashaelan asked.

"Hmm?" He looked up, pulled back into reality.

"She says you're a better dancer than me," Sunshine said.

"Come on, Whispers!" Thumbs said. "Show us how it is done!"

"Does the lady demand it?" Leslie chuckled and met her gaze.

She smiled. The night had already been so wonderful, and she didn't want it to end. She could have danced with

Dashaelan and Sunshine all night or let Toothy twirl her around the fire with Ponce a few more times. But she wanted to be proven right. So for now, she wanted nothing more than to dance with Leslie.

"Let's show these ruffians how a gentleman dances with a lady."

Leslie sighed and forced a smile. She braced herself for a no and readied to find another partner. But Leslie stood, handed his recorder to Brute and dusted himself off, as though that could make his beaten clothing more formal in some way. His approach was slow, as though giving her time to change her mind. When he held out his hand to her, she set her fingertips on his palm. He kissed her knuckles as he might in formal surroundings. She failed to contain her giggle as she gave a small curtsy. Pinch changed the song, but kept the same tempo as before.

Leslie took her into his arms and they fell into perfect, synchronized steps, gliding over the rough ground of the field as though it were the smoothest of dance floors. His eyes captured hers and held fast, searching deep as though to try reading her very soul. But she knew all he would see within was a little girl who'd consumed far too much whiskey that night to be dancing the way they were.

She searched within his own eyes to see what he thought of what little he found in hers. Something like a fire burned behind the ice of them. She saw then that urging him into the dance was a poor decision, as some unnamed torture preoccupied his mind. She knew he longed to be back by the fire and left alone to his own thoughts. Perhaps something about this night reminded him of his terrible past.

"I ain't never felt clumsy…until now," Sunshine said from the fire.

His voice pulled her back into the present and out of the dark thoughts that plagued her regarding Leslie's past. As close as they'd become, she still only knew the vaguest details of his life before. He was well-educated, that was certain. It seemed there was nothing he hadn't done, nothing he had left to see. The gentle features of his face had her assuming he was the same age as Toothy, but his eyes held a lifetime of stories he would never tell.

"There is a word for something like that," Thumbs said.

"Beautiful," Dashaelan answered.

"Beautiful," Thumbs echoed.

Song tried to block them out, but couldn't. Embarrassment flooded her cheeks, painting them pink. She was glad for the darkness of the night.

"It's like they're one person," Sunshine added.

Their comments continued to poke at her. She found them preposterous. So silly were their adulations, that her laughter bubbled into her throat and she had to purse her lips to keep it from bursting into the night. It growled through her sinuses. She turned her head into her shoulder to make sure the laugh stayed put. Soon she was shaking from the effort. Leslie released her and took both her hands in his.

"Thank you." He bowed.

She sobered just enough to curtsy. "And thank you." She leaned in close, her laughter twisted her lips into a Cheshire grin and sat tight in her chest to spice her words with it. "Sorry. I wasn't laughing at you. I was laughing at those fools." She snorted on her laughter and it broke free, echoing across the field. "That was bloody lady-like."

She returned to sit beside Dashaelan, who set an arm over her shoulders and leaned in to tell her more of how graceful the two were. It caused her face to heat and her laugh to return over such flattery. Leslie took his time returning to sit between Brute and Song. When he did, he kept his face to the fire and his eyes trained on the embers therein.

"Where did you learn to dance like that?" Dashaelan asked him.

But Leslie was so lost within his own mind he didn't hear it.

Song leaned close to whisper, "What's wrong?"

He pondered his reply. His eyes darted between hers as he again searched for anything besides a drunk little girl. "Nothing," he said. "I suppose it's just the heat of the fire."

But it didn't fool Song. His home country was a short distance north. Perhaps it was the proximity, and his desire to stay as far away from Pishing as possible.

"Don't worry, Leslie. Your secrets are safe with me," she whispered.

"Thank you." He returned his gaze to the fire.

She leaned back to Dashaelan as he told fantastic tales of his own grand adventures aboard the Stars' Bounty. She could sense it in the carefulness of his words, though, that his life before piracy would never enter his tales. Song found their secrets weighing on her own heart and wished they'd never confided in her. But that's what friends did, wasn't it? Shared their darkest secrets and trusted the other to keep them?

Song smiled and leaned her head on Dashaelan's shoulder, allowing herself to slip into dreams of his fanciful life.

Thirty-Five

S ONG SQUINTED AGAINST THE BRIGHTNESS OF THE SUN AND
tossed a blanket away that someone must have covered
her with. Gazing around the campsite, she found Dashaelan
still beside her and Brute to her left. Toothy wasn't far away,
cuddling with one of Ponce's boots. Ponce was several feet
away from Toothy, his big toe poking through a hole in his
sock. A fly landed on the appendage just long enough to
tickle his foot into twitching, then it took off and circled him,
only to land and start the process all over. Against his side,
using Ponce's arm as a pillow, Pinch curled around an empty
rum bottle and his concertina. She stood, stumbling with
vertigo from too much drink the night before. She tripped
over Thumbs. Her palms landed on some sort of burr patch
he'd covered with a blanket.

"Sorry," she whispered as he groaned and sat up. "Have
you seen Leslie?"

He rubbed his eyes and stretched, shaking his head to
answer her question. A horse's whinny carried across the
field from behind her. That's where she discovered Leslie
at the sharp end of a spear. The man at the other end was
as dark as Thumbs, wearing loose cotton pants that reached
his knees, and nothing else. His entire head was shaved, like

Thumbs, but a long, black braid draped over his left shoulder. There were five more horsemen, including one woman.

"Nomads!" Thumbs hissed. He dragged her back to the ground.

The woman turned to look in their direction. The sides of her head were shaved, too, but she'd plaited the hair down the center of her scalp in a thick braid that hung to her waist. Leslie followed the woman's gaze, then climbed onto the horse behind her.

Song sat up and Thumbs dragged her down again.

"What is he doing?"

"Stay down!"

"Let go of me!" Song shook free and raced across the field after the group as they retreated into the forest. "Leslie!"

He looked behind, but didn't respond as they disappeared from her view. She slowed to catch her breath.

Thumbs caught up and took her by the arm. "You cannot go after them!"

"What if they kill him?"

He grimaced as he thought. "All right. But only because you are both my friends. Let us get weapons—"

"There's no time!" she insisted. She took him by the hand and pulled him toward the tree line.

"What about Dash or Sunshine?"

"No time!"

He shrugged. "Fewer casualties, I suppose."

Song slowed to a walk as she followed the path made by the horses' hooves. She lifted her skirt to her thigh to show Thumbs her revolver strapped to her leg. "Give us a fighting chance."

"If that is what you want to call it," he grumbled.

The woods gave way to another clearing several times larger than the one they'd camped in. Animals of all types grazed on the tall grass—the brown ones with their striped rumps; tall ones with long necks; the horse-like ones with black stripes and stiff manes; huge grey creatures that towered over everything—the hump of the tallest one's back was at least eight meters high. Thumbs grabbed Song's wrist and dragged her into a bush. He signaled for her to stay quiet. He pointed to a path that curved along the outer edge of the trees and ended at a large encampment.

"Right." She cleared her throat of the panic knotting within it. "At least we'll go out fighting?"

"I do not want to go out fighting," he complained. "I want to go out eating."

"It's a wonder you can fit through any doors."

"Says the eilfaas in a little girl's body."

"What's an eilfaas?"

He pointed at the huge grey beasts, their stomachs wide with the grass their long trunks collected from the ground. Song shot Thumbs a bitter look. Despite the situation, he smiled. She made a slow approach to the encampment, staying inside the tree line and keeping to tall bushes and grass as cover.

"Wait!" Thumbs hissed. He dragged her into a patch of tall grass. "Look."

He pointed at the encampment where men on horseback—with crossbows, bows, harpoons, and ropes—rode out in single file. They were all clothed similarly, wearing thick leather vests and thick leather around the groin of their cotton-legged pants. The man with the long braid, though the rest of his head was bald, wore no vest. A man rode beside him, dark paint over the pale skin on his forearms and shoulders, his auburn hair loose with the top half braided, and a spear set across his back. Song gasped and surged forward, but Thumbs caught her and dragged her back to the ground.

"We have to get him!" she said.

"No."

"What?"

"Look at him. He is no prisoner. He wears their clothes and their marks. Whispers is part of the hunting party."

"What are they hunting?"

Leslie and the other man stopped to talk as the rest separated into two rows, loosely filed. Thumbs's eyes widened, his mouth dropping open.

"No," he gasped.

"What?"

"*Tal-taniico.*"

"Thumbs—"

"When I was a boy, there were stories of a man. Many thought he was just a rumor, but my friend claimed to have seen him. He was called *Tal-taniico*. It means Brother, but not by blood. More like an earned title."

"What of him?"

The hunting party charged forward, frightening the animals and weaving between them to separate the groups.

"He was a white man who rode right hand to Jiridamudor of the Kal'Bar Tribe as an honorary member. He is the only outsider to hunt the way the nomad tribes do…without dying."

"Hunt what?"

He pursed his lips.

"Thumbs," she urged.

"Eilfaas."

Song gasped. "Are you saying he's going to get himself killed?" She stood, but he dragged her down again.

Leslie and the other man joined the rest of the horsemen. They worked together to single out the huge bull eilfaas towering over the other animals.

"I think he is *Tal-taniico*," Thumbs said.

Song gave him a look. "I think you're full of it and Leslie is going to get himself killed."

"*Shh.*"

"Excuse me?" she demanded.

"I have always wanted to see an eilfaas hunt. So, *shh.*"

She obeyed without enthusiasm. Her muscles tensed as she watched.

The hunters had cleared the field and isolated the bull. They dictated where he went by pulling on ropes attached to arrows shot into his ears. His feet made the ground thunder beneath them as he charged across the field. He trumpeted his anger and swung his head in an attempt to hit the men.

"Keep your eyes on Jiridamudor and *Tal-taniico*."

"He's not—"

"Just watch!"

She suspected Thumbs assumed the man with the long braid was Jiridamudor. He held a rope with a weight at one end, which he rocked back and forth before sending it into a circling twirl. He and Leslie galloped toward the eilfaas from behind. They separated to match pace on either side of the beast. Jiridamudor released the rope, and it sailed high over the back of the bull, where Leslie caught it on the other side.

A series of shrill whistles echoed back to where the two hid in the grass. As one, Leslie and Jiridamudor stood in their saddles, other hunters taking the reins of their steeds to keep them steady. One more whistle and together they jumped, using each other's weight as an anchor. They clambered up the sides of the eilfaas and clasped forearms at the top to pull each other up. They balanced on the back of the beast as the others steered it closer to their camp.

Leslie and Jiridamudor raised their spears and together plunged them into the back of the eilfaas's head. It groaned. Its front legs collapsed beneath it. The two men leapt back onto their horses as the bull crashed to the ground, dead.

"That's awful," Song whispered into her palm.

"They do it that way because it is quick. The animal does not suffer."

She shook away the shock and made to stand. "Let's go get—"

The barrel of a rifle pressed into the side of her head. The hammer cocked with a loud *click*.

"Bugger me."

Thirty-Six

SONG KEPT HER HANDS AT THE BACK OF HER HEAD AS THE KERRI woman walked behind her, holding the rifle focused on her head. Thumbs walked beside Song, his hands up in surrender as well. She clenched her jaw. Her eyes flicked between the hunting party—who hadn't noticed the capture of prisoners—Thumbs, and the tribe's camp. The woman said something and Song looked at him to translate.

"She says—"

She turned the rifle on him and shouted. He gave a swift reply. She clenched her jaw and pushed the barrel of the rifle closer to his head. Thumbs closed his eyes.

But Song would not admit defeat. She gripped the rifle and shoved the barrel up away from Thumbs's head as the shot blasted from the tip. The crack echoed like lightning across the field. Song ripped the rifle from the woman's hands and realized it could only hold one shot in the chamber, and now it was useless.

She swung the butt around. It cracked against the other woman's jaw. She swung it for a second blow, but the woman caught it and tore it from her hands as she reached into a pouch at her hip for another bullet. They wrestled for control of the weapon before Song ripped it from her hands. It slid from her grasp and twirled away from them and landed in the tall grass.

The woman rushed for her rifle. Song shoved into her and tackled her to the ground, where they wrestled. Each of them got in a few lucky blows on the other. Song found herself beneath the woman, who pulled a knife from a sheath strapped to her ankle and pressed it into Song's neck. Before the woman could draw blood, Song lifted her skirt, unholstered her revolver, and pressed the cold mouth of it into the soft flesh under the woman's jaw.

After a moment to contemplate her situation, the woman lifted her arms in surrender. She opened her hand to let the knife roll from her palm, then backed away to let Song up. They stood an arm's length apart to glare at each other as Song kept her gun pointed between the woman's eyes.

A pale hand snaked out to twist the gun from her grasp. Leslie placed himself between the two, his palms pressed against their collars to keep them separated. He said a few stern words to the Kerri woman, then turned his angry gaze on Song. Someone had stained his face with dark brown lines in a fashion to resemble the tattoos of this land's people, a marking of their lot in life etched across their faces with burns and inks. On his forehead was an eilfaas head, the tusks stretching down the inner corners of his eyes to frame his narrow nose, where the eilfaas trunk curled over the bridge. The Kerri woman bore the same marking on her forehead.

Leslie didn't have to say anything and already she felt chastised.

"You should *not* have followed me."

She jutted her chin forward in defiance—he would not make her feel like a berated child. "You should have told me where you were going."

"I don't answer to you."

"Doesn't mean I can't worry."

Jiridamudor's steed came to an abrupt halt. The man's black eyes glared down at the scene. He and Leslie conversed before Leslie bowed his head in acquiescence. He dropped his hands and let the Kerri woman retrieve her knife and reload her rifle. She skirted behind them and held the barrel at the back of Song's head.

"Jiridamudor is not pleased with you," Leslie said. "Kiikribandarija is his sister."

"She was about to shoot Thumbs!"

Leslie turned his grim expression on him. Thumbs pursed his lips, his nostrils flared at Leslie, as though he held back contemptuous comments that rested on his tongue. Jiridamudor spoke with Leslie in clipped tones as his eyes shifted between the two. Leslie cast his gaze to the ground and gave a solemn reply. Thumbs exhaled his anger and trained his eyes on Song.

"You two are to go with Jiridamudor and Kiikribandarija and await the tribe's decision of what to do with you," Leslie said.

"Excuse me?" Song exclaimed.

"I already know what they will decide!" Thumbs barked. "Why delay the inevitable?"

"Thumbs, please." Leslie set a hand on their dark friend's shoulder and Thumbs shook it off. "Go quietly. I will be back soon."

"Where are you going?" Song asked.

"To let Dashaelan know we are safe and not to come looking for us."

Her eyes met his as he settled himself into the saddle of his painted stallion. "Are we?"

His gaze remained fixed on hers, his lips pursed in thought as the horse shifted, eager to run. Leslie sighed. He dropped his gaze and kicked the horse into a full gallop. Song looked to Thumbs for her answer.

"No, Song. We are far from safe."

Jiridamudor shouted in Kerri and kicked the side of Thumbs's head. Thumbs fell to the ground at the horse's hooves. Song threw herself to her knees over him.

"Don't worry," she whispered, "I won't let anything happen to us."

"You worry about you—"

"I promise."

Jiridamudor shouted over them. Thumbs stood and helped Song to her feet. They set their hands at the back of their heads and let the two lead them into the camp. The rest of the tribe gathered to watch, some jeering, as they led their prisoners to a large tent.

Inside, there were two poles to support the length of the tent. They stood Song with her back against a pole and tied her wrists behind her, then bound Thumbs to the other. Jiridamudor pursed his lips at the two of them, then strode outside. Kiikribandarija trained the gun on Song a moment longer as though contemplating using it, then scoffed and exited the tent.

"I'm sorry, Thumbs."

"I do not want to hear it."

"I should've listened to you."

He clenched his jaw. "Just know that when I die, it is not you I will be blaming."

"Who, then? Leslie?"

He made no reply.

"You're not going to die."

He trained his glare on the tent wall across from him. Song stared at the side of his face a moment longer before realizing all conversation was done. They stood in an uncomfortable silence for a long time before the flap of the tent flipped open and Kiikribandarija stepped in. She gripped a knife in her fist, which shook with anger. She growled something at Thumbs and spat on the floor. He met her glare, but did not reply.

"Don't you touch him."

Kiikribandarija sneered at Song. She stepped forward to set the tip of her curved blade against the soft flesh under Song's jaw. The way she spoke next told Song that it was a taunt, perhaps daring her to do something in her bound state.

"I could burn this entire encampment to the ground with one word," Song said, her upper lip curled in contempt.

"Do not," Thumbs said.

"I didn't say I would, only that—" She sucked in a breath as the tip of the blade pressed into her skin and stung it open. A single bead of crimson rolled down the sharp edge of the knife and dripped onto the carpet at their feet.

Thumbs shouted at Kiikribandarija, and she retracted the knife. She shot her glare at him.

"Don't you dare touch him," Song warned.

Thumbs said something again, a taunting tone barbed the strange Kerri tongue. Kiikribandarija strode across the room, pulling back her hand as she readied to stab Thumbs.

"Mi'h t'keht-orp!"

A shimmering sphere encircled Thumbs as Kiikribandarija's knife thrust forward. The moment the metal tip touched the sphere, shocks of lightning sparked around the weapon. The woman froze in place, her body shook in small convulsions as the sparks traveled up her blade and into her arm. Her eyes rolled into the back of her head and spittle foamed at the corners of her mouth. The sparks stopped, and she collapsed to the ground. The sphere stayed swirling protectively around Thumbs as he stared at Song.

"I told you I wouldn't let anything happen to either of us."

"Let us just hope she is not dead." Thumbs stared down at the Kerri woman, an internal struggle clouding his dark eyes.

"You fear their retaliation."

"Not so much retaliation as another nail in my coffin."

"You did nothing."

"The Kal'Bar do not care if I have done nothing or everything. They do not care that I am pirate or that I have washed my hands of my birth tribe. They only care what the markings on my face tell them." Thumbs glared across from him again.

"And what do your markings tell them?"

The flap opened again to let Leslie and Jiridamudor into the tent. Jiridamudor's gaze first found his sister lying on the floor, then it found Thumbs wrapped in a blue sphere of light. He unsheathed a dagger of his own and strode to

Kiikribandarija. He said something to Leslie, then turned his scowl on Thumbs.

"You're lucky she's alive," Leslie said.

"She'd be luckier if she hadn't attacked Thumbs. I merely protected him from her blade."

Leslie's brow knit together as he observed her, his eyes lower than her own. She looked down to find a red stain forming on the chest of her new dress, where her blood had dripped onto the fabric.

"She went for Song first, but I called her a whore and she came for me," Thumbs said.

Leslie explained the circumstances to Jiridamudor, who sighed down at his sister. He scooped her into his arms and strode from the tent. When Leslie turned to meet his gaze, Thumbs's scowl returned.

"Why did you not tell me?"

Leslie blinked at him. "Would it have prevented us from becoming friends?"

"Of course it would have!"

"That's why."

Thumbs turned away from Leslie to seethe.

"What's going on?" Song asked.

Thumbs snapped his angry eyes to Song. "He is Kal'Bar. I was Pitique."

"I don't understand."

"Sworn enemies," Leslie said. He let that sink in before trying to plead his case. "I didn't say anything because it is not relevant outside of Kerriwen. I am not marked as Kal'Bar, so I believe beyond these borders I am just another man."

"Why aren't you marked?" Song asked.

"Honorary members are never marked permanently, though we wear this stain when within the encampment."

Song understood Thumbs's fury, now. In fact, anger of her own flared into existence. "You moved the map pin. You knew where you were leading us. How could you put Thumbs in this kind of danger and still call him a friend?"

"The pin was set to take us into Quodinlau territory. If you think the Kal'Bar are bad, take a stroll around Quodinlau lands. They don't take prisoners except as livestock. They don't care about tribe or country of origin, they will kill you on sight. I moved it here so that if we encountered any Kal'Bar, at least I could negotiate for the rest of the crew. They were never supposed to see Thumbs. I did not endanger him, you did. You are the one who cannot leave well enough alone and dragged him out into the woods to chase after me."

"I thought you were in danger!"

"Song, you know better than anyone that I can handle myself."

"Why didn't you just tell me?"

Leslie folded his arms over his chest. "You were all safely asleep when I left, and I'd hoped to be finished quickly."

"Finished with what, exactly?"

"Stanjarbonima, Jiridamudor's newest riding partner, was injured. They needed to get that bull eilfaas out of the savanna because it was a threat to the tribe and to the other animals. They'd been waiting for Stanjarbonima to recover, but since I was here, they said if I helped, no one would be harmed."

"Oh, my hero," Song scoffed. "Why don't you use that special status to free us?"

"That is not my decision."

Song rolled her eyes. "If they knew who I was—"

"They would still be debating your execution," Leslie hissed. "Song, you are nobody here. There is no social hierarchy or nobility. You were born into privilege, but that privilege only reaches the borders of Andalise and holds very minor weight in Jashedar and Pishing. But in Kerriwen? You are nothing. I worked and bled for the name *Tal-taniico*."

Song swallowed away the angry knot in her throat. "It's amazing how you know exactly what to say to make me hate you."

His demeanor shifted as he unwound his arms from each other and stared at his feet. "I'm sorry, Song."

"Prove it. Free us and get us back to the Bounty."

"I'm working on it."

"Funny, looks to me like you're standing here insulting my upbringing."

Leslie sighed and strode from the tent. Song's eyes locked with Thumbs's as he stared through his swirling protection.

"*I* would've found a way to tell you," she said.

"He is right, though. I would not have been his friend and one of us would not be on the Bounty."

SONG'S LEGS GREW TIRED, SO SHE SLID DOWN THE POLE TO KNEEL. She glared at the closed flap as though willing Leslie to come through it.

"I could've untied us long ago. We could be free."

Thumbs grunted as he, too, sat on the carpet. "You do that and they *will* kill us all."

"Not if I kill everyone here first."

"Song, no. You do not want that kind of blood on your hands."

She growled low in her throat as frustration clawed at her. "We have to do something!"

"Waiting is something. Trusting Whispers is something."

"You trust him? After all this?"

Thumbs let out a breath as he contemplated this. "I would not say that I trust him as I used to, no. But he has had many chances to kill me since meeting. If he wanted me dead, I would be."

"If anything happens to you, I'll never forgive him."

"I think he knows that. I also think that is his greatest motivation to keep us both from harm."

Song rolled her eyes and leaned her head against the post. She closed her eyes, resting them against the stress of the situation.

"Song." Leslie's gentle voice woke her. He pressed his palm to her cheek, his thumb caressed her cheekbone to aid in rousing her.

When her mind grew more aware of the situation, she jerked her head away from his touch and glared at him. "Can we leave yet?"

Leslie clenched his jaw and reached around to untie her. "We're all free to go."

Song took down the protection around Thumbs. "Anyone gets too close to him and the protection comes back."

"Fair enough." Leslie crossed the tent to untie their comrade.

Jiridamudor stood over Song, his black eyes boring into her. He extended a hand to help her up. She glanced at the others; Leslie gave a reassuring nod. She set her hand in Jiridamudor's and he pulled her to her feet. Their gazes locked as they tried to read each other's intentions in their eyes. He released her hand and took an ornately carved eilfaas tusk from his belt, then took each end and pulled them apart to reveal a blade hidden within.

Song's muscles clenched and a command to her *kijæm* rested on the tip of her tongue. Jiridamudor held out both parts in his flat palms as a presentation. The blade was beaten steel that rippled along the surface where the hammer strokes had molded the metal. Song lifted the dagger and gripped it in her fist. Her eyes met Jiridamudor's cool gaze. He gave no indication that he feared she might turn it on him.

After a moment of silent tension, she took the scabbard and slipped the dagger back inside. The parts fit together in seamless perfection. Any who looked at it would never know it was a dagger, just as Song hadn't.

"He honors you," Thumbs said. "What did you say to them?" he asked Leslie.

"It's better left unsaid."

Jiridamudor led them from the tent where five horses waited outside. Armed Kal'Bar occupied two. They led Thumbs to a riderless steed as Jiridamudor took Song's elbow to guide her to Leslie's painted stallion.

"I'd rather ride with Thumbs," she said.

"Just get on the horse, Song." Leslie gave her a kind smile.

Jiridamudor took the choice from her as he wrapped his hands around her waist, picked her up, and set her behind Leslie as if she weighed nothing. The party rode in silence, following Jiridamudor's lead. When they reached the Stars' Bounty, he leapt from his mare to lift Song from the stallion. After setting her feet on the ground, he bowed. She'd no idea of Kerri customs, and so curtsied. The man laughed and looked at Leslie, who smirked and shrugged. She fingered the patterns on the handle of her new dagger as the Kal'Bar took the reins of the two empty horses and galloped back into the trees. She stared up at the Stars' Bounty to find the smiling Dashaelan waiting at the top of the ramp.

"I hope one day you'll be able to forgive me for this," Leslie said. His eyes caught Song's first, then Thumbs's.

"We'll see," Song said. She took Thumbs by the hand and walked up the ramp and onto the ship.

She didn't think she could forgive him so easily—especially not as the stain of warpaint remained on his skin for another month. She fought it every day. Until two fortnights later when she walked in on Thumbs extending a hand of friendship to Leslie. She sighed, realizing she couldn't hate him forever—not if Thumbs couldn't.

"Fraternizing with the enemy?" Song asked.

Thumbs laughed. "I see no enemies here."

She gave them a crooked smile as one side of her mouth accepted the joy of being on good terms with each other, and the other tried to remain aloof to the situation.

"Song?" Thumbs raised an eyebrow.

"I suppose I can't hate Leslie forever."

Leslie chuckled. "You can. And I'm sure you would've."

She shrugged but didn't deny the claim. "Feel like a quick spar on deck?"

He smiled. "Lead the way."

Thirty-Seven

SONG SCANNED THE OCEAN BELOW, HER GOGGLES PULLED OVER her eyes and adjusted at the farthest viewing distance. She could feel Dashaelan's gaze on her. He still did not approve of her desire to sack a sailer. She hadn't let the subject go since that night when it first entered her mind. It had never been done before, and something inside her wanted to do it, just to say she was the first. It was her Jewel of Castildi, for the time being. Though her impossible goal was not quite so out of reach as Dashaelan's.

They hadn't forgotten Duke Barton. They planned and revised their plans over and over, reviewing every minute detail. Dashaelan refused to accept any plan that left room for error, which could lead to Song's endangerment. He had Leslie training her to escape a man's grasp or knock him from atop her. Leslie didn't ask why. He seemed to agree they were ideal skills for her to have.

They'd grown closer than Song had ever expected—especially after the Kerriwen fiasco. She could have ventured they'd gone beyond the student-teacher relationship and found a rather ideal partnership—maybe even a true friendship. It was comfortable to her, though he stayed around her more since her birthday. He wanted to know more about her, about her likes and dislikes, not Tsingsei's, which expectations and privilege had forced upon her.

For all his kindness, it made her miss Altain more. She could never forget her first friend, and her determination hadn't waned in the slightest. But as they still hadn't discovered the name or whereabouts of Darian's supposed new ship, there wasn't much she could do but trust that her crew mates would keep her safe until she'd reunited with her friend.

"What are you watching for?" Leslie asked.

Song smirked. "Wouldn't you like to know?"

He left her to her gazing, but it wasn't long before the next interruption came.

"Looking for a sea monster?" Thumbs asked as he sat beside her on the railing.

"Those are just stories."

"They are real, I tell you."

"Have you seen one with your own eyes?"

"And if I have?"

She pulled her goggles up to stare at him, gauging his seriousness. He gave her a sly wink and slunk away.

Hours passed, and Song was nearing giving up. Then she saw it: a three-masted galleon flying colors of green and blue. Andalise colors. She hesitated a moment before standing and breathing deep to calm her nerves.

"Dash."

"What, Song?"

"Don't leave me behind."

With that, she leapt over the railing. The tails of her coat flapped in the wind as it whipped past her on all sides. It stung her face, biting at her cheeks and forcing her air back into her lungs. Surrounding herself in a protective sphere of mist, she adjusted the view from her goggles and braced for impact. The spiraling mist slowed her to a reasonable speed and she landed painlessly on the deck of the galleon. The men shouted and stood at the ready. One spun a swivel-gun to face her. With a quick command to her *kijæm*, the gun tore from the deck and flew into the ocean.

"Right then. Gentlemen, there are two ways in which we can do this. Option one: you all toss your weapons here at my feet and take a seat on the deck. Op—"

Three men came at her. She drew her sidearm and shot one in the chest. As she swung her arm toward the second, the third man kicked her gun from her grasp. She drew her sword to block the blade coming down above her. She parried his overhead swing and, while he recovered and brought his arm back up for another go, she sliced his hand clean off at the wrist.

The second man came behind her, swinging his sword in a wide arc to take her head. She threw herself sideways and his sword cut open the windpipe of his crewmate. Song took his distraction as an opportunity to come around behind him. She set her sword against his throat and slid it long and deep, cutting him open from ear to ear as a spray of crimson wetted everything in its path. She threw him to the deck and pointed her sword at the man at the helm.

"*That* is option two. What say you?"

The men looked among themselves, sizing her up against them and counting their numbers. The man whose cannon she had tossed into the ocean drew his sword and approached her. She readied herself, but he tossed the weapon at her feet, then returned to his post and sat cross-legged on the deck. The man at the helm was last to bring his weapon to her feet. He tilted his head to see beneath her hood.

"Who are you, boy?"

"They call me Song. Caleb Song."

He threw his weapon onto the pile and returned to sit at the helm.

"You four," she pointed at sailors near the masts. "Furl the sails. I don't want this ship moving around any more than it needs to."

She approached the man with the sliced throat. He was bleeding out, gagging on what entered his windpipe. She crouched beside him and stared into his eyes.

"I'm sorry. I truly am." She planted her sword in his chest and relief glazed his vision over.

"You little brat!" The growl came from behind her. "You come on my ship. You kill my men. For what?"

"I've come for your provisions," she replied.

She recognized this man. He'd attended one of her father's political functions—a ceremony of sorts. Song was barely thirteen, and he was drunk. He'd spent the night stalking and propositioning marriage to her until she'd locked herself in a cupboard and refused to come out until all the guests had gone. He was a renowned captain, recognized for his bravery and the success of his voyages. She was eager to tarnish his record.

"And what are you going to do once you have them, eh? Fly away?"

She couldn't have timed Dashaelan's entrance with the Stars' Bounty any better if she'd tried. He brought the sky-ship in low, casting a shadow over the deck of the galleon. Ropes fell to the deck and men trickled down like spiders descending on their prey.

"As a matter of fact, yes, I am," Song said. "Would you like to contribute your weapon to my new collection? Or would you like to join them?" She motioned at the dead men.

He glared at her as he unsheathed his sword to toss it on the pile.

She rushed forward and stopped him. "Oh, no no no! That is much too beautiful to go on that pile of scrap."

She remembered the ceremony's purpose, now, in which the governor of Garda presented him with the saber. The seal of the city was stamped into the base of the pommel. Black leather was stretched across the hilt and shaped for a comfortable grip behind an ornate hand guard.

Song took the sword from him and held it with reverence. "I'll take the scabbard, too."

He growled low as he unclasped his belt and slid the scabbard from it.

She caught it as he tossed it toward her feet.

Leslie jumped the final meter onto the deck, landing on the balls of his feet. He drew his sword and pointed it at the captain, then paused, his eyes narrowed. "You?"

Recognition spread across the captain's face. "You!" He reached for Song. "Give me that back. I'm gonna run him through!"

Song held the sword behind her back and shied away from him. It didn't deter him, though, as he reached into the pile of weapons and withdrew another. He lunged at Leslie, who parried and spun so the captain was on the other side.

"You have this, then?" Song asked.

Leslie smirked. "Oh, I definitely have this."

Song wiped the blade of her sword clean and retrieved her revolver, then clasped the saber to her belt. Her eyes flitted around to the other crew as they, like her, watched the fighting pair. Hairy took the rest of their men below deck to secure any crew still loose aboard the ship.

The captain was all force and offense, lunging and hacking in an angry fashion. Leslie was control and form—his body moved with fluid purpose, like a great feline on the prowl. Dashaelan finally made it to the deck from the rope ladder and strode to Song.

He set his hands on his knees to catch his breath. "I'm getting too old for that nonsense."

"Then why didn't you stay on the Bounty?"

"And miss all the fun?" He looked around at the passive crew all sitting and watching their captain fight with Leslie. "Where's all the fun?"

"Three men died," Song admitted. "Would you rather I'd killed them all?"

"No," he urged. "No, I think you did very good. This time." He eyed her. Then he set his attention on the fighting pair. "Is that…Pishing sorrowstone?"

Song looked sideways at him. "He oils it every day. On deck. While you're at the helm."

"Oh." His embarrassment was tangible. "Well, he'd have to. Keeps the metal good and strong. How does one in this profession come across such a rare thing?"

"How rare is it?" Song asked.

"Enough so that only the royal families own them. The craftsmanship on his… That's not a sword you go traveling around with to have it nicked by a pirate."

"Where do you suppose he got it?" she asked, though she had a guess.

"Are you two gonna stand 'round talking all day, or help us down below?" Toothy asked as he rolled a barrel past them.

"How many—" she and Dashaelan spoke at the same time. He motioned for her to take charge.

"How many were below deck?" she asked.

"Three times as many as this." He gestured at the men on deck.

"Close to one hundred, maybe more," Dashaelan said.

"Any resistance?" Song pressed.

"We told them we had the upper deck and any resistance would land them an early grave." He smiled his gummy smile. "They didn't seem too keen on the idea."

Song's brow furrowed. "This was easy."

"Aye," Dashaelan clapped her on the shoulder. "You did good."

"No. It doesn't seem right. It should never be this easy, not with such a large crew." She thought hard, scrutinizing each man. "They're hiding something."

Song closed her eyes and concentrated as Dashaelan took Toothy below deck to search the ship. She knew the rules of far-seeing, but this time she hoped those rules were breakable. She focused on Dashaelan first, looking over his shoulder around the barracks. The Stars' Bounty crew were searching foot lockers and hammocks for anything of value. She switched her view to find Hairy. He'd stationed himself in the cargo hold, searching the barrels and crates, sending the ones with something worth their time away to the deck.

She forced her vision away to search other rooms without her crew in them. Her head filled to bursting as she viewed the weapons hold from every angle at once, as though she had a thousand eyes. Her vision moved through the ship one room at a time until she realized what was off about it. There was no access to the lowest hold, though she knew there had to be one. When Song pulled herself from her state, she'd fallen to her knees. Toothy knelt beside her.

"You all right?"

"I'm fine. I was just searching the ship."

He cocked an eyebrow at her.

She shook her head.

"All right if I get more cargo? You won't keel over?"

"Have at it. I've other matters to attend to." She accepted his hand up and took a moment to steady herself. "Stop," she shouted at Leslie and the captain, but they ignored her.

They'd gotten a few good shots in on each other. Leslie's shirt was cut across the front and there was a red gash along the top of the captain's forearm.

"*Meh-th pahts.*" Their swords bounced against each other one last time before it threw both men to either side of the ship.

"Song?" Leslie questioned.

She ignored him and knelt over the captain. She took his shirt in her fist and pulled his throat up to meet the gentle tickle of his own sword's steel. "Fancy sword. I remember when it was given to you. You got terribly drunk that night and became inappropriate with a young girl. I have to wonder if you were drinking from elation…? Or from shame…" She gauged his reaction. "What are you hiding in your lower hold?"

"There is no lower hold."

She hit the side of his head with the hand guard. "I know it's there, I just can't see inside. How do I get to your lower hold?"

"I'll die before I tell you, goggle-head." He spat on the left lens of her goggles.

She pulled them over her head and wiped the lens clean on his shirt.

"You?"

"Lots of *you*'s going around. Makes me wonder just how everyone knows each other. I know you because my father hosted the benefit when you received this sword. Such a fine sword." She replaced her goggles on top of her head, out of the way.

"Song," Leslie said behind her. "The access is in his cabin."

"Is that true?" she asked the captain.

He scoffed at her.

"Let me," Leslie urged.

"No, I need to know why I can't see down there."

"Song, you don't *want* to see what's down there."

"Why?"

The look in Leslie's eyes unnerved her. Whatever the captain and crew were hiding, it was something that frightened Leslie in an imperceivable way. The mere idea of it had him on edge.

"Don't," he pleaded.

"Leslie, you stay up here. I'm going."

She hardened herself against the fear tickling the nape of her neck, and the knot in her stomach telling her this was a terrible idea. Inside his cabin, she knocked her heel against the floorboards, listening for a change in pitch. She searched under the cushions of his bay bench. A draft of putrid air tickled her cheek. A nearby pry bar fit into the crack and provided enough leverage to pull a square board loose and reveal a hidden passage down. The stairs were dark and steep, leaning to conform to the aft of the ship. From without, none would be the wiser, and within none could tell a full meter had been left vacant between the aft and the hold.

"Taini-mooli."

The area illuminated with blue light, and she found the bottom. There was a door there, and a smell coming through that sent her stomach in roiling circles. She tried the knob, but it was locked. *"Kawl-nu."* Nothing happened. Bracing herself, she kicked with all her might, calling on her *kijæm* to strengthen the blow. The door exploded inward with the lock and knob still holding fast to the latch. The smell intensified, gagging Song.

"You shouldn't have done that." The voice came from within. *"Mi'h t'sælb!"*

An undulating blue wave came at her and she braced for impact, but it blew around her, knocking her hood to her shoulders and ruffling a few stray hairs.

"Surprise, surprise. A girl. *Aibhridh ain Thuirin?*" he said with an unmistakable Pishing accent.

Song cocked her head at the unfamiliar language. *"Mi'h snehl'ys!"*

She smiled as he stepped forward into her light, shouting without a sound. He was a pudgy man, well fed in fine silks. His head was bald and a ghastly scar marred his left cheek.

"You're not the only one with tricks. The unfortunate thing is, that was your only one. And I have many. *Tainimooli.*"

The room lit. It was long, spanning the length of the hull. The ceiling was a claustrophobic height and there were rows of benches set along the sides. Every bench had several pairs of shackles, and a child occupied each pair. Their clothes were rags hanging from their malnourished frames. Their refuse had been left to slide down the angled sides of the floor into the middle, where it pooled and festered.

The Gifted gave a wicked smile as she looked on in horror. She turned away from him, but still she could feel those eyes on her.

"I bet your tricks didn't account for this," he said.

Song jolted and spun around.

He advanced on her and she backed away. "I learned long ago to counter a simple silence. You poor little girl. You have so very much to learn. *Naip.*"

Red lights shot through the air toward her and crashed against her chest, wrapping around to slither into her coat and cover her body. The sensation of ants crawling along her skin and biting into her flesh overcame her. She fell to the floor, screaming. She wanted to rip her skin from her bones just to make it stop.

"*Pawts!*" she shouted. Her sphere of protection exploded from her core, pushing the sensation of pain away and keeping it at a distance. She opened her eyes to see his *kijæm* pressing in on hers, meshing together in a purple struggle for pain and protection. They twisted together until, in a series of flashes, the entire mass turned blue and hovered patiently around her. She stood, fueled by her anger, to stare at the Touched with all the hatred she could find within herself. The *kijæm* fanned out behind her as though waiting to dart over her shoulders at her next command.

"How did you do that?" His voice betrayed his surprise. "That's…that's not possible."

She didn't know what she'd done or how, but she chuckled at his destroyed morale all the same. "Is that all you've got? *Mi'h t'sælb.*"

The blue wave of both her *kijæm* and his rushed forward to push against him, flinging him backward. He caught himself with his own diminished power and remained suspended over the pool of filth so as not to soil his fine silk robes. He came back at her with his own wave, knocking her into the side of the stairs. The wood crumbled beneath her weight. He set his feet back on the floor and advanced on her.

"*Naip.*"

She braced herself for the pain, but nothing happened.

"*Re'h r'h nger'b!*"

Again, nothing happened.

"Performance issues?" she asked.

"Silence!"

"I'm sure it happens to everyone." She pulled herself from the hole in the wall and dusted herself off. "Are you too tired for this? Do you need a nap?" A short *ha* of a laugh escaped her lips.

He ran at her, hands aimed at her neck. "I said be quiet!"

Song caught him by the arm, spun him around, and threw him into the hole she'd just crawled from. "And I told you I have a lot more tricks."

He picked himself up and ran at her again. She caught him, and in a few short moves had him lying face-down, his arm twisted up between his shoulder blades.

"The difference between us," he said with a grunt, "is that I did what was necessary. You are afraid of your own power, child."

"Actually," Song growled, "I just want to make sure you hurt as much as possible before I kill you." She yanked up on his arm, ripping his shoulder from the socket with a *pop!* "*Naip.*"

The red aura converged on him. He shrieked and writhed beneath her. He shouted commands to his *kijæm*, but nothing happened. It had abandoned him. He began to lose the words to say, until he had nothing. He was just a weak man in fine silks, trapped in a secret hold with an angry Touched woman holding him down.

"*Trah-pah mi'h reht.*"

She stood to look down at him. The red *kijæm* mist spiraled over him and slithered into his mouth, ears, and nose. His skin rippled. It bubbled and pulsed across his bones. His shrieks were inhuman. They filled the hold, echoing up the stairs. The children in the hold pressed their hands to their ears and screamed in chorus as they watched the man contort and twitch in agony.

Leslie rushed down the stairs and strode to Song. "Are you hurt?"

She ignored him, her murderous glare fixed on the man on the floor.

He stood in the doorway and shouted to the children, "Close your eyes, all of you! Look away!" He turned to her once more, taking in her unrecognizable state of malice. "Song, don't!"

But it was too late. The man exploded as the *kijæm* burst from him in a sparkling flurry. Every bone in his body had been crushed to small bits, every organ liquefied. Now he was nothing but a dark stain on the floor. Leslie took her into his arms. She wanted to shove him away, spurn his comforting embrace. But right then, it was something she needed, no matter who it came from.

"They're children," she said, her voice a whisper.

"I know."

"Where are they taking them?"

Leslie didn't reply. She shoved away and searched, discovering a list of each child within the hold. They numbered in the hundreds. At the bottom of the list, she found the destination: Pishing. Her eyes met Leslie's and sorrow filled his.

"You knew?" she demanded.

"I've encountered Captain Hugh before. I was on his crew for a short while until I found out."

"He's a monster." The look that spread across her face was telling as she spun and took the steps two at a time.

"Song, don't." He chased her up the stairs and caught her wrist.

She spun on him, ripping her hand from his grasp. "Don't touch me!" She shoved him just enough to set him off balance and buy her some time.

She ran the rest of the way up the stairs and unsheathed Hugh's sword. Without a pause, she drove it into his chest. Her fury rose as she withdrew the blade, then plunged the saber into him again and again. When Dashaelan's hands pulling at her waist to drag her away brought her back to the present, she broke down into frantic sobs. He held her to him and let her cry into his shoulder.

When she'd cried her fill, she pulled away to frown at him. A bright spot of blood stained his vest at his collarbone.

"Dash, you're bleeding."

He looked at his shoulder, and took her cheeks in his hands. Dashaelan traced his thumb under her nose. Liquid poured across her lips to drip from her chin.

"Song?"

The world began to fade.

"Whispers, take Song back to the Bounty, now!"

Leslie took her in his arms as Dashaelan steadied the ladder for him.

"Can you hold on to me?" Leslie asked.

"Wouldn't you like—" She inhaled a hiss. "Ugh, my head." Pain stung her snarky reply from her lips as the world flashed white.

"Right then." He threw her over his shoulder and clambered up the ladder.

The blood on Song's face ran the other direction, sliding across her forehead and crawling into her hairline. He transferred her to Maps, who laid her out on the deck, then ran below. Leslie pulled his shirt over his head and used it to clean the blood away. He pressed it under her nose to catch the flow still oozing out.

"Stay with me."

"I don't want to," she complained.

"Do it anyway."

"But I don't like being a lady."

Leslie blinked. "No one is saying you have to be a lady. Just stay awake."

"Will Daddy be home this week? Johanna, tell me."

He paused before answering. "I'm sure he will."

She smiled under the shirt and it shone in her eyes. It was the sort of smile one never forgets is being shared with them. She turned her head to look at Leslie, lifting her hand to set it on his cheek. She attempted to murmur something, but immediately forgot what as her lips refused to form the words. Not that he would have understood her past his shirt, anyway. Her hand fell away from his cheek, the back of it slapped against the deck as she lost consciousness.

Thirty-Eight

SONG WAS NEVER ALONE AS SHE REMAINED UNCONSCIOUS FOR days. When she woke, it was Doctor who watched over her. He had his feet propped on the table as he read. She was in Dashaelan's hammock, cocooned in warm blankets. He turned a page; it scraped along his shirt, disturbing the silence for only a second.

"How lo—" Song attempted to clear away the scratch of her dry throat. "How—" It hadn't cleared.

Doctor stood and poured a glass of water from a pitcher. "Three days. Ah-ah, sip it. Don't want to upset your senses."

She lay back after handing the glass back to him. She breathed heavier as the small action of sitting up to drink had drained her energy. "Where's Dash?"

"On deck." He slipped a scrap of paper between the pages of his book and tucked it under his arm. "I suppose I should go get him for you."

"Please."

"Dash!" Doctor called as he opened the door.

Footsteps thundered overhead, down a flight of stairs, and to the door. Doctor pressed himself to the wall as Dashaelan shoved past him. Worry had left her captain sleepless and haggard. He pursed his lips, taking a few deep breaths to control himself.

"Don't you ever do that again."

Song scoffed. "You act as though I did it on purpose."

But Dashaelan was in no mood for humor. "Song, I'm serious. We nearly lost you."

She swallowed, her eyes darting to where Doctor leaned against the wall. "What's wrong with me?" she whispered, all fear now.

Doctor sucked in a contemplative breath. "I don't know. Whispers said you used an incredible amount of *kijæm* on the Garda's Pride. Last time you used a large amount was in Talegrove, with the snow—though that was significantly less. Before that, it was the incident with the visions, which he told us about." His breath whistled through his nose. "My best guess is…your *kijæm* is killing you."

Song snorted on a laugh. "If this is some half-baked ruse to get me to cut back on—"

"Song." Dashaelan gripped her shoulder. "I don't know if Doctor is right. I don't know if he's wrong. All I know you very nearly died. And I'm not willing to take that risk again to find out if it's the truth."

"Dash, you're being silly!"

"Song!" he snapped. He turned his head to glance at Doctor, who took the hint to leave. "I told you I failed my son. For all I know, he could be dead, or worse, still trapped in that purgatory I surrendered him to. Gods willing, he escaped. I will never know. If he's…and I wasn't there to prevent it…?" He cleared his throat, fighting against his emotions. "I will not make the same mistake with you."

She swallowed, tears threatening to well in her eyes. "Dash—"

"Don't you 'Dash' me, young lady. I will not let you kill yourself over this…abomination of a Gift!"

"I'm an abomination?"

"No!" He rubbed his palms down his face in frustration. "Gifted did not exist before. Everyone knows that as well as they know the sun rises in the west. It's not of this world, Song. It's not natural!"

She scoffed. "Don't be ridiculous."

"My point is, nobody knows the true nature of this *kijæm* stuff, so don't go assuming it's safe to be using so much. Most Gifted use it on superficial things, never taxing themselves as you do."

"How can I know what I and my *kijæm* are capable of if I don't test it?"

"You're beyond testing, now, Song. You're taking unnecessary risks. And for what?"

Song set her jaw and cleared her throat as she realized he was not angry with her. He was terrified of the consequences of using so much of an unknown thing—and of losing her. "I did it for the children." She stared at her fingers and picked dirt from under the nails. Then she jumped. "The children! Where are they? What of Garda's Pride?"

He reached his arms out and motioned for her. "Come."

She wrapped her arms around his neck as he lifted her from the hammock and strode to the bench along his bay window. He set her down and sat beside her. Together, they peered out the window, down to the ocean below where the Garda's Pride kept pace with the Stars' Bounty. Even from high overhead, she could see the sun glinting red from Leslie's auburn hair as he manned the helm.

"He knows the ship, apparently," Dashaelan said. "Had him take half the crew to man it. The Pride's crew is all locked up, save the ones who offered to help."

"So…what are we doing with it?"

"Taking it—and the children—back to Garda, of course! Give her to someone that wants her, I suppose."

Song twisted her lips as she thought. "My father was close with Hugh. I don't know if he knew of the slave trade, but he'd be the one to return the ship to." She sighed as she thought of her parents. "Could I write him a letter?"

"What about the reward on your head?"

"As Caleb Song. Present him with the ship and the children as a sign of good faith. Just because pirates sacked a ship he commissions, doesn't mean we don't have to explain the situation. Then our men can escape before anyone boards in Garda. It might help keep us out of his crosshairs."

Dashaelan played with the idea, running his tongue along his yellowing teeth. "You argue a fair point. Just be careful what you say."

He carried her to his table and produced a dip pen and inkwell, and a sheet of thick paper. Song stared at the page for a long time, thinking hard about what she should say.

Senator Elroy Gould,

Please accept my humblest apologies for the state in which I am returning your vessel and crew. I do not ask forgiveness for Captain Hugh. He deserved it. For some time now, Garda's Pride has been involved in the trade of orphans from Andalise to Pishing as slaves.

I could not control my anger at the discovery. I wouldn't take it back if I could. My crew and I are not the most upstanding of the world's citizens, but we do have honor. I hope you do, too. What happens to the ship now is up to you, but trust me when I say that if it returns to its previous activities, I will find out and I'll sink it. After which, I'll be paying you a visit.

We can be enemies, or we can be friends. Think on it.

Regards,

C. Song

"Eloquently stated," Dashaelan said after she read it to him. "Not many are bold enough to threaten a senator so openly."

"It didn't sound like a threat to me."

"*Because* he's your father." Dashaelan laughed as he folded her letter into a small packet.

He spilled golden wax over the seam and pressed a metal stamp into the soft wax. Before it hardened completely, he pulled the stamp up and carved her false initials over the North Star imprint the stamp had left. Song hunched in her seat. He stood to catch her as she teetered sideways, spent from the effort of sitting upright. He set her back in his hammock and brushed away hairs that clung to her damp forehead.

"Get some rest, my dear. I'll make sure this gets down to Whispers."

She smiled, fading into sleep too fast to respond.

By the time Song woke again, they'd already returned the other ship to Garda and had made a clean getaway. Dashaelan was watching over her this time, his Duke Barton research splayed across the tabletop. Leslie had been the one to deliver the ship into the harbor after the rest of the crew returned to the Stars' Bounty.

"I thought he was going to crash right into the docks!" Dashaelan laughed, his face red with breathless humor. "That boy's got the strangest kind of luck about him. At the last minute, he dropped anchor and blew a whistle to call the guards. They came running, and he jumped onto the ladder and held on for dear life. Thumbs was yelling the whole time to get him up before he fell." He laughed again.

"It's a shame I missed all the excitement." She gave him a crooked smile. "I told you he knows who's in charge."

"I know that, Song. I've always known."

"Then why do you pick on him?" She laughed.

Dashaelan shrugged. "I have my reasons."

She climbed out of the hammock and slid into a nearby chair to look over the papers on the table. They remained that way for a long time, silent in their own contemplations of the information in their hands.

"He's a good man," Dashaelan said.

"What?"

"Whispers. He's a truly good man."

Song cocked an eyebrow at him. "What's this got to do with…anything, really?"

"He cares about you, Song."

She stared at him. "Of course he does. We're partners. We look out for each other."

"You really are a blind idiot, aren't you?"

"I'm not an idiot. You are."

"I'm not the one looking right through someone as though I can't see them," he growled across the table.

"Really? Because you do that all the time. Name every man on your crew."

He stared her down. "This has got nothing to do with that."

"Then what has it got to do with, Dash? Because I am so lost, I might just find Balamora's treasure accidentally." She flipped the cover of a book over, peering as though she might find a treasure chest hidden underneath.

He rolled his eyes at her dramatics. "I have reason to believe he cares deeply for you."

"Who, Balamora?"

"No!" He sighed in frustration. "You know exactly what I'm talking about."

"Doesn't mean I have to acknowledge it," she said.

"Doesn't change that it's there. What about you?"

"What about me?"

"Do you fancy Whispers?"

She stared out at the blades of the propeller. She wanted to say no, of course not. But doubt wove through her mind, staying her tongue from objection. Did caring for him the way she did count as fancying? It wasn't anywhere near the way she'd fancied Isabelle, the first girl she'd kissed and the reason she was out in the skies with pirates instead of tucked into a warm, cozy bed and doted on hand and foot. It was also different from the way she'd fancied Amelia, the farm girl who'd retrieved her from the beach and watched over her. But Leslie was not a woman. Care for him as she did, the idea was preposterous. She took the glass of whiskey Dashaelan had been swirling against the tabletop and swallowed the contents.

"I fancy ladies," she said.

Dashaelan observed her for a long beat. "Complicated, isn't it?"

She glanced at him from the corner of her eye.

He poured more whiskey in the glass and swallowed it before she could take it again. "Life is always changing, Song. Opinions and fancies can change at the turn of a wheel. Nothing is set in stone, and you don't have to settle yourself on one thing if you find yourself intrigued by another."

She stared at him long and hard, letting his words soak into her mind. She would not tell him her thoughts—that it wasn't as easy as he thought. Not this time. She stared back out the bay windows.

"I fancy ladies."

"Shame, really. Not sure you can do much better than him."

"Are you suggesting I couldn't get a proper suitor if I wanted to?" she demanded.

"No. I'm sure if you went back home, they'd line around the city square to beg your hand. What I'm saying is, Whispers is the kind of man that only comes along once."

Song pushed herself from the chair and hobbled to the bay bench to lie back. "When did you become a matchmaker?"

"Not matchmaking," he muttered into the glass. "Just trying to figure things out. Make sure you're happy."

"I *am* happy! I've got a captain who is like a father to me…better than a father! A partner that I trust with my life—and do *not* fancy. And a crew I can depend on. What more could I ask for?"

"Song, I won't always be—"

"Shut up, old man."

"—around. I'm old, Song. I've had a good run, but—"

"I said shut up!" She sat up and grabbed a pillow to lob across the room at him. "You're not going anywhere. You're staying here with me. I will not be handed off as a bride to a man, no matter how honorable!"

"Just listen to—"

"No! You listen to me!" she was downright shouting at him. "I will not be forced to play house with a man just so you can retire and I'm not left up here getting into trouble. You don't want to have to worry about me? Then you keep your bloody arse on this skyship and *you* keep me out of trouble."

"Song, that isn't what I—"

"You can't hand me off with the bollocks notion that he'll make me stay put."

Dashaelan opened his mouth to argue, but she shouted over him, her head growing light.

"I won't do it, Dash! I won't!"

"The Bounty will need a new captain one—"

Song growled to interrupt him. "So that's it, is it? You retire and hand him your ship and your precious little Song and tell him to make sure I stay out of it all. Turn me into the plain girl, watching the skies for his return."

"You're the one with the bollocks notions, here, Song!" Dashaelan shouted.

"Just shut your bloody face up!" She threw herself back onto the bench and turned on her side to stare at the propeller. Tears slid across the bridge of her nose and onto the cushions.

"Toothy's rubbed off on you a bit too much, I think."

"Bugger off!"

The door slammed behind her, and her ears rang in the silence that followed. Her chin quivered; she gripped it with her thumb and forefinger, pinching it to make it stay put. She would not sob. Dashaelan couldn't leave. And if he did, what made him think she would leave, too? Did he think the men on the crew would then see her as something to abuse? And that marrying her off to the man he appointed as captain would keep them at bay? What was running through that vault of a mind that had him saying such things?

The door opened and shut. Light footsteps crossed to the center of the room. She wiped the tears from her face but didn't turn around. That quiet walk could only belong to one person on board.

"Are you all right?"

She closed her eyes and released a frustrated sigh. "Go away, Leslie."

"Dash said you were awake, though the entire ship and a few frightened birds already knew that. He said I should talk to you."

"Of course he did."

She could feel his eyes on her. She wanted to roll over and look into them to see if she really could read within them the truth in the stories Dashaelan was weaving. But she didn't. She kept her back to him and her sight on the horizon. Song didn't want the preposterous claims to be true. She wanted him to go away and leave her to cry and be angry at Dashaelan.

"Would you like to tell me what's wrong?" He used his fingertips to move stray hairs away from her cheek and tuck them behind her ear.

She wished he hadn't. Wished he would keep his hands off her in the tender way he'd begun to do. She would rather he'd punched her in the shoulder and told her to buck up, like men would do to one another.

He remained beside the bench, waiting for an answer she didn't want to give.

"No, Leslie, I am *not* all right. And no, I do *not* want to talk about it. So just go away."

"Dash hasn't given his approval for you to be left alone. I'll stay right here."

Song pressed her face into the cushion and screamed her frustration into it. She pushed herself up to her knees and reached out to slap him. He pursed his lips and adjusted his jaw as though anger might show itself—something besides his usual calm.

"I'm not sure what I did to deserve that." He stared into her eyes, looking for her reason.

She swung her other hand around to slap his other cheek. Before he could recover, she slapped the first cheek again. She knew he could have stopped her every time, and yet for some reason he'd taken the strikes. This angered her even more. She didn't want him to take the beating, she wanted him to grab her wrist and slap her back. She wanted everything to go back to how it had been, before she'd become acutely aware that he'd begun to treat her more gently.

She choked on her angry tears and launched herself at him. He caught her around the waist and they fell to the floor in an angry heap. She knelt over him and sent pathetic punches into his shoulders as the effort caught up with her still-recovering body.

"I hate you," she growled. "I hate you!"

He grabbed her forearms to keep her still.

"Let go of me! Damn you, Leslie." She fell forward to cry into his collar.

He wrapped his arms around her, enveloping her in comforting warmth. Song relaxed. For the smallest moment, she felt comfortable in his embrace. And she hated Dashaelan for putting such ridiculous notions into her head.

"Damn you."

"Do you still hate me?" Leslie asked.

Song had returned to lying on the bay bench. Leslie sat on the floor with his back against it. She made no reply. Her gaze was fixed on the ceiling, thoughts tumbling through her head.

She contemplated his question for a long while. How could she explain that she didn't hate him? He was, in fact, precious to her in a way she didn't understand and so couldn't voice. She turned to meet his gaze and held it steady for a long time.

"I'm not sure, yet." It was the only answer she had, even though it wasn't for the question he'd asked.

"Why?" he asked after she turned her attention to the windows.

"Do I hate you?" She turned back to him.

His expression was an implied affirmation.

"Why shouldn't I?"

He stared across the room, unable or unwilling to answer her. They stayed in that strange silence for a long time. When Song looked down at Leslie, he'd unsheathed his sword and had set to polishing it. Without a word, she lowered herself to the floor beside him to watch. He stopped and turned his attention to her. She glanced up at him, then took his cloth in her own hand and began working it across the sorrowstone.

"Here." He set his hand over hers. "Like this."

She lost track of time as they polished his blade. His warm hand remained wrapped around hers, guiding her fingers. She understood why he would mindlessly work the blade when he'd nothing better to do. The action was soothing and almost meditative in its repetitive simplicity. He sheathed the sword and put the items away. Song set her cheek against his shoulder and stared at the table. Leslie observed her in his own silent contemplations for a long while.

"Do you still hate me?"

She met his gaze. "I never did."

Dashaelan found them that way some time later, sitting on the floor and staring off into empty space as the comfortable silence settled over them. He said nothing, just set two bowls of the day's lunch on the tabletop, then made a quiet exit.

IT WAS MORNING. SONG HADN'T REALIZED SHE'D FALLEN ASLEEP propped against Leslie's shoulder. But now she lay on the bench beneath the windows and had Dashaelan for company. He was hunched over his Barton paraphernalia, lost in his own thoughts. He reached for another paper; the Garda's seal saber shifted from atop it. Song stretched, a small squeak and a grunt forced from her throat. Dashaelan smiled at the papers, then turned the smile on her.

"Good morning."

"Morning."

"Are you quite done sleeping for unreasonable amounts of time?"

Song thought about it. She sat up, then stood. Her head did not spin and her legs remained beneath her. "I just may be."

"Are you also done being impertinent?"

She narrowed her eyes at him. "Are you done trying to hand me off to someone else?"

He rubbed his palms over his face. "That's not what I was—"

She cocked an eyebrow at him and folded her arms over her chest.

"Yes, all right. I'm done talking about Whispers."

"And retiring."

He groaned out a sigh. "And retiring."

"Then yes, I am done yelling at you."

He stood. "Good. Then I have something for you."

"What is it?"

He gripped the Garda saber by the scabbard, pointing the handle toward her. "Every good pirate needs a good sword."

"I couldn't possi—"

"You are from Garda and, in fact, are part of the most famous family there. Your own father is part of the senate which commissioned this blade. And you killed the owner. This sword is more yours than any has ever been to another."

She twisted her lips and scoffed. "It should belong to the captain of the ship."

"It belongs to you, Song. I've plenty of swords. You have none."

With a sigh, she took it by the scabbard and stared at it. "It's different from the one I use."

"A saber is more similar to an Armalinian flatblade than you think."

She unsheathed the sword to stare at the shining steel. "Why don't we go on deck and test that theory?"

They shared a wicked smile.

Thirty-Nine

THE HAMMOCK SWAYED LEFT AND RIGHT AS SONG MOVED HER legs in rhythm. She sat sideways in it like a swing, reading a book she'd borrowed from Doctor. They'd docked in a harbor city at the northern curve of Andalise. The air was bitter with the crushed leaves of fall and the threat of winter. While the crew sold their goods, resupplied, and slept in warm beds with stout meads to fill their bellies, Song was stuck on board, as usual. She wasn't bitter about it, but she couldn't deny the desire for fresh, hot bread and a foamy ale to wash it down. Leslie cleared his throat over her and she smiled at him.

"Enjoying yourself?"

"I had a swing in a tree back home," she said. "I didn't realize how much I missed it until now."

He chuckled. "I never did swing as a child."

"Never too late to start." She slid sideways, and he joined her. They sat in silence, Song reading and Leslie staring up at the floorboards above them. "So," she said, finishing one last sentence, "how do you like swinging?"

He shrugged. "It's all right."

"It's fun."

"Perhaps I'm just too old to fully appreciate it."

"Dash would appreciate it."

"I'm not Dash."

"No, but he's much older." She laughed.

"Nobody seems to know how old he is."

Song thought about it. "I'd put him in his fifties."

"That's a lot older than anyone else says."

She sighed. "Your secrets are not the only ones I keep, Leslie."

He nodded. "Fair enough."

She returned to her reading, and he returned to staring at the boards overhead. But something continued to nag at her in the silence made comfortable by his presence. She sighed and snapped her book closed. Leslie flinched at the noise.

"What was that?" she asked with a laugh.

He tried to hide the small smile. "In the past, when someone snapped a book closed like that, they would hit me with it."

She snorted. "Should I hit you with mine?"

"I'd rather you didn't." He studied her. "What's got you so bothered?"

"You."

"Oh. Did you want me to leave?"

"Nothing like that. When we met on deck that first night, you were kind to me, like you are now. The next day, you began treating me like I was a nuisance—some silly little brat in over her head."

"Are you saying you weren't?"

"No, I'm saying you were the only one to do it—*after* treating me like a friend."

He smiled as he thought. "Because I had to break you."

"Break me?"

"I had to make sure you were up to the task by treating you like a student, not a friend. If I'd gone too softly, would you have put as much effort into our lessons?"

She thought. Her mouth twisted into a conceding smirk. "Probably not."

He chewed on the inside of his bottom lip, eyes scanning her face as thoughts clouded the blue of his eyes to a smooth gray. "Song…" He stopped, as though unsure about saying what was on his mind.

"Now it's my turn to ask. What's got *you* so bothered?"

"Just something I've been thinking about for…a very long time."

"How long?"

"The day the Jashedar ship took Dashaelan—"

"That was months ago!"

"And I've been observing you since."

She cocked an eyebrow in suspicion. "Why?"

He picked at his already clean fingernails. "When Dash was taken, how did you know?"

"I was far-seeing because the deck grew so quiet."

"Well, I'm not sure how it happened or why, but you were not just seeing things from nothing. You saw through Bruce's eyes. At least, you did that time."

She furrowed her brow. "That makes no sense. How do you know that?"

"Because his eyes are not blue, but that day they were. The same blue as your *kijæm*."

"Well, I'm not doing it on purpose! And I'm not hurting him, either!"

"I didn't say you did anything intentionally or with malice. I almost wonder if it's something to do with Bruce."

"What sort of something?"

Leslie thought about this. "He sees things. Knows things. He told me the first night aboard that you glitter. It made no sense to me at the time. But when you use your *kijæm*, you glitter. He knew, Song. You hadn't even said a word, and he knew you were a Gifted woman, rather than some cabin boy."

Song stared at the book in her hands, her fingers traced the spine in absentminded preoccupation. This was so much to take in and really think about. What made her or Brute so special that she could see through his eyes and even urge him to go where she wanted? Her mind flew through all the possibilities and opportunities such a connection could provide. She also knew in her heart that taking advantage of Brute would be unfair.

"Soup's up!" the muffled shout of Thumbs drifted down the stairs to them.

"It's about bloody time!"

Song leapt from the hammock and took the stairs two at a time. Leslie appeared several moments later. He sat across from her as Thumbs dished out plates for the two, plus Pinch and himself. Each plate had a sizable steak, potatoes topped with butter and chives, and vegetables roasted with pungent spices. Thumbs set her plate before her and she shoveled the food into her mouth, groaning at the delectable feast he'd brought. Pinch set a large stein of ale beside her plate and she guzzled half down before clearing her throat.

"Did you make all this?"

Thumbs smiled with pride. "I did. Taught the cook at the inn a thing or two." He winked at her and sat to eat his own meal. "Pinch brought your drink."

"Ha!" he said. "I brought it for meself. Just thought I'd share."

"Only because she would beat you into the floor and take it all if you did not," Thumbs mumbled into his own stein of fresh water.

"What was that?" Pinch asked.

"Nothing. You are just so generous, is all."

They ate in silence, savoring every bite. When their paces slowed, Pinch twisted the corner of his mouth up in thought.

"Nice brothel here. Saw a few ladies worth the price." He stared at Leslie. "Would you like their names?"

Leslie remained stoic, swallowing the food in his mouth before he answered. "I've no interest in any of that."

"Oh, come on, man. There's no shame in paying for company!"

Leslie kept his face aimed at his plate and glanced at Song through his eyelashes. "This is not a good conversation for present company."

"Ain't you ever bought companionship before?"

"No."

Pinch looked to Thumbs for support.

Thumbs shook his head. "If you see the way things go in Kerriwen, and have any sort of conscience, you do not buy a lady's love."

Pinch laughed. "Not buying love! You're paying for—"

"Enough!" he shouted. "You are bothering Song."

Song looked up from her plate, eyes wide and confused. "Don't drag me into this!" she said over her food. She swallowed. "You want to go buy a lady? Buy a lady! Don't refrain on my account!" She directed her stare at Leslie.

He pursed his lips. "It is not for you that I refrain."

"Then who?" Pinch asked.

"I knew a woman from Kerriwen. She was marked as paid pleasure." He shook his head. "Like Thumbs said, when you see the way things are in Kerriwen, you do not pay for a woman."

They sat in the heavy silence, chewing their food in awkward thought.

"I was to be marked a warrior," Thumbs said, smiling. "I cried so hard after killing my first man that they sent me to the kitchens. Turns out I had a knack for cooking."

"You've killed a man?" Song asked in disbelief.

"We all have, haven't we?" Leslie said.

"How old were you with your first?" Pinch asked Leslie.

"Nineteen? I think."

"You think?" Song laughed.

His smile was tight. "I don't actually know when my birthday is."

"Oh." She swallowed her embarrassment with some ale. "Well, we all know exactly when I killed my first man."

Pinch scrunched his face in thought. "Who was that?"

"William," she said.

"Dash killed William," he objected.

Song's lips drew thin with her strained smile. "Dash threw him overboard. My words drowned him." They stared at her in astonishment and she shifted on the bench. "What about you, Pinch?"

"Oh, um." He thought about it. "Sixteen, I believe."

She whistled. "Started young."

Pinch laughed and jerked his chin at Thumbs. "What about you, mate?"

Thumbs didn't look up from his plate. "I was seven."

The conversation became one none of them wanted to have. Pinch speared vegetables onto his fork until it was so full they split in half and fell back to his plate as he forced more onto the end. Leslie held his fork in his fingertips, dangling it between his palms, his lips pressed to the side of his hands. Song continued to pick up even the smallest bits of food left on her plate in an attempt to clear it. Thumbs leaned his jaw on his fist and stared at each one in turn. His eyes met Leslie's, and they shared a smile.

"Strange..." Thumbs mused.

"What?" Song asked.

Leslie chuckled. "How easily your opinion of someone can change—"

"Once you've learned their past." She turned her sights to Thumbs and smiled. "My opinion hasn't changed a bit."

"Only because I feed you."

"You know me too well."

They all laughed together, the weight of the conversation lifting from their shoulders. Pinch stood and stretched.

"So," he said, "invitation is still open."

Leslie glared at him. Thumbs shook his head.

"Song? Care for a romp with some lovely ladies?"

Her cheeks warmed, and she cast her gaze back to her plate, searching for something, anything, to pick up with her fork. But her plate was empty.

Leslie cleared his throat. "I think you're in the wrong company to be asking that question."

He shrugged. "Suit yourselves, lads." He started up the stairs before tossing out a quick, "And Song."

Leslie eyed Song as she stirred the leftover juices on her plate. "And on whose account do you refrain?"

"Who said I was refraining?" She hoped the warmth crawling up her neck hadn't cast her skin in a telling shade.

"There is no shame in it," Thumbs said.

"I just don't want to—"

He shook his head as he chuckled. "I was not talking about that."

She met his gaze. His dark eyes crinkled at the corners as he smiled. She glanced at Leslie, who was observing her in quiet, nonjudgmental thought.

"Well," she sighed, trying to mask her embarrassment. "It's good to know Dash isn't the only one overly concerned about my chastity." She rushed below before her mouth decided to say anything more embarrassing.

Song slipped back into her hammock to resume swinging and reading. It was some time before Leslie appeared in the doorway. He leaned his shoulder against the frame as he waited for an invitation. She pretended not to see him, as though ignoring the problem would make it go away. But he didn't budge. She growled and set her book in her lap.

"What?"

"Thumbs is gone. Bells is on deck. And I have nothing better to do."

"Nothing better than staring at me?"

"I wasn't staring."

She narrowed her eyes at him. "Go read a book or something."

"I don't have one."

"Liar."

"I'm not lying. I don't have any that I haven't read." He chuckled.

"Go get one."

"If Roman put out a bounty on me, I'd rather not risk going out into the world."

"We're at the farthest north of Andalise," she said. "I highly doubt word has spread this far."

"Your posters were in Jashedar. Trust me when I say he wants me more than your parents wanted you." He strode to the cannons and took a seat on a dolly.

After a length of silence, Song pursed her lips. "Are you just going to sit there?"

"Do you want me to go away?"

She shrugged and raised her book. "I don't care either way, as long as you're quiet."

"As you wish." He unsheathed his sword and began polishing it.

Song peeked over the top of her book at him. He gave her a sly smile. She ignored him for the better part of thirty minutes. Every so often, she would peer around her book at him. She set her reading aside and folded her arms over her chest.

"How do you wield a sword like that, anyway?"

His smile was bright and eager. "Would you like to learn?"

She twisted her mouth sideways in thought. "Sure, I'll give it a go."

They stood and met in the middle of the room. He set the sword in her hand. It was lighter than she'd expected, but still heavier than any she'd used before. Leslie positioned himself behind her, pressing his chest to her back and snaking his arm alongside hers to wrap a hand over the one which held the sword. His other palm set on her waist to urge her to move a certain way.

"You have to be careful," he said. His breath tickled her cheek. "The only safe part of the blade is the flat of it. Even then, it's easy to make the smallest mistake and lose something important." He moved her sword hand with his in a slow demonstration of the proper way to swing his sword. "Unlike your saber, a Pishing blade can attack from any angle, so your wrist movements are not as important for switching direction of the edge. But it requires concentration and absolute control."

"Get my saber. Let's spar."

"Not yet."

Song laughed. "Afraid I'll lose a limb?"

He smiled and sheathed his sword. "A hook for a hand wouldn't be very becoming on you."

"A hook for a hand is not becoming on anyone!" Thumbs laughed from the doorway.

"I thought you'd gone back to the inn," Song said.

"I did. But I came back to show you something." He held up a large sheet of rolled parchment gripped in his fist.

"Reward posters still floating about?"

"Yes, but none for Miss Gould."

She glanced at Leslie. He pursed his lips in anticipation of his own inevitable bounty. Thumbs unrolled the poster and held it beneath his toothy grin. Song's mouth dropped open in shock.

Leslie read the poster aloud. "Wanted dead or alive on charges of piracy, torture, murder, et al. Proceed with caution. Subject is armed and extremely dangerous. Name: Caleb Song. No known aliases."

They stared at Song as she kept her sight fixed on the sketch of a hooded figure.

She furrowed her brow and met Thumbs's and Leslie's gazes in turn. "Is my jaw really that…masculine?"

Thumbs laughed.

Leslie cleared his throat. "It is a bit harsh for a woman."

"I mean, I know I look a lot like my father, but it seems to have…worsened… What about my nose? That nose is completely heinous!"

"The nose is all wrong," Thumbs agreed.

She took the poster from him to reread the text. "Am I really only worth two-thousand quoine?"

"You haven't killed enough people," Leslie said.

"Ha! We'll just have to fix that." She nudged him in the ribs with her elbow.

He scoffed through his nose and shot her a humorless glare. "Wearing a bounty like a badge of honor isn't very becoming for a lady."

"But it's bloody brilliant for a pirate." Toothy smirked from the doorway. "Just came to make sure you heard.

Makin' a name for yourself in this world. I'm damn proud."

"Where shall I hang it?"

Without Leslie's approval, she and Toothy nailed the poster to the wall beside her hammock. Song's stomach fluttered with apprehension and joy. She was no longer a sought damsel in distress, but a feared and dangerous pirate. She didn't expect Leslie to understand. It wasn't about the bounty or the amount; it was about being something more than a little brat. She was making a name for herself, not relying on the Gould fame to be noticed. It wasn't the best sort of attention, but to her it was enough—an affirmation of her existence beyond the Garda manor.

Song stood at the helm with Leslie at one shoulder and Maps at the other as they tried to teach her how to chart a course and adjust the ship to take it. Sunshine stomped above deck, a thick piece of folded parchment gripped in his fist.

He observed the three of them. "Dash?"

"In his cabin," Song replied.

"Why?"

She shrugged. "I didn't ask."

Sunshine fixed his black eyes on Leslie, who stiffened under the intense scrutiny.

"Can I help you?" Leslie asked.

As reply Sunshine scoffed as though it was the most ridiculous thing he'd ever heard, then stomped down the steps to knock on Dashaelan's cabin door.

"He hates me."

"Hates me, too," Maps said with a chuckle.

"He hates everyone," Song said.

Leslie gave a gentle laugh and shook his head. "Except you." He set his hand over hers and righted their course just a little. His palm lingered longer than necessary.

The back of Song's hand tingled with the pins of discomfort, so she nudged him away with her elbow. "Even me," she said.

The whistle pierced the air above them. Two pips. Pirates. As though through a set choreography, Song pulled her goggles down over her eyes as Leslie tucked her hair into her collar and flipped her hood over her head. Maps took the wheel as Song spun to search the horizon.

"Port side!" she shouted. "Make ready!" The men scurried about the deck. A thrill ran through her as they obeyed her order without hesitation.

"Belay that order!" Dashaelan shouted from his door. He hurried up the steps and pointed to Maps. "Hard to starboard!"

"But Dash—" Song began.

"That's an order!"

"Aye, captain," she replied.

He turned to study Leslie. Again it unsettled the man, his shoulders squaring and his hands finding items to fidget with, as a senior crewman took such time with his features.

"Whispers," Dashaelan said.

"Captain?"

"I need a word with you—"

The whistle pierced the air with another two pips. Song returned her gaze to the horizon and observed the other vessel speeding toward them with determination.

"They're moving to intercept!" Song said. "Get Toothy down, Dash. We cannot outrun them."

"I'm the captain of this skyship," Dashaelan warned.

"That is why I'm asking you to give the order to come about and make ready!" she replied.

"Steady on, Maps."

"Come about!"

"Song, I am warning you—"

"It's a clipper!" she growled. She gripped his shoulder and turned him to look into her eyes as she lifted her goggles to her hair. "Dash! We can't outrun them!"

"When did you get to be such a good pirate?" he asked in astonishment.

"I've had exceptional teachers."

"Maps," Dashaelan set a hand on the man's shoulder. "Bring us about." Next, he shouted to the crew who stood on deck awaiting his orders. "Make ready, gents. Let's make this fast and clean so we can tend to more important matters." He turned to stare at Leslie's back as the latter stood at Song's shoulder, a spyglass set to his eye.

Song gave Dashaelan a strange look. He shook himself back to the task at hand and put the whistle to his lips to call Toothy from the crow's nest.

"I'll go warn the crew below," Leslie said. He compacted the spyglass and handed it off to Maps.

Dashaelan gripped Song's right biceps. "Lock him in the cage."

She stared into his eyes, trying to find some humor within, but there was none—only some unnamed terror that had sobered him more than she'd ever seen him. "Leslie?"

"Aye."

"Why would I do such a thing? What did you and Sunshine talk about?"

"He merely gave me a poster," Dashaelan said.

"And what was on it?"

Dashaelan thought for a moment, his eyes flitting to the horizon where the other vessel was closing the distance between them. "Let's just say I'd feel a lot better with him locked up."

"You'll tell me, right?"

"After," he assured.

She gave a single nod and rushed below to find Leslie. He was laughing with Brute and Doctor in the crew's quarters. Brute observed her. His smile faltered before he stepped forward to set a massive palm over her shoulder.

"Smile, Song."

She gave him a half-hearted smile before he and Doctor made their way to the lower cargo hold. Leslie made to go above deck. Song stopped him with a hand on his elbow.

"I need you to come with me."

He didn't question her, just followed as she took him down to the weapons hold. The cannons were unmanned — Thumbs and the others would be there any moment after they'd finished securing cargo. Leslie stopped in the middle of the room and looked around. Song withdrew her sidearm and pointed it at the back of his head.

"Are we manning the cann—"

Song pulled back on the hammer of her revolver. The metallic *click* broke the silence and sent ominous waves pulsing through the room.

"What are you doing, Song?"

Muffled shouts came from above deck. They'd run abreast of the clipper and soon the fighting would begin.

"Just following the captain's orders," she replied. Her voice betrayed her desire to ignore the order.

Leslie turned to stare at her. "And what exactly are your orders?"

"To lock you up. Get in the cage, Leslie."

"Why?"

"I didn't ask."

"Maybe you should start asking questions."

She took a step forward, pressing the cold metal to his forehead. "I'll get my answers later. Now get in the cage."

"You're not going to shoot me."

"Not if you get—"

His left arm snaked up to grip her right wrist and twist it until she lost her grip on the gun. It clattered to the floor. He shoved at her shoulder and sent her to the floor as well. Leslie strode past her as Thumbs entered, leading the pack of cannoneers.

"What is going on here?" Thumbs demanded.

"Stop him!" Song shouted as Leslie sped past the group. She lifted her revolver and shot after him.

The cannoneers ducked and moved out of her way.

"Get to the cannons, lads." She raced after Leslie.

Song emerged on deck, where the sun immediately blinded her. Swords clanged together over her head. She spun to see Leslie's sword crossed with another.

"Watch your back!" he shouted.

"You're doing enough of that for both of us."

He kicked the man away and turned to confront her. "Which I wouldn't be able to do if you'd killed me."

"I wasn't going to kill you," she said. She drew her sword and batted the man's saber away. "Dash wanted you locked up. You know better than disobeying orders."

"This one is worth ignoring. It makes *no* sense!" Leslie parried sideways, taking the man's momentary loss of footing as an opportunity to wrap his arm around the other's neck and hold him in place. "Why would he lock up his best fighter?" Leslie demanded.

"Why don't you tell me!"

"No!" Dashaelan shouted. He thundered across the deck and shoved Leslie to the floor.

Gunfire split the air. Leslie untangled himself from the other man.

Dashaelan turned to lock his sad eyes with Song's.

"Dash?" Song squeaked.

"Not...not again."

Another gunshot boomed and Dashaelan grunted, his eyes wide and focused on her. He crumpled to the deck. She crawled to him and ripped his coat open. Crimson seeped across the white of his shirt. Panic settled into Song's bones as her hands shook. She pressed her palms to his belly. She muttered *kijæm* over him. His flesh burned, leaving a pungent stench in her nostrils.

"Stop," he grunted. "It's too late."

"Shut up, old man." She tried to remain calm, but her throat tightened in panic as her sight clouded with tears.

His hand reached up to rip free the captain's cabin key from around his neck, which he pressed into Song's hand. His eyes roamed just over her shoulder to a point behind her. "I'm proud of you," he said.

"Dash, stop it," she begged.

"I'm proud of you, son," he said. His eyes drifted back to meet hers. "Song."

The life in his eyes dimmed, and they focused on nothing. Song shook him, speaking words so garbled with grief they were incomprehensible nonsense to everyone, even herself. Somewhere outside her, a battle still raged. Blurry figures and distorted sounds echoed all around. Men shouted, swords clanged, and a handgun fired its last remaining shots. Song, however, felt separated from it, as though time had slowed to a morose crawl.

Someone knelt beside Song. She turned and shoved her face into his shirt and screamed until her throat hurt. When she pulled away, Leslie's gentle eyes met hers. She stared at the key sitting in her bloody palm, then back at Leslie. Her mouth opened and closed as words tried to come out, then thought better of it. She pushed herself up and dropped the key as though it was poisoned.

Her shaking stopped and heat raced through her veins, her blood set ablaze and her mind consumed by the fire. She turned away from Leslie to scan the other vessel. Her eyes met those of the man who'd shot Dashaelan. She walked to the edge of the ship and he smirked. But his cockiness fell when she stepped out into the open air and her *kijæm* caught her as she whispered for it to carry her across.

A man rushed at her. She turned to stare into his eyes. He faltered and stopped as she whispered commands to keep anyone from reaching her. Her *kijæm* obeyed when she told it to dismantle the shooter's gun, which fell to his feet in useless pieces.

Her *kijæm* returned to her. It swirled around her, blinking and shimmering in its beautiful blue. No one moved—all too afraid to attack a Touched with *kijæm* at the ready. Her slow advance sent his boldness out into the empty air, abandoning him to his fear.

She reached out to squeeze the collar of his shirt in her fist as she set her blade to his throat. "You killed him."

"I wasn't aiming at him!"

"You killed Dash."

"Mercy, please!"

"No," she whispered.

She pressed her blade into the side of his throat, cutting his jugular vein, which fluttered against his skin in frantic palpitations. Red oozed from the wound before the edge found his carotid artery. Blood spurted out around the metal of the saber, splashing across Song's lips and dripping down into the consuming blackness of her coat.

The man grunted, his lips still forming the word 'please', though he'd lost all hope of mercy. She released his shirt. He sank to the deck, his eyes wide and fixated on hers as though awestruck by the hands which had killed him.

She spun to glare at the rest of the crew. They kept their distance, swords ready in their fists. She looked each of them in the eyes, her upper lip curled in loathing. *"Meh-th n'rb. Law meh-th n'rb."*

The blue mist swirling around her flickered between white and blue in quick succession, then turned to a red that shone like the embers of a fire. For a moment, what appeared to be a purple mist surrounded her, before the rest followed suit and the shining spirals twisting all around shone crimson with rage. They snaked in slithering trails away from her to find their victims.

The first of the men didn't move, but watched in terrified curiosity as the mist wound its way up his sword arm. It covered every inch of his body before the red obtained an orange hue like heated metal and pressed in on his skin. He screamed and dropped his sword to the deck. He slapped his hands over his body in a futile attempt to brush away the pain.

The rest of the crew dropped their weapons and scattered about the deck as the trails chased them down. The *kijæm* caught and consumed them. One man tried to leap over the side toward the ocean below. The mist converged in a bright blue mass as a guardian angel to keep him on the ship. Once he was safe, the beauty twisted into the angry scarlet devils and swarmed him.

"*Law ti n'rb.*"

Smoke rose from a blackening patch in the center of the deck before finally giving way to yellow flames. They danced across the deck, igniting everything they came into contact with—including the men.

People rushed from below, their skin purple from the mutilation and their clothing ablaze. Once discovering there was no refuge above, they threw themselves to the deck to succumb to their wounds. Some tumbled overboard in hopes that the ocean below might extinguish them.

The flames grew taller as Song stood her ground upon the only unscathed area. She watched with a vicious satisfaction as the damned souls wailed at the Hell she'd sent them to.

"Song!"

The voice seemed far away—somewhere beyond the wall

of flames that flickered toward the zeppelin overhead and gripped the ropes to begin the climb upward.

"Song!"

The desperation pulled at her, but she ignored it as her heart beat fire through her veins.

A figure exploded through the flames. He landed on the crumbling deck and shielded his auburn hair from the cinders that rained down on him from the mainmast. Leslie picked his way across the fragile wood. He shied away from the flames attempting to lick him. Song said nothing as she watched.

When he reached the safety of her unscathed area, he looked into her eyes, frantic as he caught his breath. His face was red from the heat. His skin was black in places the flames had gotten a bit too friendly with him.

"Song," he whispered.

But she returned a blank stare. The deck groaned as the planks weakened. The circle of untouched boards shifted and dropped a little as the surrounding wood crumbled. Leslie tensed and caught Song as she lost her footing. He scooped her into his arms and leapt across the crumbling deck.

At the edge, he gripped her around the waist. He used his free hand to catch the rope Sunshine swung across the distance for them. The moment their feet left the other vessel, Maps put the Stars' Bounty into motion to get them away from the blaze.

The crew ducked as the other zeppelin exploded, sending debris at them. Song remained standing. Her tears reflected the bright blast in glittering echoes of itself. Even though she hadn't said a word, debris slammed against an invisible wall which shimmered blue at the impact as her *kijæm* protected the Stars' Bounty.

Her body numbed, her ears fell deaf, and she floated as though lost in a strange limbo. Her feet carried her to where Dashaelan lay. His skin paled as the blood he'd lost seeped across the deck, searching for an escape over the side. She dropped to her knees in the middle of it and took his hand in her own. It was cold in her grasp. Her thumbs rubbed across the back of his hand as her throat came to a painful close and the agony tightened in her chest. She held her eyes to his as a desperate hope willed them to turn and look at her. His gaze remained fixed somewhere past the stars on the zeppelin.

A mournful silence pressed the voice from every man on deck. One by one, the crewmen from below emerged, only to be caught in the same quiet as the others. Sunshine set his hand on Song's shoulder and shed his own silent tears for his dear friend. Time held its breath for them, letting the moment go uninterrupted by the rest of the world.

Song gasped on the pressure building in her chest, suffocating the air from her lungs and the joy from her heart. Sorrow rose up as a wave in a tumultuous ocean, swelling higher than she could've thought possible before it came crashing down to drown her. All she could do was gasp as the heart within her was crushed beneath the weight. She rocked forward to press her tears into his shirt, weeping loud and open against his chest. Her mind raced to think of words that might bring him back. Something her *kijæm* could accomplish. But there were no words. He was gone and would remain so.

When Song was weary from her tears, her eyes sore and red, Sunshine knelt beside her. He rubbed his palm across her shoulders and met her gaze. His other hand reached over to close Dashaelan's empty ice-blue eyes.

"We've got to clean up."

She gaped, her mind blank. "No," she squeaked.

"Song, you need to—"

"No!"

He reached for her, but she gripped her fists around the cloth of Dashaelan's shirt. Hands set upon her, tearing her away from Dashaelan. She screamed out in anger and sorrow as she fought against the men. Leslie whisked her into his arms and carried her—kicking and screaming—down to the small area of the weapons hold she called home. He set her on her feet and she collapsed to the floor. Lethargy swept over her, weakening her limbs and warning of the coming darkness. She gritted her teeth and forced herself to remain conscious.

Leslie helped her out of her boots and trousers, setting them in an empty bucket. He lifted her shirt over her head and their eyes locked. Her chin crinkled against her will, and she fought against the sobs fighting to return. He circled around her and unbraided her hair. Thumbs set a bucket of steaming water beside them, taking a moment to rest his hand on her shoulder before taking her soiled clothes away.

Leslie reached into the bucket, wringing the water from the cloth. He set it against her scalp. She ignored the heat of it as he worked the blood and ash from her hair. When he knelt in front of her to clean her face, she cast him an accusing glare.

"It's your fault."

He didn't acknowledge her.

"Did you hear me? I said—"

"I heard you, Song."

"And?"

"And what?"

"What do you say?"

"I know."

Her jaw quivered as a fresh tear rolled down her cheek. "Why didn't you just do as I said?"

"You didn't give me a good reason."

"It was an *order*." Her eyes bored into him as he focused on wiping away every last drop of blood on her face. "And now?"

He rinsed the cloth and set his attention on her neck. "What?"

She set her hand on his to stop his actions. "It doesn't bother you? You wouldn't take it back?"

"It bothers me plenty, Song. But it can't be taken back."

She yanked the cloth from his grip. "Leave me alone."

He thought for a moment as he studied her expression. "All right, Song. But I'll be right outside the door if you need me."

She shook her head. "I will never need you, *Whispers*."

He pursed his lips and cast his gaze to the floor between them. Leslie swallowed away everything he might have wanted to say. He nodded and stood, hesitating for a second before he strode from the room. Song hung her head. She wiped her running nose with the rag; it came away red.

"Not yet," she hissed.

THE CREW HAD GATHERED ON DECK. SONG SAT ON THE STEPS, HER limbs heavy from fighting off the darkness trying to consume her. She kept a small cloth to her nose, the flow of blood increasing each second she fought against her own body. The crew had sewn Dashaelan's body into a canvas tarp and laid it out on the deck. They had scrubbed away the blood and washed it over the side.

Thumbs gave each man a cup of some sort with a shot of whiskey. Song gripped hers, rubbing the side of her thumb against the cool glass. She kept her eyes trained on Leslie, who accepted the drink, then stared at it as he lost himself in thought.

They were going to bury Dashaelan at sea. If they buried him anywhere else—even Talegrove—his grave would be defiled or robbed. She could protest all she wanted, but in the end, Sunshine was right. Dashaelan deserved better than that.

The men each said something about him, going around the deck with little anecdotes and memories. When it came Song's turn, she said nothing. Anything she wanted to say, she wanted to say to Dashaelan, face to face. They raised their cups.

"To Dash," Thumbs said.

Song swallowed the whiskey, recognizing Dashaelan's favorite. Her eyes locked on Leslie. He stared at the drink for a long time. He swallowed the whiskey, glancing at her before returning his gaze to the empty glass in his hands. His face gave nothing away. No hint to a secret he was hiding or ill thoughts. He, like the rest of the crew, was paying his solemn respects.

Sunshine and Toothy hoisted the tarp-wrapped body to the railing.

Song screamed out. "No! You can't!" The glass shattered as she dropped it to the deck and threw herself down the stairs toward them. "You can't take him!" She grasped at the canvas with feeble fingers. "Don't take him from me."

Weakness weighed on her limbs and she dropped to the deck. One of her hands scratched at the canvas, attempting to grip something and prevent the loss of the father she'd always wanted. Her other hand pressed to her eyes to catch her tears.

The most gentle of touches set on her shoulders. She looked up to glare at Leslie, but it was not his eyes she met. Sunshine frowned, his black eyes holding her gaze to his.

"Dash was like an extension of me. I ain't takin' him from you. I'm sayin' goodbye to my better half in the most honorable way I can."

He wrapped his arms around her, letting her cry into his shoulder. After a few silent minutes, he lifted her to stand and set his palm over hers on the tarp. She stopped trying to grip it and instead splayed out her fingers.

"Help me say goodbye?" he asked.

She nodded and held her breath as together they pushed Dashaelan's body over the side and down into the dark waters, where the cannonballs sewn in with him would take him to a final resting place at the bottom of the ocean.

Her hands and feet tingled. Her eyelids fluttered. The blood dripping from her nose came as a steady stream that ran onto her chest, ignored. Her vision fogged. The blackness crept in from her periphery as it threatened to drag her under once and for all. She was able to gasp one last thing before the darkness enveloped her and sent her limp body crashing to the deck.

"Goodbye, Captain Dashaelan Krell."

Enjoyed the book?
Please consider leaving a review!

Acknowledgements

A HUGE THANK YOU TO LAURA FOR PICKING THROUGH THE original novel and beta reading the second edition. I have to thank my writing friends who helped keep me on track, and encouraged me every step of the way. Sometimes we all just need a good kick in the pants. And finally, thank you to my fans and readers. I love you all. Your excitement over anything I write makes it worth it.

About the Author

Shalaena Medford is an American author, editor, researcher, desktop publisher, artist, and definitely not a lizard person. She has attended university for creative writing, with focuses in fiction and screenwriting. She has always had a passion for books and the written word.

Visit her website at:
www.shalaenamedford.com

9 781970 291032